The Owl and the Oak
The Climate Change Novel

by Robert Emmett Morris

PublishAmerica
Baltimore

ISBN: 1-4241-6709-4
PUBLISHED BY PUBLISHAMERICA, LLLP
www.publishamerica.com
Baltimore

Printed in the United States of America

Dedicated to Barbara and Josh,
whose faith frees me to undertake any venture.
Our family bonds are unshakeable
despite distance, time or circumstance.

Prologue

Owl sat on a bough of the Oak halfway up the hill. That Oak had been the family roost for 200 years. Owl's gaze pierced the thin woods in the shade of the Oak, fixed on the naked boy in the open space, down on the trail that ran next to the creek. The boy stared back. Heavy summer leaves hung listlessly in still air, stirred by the ratchet of cicadas, rustle of squirrels, flutter of birds in the high shading canopy. Motionless, Owl and boy measured each other for long minutes, each assessing if they saw threat or prey.

Through seasons of stalking, sliding, watching, listening, smelling, feeling, the boy had learned timelessness and had become part of the woods and it part of him. He absorbed the very air of the woods through his sun-browned skin. His stance balanced and hands open, he projected confident dominance of the wild glade, challenge without threat.

Owl blinked first. The boy had won and now the Owl was his: part of him just as the rough bark and high leaves of the Oak, the rich forest earth, the butterflies around the black cherry, the meadowlark on the dogwood and the hummingbird sipping from the white flowers of the black hawthorn had all become part of him, and he became part of the Owl. Owl finally turned his head left, then right, spread wings broader across than the boy was tall, and sailed through the tangled wooded canopy, a brown ghost with yellow eyes.

Over the next years the boy spent countless hours in company with the Great Horned Owl, escaping a large family in a small suburban home. At night he waited, pressed close as bark to the Oak and saw the Owl drop on an unwary rabbit. A thud, a scuffle and then two, three silent wing beats and it was gone. The boy raced through the brush like a shadow under the Owl, twisting, turning and feeling his way through underbrush, ash, pine and oak, footfalls quiet and sure, but always he would get caught in a bramble or lose sight in the dark woodland roof and get left behind. Even as he grew, try as he might he was never fast or strong enough to follow all the way to Owl's nest. Scratched, dirty, ticks and burrs in his hair, the boy would go back home and face questions about what he was doing running around in the woods at night. There was no answer, so he stayed silent as the Owl.

He was drawn away by the demands of growth, school, jobs, friends, family in the suburban world that started just a hundred yards away, where houses pressed against the woods. But the Owl never left him, even when he returned years later and found the woods had been turned into apartments to house the large families of immigrants from far, dusty, hungry homelands. Only the Oak had been spared, ancient, tall and strong, shading a playground filled with happy multi-hued children. He had been to those foreign lands and seen the poverty the immigrants were escaping. The loss of the woodland where he had spent the best days of his youth cut deeply, but he accepted the needs of those making new homes there.

He made a vow. He would make sure there was always a home for the Owl, too.

Chapter 1

"Where the fuck is that kid!" Aaron Woods cursed vehemently as he snapped the cell phone shut.

"You have a kid?" There was surprise in Wendy's voice, an elevation of the wariness he had sensed from her since they started working together three days ago. "I thought your son was older."

They had just stopped on their hike, halfway around Roosevelt Island on the Potomac River. The warm sun soothed knotted muscles while the light brush of the cool spring breeze refreshed them, whisking away the dullness and tension that came from too much time in stale offices and meeting rooms. As they rested they looked across the wide river to the graffiti-covered wall of the Georgetown waterfront with Whitehurst freeway suspended above like a concrete brow, the modern plazas and high rise buildings of Washington Harbor, busy Thompson's boathouse, the classic Kennedy Center, the Lincoln and Jefferson memorials and the spire of the Washington monument. The bustling and famous federal city across the water made a tasty contrast to the cool riverbank rocks in the shade of beech and oak trees where they listened to the rush of the water and meadowlark songs. After two days of plan writing, staff meetings and working lunches at the Natural America Club, he had asked Wendy Sparks to join him on this little trip to knock the cobwebs out of their brains and see "the best view in Washington D.C." He felt like he had gained some trust from her as he made his pitch to her and the other members of the Campaign Action Office she led, and then when she had taken him to meet with Directors, Board Members, and finally, this morning, with Phil and Tony, the Board President and the Executive Director. That feeling was confirmed when she agreed to come along on the walk and he expected the time outdoors would help build on that trust. Now he realized that she was less comfortable as he lapsed from his social persona into his more customary reserve, intently observing but not feeling the need to comment or provide a background of what he considered to be empty chatter.

And she really wasn't comfortable when that quiet was broken by a frustrated F-bomb thrown at a heretofore unsuspected kid.

"Ah, well it's complicated," Aaron said lamely. He bit his tongue, and she looked like he had bitten her, too. Damn it, he needed her help if he was going to get this project off the ground. Now he was going to screw things up after spending three days of carefully building a basis for a working relationship. He didn't want to admit that he was, as usual, a little off balance when dealing with an attractive, smart woman. He had always been able to keep professional relationships professional, but that was on the outside. The eager, awkward and inadequate teenager that resided inside his middle-aged body had a way of popping out at inopportune moments.

"Let me explain," he said, trying to project his sincerity. "My son, Ted, whom I think I mentioned before, is 30 years old and long gone out on his own. Squeak is a kid that I kind of just, ah, picked up a few years ago and eventually I adopted. I take care of him, or try to as much as he'll let me. He's 12 now and I think he's out on the streets again."

Explaining himself was never comfortable, and he felt like he ran out of breath getting it all out. At the same time, he knew he hadn't said half enough for her to really understand the very complicated and unusual circumstances surrounding his relationship with his adopted son. Hell, the fact was he wasn't sure he understood it well enough to articulate it to anyone.

"Hmm…" Wendy paused and pushed back her hair. He liked her hair, thick, dark, untamed and curling. He liked her neck, too. Shit, he had to keep his mind on her as an ally, not a woman.

"Isn't there anyone there to watch out for him? What kind of a name is Squeak, anyway?"

"No, no. There's just the two of us. It is complicated. He was a street kid and now he sometimes just goes back to the streets. To reconnect with what he came from. Squeak was his street name. Hell, it was his only name until I adopted him. He's supposed to carry a cell phone, but usually doesn't because he, well, I guess he doesn't want to feel tied down. Same reason I don't always carry my cell. So I just stew and cuss until he comes back. And hope that he does come back."

"Wow. That's…I don't know what that is." She pushed her lips out and raised her eyebrows. There was a long silence, during which Aaron could feel himself getting more and more irritated. What business of hers was his relationship with his kid? She probably thought he was some kind of pervert or something. He was just worried about his kid running the streets and he felt like she was judging him.

"Yeah, well, we better get moving on through the wetlands so we can get back to the city before the evening rush hour starts to build up." Screw it. He needed to get the conversation back to the big topic that had brought him to her and the NAC. He stood up from the rock, swung the small backpack to his shoulders and stood aside to let her lead the way.

"We need to move pretty fast or we'll be sitting in the car for an hour getting across the bridge."

Her face was tight and it didn't loosen as she got up. She didn't like being told what to do and it showed.

"Well, we don't want that!" Wendy snapped coldly, and set out with quick, choppy strides, pushing branches angrily aside, letting them snap back behind her.

Aaron followed with a sigh. He tried to absorb the calm of the wetlands, the ebb of the tidal flow, the birds flitting through the trees, dragonflies in the marsh grasses under a fine April sun and sky as he followed with a loose, quiet stride. When they got onto the main path with its wooden walkway across the marsh, Wendy's tromping march and the occasional roar of a jet overhead flying into National Airport (he would never acknowledge the addition of Reagan to its name) distracted him, "disturbed his wa" as his spiritualist friends would say. He found himself focusing on the roll and tilt of Wendy's ass and hips, the swing of her shoulders and bounce of that nightfall of hair. She moved like an athlete, strong and certain but with fluid grace, head high and shoulders supple and square. *I'll bet she was a figure skater, maybe still is*, he mused, comparing her butt with memories of Katerina Witt and Nancy Kerrigan from past Olympics. Pleasant thoughts, but not helpful in getting things back on a productive track.

When they got back to the parking lot they silently got into the car and edged back onto the George Washington Parkway. He turned on the CD as they drove up Spout Run to make the turnaround and go back down to the river and the ramp to Key Bridge. By the time they got into the heavy traffic on the bridge he saw her nodding and tapping her fingers to the sweet rhythms of Van Morrison singing "Tupelo Honey." Maybe she was ready to give him a chance to redeem himself. They crept along bumper to bumper, going right on M St. and then left up Wisconsin Ave. When the song ended and they made their slow way back to the NAC offices, she reached over and turned down the volume. She looked at him for the first time since they'd started back to the car and he felt like some of the chill had gone out of the air, like the spring sun warming the breeze. Wendy Sparks had been a big help and he was going to need her if he was going to translate his admittedly half baked ideas for building a new grassroots movement into real action across the country. NAC was the biggest environmental organization in the country, with almost a million members. Aaron had surveyed the field and concluded that it was the only one with the reach, structure and reputation to pull off the kind of campaign he envisaged, and Wendy was in the ideal position to make it happen.

"I think that Tony was really interested in the boycott," she said. "He kept on asking you questions and that's a good sign from him." Her voice was calm and neutral and he was grateful to have the topic back on non personal issues where he felt more comfortable. He forced distracting thoughts about her as a woman out of his consciousness and focused on her as the savvy, accomplished professional grassroots operative. That was the part of her that was important to him. Over the past two years the drumbeat of reports citing the dangers of climate change due to greenhouse gas emissions, and the willful lack of action or even thought being given to dealing with it by the government or the American people, had crowded out the more normal concerns of his life, like a job, his family or social life. He needed to keep his mind, and hers, on the issue.

"That's great. I really appreciate you giving me your take on him. It's pretty frustrating to read all the facts that show we have a big problem and not have anyone want to listen when you talk about what needs to be done about it. There's a guy that stands outside Union Station with a Bible, telling people, 'You're going to burn.' I told Squeak the other night that I was afraid that I was going to become that guy, preaching away and nobody listening. He told me I already was that guy. Since I talked with you I feel a little less like some crackpot."

They both laughed lightly, and spent the rest of the ride talking about how to build their campaign. Aaron was trying to get the NAC to directly confront the corporations that profited from and were responsible for emissions that were disturbing the delicate balance of earth's climate. That balance in the ecosystem was necessary for life in its many forms, including human. He hadn't had much success other than becoming known as "the grassroots energy guy," but kept plugging away until he connected with Wendy. Six months ago, shortly after he was hired as Executive Director, Tony Albritton hired her to help him with his own plans to reform the NAC. That venerable organization had built its national reputation on grassroots organizing to fix local or regional environmental problems but, as it grew bigger and sought more national focus, it had strayed away from traditional grassroots organizing. They had expanded their financial base and hired on a large staff to write policies and lobby Congress, but NAC just didn't have the money to compete with the industry lobbyists, and money was what bought influence in Washington D.C. The old time activists had become frustrated as the NAC failed to succeed on national issues the way they had in earlier decades with their local campaigns. Those old timers made up a small percentage of the total membership but were highly vocal and held some of the leadership positions. Not surprisingly, the staff were wedded to the lobby and think tank model, and had little talent or inclination to change careers and go do old fashioned grassroots organizing. Aaron had struck the right cord with Wendy and Tony when he presented his ideas for using climate change issues and grassroots techniques to make NAC the leader of a new movement.

"You just happened to hit us at the right moment," she told him now with her refreshing frankness. "We needed someone like you to bubble up from the membership so that Tony and I weren't seen as newcomers trying to force this on the staff and insider volunteers. Not that changing things will be easy or that people won't bitch about it and try to sabotage us, but if you're prepared to stick with us on this then maybe we can do some great things. We think that enough frustration has built up that the members will accept new ways of doing things as long as they don't see it as being dictated to them."

Aaron smiled for a minute and then nodded his head. "Oh, I'm ready to stick the course. I've been trying to change the world my whole life. Been a part of successful efforts some of the time, in small ways. I was a tiny part of the Peace movement that got us out of Vietnam and the Civil Rights movement that moved us forward on race, so I know the culture can change if enough people are willing to do whatever it takes. I'm willing."

When he dropped her off at the office they shook hands and exchanged promises to get back in touch. Aaron felt he was back where he needed to be with her. He'd keep his mind on the big picture and stop thinking about her ass from now on, he vowed as he headed across town towards Capitol Hill and home.

It would have been a good day and had him singing along with Bob Dylan's "Talking Blues No. 10" if he wasn't so worried about Squeak being out on the streets again. He hadn't come home from school last night, and school was out already today and he still wasn't back. It was getting close to dinnertime. If the kid had been picked up by the cops then things would really get messed up. His being a single adoptive father made him vulnerable to the screwed up but still autocratic Child Family Services Division if the kid got caught up in "the system." Or he could have gotten mixed up with some of the unemployed hoods and gang bangers hanging around, selling dope and mugging commuters. He and the kid had come a long way in the last five years and the boy had a real future if he could just get through the next few years. Damn…he'd just have to hit the streets himself to see if he could hunt the kid down.

He settled back and cleared his mind and focused on fighting his way past the taxis that took a 25% down payment on his lane while owning 75% of the other in case they needed to switch lanes. He enjoyed driving and had a nice little Beemer sport wagon, but he seldom drove in town because the traffic was such a pain in the butt and using transit, biking and walking was more fun and part of "walking the talk." "Overfed ego wagons," he called the big SUVs that many commuters rode into town for work, and he didn't like being part of that pollution-producing traffic stream. He had driven today on the chance that he might get Wendy out of the office and walking in the woods. People thought clearer and deeper when they got out in nature. At least that was what he told himself. Probably would have worked if he hadn't lost his cool.

Aaron stopped at the Whole Foods to pick up some ready cooked chicken and vegetables for dinner. Getting back in the car to fight the commuters the rest of the way to his little row house on Capitol Hill, he went back to musing on what had become his life mission.

He knew that the only way for people who didn't have a lot of money and power to make big social changes was to organize. His years in business, where he had earned the money that supported him now, gave him an edge on other grassroots activists. He knew how vulnerable seemingly invincible corporations were to organized actions that would affect their share prices if you isolated them, cut one out of the herd and attacked. Start with a consumer boycott, work on shareholders, especially the pension funds and other big institutional investors, hit the insurers and financial institutions that provided the money, talk to the workers and unions, the service providers; a big enough campaign could bring down the share prices of any corporation and that would bring the executives to the table. Then you make them responsible for leading the change to a clean power economy that would minimize and mitigate the consequences of climate disruption. That was only fair, since they had the expertise and money to do the job, resources gained by causing the problem in the first place. Just like in the old days, when the way to change was clear and people power would make the world better.

With Wendy and Tony and the NAC to use as a tool he thought they had a head start, not having to build brand new organizations like movements in the past. They were going to surprise the big multinational corporations who had been profiteering on the oil and coal economy while spending millions to keep their political stooges in office and hiding the need for change from the public.

He broke off his musings and came back to reality when he got to his driveway, punched the door opener and pulled into the garage behind his townhouse. The garage was stuffed with bikes, gear for camping, fishing and snorkeling, kayaks, skis, hiking boots and poles, and assorted balls and gloves. It wasn't neat, but he could quickly grab hold of whatever he needed when he or Squeak got an urge to get out and do something.

After punching the garage door closer with his thumb and opening the door that led to the postage stamp back yard, he heard Squeak fiddling around on his saxophone up in his second floor room. Tension eased out of his shoulders. This might turn out to be a good day after all, he thought as he opened the back door (darn kid left it unlocked again) and pushed through the little mudroom and into the kitchen.

Let's see what we can throw together for supper, he mused. Nothing like a little rice, salad and chicken. His repertoire also included tuna noodle casserole, ham steaks, and bacon and eggs any time of day. Other than that, it usually was pick-up from Young Chow or a pizza. He happily set to work fixing dinner for his little family. It had been too much carryout and not enough home cooking lately. He considered the pre-cooked rotisserie chicken home cooked because he put it in a pan and heated it up in the oven. Squeak sounded pretty good on the sax today, smooth runs and riffs. When he was mad he would blast out angry, sharp notes, hard and fast with rough, broken rhythms. Tonight it sounded like the kid was in a good frame of mind. Of course, with a 12-year-old you never knew when he would turn into a raving, hormone driven lunatic, but Aaron tried to enjoy the good moments and forget the bad ones.

"I guess I didn't blow it too badly with Wendy, after all," he reassured himself. "I'll give her a call tomorrow so we can nail down the plans to get out and start organizing."

He often said that the worst day he had ever had was pretty good and today had turned out to be more than pretty good. The clouds that had been building up through the ride home finally got heavy enough that they had to open up with a crack of thunder and dump a torrent of rain as he called Squeak down to dinner.

Chapter 2

Squeak heard Gray come through the garage and into the kitchen. "Gray" was Aaron's street name. He was well known in the black community, both those who lived on the street and the old time residents still resisting the push of wealthier, mostly white people, like Aaron, who were buying up the old houses in the neighborhood. One of the things Squeak and Gray talked about was being tuned in to what was going on around you. Squeak respected that. Hey, that was how he had stayed alive before Gray came on the scene. That's why he heard the garage and kitchen door noises even when he was playin' the horn. Look, listen, smell, touch, taste and soak it all in, let it be part of you, some kind of Zen thing, Gray would say, taking what he called "awareness" to a whole new level.

He'd never forget the first time when Gray took him out to the woods, back before the adoption, and went on about all that stuff. He'd been scared to death just to be out in the woods with bears and deer with big antlers, wild dogs, bugs. And snakes! Lizards! So he'd paid close attention, oh yeah! Watched the old dude and did exactly what he said.

Man, it was wild, that first hike. 'Cause old Gray, when he was out in the woods, it was just like he was in his living room. That's what Gray had told him. "When I was little and I wandered out into the woods, I knew that it was my place in the world. Think about it, my name was Woods, so to me it was just natural that this was the place where I really belonged."

Even though he looked like he was moving slow, Squeak had a hard time keeping up with the big old guy, or at least without making a big racket. And really crazy, when it got dark they just stayed there! Ate some sandwiches and fruit and then kept moving up the mountain following some stream. Not even on a trail, just right through bushes, stickers and all, although big old Gray somehow seemed to slip through without getting stuck. Sometimes they were walking right up the stream, rock to rock or right in the water.

Finally Gray had stopped still and just held his hand out behind him, so Squeak had stopped too. Slowly, like it took a whole minute or two, Gray moved his hand and touched Squeak right between the eyebrows and then pointed it up to a branch up in a big old tree, and then held still again. Squeak didn't see nothin'! Not for a while, anyway. But he kept still, just like Gray. And finally, something big up there, sitting on the branch, blinked the biggest, yellowest, scariest eyes he had ever seen. Then he could make out, against the night sky and darker trees, a big, round head with tall, pointed ears and then the body, looking tall and somehow all the power of the moon and stars were concentrated in that still, dark shadow, just waiting to spring loose. Squeak didn't move a muscle, barely breathed. Gray seemed, without moving from right beside him, to have disappeared, become a tree himself.

They watched that owl for what seemed like an hour. And while they watched the owl, turning its head every now and then, Squeak began to feel what Gray had been telling him about. He felt the life that is in the woods, all around you, more than anywhere else, a force that you can let sink in to you and make you part of everything there. He could see some kind of brown, round, looking animal nosing through the leaves just ten yards away, hear the bats squeaking and swooping as they feasted on the bugs (some of which were feasting on him!) And now he wasn't scared anymore, he was just a part of all that life, the trees and plants and worms and snakes and fish and bugs and birds and bats and even Mr. Woody Woodchuck or whatever that thing was and it was part of him. So how could he be scared?

Well, ok, so he finally smacked one of the mosquitoes that was sucking a gallon of blood right out of his lower lip, and then the big owl spread wings as big as Squeak was tall, bigger even, and somehow flew away with not one little sound, right through the most tangled mess of branches, leaves and tree trunks you could imagine, never stirring a leaf or bumping into anything, then suddenly disappearing.

"Great Horned Owl," Gray said. He put his hand on the back of Squeak's neck and gave him a big grin. "You did great. You're a woodsman."

Squeak didn't really know what that meant but it felt good and he was proud, maybe the first time in his life that he had felt like that.

Then darn if the old dude didn't pull the bedrolls out of his big, red pack and throw them on the ground and they spent the night, right there, in the woods, and he slept as sound and deep as he had ever slept. It was like old Gray said, they belonged.

Thinking about that first outing made Squeak feel good now, and he knew that Gray liked to hear his horn when he was feeling good. He lost himself in the sound and feel of the music, making it up as he went along until, Boom! Boom! Boom! Gray was banging on the door.

"Hey, dinner's just about ready. I've been calling you. Come on down."

That was all it took. Squeak didn't know why or how or what it was that made him blow up this time any more than any of the other times. He'd been working on it, like Gray had talked to him about after the last time he exploded.

"Of course you've got anger pent up and it has to come out and explode sometimes," Gray had told him; quiet, peaceful, not mad. "You have a right to more anger than ten, fifteen, hell a hundred people."

That was the time, the worst one, a year ago, about. He'd got set off by something, he didn't know what exactly but partly it was like Gray was such a big guy, not just big like tall and big but big like he filled up every space of a room when he just walked into it. And there was no place to hide what you were thinking or anything from him, he saw through bullshit like it wasn't even there. He didn't just look at you he sucked your brain right into his eyes, absorbing you, steady and really focused, seeing and hearing everything. Not like other people who were 90% thinking about themselves and didn't really look at you. Other people didn't threaten to soak up WHO YOU ARE and leave you with no secrets, maybe leave you with nothing at all, just gone like an empty little hole where a puddle had been but it gets sucked up by the sun.

That time when he blew up they were in the living room. He had thrown stuff, busted a lamp and a statue of Moses from Italy that he knew was special to Gray, tore some books, broke a window, yelling. He didn't know what he was yelling or doing while he was doing it, didn't find out until he looked around after the rage had passed and he could see again, just a little and then more clearly, and then he could hear again and, damn, he had the fire poker in his hand and old Gray was bleeding from his head and holding his left arm funny. But Gray wasn't yelling or mad or anything, he was just talking to him.

"You've just got to work at directing how and when the anger comes out, Kenya." Kenya was his real name, or at least the name he and Gray had made his real name a year after he took him in from the streets and had found his mother and gotten her to hang around long enough for the lawyers get her to let him adopt him.

"I had the anger, just like you, but not as much because I didn't have all the stuff to be mad about that you've got, buddy. Got in fights. Hurt people. I still get it, but it comes out differently. I still hurt people, not with my fists but in ways that are still cruel, even though I know I don't want to do that. Just like I know that you didn't want to hurt me right now. You've just got to recognize when the rage is coming and find a way to move it to a space where it can stay until it can come out in a way that won't kill someone, a way you and I and the world can live with."

Squeak had dropped the poker and noticed that he was breathing real hard. He was scared of what he had done and maybe this was it, he'd get kicked out on the streets again and this life was over, he was back into the old hustle and scrape. That was always in the back of his head, that he didn't really belong in this life he lived now with regular meals and books and music lessons, a room and a real father, even if he was an adopted father he was the only father he had ever had. But old Gray just kept talking and finally Squeak had been able to listen and hear that Gray really knew what the anger was like and he wasn't going to kick him out. Gray sat down on the couch. He put his broken left arm on the armrest and then reached up and touched his head where it was bleeding.

"Ok, now that we're done with the drama, go get me a towel, run some cool water on it, and get some of those Ace bandages out from the drawer in the hall bathroom and bring them here. I'll call Antelope to come pick us up and we can all go spend some quality time in the emergency clinic." Gray had paused and just looked at him. "I guess what you were trying to say is that you don't want me to decide what you should wear to school tomorrow, right?"

Then they had looked at each other, mouths slowly curling up into smiles, and started laughing, so hard they couldn't stand up and he collapsed on the sofa and leaned up against old Gray until it passed and they went about putting the pieces of themselves back together again.

Over the years old Gray had talked with him about how other people had gotten control of their anger and channeled it, all kinds of people. Martin Luther King, Gandhi, Cesar Chavez; they talked about how they had used non violence and peaceful demonstrations to fix the things that made them angry. But they also talked about Che Guevara, Osceola and Crazy Horse, the guys at the Alamo, John Brown and J.E.B. Stewart and other guys who were warriors. They read books about those guys and it confused Squeak about what was the right way to use his anger. Should he be peaceful or a warrior? Gray just told him that he would have to find his own way, but the first step was to take control so he could use the anger to accomplish what he decided he needed to do with his life.

Those memories flashed through Squeak's mind in the instant between when the "boom, boom, boom" of Gray's fist hitting the door made him jerk the sax out of his mouth and he felt the wave of fury start to fill him. Gray started to push the door open. His face loomed huge in the opening, crowding Squeak out. Squeak went from musing and noodling on the sax, warm and safe feeling in his own private room after a day and night out on the crazy streets, to wild rage. Everything looked like it was shiny and brittle like ice but the images were hot and burned into his brain through his eyes. He threw the horn away from him but this time, unlike the other times, he saw what he was doing and he threw it onto the bed, where it bounced before it went against the wall and back to the bed.

"The fuck you doin', motha' fuckin' bastard, get out, bitch, asshole…" The words just blasted out of him from someplace deep down inside, the foulest, most hurting words from the worst times of his past. Then not even words, just animal grunts, shrieks and shouts. His body launched from where he had been standing beside the bed looking out the window across the room and slammed into the door, leading with his forearms but smashing his head into the solid wood panels, then scrambling to his feet and doing it again and again. Then, dizzy and exhausted, just hitting it with his fists, finally falling to the floor and kicking it with the last of the rage until it was spent.

Gray kept the door open a little, absorbing some of the impact with his shoulder and arms. Then, when it was over and Squeak stopped kicking, he just said, "Ok, that's ok, just clean up and come down when you're ready. I'll be down there for you and it'll all be ok." He repeated it, once, twice, three times until he was sure that Squeak could hear him.

Then he closed the door and went on down the stairs.

When Squeak got his breath back, and everything got back to looking normal, he looked around the room. His hands, arms, head and left knee were sore and he was bleeding from his forehead, one elbow and a couple of knuckles. He looked over at the sax until he felt ready to move, then slowly pulled his knees and hands under himself and pushed up from the floor. He crawled to the bed and pulled himself up to sit on the side of the bed. He reached over and picked up the sax, afraid that he had busted the best thing he had ever owned, almost the only thing. He saw that it was ok, just a little ding on the bell but no real harm, and he remembered how he had known what was happening and he had controlled where he threw the horn, aiming for the bed so it wouldn't get damaged. He looked around the room and nothing was really messed up except him, and he thought, *Whoa, I knew what was happening. I saw it coming on.*

A ghost of a smile crept across his face. *And I controlled it some. I didn't smash the sax.*

He put down the horn and got up. *Ok,* he thought, *I got to go down and let Gray know. I'm getting control of it. I'm getting in control of who I am an' what I do. I can do that.*

Squeak went into the bathroom and washed off the blood from his forehead and elbow and knuckles. He taped a gauze patch on his forehead, admiring how it looked in the mirror. It really only needed a band aid, but the patch was tough looking and it would make people think he had been in a fight. When he finished he went down and they had a great dinner and then played a game of chess to finish off a very good day.

Chapter 3

Everyone liked Perry Pierce Richardson and it had always been so. Throughout his school years he was always among the most popular with teachers and classmates alike. Election to student government offices was a matter of course. He was always "classy," with pressed khakis or jeans, button down blue or white dress shirts, well shined penny loafers and a trim but fashionably shaggy haircut while his classmates sported either bell bottoms and psychedelic shirts or punk jeans and tee shirts. The idealism of the 60s had died out in his suburban high school in Silver Spring, replaced by the selfish and shallow cynicism of the 70s. The few black students were ignored even as the white students danced to the Motown sounds of the Supremes and Temptations. Perry had a ready smile for everyone, a joke on his lips and an "aw shucks" way of avoiding confrontations. He smoothly moved through the "brains," the "jocks," the "heads" and the "punkers" with light patter, a friendly pat on the back. He was a perfect product of his time: not embroiled in any deep causes, untroubled by events that didn't affect his social status or his future ambitions.

Today as Perry cruised along in his Lincoln Navigator from his house in toney Bethesda, down Wisconsin Avenue to the equally well located offices of American Power Resources Council, abbreviated as APRC, he found himself flashing to images from those 1970's school days. Those had been fine times for him, forming his character while enjoying the friendship and sometimes a bit of awe from his generally less comfortably situated classmates. Not that his family had been wealthy. They were just a little bit more secure than most of the middle class in Silver Spring, and as an only child Perry had not lacked for anything he really wanted.

Perry Pierce Richardson was no less a fashion plate now. His custom tailored grey wool suit with the thin blue stripe, white Sea Island cotton shirt with blue sapphire cufflinks and European collar, also custom made, Hermes blue and grey striped tie and bespoke black Church oxfords combined perfectly with his boyish but meticulously styled sandy hair, sapphire blue eyes, and open face with just a hint of crook in his nose from an elbow he had caught in high school basketball practice as a third string forward. As the senior lobbyist in APRC, Perry was the face of major corporate oil, coal, natural gas, electric, and nuclear utilities in their dealings with the top layers of federal government and Congress. His carefully sophisticated but understated look was as critical as his smooth and flattering charm when providing the politicians and regulators with perfectly patriotic and reasonable sounding excuses to throw ever more billions at his multinational clients, augmenting their combined revenues of over a trillion dollars a year. Often those glib rationalizations weren't even necessary. The availability of unlimited campaign contributions, using multiple sources to insure compliance with annoying but easily circumvented legal limits, was sufficient to get the desired language inserted into legislation, the favorable interpretations of regulations, the convenient timing of mineral rights leases or sales. There were a myriad of subtle and blatant ways that the government provided subsidization and security to the wealthiest corporations in the world and Perry's mission in life was to keep the gusher of tax dollars flowing. He prided himself on doing it in a way that made everyone feel good about them selves and about him. The payoffs in campaign money that he made possible never appeared in the same conversation as the legislation or other favors his clients were seeking. Many times he didn't mention the name of his client. He didn't have to. Everyone knew whom he represented. Perry Pierce Richardson was reliable, a real team player, a stand up guy and a true American.

Since the election of a President and Vice President who owed their great good fortune directly to their sponsorship by the barons of the oil industry, there were virtually no limits to the favors Perry could gain for his clients. Having been bestowed time and again with ever greater rewards despite their own bumbling failures in their personal business careers, this President and Vice President were totally committed to insuring that their carbon based industry sponsors got the first and biggest portions of pork served up by the government. Perry was well known to both the President and Vice President. The young President had even spent some time hanging around the APRC office drawing a hefty salary while in between failing oil ventures, back in the 80's. Perry was working his way up as a lobbyist back then and he and the future President had gone out together, had some good times. Big Ed Tower, then and still the Director of APRC had taken him aside and told him to keep "our young investment's nose clean." Perry knew what that meant and steered their partying away from the coke sniffers and towards the old fashioned drinking and screwing set. Of course back then he didn't have any idea how far the overgrown frat boy was going to go. Like everyone else, Perry had just treated him like a speculative investment and shared their surprise when they hit a home run.

So it was no coincidence that the past three years had been the best ever for the oil and other big time energy industries, and that a good portion of that good will and even better cash had flowed through APRC. And now it looked like the President that Perry still called by the nickname "Randy" from his younger days was going to roll to comfortable re-election and provide four more years of corporate bounty. He certainly ought to, Perry thought to himself, considering all the money that he had gotten his clients to funnel into the re-election campaign. He figured that he had been responsible for channeling at least $110 million through either legitimate or hidden hands to insure they had another four years of access to the federal candy store. Perry had every reason to feel good about his rise from his modestly comfortable background to being a top power broker in Washington, D.C.

He whistled lightly through his teeth as he navigated through the traffic that was still heavy at 9:45 on a Thursday morning. The sky was blue and the sun was shining, but a front was coming in and a few clouds starting to build up, with rain a possibility later on. Perry's thoughts mirrored the weather. There was something back behind his enjoyment of his general good fortune and the prospects of another pleasant day of wheeling and dealing that felt like trouble just over the horizon. Perry's instincts had been honed to sort through subtle nuances and seemingly innocuous actions and he trusted them to let him know when there was any danger to his charmed and lavish existence. His thoughts kept coming back to his dinner companion of the previous evening and something she had mentioned.

He had started taking Wendy Sparks out in January, four months ago, and was still intrigued by her combination of earthy beauty and sharp, critical wit. She challenged him in a way that other women didn't and he kind of enjoyed the edge that it put on their relationship. His colleagues, which is as close as you get to friends in the lobbying business, all kidded him about bringing an avowed tree hugger into their circle, including occasions such as last night's dinner with the junior Senator from New Hampshire and two investors eager to put a Liquid Natural Gas terminal right off the Portsmouth, New Hampshire coast. Perry didn't mind the kidding. He knew that bringing a staffer from Natural America Club as his dinner companion gave his clients and the Senator a feeling that they were being open minded and considering the importance of the environment. They gave serious consideration to her remarks about reducing dependence on fossil fuels, on the need to secure the people who lived in the area that would be burned to a crisp if the plant ever exploded and protect the rugged New England coastline from the dangers posed by the LNG plant. They thanked her for helping them see that they would have to move very carefully on this project if they did it at all.

Which, they knew, was as sincere as a political campaign promise. All that Wendy's arguments did was to allow them to prepare for the inevitable outcry that the usual green whackos would bring up, just like they did with every advance to modern technology. So even while acknowledging the need to consider the wider and broader considerations of building a giant LNG terminal that would destroy everything within one mile or more if it blew up in close proximity to shipping yards and Navy yards, recreational harbors and thousands of residences, they still were able to feel each other out about what kinds of "improved cost structures," "residual benefits" and "energy depletion allowances" would allow them to mutually prosper.

Perry had never claimed to be the smartest guy in the room, and he wasn't a bookish sort. In fact, he had never read a book for pleasure, sticking to the news clips he got on the internet that covered the political, social and economic world in which he worked and lived. But he had a certain genius, nonetheless. Perry could take part in hour after hour, day after day of conversations; much idle small talk, some technical jargon that he little understood, sophisticated and crude dominance posturing, lots of social mixing and matching and mating rituals. From that numbing mix he could glean the one or two small but very important pieces of information that could help or hurt the symbiotic relationships of his clients, their governmental servants and the rest of the world at large.

Like Big Ed would boom, "Perry can root through two barns of bullshit and come back with the Hope diamond." Upon which Perry would nod and join the robust laughter with his best aw shucks guffaw. Ed was short, wide, loud and fat and had the perfect "cowboy in the locker room" demeanor to keep their clients happy. His combination of ruthless cunning and good old boy charm had kept him in the top job at APRC for two decades. "Big Ed would throw his mama off the train to get an upgrade to first class," Perry had heard men confide on more than one occasion. He was pretty sure that Big Ed had started that line going around and kept it alive to scare off competitors. Perry imagined that one day he would move down the hall to Big Ed's palatial office, but he wasn't sure he wanted that responsibility and was content to be Big Ed's number two for as long as the boss wanted to stay on.

Perry was pulling into his reserved parking place in the garage under the 14 floor office building at 15th and K St., N. W. when he finally recalled the one little comment that Wendy had made that had been irritating him like a tiny stone in one of his perfectly fitting custom made shoes. Now he sat in the plush seat of his Navigator and played it back in his mind.

"You guys are pissing me off," she'd said, getting flushed. "You know the facts and you pat me on the head and then continue to plan on a new way to ride the carbon gravy train until…until what? Until the public gets wise that you've been playing them for fools while your emissions cause worse and worse hurricanes, floods and droughts? Is the money worth all that?"

Perry could see that she was making the Senator and gas men uncomfortable and he needed to step in. Over the months she had challenged him and his friends before, but it had been done more in the sense that they were all reasonable and she thought she could get them to see the light. Now he sensed that she was beginning to give up on that and understand that they were just not ready to believe that the economic realities of the oil century had changed. Yeah, they knew the scientific facts, but they just didn't see that it was up to them to change the world, if it could be changed. She was a great date and an even better lay, but he wasn't going to let her screw up his deal making. No woman was worth that.

"Ok, Wendy, we get the picture, but we aren't going to change the world tonight," he interjected. Turning to the Senator he said, "Anyway, Jake, I wanted to ask you about the golf trip to St. Andrews last month."

"Before you change the subject," Wendy had interrupted coolly, "I just want to warn you that the times are going to be changing. People are starting to wise up and I think we have found the guy to pull the enviros and the public together and he knows where you guys are vulnerable. You better be thinking about your place in a new, clean energy economy now."

And that had been it. They had hurried to assure Wendy that they were all good guys, trotting out the usual "green wash" of the pittances they spent on clean energy like solar power and the hydrogen research they were supporting, and how they all loved the trees and were going to stop climate change emissions as soon as they could do it without causing "undue economic disturbance." Then the talk had turned safely to golf and before long she had signaled to Perry that she was tired and needed to go home. They all were ready to call it a night anyway and said their goodbyes. Perry thought to himself he was going to have to be more careful about the occasions when he mixed Wendy with his business. She was crossing the line from being a pleasantly charming challenge to his clients to being an irritating scold.

Wendy was a smart woman, but she just didn't understand the way the world really worked. The global warming Pollyannas wanted to move to an economy where energy efficiency measures cut consumption by 60% and most of the energy was created by wind and solar operations dispersed all over the place. In that economy the big corporations would no longer hold the political and economic reins of the world in their hands, and the result would be chaos.

Millions of dollars had been spent to convince the public that there was doubt about global warming and climate change. That's what people wanted to hear, because it meant they didn't have to think about changes in their lifestyle or the economy. People just wanted to think about their job, their families, football and golf. The American news media had been played and paid and threatened and so far the big coal, oil and gas corporations had been able to control the message and keep the public from getting alarmed. With the takeover of the government by the "oil administration" they had hit their peak in this campaign, and they were darn sure going to keep things the way they were for as long as possible. It was good for America and it was definitely good for them.

Still, Perry was aware that all of Europe and now even China were going full bore into plans to reduce carbon emissions and it wouldn't take much to tip the scales in the US against his clients. They had only been successful so far by being very aggressive in counteracting any threat before it became a problem. "Pre-emptive attack" was not only the new national strategy regarding threats to the foreign oil supply; it also was the strategy for threats to their hold on the minds of the American public. That is why Perry made a note to check into this little pebble of a possible problem hinted at by Wendy, her "guy who could pull the enviros and the public together," and make sure that it wasn't something that could upset the delicate balance of misinformation and insider influence that supported him and his wealthy clients. Any threat that sought to replace the system that was working so well with some utopian idea of dispersed power and wealth was unthinkable and not the American way. It was communism and would have to be dealt with. With that decided he opened the door of the Navigator, grabbed his fine leather portfolio and stepped into his day with his usual cheerful and clear purpose.

Chapter 4

After being dropped off by Aaron on Thursday, Wendy had gone right home to get ready for her date that evening with Perry Pierce Richardson, the Senator and the two Gas men. She had met Perry four months ago outside a hearing room in the Rayburn House Office Building and was immediately charmed by his humor, sophistication and good looks. Wendy wasn't dating anyone at the time, and she made no attempt to hide her interest in this urbane and cheerful man. Women had to be aggressive in Washington if they wanted to be serious players, socially as well as professionally.

"What do you think, is the Chairman trying to make this hearing into a career?" she had asked Perry while they went into the hall to check their cell phone messages.

"If we could just hook him up to a pipeline we wouldn't need to pump any gas out of the ground," Perry told her with a lopsided grin.

"Which end would you hook up? He's as flatulent as he is fatuous," she had responded. The Chairman was famous for episodes of loud farting during his hearings.

"Oh, that's good!" Perry joined her in a good laugh.

They had exchanged names and chatted and before they went back in to the hearing room he asked her if she would go to dinner on the next Friday, "so they could find more ways to solve the energy crisis, and at the same time find useful employment for great leaders like the Committee Chairman."

She knew from the beginning that he was involved with lobbying or legal support for the energy industry, but in Washington it wasn't uncommon for people that had professional positions on opposite sides of issues to date or even have serious long term relationships. Besides, it had been six years since her short, post college marriage ended in divorce, a year since her last real relationship and three months since her last date. She didn't have to think twice before saying yes.

The relationship had developed into something between casual and serious. Perry was also divorced once, with two children who stayed with his remarried first wife. He had married his second wife, Dusty, three years ago, but they were separated now and she was living in Florida while the lawyers worked out the terms of their divorce. She had been his "trophy wife" he confessed to Wendy. She had seen a picture of her at his house, in the Dallas Cowboy cheerleader outfit she had been wearing when he met her. Great body, big hair and, Perry related freely, an attitude towards life uncomplicated by morals or intellect. Unfortunately Dusty had become too fond of booze and nose candy and became a problem. She would get stoned and come on to Perry's clients and the legislators and officials he entertained. Wendy suspected that he was more upset about Dusty's lack of discretion than the infidelities themselves; his complaints centered about the occasions that had caused him to lose face among his friends and colleagues. He couldn't afford to look foolish, he told her. Once people started laughing about you, rather than with you, they stopped entrusting you with serious business. Dusty was now ensconced in an decent apartment in Miami, supporting her cocaine habit with a nice temporary settlement Perry's lawyer had worked out while waiting for their divorce to become final. Perry was open and humble about allowing shallow ego gratification to lead him into a bad marriage, which struck a responsive chord with Wendy, who had her own marital regrets.

On her second date with Perry, after a superb dinner at Vidalia in the Dupont Circle area, Wendy had taken charge. When he took her to the door of her Wisconsin Avenue apartment she had opened the door, stepped inside and reached to pull him in by his necktie. Perry seemed prepared for some kind of smart seduction, but she had a different approach.

"That little cognac seems to have warmed you up," he murmured smoothly with a suave smile as they embraced inside her door. "No telling what another little glass of wine would do..."

He never got "now" out of his mouth before she pulled his head down and gave him a fierce, open mouthed kiss. Before he could get his bearings she pulled his shirt out of his pants, running her nails along the small of his back and then reached down to encourage his growing erection.

"Whahnh!" she groaned. Grabbing the back of his neck with her left hand, she pulled him through the small entry, across the living room and into the bedroom, reaching behind with her right hand to unzip her dress.

Embracing again, she pulled the knot of his tie loose then fumbled at his shirt buttons while probing his mouth and lips with her tongue. She liked his smell and the roughness of the slight evening stubble on her tongue and chin.

"Off," she said urgently in a husky voice. "Take it off." She pulled away again, stepped out of her dress and stripped away her bra and panties.

"Yes, ok, all right, oh man!" Perry puffed out a little nervously as he struggled out of his tie, suit coat, shirt, undershirt. He was sweating as he pulled desperately at his belt and tugged down his zipper. His pants got down to his knees before she came back to him, naked and they tumbled onto the bed.

She climbed on top, pressing her breasts into his face, first one than the other demanding his tongue and lips. After a moment she raised herself to her knees and reached down to push away his boxer shorts. When she lay back on top of him, she pulled on one shoulder, rolling them to their sides so they could embrace and kiss and explore with their hands, touching, cupping, stroking.

"Wait, wait," she said with urgency and reached across him, opened the drawer on the lamp table and pulled out a condom. "Here." She handed it to him and Perry put it on. She straddled him again and he pushed up and entered her. Then there was no thought, no words, no idea of rhythm or technique, just her raw hunger to possess and his need to show his force and strength, one need filling the other for a time with no boundaries.

That first time had been the best. Four months later, the sex was still nice and comfortable, but she had come to feel that Perry was a bit too, well, conscious of what was happening, like he was watching it happen to him, selecting from a menu, admiring his performance and judging hers. For her sex was instinct, not that conscious at all. Intellect had nothing to do with it. It was nothing she could or even cared to put into words; that surge of overpowering physical and emotional feelings that combined to wash away everything else; feelings that were getting smaller and less overpowering lately. It was nice, but Wendy really wanted more than nice.

Friday morning Wendy got to the office shortly after 7:00 despite the late hour that Perry had left her Northwest apartment the night before. It had been after 1:00 when she got back to bed and tried to get some sleep. Then she tossed, twisted and finally just sat up and tried to sort through her thoughts and emotions from the previous day. How in hell had she let Perry talk his way back into her good graces and her bed after his smug put down at dinner? This was going to have to stop. On the other hand, there wasn't any urgency about it. She felt in control of their relationship, and it was…she searched for the word and finally settled on comfortable. After all, he was good looking, charming as hell and she got to go to great places and meet with real decision makers. How many other environmental lobbyists were able to have dinner with a Senator and two top level energy executives and engage them in substantive talk about major projects? None! She still had hopes of being able to get Perry to see the need for a more responsible approach to man's relationship with the natural world, and by extension influence the thinking at APRC. Sometimes it seemed he was moving in the right direction, gaining an appreciation for the need to work on transitioning to a new energy economy based on clean power and climate protection. At those times she fancied herself as some kind of agent provocateur, effecting change from within the camp of the enemy, but at other times she just felt cheap and frustrated, a foolish girl from small town Vermont playing out of her league.

When she had gotten this job as Director of the Campaign Action Office of the Natural America Club she had been ecstatic. She had been an activist as long as she could remember. Through high school and college she supported all the good causes but really devoted herself to keeping the "fuzzy critters" safe. She organized a "Students Against Hunting" club in school that demonstrated at gun shows, lobbied the governor and state house and even marched with drums through a hunting preserve before dawn on opening day, scaring the deer into hiding and enraging dozens of drunks with guns hiding up in their deer blinds.

After college she had married her senior year sweetheart and they went to D.C. looking for work with one of the countless non profit organizations headquartered there. She had waited tables, sold gym memberships and submitted resume after resume. She, husband David and two friends shared a dumpy two bedroom apartment on Georgia Avenue in a crime infested neighborhood for a year and a half. Although there were a thousand non profits dedicated to doing good work in D.C., there seemed to be at least a hundred people ready to apply for any position that came open, all of them with advanced degrees, internships and connections. When she finally landed a very bottom of the pecking order job as receptionist with Friends of the Earth she had told poor lost David (who was on his third consecutive unpaid internship and thinking about going back to school) that the marriage was over. David headed to Ohio for graduate work, and she threw herself 24/7 into becoming indispensable at Friends of the Earth. Her willingness to do any task at any time, experience with demonstrations and direct public actions and innate empathy and intelligence helped her move up step by step, and eventually direct the public outreach office. She was happy to call a hundred people to get a half dozen to show up for a meeting or man a picket line, while other so called organizers felt that sending out emails was how to make personal contact. She built a reputation as someone who had the grassroots touch, and in fact she had discovered the secret of organizing was that you had to get down on your knees and dig into the soil with both hands if you wanted to get at the grass roots.

Wendy had been surprised to get the call from Tony Albritton to D.C. and interview to be National Director of Campaign Action Office at NAC and absolutely astonished when she got the job. NAC was the most widely known and respected environmental organization in the country with almost a million members and a long history of saving endangered species and preserving wildlife habitat. They had also gained a reputation as a major proponent of anti pollution laws and the best at bringing litigation to enforce those laws. The National Campaign Director job was a career peak that exceeded her highest expectations and put her on a whole new level in the environmental community pecking order. It seemed that now she could really make a difference in changing the culture of America to one of living in harmony with the natural world.

When he told her she had the job, Tony had both supported her expectations and cautioned her about the difficulty of meeting them. He had only become the Executive Director of NAC two months before hiring her, having moved from a very high level position at the Environmental Protection Agency.

"Don't believe the hype you have heard about NAC," he told her. "They have a great history based on local issues, and we are widely feared because we are good at suing polluters and logging companies, but on the national stage NAC is as ineffective in shaping policy as the other environmental organizations. We're just bigger. This organization is stuck into the status quo. We get money from donors and grants targeted at narrow and specific political and legislative objectives and try to reach those objectives by writing policies and lobbying to get them enacted and enforced, or suing when someone breaks the law. NAC says it is a grassroots organization and sometimes works that way on the local level, but on the national level we're a weak imitation of the special interest lobbies without the money to compete effectively. I brought you in to help me shake this place up. You're new, energetic, experienced and you have more balls than any other activist I have run across in D.C. When I heard the story about your action chasing away the deer in front of drunk hunters I knew you were the one for the job. Now you and I have to find a way to move NAC out of their comfort zone. They need to do their lobbying on the streets and pack the home offices of the congressmen, not here in D.C."

Then he smiled and put out his hand. "Welcome aboard! We'll either turn this ship around or we will be walking the plank. It should be interesting."

They had bided their time, learning who was open to new ideas (very few, mostly young interns and new hires) and who was not. She got to know key leaders among the volunteer membership, looking for those who would be allies in an organizational shakeup and who wouldn't.

This past Tuesday Aaron Woods had poked his head into her office; no appointment or even notice that he was coming in.

"Excuse me, are you Wendy Sparks?" He moved into the office as he spoke, tall, shoulders filling the door, a mobile, well worn face with tousled brown hair turning gray. His heavy brow shadowed intense eyes, brown with green and some yellow, like moss on an old log. He was dressed as though ready to go hiking in the mountains, and so much at ease that he made her own office attire feel overly formal. The closer he got the bigger he looked to her.

"I'm Aaron Woods," he added, not waiting for her to respond. "We've corresponded a bit and I thought I'd stop in and see if you've had a chance to think about what I've been proposing."

"Hi," she answered, standing up to take the hand he held out. Her hand wasn't delicate by any stretch of the imagination, but it disappeared into his firm grip. She tightened her own grip, finally placing his name and recalling email messages she had gotten from him. When she had read them she'd noted that this was at least one person who shared Tony's vision of using NAC to start a new environmental movement in America. "Yes, I'm Wendy. It would have been better if you had called ahead, but I have a few minutes. Please, have a seat."

He sat in one of the two chairs facing her desk. Her office was small, and cluttered with posters, pamphlets, books: all the accoutrements of putting together campaigns. A bulletin board on one wall was filled with newspaper clippings with overflow taped to the wall itself. There was a white board on the other wall where she kept track of her priorities. It was filled, too. A window behind the desk looked out on a small air shaft and the brick wall of the next building. Phone, computer, flyers, stacks of handouts, notebooks, and loose paper filled her desk, with more books, flyers and papers haphazardly stacked on the unfinished wooden shelves under the white board. She had no room for knick knacks, pictures or any of the usual personal things that would make this anything but a work space, and that was the way she liked it. Her work place was for work; her apartment was the place for personal decoration. Her clothes showed an equal focus on the work at hand, a simple but elegant black pants suit and soft white blouse, the jacket hung on the back of her chair and her sleeves rolled up to below the elbow. She sat down and waited as he frankly looked all around, taking everything in before turning his steady gaze directly into her eyes.

"Wendy, I appreciate you giving me a few minutes and apologize for barging in on you, but if I called ahead I would've gotten your voicemail and we would have danced around by phone and email for longer than my patience will last. At least now I can see who you are and you can see who I am and we can make some preliminary judgments about whether we may be able to work together going forward or not."

She smiled. "Not too big on bullshit, are you?"

He returned her smile, leaning back and stretching his legs out in front of him. "No, I guess I'm not. This is already a good start. Have you had a chance to read the stuff I sent you? Do you have a few minutes to talk about NAC directly engaging the corporations that are causing climate change? About organizing a real national grassroots movement? Your answers to my emails, and I appreciate you responding, something your predecessor never did, your answers lead me to think we share some common views."

As they talked over the next hour Wendy found her excitement building. Aaron understood real old time grassroots organizing: house meetings, street rallies, pickets, packing public meetings and corporate offices; above all sparking enough loud public events to get the media interested and get stories in the papers and on the evening news. He not only understood it, his enthusiasm was infectious. Tony had told her to be on the lookout for a volunteer like Aaron to front the recruitment of the other NAC members.

"Don't just bring me some schmuck," Tony had said. "We need someone who can stand up to the opposition that the staff and a lot of senior members are going to put up because they don't want to get involved in messy grassroots organizing stuff. Someone smart enough and tough enough to handle tough questions. They'll need to have good leadership qualities, but it still has to be someone that you and I can manage and put into the background when we're ready to go public."

Tony was a legend in D.C. for his subtle manipulation of people and organizations. Wendy was thrilled to be his confidante and anxious to learn the arcane nuances of D.C. politics from such a mentor. She was going to put this prospective stalking horse through his paces before she took him to Tony to check him out.

"Tell me what really pushed you to recognize the need to try and build public awareness of climate change," she asked Aaron. "What was the one fact that tipped you into being an activist, and how important is this to you?"

Aaron pulled his feet in, sat up straight and focused intently. "I'm not a scientist, but since, oh, way back, before college, I've been deeply interested in ecology: how everything fits together and the dynamic balance that supports life," he answered. "You could call me an amateur social ecologist, and that is more like a religion to me than what you would call an 'interest.' You know Murray Bookchin? Been reading his stuff forever. I started digging into climate change maybe five years ago. The more I learned the more I got alarmed. Climate change affects everything and it's speeding up. I found out the big oil and coal corporations have spent millions to create doubt and hide the truth from the people, so they keep on making dumb choices that burn more carbon and make more money for the corporations. And this damn administration and congress are totally co-opted by the carbon based industries. So I've been trying for the past couple of years to get NAC to take the lead in building a new energy future based clean power and climate protection. Without much effect except to get some notoriety as a Global Warming guy among activists and a pest among the staff."

He smiled again. "Until now, I hope."

Wendy studied him for a minute, and he waited, patiently allowing her time to consider. She wasn't thinking about what he'd said. That was all pretty

35

common knowledge among environmentalists and the carbon industries. She was impressed with how he said it. He was direct, matter of fact, but calm, reasonable; not strident, hysterical or preachy. He wasn't subtle and didn't come across as an intellectual, but he had a good grasp of the facts, a strong presence and a comfortable manner. He seemed like someone who people just naturally looked to as a leader, and who thought of himself that way, too. Still, Wendy felt that she could manage him, remembering how important that was to Tony. He seemed respectful of her position and she could control most men (except for Tony, who was famously gay as well as being smarter than anyone she ever had met).

What the hell, this guy looked like the real deal and was already a true believer. She might as well fish or cut bait. She returned his smile. "Ok, I'll level with you. Tony and I have wanted to move in exactly the same direction you want NAC to move. We want to start a new movement in America on climate and energy, but we needed to find someone who can be the leader among the volunteers. I've heard about you from other volunteers and your reputation is better than you think it is. People respect you as an effective Global Warming activist. And a pest among the staff, as you say. By the way, I like your 'clean power and climate protection' phrase. We'll want to test it, but I think maybe it can be a key catch phrase for the campaign. For a movement, even. Anyway, let's take some steps, try it out and see if this thing has legs. Can you come back in tomorrow for the day, and Thursday, too?"

"Yup!" he shot back. "What do you have in mind?"

"I'm going to work out an outline for introducing this campaign. Actually, I have already given it a good deal of thought. I'm going to set up meetings with groups of the staff tomorrow and let them know that we are going to be launching a, ah, Clean Power and Climate Protection campaign, starting right away targeting the fossil fuel corporations. Introduce you as the volunteer leader of the campaign. Right away that will piss them off, since they don't think that non professionals have any business messing in the decision making or leadership of a campaign. Then we'll really upset them by telling them that they are going to be asked to help organize the campaign: contact volunteer leaders across the country; integrate Clean Power and Climate Protection into their own work; identify and nurture more new volunteer leaders and allies; plant information in the media; set up meetings and public events. I expect that much of the staff will blow their tops, try to sabotage us or retreat into their shells, depending on how each one handles getting yanked out of their comfort zone. If you are really committed you are going to have to help me deal with that and we might as well start confronting it right away. On Thursday we'll meet with Tony, and I think later in the day Phil McPherson will be coming in."

"I know Phil," Aaron interjected, referring to the President of the NAC Board of Directors. "He understands the issue. Like a lot of activists, he complains about the separation between the local campaigns and the national office. I think he just doesn't have much of a taste for, uh, I guess for being out front in changing things, in confronting people."

"Unlike you?" Wendy asked, raising her eyebrows. This was the key moment. Was he ready to take on the work and hassles of leading a campaign that would alienate entrenched staff and that would need to be sold to the ten thousand really active volunteers across the country, the million who sent in their dues and occasional donations and the big donors who would need to provide heavy funding?

Aaron didn't hesitate. "Yeah, unlike me. Hell, I'm an agent of change. Always have been. Vietnam War, civil rights, workers rights, pollution, saving wild places…in my business career I was known as a real kook, a rogue elephant. But people let me do my thing because I was good at building businesses and making money, so yeah, I'm used to change and helping people get through it. And confronting those who try to stop it."

"Ok! Anyway, we'll see where we are after Thursday. If you survive, ha, if we survive, then we'll talk about getting out and organizing the Chapters, getting them to set up events, contact other groups across the country. Can you travel?"

"Yeah," Aaron said. "I'll have to have some advance notice so I can make arrangements. And, uh, I don't want to be gone more than a couple of days a week, at least most times."

"You married? Got kids?"

"Yes, I mean, no. I, uh, was married but got divorced some years ago. My wife, I mean former wife, lives in France and our son lives in Switzerland. He's in international finance: stuff that's over my head."

Wendy stood up and put out her hand. Aaron stood and took it. This time she made sure that her grip was harder than his as they shook hands.

"Ok, why don't you come in at 10:00 tomorrow? That'll give me time to set things up."

Aaron held her grip for a moment. "Thank you, Wendy. I'm, I'm really pleased and grateful. I think we can do some good work."

"We'll see how you feel after the staff get through with you," she said wryly, letting his hand go after a final shake.

They exchanged goodbyes and she watched him walk out of the office before sitting back down and reaching for the phone to call Tony and let him know they had their stalking horse. It was time to get into action.

Chapter 5

When Anthony Albritton came into his office on Friday morning and saw Wendy chatting with Arch, his administrative assistant, in the anteroom, he knew she had been waiting for him.

"So finally you are going to talk to me and fill me in on why all my most prominent issue experts are parading into my office and either threatening to quit or trying to get me to fire you," he said to Wendy as he walked steadily past them and into his office.

Wendy slid off of Arch's desk where she had been perched. "Tony, I've been waiting for you for half an hour. Who's saying they want to quit? Are you going to fire me?"

Tony led her into the office and put his briefcase on the desk as Wendy's words continued to tumble out. "I hardly slept last night because I was so excited. I was up and out jogging by five and got here an hour ago. I didn't get a chance to see you before you left yesterday because I went out to walk around Roosevelt Island with Aaron and talk some more, then I had an evening engagement. I think he's the guy we need to head this thing up and it's time for us, you know…this is our chance to get some real traction, to start an environmental movement, like the Civil Rights movement back in the sixties or the Anti-Vietnam war movement."

Tony held up both small, neat hands and smiled.

"Whoa! Good morning. I guess you already had your coffee. Maybe you had some of mine too. Sit down and hold on a minute while I see if there is any left. Do you want some more?"

Wendy took a deep inhale and exhale, and turned back to the sofa that was part of the seating arrangement in front of Tony's desk, perching onto the front of the seat. "I'm sorry. I didn't mean to come at you with such a rush. Please, get your coffee and then could we talk about this? I think I've had enough coffee for now. I just really need to know what you think."

"I think we are going to be talking about this most of the morning, so just take it easy and I'll be right back so we can get into it," and Tony chugged out to fill his coffee mug while Wendy leaned back on the sofa and let her shoulders relax a bit. Tony could see she was really jacked up and that was good. He knew that he would need her and every other ally he could get if he decided to take this big, very traditional organization into new and unknown directions.

With his small, neat appearance, quiet manner, small steps and the graceful way he moved his hands and crossed his legs people often underestimated Tony's tenacity and courage. Tony Albritton had to fight for every step as he worked his way up the career ladder to becoming the first openly gay Executive Director of the Natural America Club, or of any other large national environmental organization. He had moved back and forth between jobs on congressional staffs, government agencies and non profit think tanks, each move carefully calculated to enhance his resume and prepare for the next upward step.

He had never been afraid to take a chance when it looked like he could move higher, even though it would expose him to the usual professional jealousies and attacks from people he stepped over or those who just couldn't tolerate a gay man in a position of authority. He mastered every little nuance of governmental policy making, choosing to focus especially on environmental issues. He had moved to the ED position at NAC from a senior executive position, just below the political appointees, with the Environmental Protection Agency just eight months ago, with the hope that this job would give him his chance to do something historic, something that would set him apart. Tony Albritton wanted people to read about him long after he was gone.

In his twenty-year career in Washington, Tony had ruthlessly employed the stealth attack technique to advance his career. Because he was an excellent and sympathetic listener, he had frequently been privy to advance knowledge of planned addresses, or position papers being prepared by other staff members as he worked his way upward through the closely related political, governmental and non profit sectors of Washington's bureaucracy. If he got word of such a plan and he felt it presented an opportunity for his advancement he would apply his tremendous capacity for research and analysis to probe the issue, find the flaws in the planned position and devise remedies for those flaws. He would then wait until the policy proposal was presented by the unsuspecting colleague and, with well feigned diffidence, express some misgivings about the weak points he had discovered. Carefully baiting the hook, he would get the top level official or panel to whom the presentation was being made to force him into delivering, seemingly without preparation, an alternative that would be an obvious improvement on the position presented by his hapless colleague. He then received wide acclaim for his seeming encyclopedic knowledge and for saving those officials from taking terrible missteps. All the while he maintained his working relationships by insisting that the original presenter had "pretty much gotten it all right except for a few details." Of course, those arcane and often obscure "details" were just the sort of things that would make the difference between a policy that would give the Congressman, Senator or agency chief political and career victories, or would cause them to suffer embarrassing defeats.

Tony kept a plaque hanging over his desk with the quote from Henry James that "What is great about a life is doing something that will outlast it." Sooner or later he knew he would find his chance to break out of the tiresome Washington policy writing, apple polishing and career backstabbing and really do something that would make his life great. When that chance came along he was going to be ready.

Yesterday he had felt the hair on the back of his neck and along his arms rise up when Wendy brought Aaron Woods in to talk with him, Phil McPherson and a few other key volunteer leaders in the conference room. He knew that Wendy had been having meetings with Aaron and the top staff members throughout the day and he was glad to see that neither of them seemed fazed by the largely antagonistic reception he was sure they had been given.

"We are locked in to climate change on a level that will have enormous impact on every living person and being on earth," Woods had summarized at the end of his presentation. "In fifty years the sea level will rise at least 3 ft., displacing tens of millions of people around the world, from Washington D.C. to Bangladesh. Oceanic salinity, currents, temperature and acidity are all changing and life forms are already starting to die out. Insect biting and breeding rates will double, causing massive loss of forests and increases in disease. A million acres of forest in the northwest part of the continent have already been lost to the climate change induced increase of bark beetles, and D.C. is seeing malaria for the first time this century. Hurricanes and tornadoes will increase in frequency and intensity by 50%.

"I could go on, about impacts on rivers and croplands, floods and droughts, but that would be an insult. We all know about this. We know it will change every person's way of life. What I am here to ask you is this: why aren't you doing anything about it? What will people say about you fifty years from now? Will they ask, 'How could the Natural America Club have known about this and not done everything possible to slow it down, reduce the impacts, shorten the centuries of travail that all living things are going to have to bear?' Was it because in 2004 people did not have the courage to change the way they get and use energy?"

Woods had paused here. Then he punctuated each point of his last sentence with a chop of the edge of his opened hand on the table.

"How will the Natural America Club answer those people who ask, 'Who were your leaders? Why didn't they take action at the critical hour?'"

Woods had paused again. "I know that you are all good people doing good work, and just haven't tackled climate change because you didn't see a way to do it effectively. Please, look at the brief proposal I left you. We can do this. Let's talk about this again."

With that he had asked if they had any questions, thanked them for their time, gathered his papers together and left the room.

Wendy had said, "I'll see him out," and hurried after him. That was the last he had seen of her until this morning. Phil and the others at the briefing had not been comfortable with the direct way that Aaron had addressed them, fixing them with responsibility for past inaction on climate change, but as they discussed the campaign they came to see that it was just that kind of tough talk that was needed. Tony felt sure that they were going to give him enough rope to either tie this campaign together or to hang himself. Phil and the other lead activists were trained in the law or public policy, or the scientific, academic and research arenas. They were not risk takers themselves, but they weren't opposed to someone else going out on a limb. After getting Phil and the others to give him the go ahead, he had gone back to his office to find that Arch had a list of the staff who wanted to talk to him about the proposed direction changes for NAC. He had brought his upset staff people into his office one at a time and heard their complaints until almost 8:00 PM last night.

"All right, Wendy, let's talk about Mr. Woods and his ideas for a new role for the Natural America Club," Tony said as he came back into the office and settled into the easy chair set at right angles to the sofa. He took a sip from his coffee and continued.

"It appears to me we have three things to consider. First, should we redirect most of our focus to climate change while abandoning or at least lessening our attention to the many other issues of wild land and species preservation, clean air and clean water? Second, can or should we change our highly paid issue experts and lobbyists into grassroots organizers to build the base of public opinion and directly engage the corporations that create the pollutants and greenhouse gasses? Third, will our members and donors embrace this campaign and form the nucleus of a national popular movement? In sum, can this be done or are we and Mr. Woods out of touch with reality?"

"I think we need to ask a fourth question," Wendy said thoughtfully. "Will our professional staff be willing or able to change their whole career path and become populist organizers?"

"Oh, please," Tony answered. "While you were cruising around Roosevelt Island enjoying the scenery Ruthann Horowitz and Jeremiah Aki Shabaka were in here raking me over the coals for destroying NAC and flushing their six years of work on the Everglades restoration project down the drain."

Ruthann and Jeremiah were the most powerful staff policy experts and lobbyists on the payroll. They were always mentioned in the same breath even though on the surface they couldn't be more different. Ruthann was a thin, beige, vegan with a shrill voice roughened by an overly fibrous and under nourishing diet that was going to let her live for 100 years but be plagued with headaches, cramps, tiredness and low libido for all of them. She came from a conventional suburban Jewish family that based their identity as such on ethnic and liberal political factors rather than on religious observance. Jeremiah was a heavy, handsome, light skinned black man who invariably wore a colorful African fez and shawl with a cotton dashiki and matching pants. Coming from a large and low income family in Memphis, his powerful pronouncements fluctuated between a baroque southern gentleman drawl and the staccato nasal Boston tones he picked up as a scholarship student at Harvard. Ruthann and Jeremiah had been working together on the campaign to restore the hydrologic function of the Everglades for the past six years. They were part of a contentious but interlocking alliance that included the Army Corp of Engineers, the Florida State Department of Natural Resources, the Environmental Protection Agency, the federal and state Departments of Agriculture along with other agencies, environmental and political groups, public utilities and, of course, lawyers of all stripes who had cobbled together an $8 billion dollar plan to renew the flow of fresh water into the Everglades thereby stopping the steady incursion of the saline Gulf and Atlantic waters that were killing this vast grass ecosystem. And, of course, provide a source of income for them all. Ruthann and Jeremiah were constantly at war with each other, but they formed a solid back to back front when dealing with outsiders, including any of their "allies" and especially in the face of any threat to their significant funding stream.

"Your boy Aaron certainly pushed their buttons when he challenged them to describe what provisions were being made in their plan to account for the projected rise in sea levels over the next five decades, to say nothing of years beyond. Ruthann told me that he said their eight billion dollars was going to get flushed out to sea, and it could be put to better use by making more energy efficient buildings. Of course, the fact he is right and that they had no answer is what really pissed them off. They are scared, and rightly so, that if people start talking like that their funding sources will dry up and no one will be interested in all the knowledge they have about the wetlands. If we don't handle this right we'll be cutting off all our donors without any guarantee that they are going to fund our new grassroots organizing campaign on climate change."

Wendy didn't have any immediate answer. They all knew that their careers depended on them getting big donors to fund the NAC. Even with a million members paying dues, they had to raise another $70 million a year to keep the organization going. Ruthann and Jeremiah and the other policy experts all had a part in raising that money. If all the policy experts moved to other organizations rather than embracing the new call to enlist the American public in reducing carbon emissions NAC would really be scrambling to get the money they would need. She thought the private and organizational donors would see the benefit of using the NAC to build up a real grassroots movement, but there were no guarantees. If the policy experts turned on them then it could really hurt their fundraising.

"Well, the hell with it!" Tony said, breaking the silence. "If we don't do this, then who else will? We have the knowledge. We have the membership organized into State Chapters and local groups. We have the reputation, even if it is mostly based on local and state victories instead of national ones. The active volunteers have been pushing for some way to make the Club unified and exciting, bring the local and national campaigns together and take the leadership in a revitalized environmental movement. I've heard a hundred times that people want to do more than write postcards to regulators or send e-mails to Congressmen. They are fed up with our professional staff who don't have time to work with the activist volunteers because they are busy being experts on some policy or another. The hell with the money. Cesar Chavez didn't worry about money when he started the United Farm Workers. Movements don't start with money; they start with an idea, a vision. I think our donors will buy into this, but if we are going to do this we just have to go ahead and do it and figure out the money angle as we go along."

Tony ran his hand delicately across his forehead. "Damn, I'm getting worked up about this, too. It feels good!"

He got up and walked over to his desk to look at his plaque. "The only way we'll see if this can be done, is if we just go ahead and do it," he repeated, working to convince himself as much as Wendy. "We're going to take on the biggest multinational corporations in the world, one at a time, and tell them that if they don't move to new energy sources that don't pollute or cause climate change, we'll expose their responsibility for the harm being done to people, the earth and the atmosphere. We'll pick one, SPECO, the biggest and baddest oil corporation. We will engage their shareholders and drive down their stock prices. We will organize boycotts of their products across the country and around the world. We'll pressure their insurance and financial backers, their suppliers and workers with legal and public actions. We will initiate litigation just like it was done to the tobacco industry, making them financially liable for the rise in sea level, the flooding, the disease, and every other consequence of the use of their products."

He turned back to Wendy. "That's about right, isn't it? That's what we are thinking of doing?"

She just shrugged and held out her hands with her palms up. It was going to be up to him to make this decision and she wasn't going to take any of the pressure off him. She knew that if she didn't let him make the decision totally on his own then when things got tough he would be more likely to back off and use her as a scapegoat. He'd probably do that publicly anyway, but this way he would have at least made the commitment in their private relationship. She needed to know that he was committed that far, so she just waited on him.

"Well," he said, "damn it! That sounds just about right to me. It is high time for us to take the horses off this merry go round and see if we can ride them somewhere."

"Yes!" Wendy jumped off the sofa, spread her arms high and wide, took two steps over to Tony and folded him in a tight embrace; then she gave him a big, sloppy kiss on the lips. "I am ready!"

Tony returned her embrace for moment, then pulled back, taking hold of her hands. He took in the hot flush of her cheeks and neck, the upturned corners of her dark, flashing eyes. "Ah, yes!" he noted dryly. "Even I can see you're ready."

"Ha!" She barked out a laugh at the unexpected riposte from her cool boss who had up to now not taken part this sort of earthy and personal give and take. Aside from his well known homosexuality, any kind of sexual innuendo between a male and female in the straight laced world of environmental non profits was definitely politically incorrect.

"You bet I am," she shot back at him. "What do you propose to do about it?"

"Touché," he retorted, dropping her hands and moving back behind his desk. "I think what I will do about it is direct you, as our Campaign Director, to work out a campaign plan to get the BOD to agree with this and get the activist members excited about it. You will need to do an internal organizing campaign to prepare the NAC to lead a grassroots movement and build up Mr. Woods as a credible figurehead. At least initially the members and even the public will be more accepting of him than they will of professionals like you and I. We will have to prop him up and support him until the right moment comes for us to take the lead. You will need to get the media staff to work on a publicity campaign that builds up to a big press announcement to kick it all off, say by September."

He paused and then looked back in her eyes with a smile. "Is Mr. Woods ready to capitalize on your state of readiness."

She laughed again, not taking the bait. "We'll see about that. What are you going to do?"

"Of course, I'll be keeping track and helping you with contacts as needed, but my main job is going to be to work with our current donors and find some new ones who will provide the funds to build this movement. Plus I have to get our highly paid and wonkish staff away from their computer screens and face to face with the members and donors. They will now have to be organizers instead of experts, and I will have to lead the way. It is going to take a lot of energy to make that happen."

"Do you think they'll buy into this? Won't they try to sabotage the campaign?" she asked.

Tony raised his brows and gave her a thin smile that revealed the ruthlessness that lay beneath his cultured exterior.

"Oh, some will be ok and some won't. Once we get the Board of Directors excited about it, staff will take stock of the excellent pay, benefits and prestige of working with Natural America and they will at least take a stab at it until they can find more traditional policy jobs elsewhere. If they don't I can replace anyone who leaves with two or three low paid, idealistic young organizers who are ready to sleep on floors, knock on doors, make hundreds of phone calls and lead volunteers on picket lines and demonstrations."

"Ok," he said, having fully recovered his normal neutral façade and bringing the discussion to a conclusion. "Let's get busy. Today we start to change the future of America."

After Wendy practically skipped out of the door to do just that, Tony sat down at his desk, leaned back and gave a large, satisfied sigh. At last he had his chance to do something on the very biggest stage of the world. He vowed to stop at nothing to achieve his goals.

"One small step for mankind, and one big step for Anthony Albritton," he said softly.

Chapter 6

Aaron got up early the morning after his Thursday meeting with Tony Albritton and the movers and shakers at NAC and Squeak's breakthrough "controlled rage," as they decided to call it. He enjoyed putting together a sandwich for Squeak's school lunch, and as usual fixed one for his own lunch at the same time. Multi grain bread, some sprouts and maybe some goat cheese and olives, or turkey and cheese, or just peanut butter and jelly: he preferred a good sandwich to most of the meals he'd had at the best restaurants in town. He had pretty much stopped going to the better restaurants since his divorce. Elena was the one interested in fine restaurants, opera and cocktail parties, while he preferred Chinese take out, Joni Mitchell and a joint with a friend. When he had figured out he had built up enough investments to provide a modestly comfortable lifestyle and retired from his business work, their different tastes and expectations suddenly became a problem. The refined social life had always been a necessary part of doing business; painless but not as eagerly anticipated as reading a good book or jogging a riverbank trail. As soon as he didn't need them anymore he gave away his suits and the contacts that went with them. Elena quickly tired of their new life with its casual social style and before he realized they were in trouble she was gone. Five years later he still found himself standing at the kitchen counter or blankly sitting on a bus going past his stop, wondering what had happened, his head filled with the empty hole she had left behind.

He added an apple, peeled and packed a big carrot and put it in a bag with the sandwich. Unlike his young friends, Squeak preferred his home prepared and packed lunches to the offerings of the school cafeteria, which tended to be over processed and less nutritious. While other kids ate meals of chips, pizza and soda, Squeak savored his sandwich, fruit and vegetable washed down with two chocolate milks. Aaron figured that the kid's respect for good fresh food came from his first seven years on the street where meals were uncertain and seldom clean or fresh. Squeak hadn't spent much of that time with his crack addicted mother, who mostly just used him to gain entry into shelters and free kitchens. As an infant he was passed from one "Auntie" to another in the drug and sex trade community, somehow never getting picked up by the "system." For at least the last two years before he met Aaron he had been a true street Arab, surviving through a combination of luck, innate intelligence, physical toughness and the kindness of strangers. He begged, stole, danced for quarters, went through trash and spent too many days hungry. Squeak gave Aaron a heart tugging hug and kiss on the cheek every day when he handed over the lunch bag as the boy left for school.

Now that the kid was in middle school he just had to go across the street and around the corner. Elementary school had just been a two block walk up the street and across Stanton Park. Aaron couldn't understand why so many young adults who enjoyed the urban lifestyle picked up stakes and moved out to the suburbs as soon as their kids reached school age. He had been able to spend lots of time in the school, especially the first couple of years, making sure that Squeak was getting treated right and working with the teachers to get him caught up with the other kids.

Squeak was the oldest in his class and way behind when he started in first grade. Couldn't read anything, couldn't write, pure street for a vocabulary. Even Aaron had to work hard to understand much of anything he said. The only thing the kid could do well was count money and add and subtract it. He caught up fast, though, moving through four grades in three years until he was in class with other kids his age. Now it was a problem to keep him from getting bored with the schoolwork. Aaron set up advanced reading, math and science projects with the teachers at the beginning of the year, visiting teachers every day until he built a good working relationship. Sure, he knew that they often thought he was a pain in the ass, but he didn't care as long as Squeak got the best education possible. In return, he volunteered as a resource, tutoring other kids and being a chaperone for field trips. Squeak completed Algebra I last year in the fifth grade; working entirely on his own with Aaron's help, and this year was doing Algebra II with the eighth graders. Aaron figured most kids in the suburbs weren't getting a better education than that.

After seeing Squeak off to school he walked to the pool at Eastern Market and swam a hard mile to loosen his joints and clear his head. He hadn't gotten in any kind of workout the past few days because of all the time he'd spent in meetings. He felt physically and mentally rusty when he didn't engage in some kind of vigorous activity; biking, kayaking, climbing, swimming, running, hitting the heavy bag, splitting firewood or lifting weights were the usual outlets. He vowed to get up at 5:00 while this campaign went on if needed to get in his workouts and keep his engine going, because he sure wouldn't have the patience to sit in meetings without regular hard physical release.

After jogging back home he tuned in to the commercial free digital jazz channel on cable and settled down to a leisurely breakfast with the Washington Post. Jazz tended to feel too much like someone was just wasting their time doodling around and not getting anywhere if he just sat and listened to it, but it was great as a background when doing household chores, reading or working on the computer. He occasionally broke into free form dancing when a particularly good John Coltrane or Thelonious Monk tune came on, or sing along with Louis Armstrong or Ray Charles. Squeak called his dancing "crazy honky heebie jeebie" and just rolled his eyes at his singing and left the room. That reaction was pretty typical of what he had gotten all his life, so he didn't dance or sing in public places.

He had a long relationship with the Post, dating back to when he delivered it as a kid. It was one of the things that had helped him decide to settle in D.C. when he dumped his far flung business career to live off his investments. The Post was both a source of information and a platform for his positions on issues ranging from storm water management standards to provision for low income housing in any new residential projects. He was a good source of quotes for reporters and was quickly welcomed by his neighbors as a leader. He got to know the neighborhood cops, the head of the PTA, the pastors of all the churches and the longtime residents. When pressure was needed, people would call Aaron and he would organize a delegation to go and sit in the office of the City Councilwoman or some unsuspecting city official, right up to the Mayor. There they would stay, calling reporters and demanding an audience.

Once they got in, they were always prepared with a timetable and task list and they didn't leave until their hapless target agreed to take action.

Over the past couple of years, Aaron had become more involved in the bigger issues of the degradation of the planet in general and global warming in particular. The poor media coverage really frustrated him. In fact, today's paper reported that profits for the oil industry were at record highs due to high prices at the gas pump, with no reference to the real issue of how neither industry nor government were preparing for the even higher prices of the future, as the world ran out of oil, or the consequences of burning oil instead of using less and cleaner energy. He'd have to write another letter to the editor.

He threw down the paper with disgust and spent the day catching up on household chores, paying bills and avoiding his e-mails, which he knew would have piled up over the last two days. When Squeak came home he changed into basketball shoes.

"Want to go shoot some hoops?" he asked as the boy put down his backpack and looked in the refrigerator.

"Are you and Antelope going to play?" Squeak asked.

"Yeah, we're going to meet there."

Squeak shook his head. "Uh, uh! No way I'm playing with you guys, and no one else is going to either. I'll go out later when you two are done beating up on each other. Don't even know why you take a ball and take up court space. You should just go out on the corner and hack away at each other. I'm gonna do my homework and some Play Station. After I have a snack."

Squeak's snack was starting to look like a sandwich, glass of milk, some grapes and anything else he could find.

"Don't know what you're talking about," Aaron said as he went out the door. "That's the way men play ball."

"Right, if you call it mangle ball. It ain't basket ball," he heard Squeak say as the door closed.

Aaron chuckled as he walked across the street, through the gate to the teacher's parking lot and around the back of the school to the outdoor courts. These basketball courts were the center of his engagement with the neighborhood. It was on this playground, in the second year after he had moved to D.C. and the first year after Elena had left him, that he met Squeak and Antelope. Often as he walked over to the courts, or while he was idling there waiting for a basket to be free or to join in a game, he felt the comfort of his personal roots in the neighborhood, and he would muse on events that had occurred there.

When he moved here seven years ago, none of the four baskets on the two courts had been useable. Two of them hadn't even had backboards, one didn't have a rim and the other rim was bent down perpendicular to the ground. A mix of thugs and kids hung out there. He bought a couple of heavy duty backboards and rims and hired a guy to come and hang them. The thugs and kids who hung around there had just watched, but as soon as they were up and he started playing, a few of them came over. First they just joked and laughed about his old school game.

"Hey, man, what kind of shit is that. That ain't no shot," one tall kid in a do rag, baggy jeans and long tee shirt called out. His buddies laughed with him.

Aaron retrieved the ball from his latest miss. He threw a bounce pass at the kid, who had to put his hands up to keep it from hitting him in the chest.

"Let's see what you got, big guy," he'd said mildly. Pretty soon there were five or six of them playing twenty one, mostly styling, not really willing to try hard. That's the way it is most of the time in street ball. If you show you're trying too hard and you fail people rag on you, so you have to play it cool, show off your moves but don't get caught up in winning.

Aaron wasn't cool, never had been. Cool bored him. He thirsted to win at whatever he tried and never concerned himself with how he looked doing it, but on that first day he took it easy, just to start to get to know the people in the neighborhood. When he'd had enough he tucked the ball under his arm.

"That's enough for me, guys," he said. "I just moved in. I like to play hoops, even if I don't have much of a game, so I paid to get these baskets fixed. I hope you'll help me take care of them so they stay up for a while, 'cause I'm not rich and can't be replacing them all the time. Then we can all enjoy playing some hoops."

No one said anything as he walked away, but those first hoops had lasted for three months before someone pulled down one of the rims. He fixed up the other two baskets, too, and over the years only had to replace an average of two a year to keep all four playable.

Soon after he started going to the playground regularly he noticed one particular boy with shabby looking clothes who hung around the courts by himself a lot, but sometimes joined the game when Aaron invited whatever kids were around to play with him. The boy was small, quiet and serious, and didn't really seem to know or fit in with the other neighborhood kids, but he was a quick little guy with natural balance and that indefinable but definite sense of himself as an individual that some people are born with and some never get. On a couple of occasions when Aaron was shooting by himself the kid had shown up and just started retrieving the ball until Aaron invited him to join in and take his shots. Aaron showed him a couple of things about shooting, no big deal, but the kid listened intently and would try things that Aaron suggested.

Occasionally another older guy would be on the courts, maybe in his thirties, a little over six foot and thick in the shoulders, chest, butt and thighs, but Aaron had never talked with him. The guy usually brought a mixed breed dog with him, tied him up to the fence that surrounded the playground and played alone, leaving if the courts started to get crowded. Same thing happens on basketball courts all over the world and Aaron never bothered the guy. Lots of times he just liked to shoot around by himself, too, the way he and millions of others had done as kids all over the world, acting out imaginary games.

About 6:30 in the evening one fall day in the year when Elena had left, when there was still just enough light to shoot, Aaron had gone to the playground to loosen up after a day of work. Some of the companies he had worked with in his first career, before he had pulled the plug to concentrate fully on the ecological and social justice issues that were his passion, called on him now and then to help them with advice. They were old friends and good people and it was difficult to turn them down, but doing corporate problem solving while being committed to righting social inequities rooted in the system that placed profit before people created stressful contradictions. Those were the very strains that had led him to leave his business career in the first place. Shooting hoops helped him relax before dinner and kept his mind off of the long night hours when sleep wouldn't come and his mind filled with the silent roar of emptiness in a lonely house.

The big guy with the dog was shooting at one basket and the others were occupied by kids, mostly middle school students.

"Mind if I shoot with you?" he said to the guy in the standard greeting.

"Sure, free world." The guy stopped and put out his hand. "I'm Antelope"
His raspy voice came from deep in his thick chest.

"Aaron," he replied. They exchanged firm grips, but didn't engage in any strength contest.

They shot baskets for a while, retrieving balls for each other.

"I hear you put these baskets up," Antelope said after a while. "That was a cool thing to do. I appreciate it."

"You're welcome," Aaron answered. They shot for a while more as it got darker.

"What kind of dog have you got?" he asked.

"Mixed, like me," Antelope answered. "I think he's part lab and part German shepherd."

"So what are you?" Aaron asked.

Antelope looked at him for a few seconds, but Aaron was just took another shot and ran down his ball.

"I'm part Cherokee and part African American," he said. Then he laughed. "People don't usually ask that. At least not white people."

"Well, you mentioned it," Aaron said after he retrieved his ball. "I didn't mean any offense. I'm mixed, too. Part Irish, part I don't know what and part fool."

They were interrupted by a loud squeal coming from the shadows by the corner of the school building. Aaron stopped and looked, but he couldn't make out what was happening.

"No! Eeeee!" he heard. It was definitely a kid who was squealing and he could make out a group of thugs back there in the shadowed corner of the building; punks who sometimes hung out around the courts. They had been hanging out there less often since the courts started being used more. He heard them laughing and shouting."

"Hol' still, li'l prick. This won't hurt much," and more laughing and hooting.

Aaron rolled his ball over to the fence and walked over to the building and into the shadows. Now he could see there were four of the thugs, young men between 18 and 25 who belonged to what he called the "lost generation." They were some of the ten thousand young men in the District that had no jobs, weren't in school, weren't in any job training program, didn't have a high school diploma. Aaron wished he had a solution for them, but he didn't and he mostly thought of them as the source of crime and trouble in the neighborhood. And right now they were causing trouble.

Two of the thugs were holding on to the little kid he had seen around and on the courts, while a third was holding up the kid's left sleeve. The fourth, the tall kid who had first come over to hassle him on the day he had put up the baskets, was trying to burn the little kid's upper arm with the lit end of a cigarette. The kid was struggling, yelling and squeaking out his high pitched squeal, and the thug and his crew were cussing him and laughing.

"Oh tha's good. Lis'en a you squeak like a li'l bitch," the thug with the cigarette said with a sneering laugh.

"Ok, hold up here right now, fellas," Aaron said as he came into the shadowed corner and walked up to the thug with the cigarette. His voice was calm but hard and firm, cutting through all the noise. Surprised, the hoods stopped laughing and looked at him as he stopped just four feet away from the ringleader. Aaron stood comfortably, left foot forward, knees flexed, hands at his side. He showed no doubt, no fear, no anger.

"This kid is a friend of mine and there isn't going to be any burning here tonight. You let him go now. Let's not have any drama."

"Who the fuck'r you, old bitch," the tall kid said, shaking off the shock of being confronted and turning to face Aaron. "This ain't your fucking neighborhood, white-ass cocksucker. You gonna get fucked up, motherfucker."

"This neighborhood belongs to all of us. You know I'm the Commissioner here and if you fuck with me you'll get the same kind of hassle as the dealers did around the elementary school. Cops will be all over you."

Aaron wasn't the Commissioner, a kind of elected but unpaid ward boss, but he had organized the neighborhood to drive away the drug dealers that had been hanging out around one of the elementary schools a few blocks away. He'd knocked on doors, held meetings, prepared news releases and letters to the editor and organized visits to officials by neighborhood groups, putting so much pressure on the Metropolitan Police Department and the City Council that they stationed cops at the school ever since and moved the drug trade three blocks away to H Street. He was bluffing and had just used the Commissioner title because it popped into his head and sounded good and it was an office respected in D.C. neighborhoods. He hoped these thugs had heard about that little project and wouldn't want to hassle him.

The two thugs holding the little kid let him go. He slipped away, but turned around to watch what would happen. The four thugs started to form a circle around Aaron. It looked like the bluff wasn't going to work. Aaron took two steps back to keep them all in front of him, flexed his knees more, got on his toes and brought his hands up and half open in front of him. He had boxed in college, not on a school team but club fighting, where the ring was often just some ropes strung from chair to chair, the air was heavy with smoke and there were few rules. It was a way to make some extra money to supplement his part time job. He hadn't been a great fighter, but he won a little more than he lost and his fights drew good crowds because there weren't many white fighters around and he had what they called heavy hands and a brawling style. He hoped that he'd be able to get in a few punches, but he'd never been very fast and these young hoods would be all over him. There were just too many of them.

"Yo, young bloods," came a deep, loud rasp from about ten feet behind Aaron. It was Antelope, the big guy. Aaron didn't turn to look, but the thugs all shifted their eyes that way, except for the ringleader right in front of Aaron.

"You studs can probably fuck up my white buddy by himself, but you better think twice about fucking with him, me, this piece of pipe and my dog," Antelope said. "Now get your sorry asses out of here and find someplace else to stink up with your shit."

There was a pause when no one moved. Antelope's dog growled a low, menacing threat from behind his legs. Aaron felt the sweat trickle down his sides from under his arms.

"Fuck, man. We just havin' fun. We wasn't gonna hurt the kid," said one hood on Aaron's left. He turned away and started to walk towards the basketball courts.

"Right, man," said another. He, and then the third moved towards the courts, leaving their tall leader alone in front of Aaron. They gave Antelope and the dog a wide berth.

"Dis fuckin' neighborhood's gone to shit anyway. White bastards comin' in pushing us out," said the last of the departing three.

He feinted at the kid, who was off to the side watching. He scampered a few feet away from them and back towards Aaron and the tall ringleader facing him. The other three continued on their way across the courts.

"Come on, dog," one called back to his buddy. The tall kid spat on the ground and then walked past Aaron, brushing against his shoulder. Aaron felt his face go hot. His fists clenched and his arms ached to lash out, but he held it back and let the punk go.

"Ugly bitches," the thug threw over his shoulder after he was well clear of Antelope. Aaron turned, watching the punks move away and finally seeing Antelope. He loomed very large and solid against the light behind him, holding a two foot length of lead pipe with a turnbuckle on the end in one hand and the leash of his dog in the other. He watched as the five thugs moved together crossing the courts and starting to jive each other. The kids that had been playing there had disappeared. As the hoods passed the last basket one jumped up and grabbed hold of the front of the rim, trying to bend it down, but he didn't have the weight or strength to do more than make the pole that supported the backboard and basket sway. He dropped down and they shuffled out through the gate and down the street, yelling insults over their shoulders and telling each other that they would have really fucked up those old bastards but they had to go down to H St. to see what was happening there and they didn't have time to mess with the old fools.

"Wheeeooo," Aaron let out a long breath. Now his knees felt weak, almost buckling as he relaxed out of his stance. He bent over for a minute with his hands on his knees and took a couple more deep breaths. "Thanks for stepping in, Antelope. I was about to get a real ass kicking." Aaron pronounced the three syllables of the name clearly: An-tah-lope.

"Well, Aaron," Antelope replied, starting to smile and exaggerating the "A," making it sound like two names: A-ron. "You probably had things under control, being the Commissioner and all."

"Hah! That was just a bluff. I'm no Commissioner. It was just the only thing I could think of that might hold them off. It didn't work for shit."

They started to walk towards the basketball courts.

"I think it was your dog that got their attention," Aaron said.

"That was a bluff, too," Antelope replied. "Damn dog would run for home if they raised a hand to him."

They looked at each other and laughed, releasing their adrenalin charged tension.

"Hey, kid," Aaron called to the boy, who was still over by the wall of the school, watching them, "come on over here."

The kid sidled over to where Aaron and Antelope were collecting their basketballs without saying anything. He watched them warily.

"Let me look at that arm. They burned you, didn't they?" Aaron said.

"It nothin'," the kid mumbled, but he walked over to Aaron and pulled up his sleeve. "Dey rip mah coat."

Aaron looked at the burn, an angry, circular red welt two inches down from the kid's shoulder.

"Let's go over to my place and put some first aid cream on this," he said. "What's your name, kid?"

"Squeak."

"Squeak? Is that your real name?"

"Yeah, 'cus, ya know, how I sound."

"Ok, go get your coat and we'll dress up that burn. Maybe we can fix your coat where they ripped it."

Squeak walked back into the corner to get his coat. He paused for a minute, then made up his mind and walked over to the two men.

Antelope had put his pipe into a gym bag and turned to go. He took the dog's leash.

"Come on, Boner, let's go eat."

"What's your dog's name?" Aaron asked.

"Boner," Antelope said with a straight face. "He just loves bones."

The two men exchanged a look. Aaron started laughing again, and then couldn't stop. It was the first time he had really let go and laughed since Elena left him and he felt tears leaking from his eyes. Antelope and Squeak looked at each other with a shrug.

"Boner, huh," he managed to get out as his laughing finally subsided and he pulled up his tee shirt to wipe his face. "That's a great name." He reached out his hand to Antelope and they shook. "Look, man, I've got a whole roasted chicken, some salad and plenty of rice. I live right over there. Why don't you and Boner come over and eat?"

Antelope looked at Aaron for a minute, then nodded, making up his mind about more than dinner.

"Ok, A-ron," he smiled. "I don't mind if I do. No one's waitin' for me to come home."

Squeak joined them and they started over to Aaron's house.

"How 'bout you, kid," Antelope asked. "Your mama waitin' on you to get home?"

Squeak shrugged his shoulders, but didn't say anything.

"Come on, Squeak. Where do you live, anyway?" Aaron asked.

"No place," he finally mumbled. Then he turned to Aaron and, for the first time, looked him in the eyes.

"Don' got no home," his high voice angry now, challenging. "I on ta' street. My mama," he shrugged again, "don' see 'er much."

Aaron nodded. He had one homeless acquaintance, Vincent, who sold *Street Sense* on the corner outside his regular Starbucks. They had talked some, both on the corner and sitting inside a couple of cold days when Aaron had asked him to join him for a cup of coffee. Vincent was an addict, alternating between recovery and relapse like many of the homeless, a bright and engaging guy who was an aspiring inventor. From his acquaintance with Vincent and from what he had read, Aaron knew that half the homeless were under ten years old, but he, like most people had just assumed that the kids were all part of homeless families.

They got to the house and he unlocked the door and opened it up.

"Well, then, let's fix up that arm and then we can all eat and talk about why three fine men like us don't have any women around."

"Four men," Antelope said. "Don't forget Boner. He's got an excuse, though. No nuts."

That had been almost five years ago. Squeak stayed in Aaron's spare bedroom that night, and one night turned into a week and a week into a month. Squeak reluctantly helped Aaron find out where his mother, Dorinda Johnson, was staying. Aaron made the rounds of the workers at the shelters and homeless people that Squeak knew or that Vincent introduced to him, learning that Dorinda was a long time addict and alcoholic and she was staying "with some guys" at the old Arthur Capper project in the near South East part of town, just off of Capital Hill. Aaron paid Vincent to check around there and get him the address, because he knew that the people at the project weren't likely to volunteer much information to him. He didn't take Squeak with him when he went to talk with Dorinda, and Squeak gave no indication that he wanted to go.

Dorinda's apartment was the left side ground floor apartment in a two story, square, brick, four unit building. The other three apartments were vacant, as were most of the buildings on the block. Many windows were boarded up and the battered front door to the hallway hung open, the lock broken and a "Condemned-Do Not Enter" sign taped to it. The Arthur Capper project was slated to be demolished and replaced by new mixed income public housing. Everyone was supposed to be moved out of the east side of the project and just a block away all the buildings on one side of the street had been demolished, like a bombed out site in the war on poverty. No one had answered the first two times he came by and knocked on the door, but on the third visit Aaron could hear the sound of a television from inside. He was surprised that they still had the electricity coming into this building. He knocked.

"Dorinda, I'm Aaron Woods and I want to talk with you about your son, Squeak. I'm not with the city. I'm just a friend," he said loudly.

The TV sound stopped and he couldn't hear anything. "I'm not with the city. I'm just a friend here to see Miss Johnson about her son. Please open the door," he called out.

He heard some low murmuring and waited while a discussion went on for a couple of minutes. Finally a man's voice said, "Well go ahead," and after a pause and he heard shuffling steps and then someone sliding open the chain and turning the lock. The door opened six inches and a, thin, medium brown woman of average height looked out at him suspiciously. She had an oval face with sparse reddish hair worn close to her head. Her skin looked dry and cracked at the corners of her wide eyes, lips and nostrils. She wore terry mules and a plain blue house dress, buttoned up the front and clutched closed at the top by her right hand while her left tightly held the doorknob.

"You look a lot like your son," Aaron blurted out without thinking. When she drew her head back he silently cursed himself for being so stupid.

"What you want?" she demanded.

"Please let me in so we can talk about Squeak," Aaron said. He didn't crowd the door, and stood with his hands at his sides, open and turned forward. "He is ok. He's been staying with me for about six weeks now and I want to talk with you about school, and, well, just about taking care of him. Please, I just want a few minutes of your time."

Dorinda looked over her shoulder and must have gotten a signal from whoever else was in the room. She stepped back and opened the door, then turned and shuffled four steps and sat on the arm of a threadbare and sagging sofa that faced a TV. Two men were sitting on the sofa. The one on the side where Dorinda perched herself looked more Middle Eastern than African. Sallow and cadaverously thin, he was bald on top with long, stiff, straight hair on the sides and back. His dull skinned pate led into a high forehead, extending a long, narrow face with a scimitar nose, thin lips and a pointed chin. The long, tapered fingers of one hand lightly held a can of beer, as did the short, pudgy hand of the man next to him. He was a doughy figure, dark skinned with sagging cheeks, thick thighs and short legs. They both were dressed in clean but worn and oddly matched clothes. They silently watched Aaron enter and close the door behind him. The heavier man occasionally glanced at the muted TV that was the only other piece of furniture in the room. Through the open doorway of one bedroom Aaron caught a glimpse of two stained bare mattresses on the floor.

He walked over to the sofa and held out his hand to the thin man first. "I'm Aaron Woods," he said. The man shifted his beer to his left hand and languidly reached his hand up, giving Aaron just the limp fingers to grip and not saying anything. The second man was equally noncommittal and silent when Aaron offered his hand to him in turn. He stepped back to the side where Dorinda perched, where he wasn't blocking the TV but where he could make eye contact with all of them. He offered her his hand to shake, but she ignored it.

"All right, so you in now. Wha'chu want?" Dorinda asked flatly.

"I appreciate you talking with me," Aaron started. "Like I said, Squeak has been staying with me for over a month now. I, ah, I think that he has a lot of potential, but he needs to get off the streets. He needs school and a place he can call home. I've got room and I like him. My own son is grown and gone and, well, I'd like to take Squeak in and, ah, Squeak said he would like to, ah, stay with me and try to go to school and all, you know, have a regular life."

"You ain't no pervert, are you?" the thin man asked. His manner was calm and his gaze direct.

"No," Aaron turned to him. "I just, I've raised a son and he's all grown and away. I just would like to give Squeak a chance to get off the street." He paused and then lifted his shoulders and opened his hands. "Hey, I like the kid and I want to help him out. Maybe you can relate. He ought to be in school and, you know, have regular meals and just be a kid."

The thin guy looked Aaron in the eye and nodded.

"So you gonna be his daddy, huh?" Dorinda said sarcastically.

"Yes," Aaron answered. He knew that he wasn't going to get anywhere trying to bullshit them or beat around the bush. He wasn't any good at it, anyway. Only way he knew was to confront things head on. "Yes, I will be his daddy and take responsibility for him. I think I can give him a chance at a different life. But I need you to help. I need you to help me with the paperwork and talking with the judge and the city, turning responsibility for him over to me."

There was a long pause. "So," Aaron finally said. "Can he stay with me?"

"So you gonna take care a him, huh?" Dorinda said, angry now, standing up and flinging one hand at Aaron. "Sho' he can go stay with you and get school and all, but tell me this. Who gonna be my daddy?"

She looked with contempt at all three of the men in turn, Aaron last. "Huh? Who gonna take care of me? You, Mister Aaron? What you gonna do for me, big daddy Aaron?"

Aaron fought to keep from recoiling. She's bargaining with me for her son, he thought to himself. She wants me to offer her something in order for her to sign the papers. He bit down on his lower lip to keep from saying anything. He needed to get her to agree to let Squeak live with him and start a real life, and it wouldn't do anyone any good for him to judge her. Or judge him, because, goddammit, he was going to do whatever it took to help this kid get off the streets. Time enough to examine motives and seek justification when the job was done.

When was sure he had control of himself and his voice he carefully measured his words. "Dorinda, I know you've had it rough and you have to deal with things I can't even imagine. Tough things and I know you want to get Squeak away from, ah, from drugs and all the hassle on the streets. I'm not a rich guy with a lot of money. I've got enough to get by and take care of the kid, but I can't save the world. I do want to help you, because I know you've had it tough, but also for Squeak's sake. What I can do is to pay for you to get into treatment when you're ready to do that. You just have to let me know and I'll find a program and pay for it. And to help you keep food on the table I'll help you set up an account at a bank and I'll make sure that fifty dollars goes into it every week for you to take out and use for food and such."

He paused. No one said anything. He went on in a firmer tone. "Hear me now, Dorinda. I'm not bargaining with you on this. This is all I can do for you and I'll do it. So how about if I pick you up tomorrow at ten and we'll go see my lawyer and get the papers started and we'll get things set up at the bank."

He said this last as a statement, not a question. The look in Dorinda's eyes made something inside of him shrivel. Her eyes accused him of every act that that had ever hurt her or made her feel ashamed. She held his eyes in her gaze for maybe fifteen seconds, but it seemed like minutes to Aaron. Then a shield came back over her face, covering the hate.

"Ok, Mr. Aaron," she said, her voice friendly now, although they both knew the feelings behind her light smile. "But you got to give me this week's fifty now. We a little short."

Aaron pulled his wallet from his back pocket. He only had four twenties in his wallet, so he pulled out three. He handed them to Dorinda, who snatched them from him and put them into the pocket of her housedress. Her chin was high and her eyes hard, daring him to say anything about the ten extra dollars. He'd rather bite off his tongue.

"Ok, then," Aaron said. "I'll come by tomorrow morning."

Dorinda and the men just looked at him, but the thin guy gave a small nod when Aaron caught his eye. That made him feel better. He was just doing what had to be done for the kid. Dorinda was doing what she had to do to survive, and he thought she knew that this was what was best for Squeak, too. However it looked to anyone else, he thought the thin guy was looking at it the same way he was. He stood a little straighter.

"Thank you, Dorinda. And thank you, gentlemen, for your time," he said simply. He turned around and let himself out of the door, walking with a firm step and not looking back.

Dorinda made the rest of it easy. She only missed one appointment, with a social worker. She had shown an almost regal bearing in talking with the judge, the lawyer and the agency people, admitting her addictions and stating that she "chose Aaron Woods to raise her boy up right" because she couldn't do it and it would be best for "all of us." On the occasions when she and Squeak were required to see a social worker and the judge together, they were awkward and formal with each other and Squeak would be silent for hours afterwards. Only once did Aaron see Dorinda's eyes start to blink and moisten, when Squeak was talking to the judge about his life on the street and she didn't think anyone was looking at her. When she saw Aaron observing, her face went hard and her chin went up another notch. Aaron's lawyer also proved to be worth the considerable fee she charged and no one in the District bureaucracy decided to put any obstacles in the way, despite Aaron's status as a single man. Squeak became his ward for one year and then the adoption of "Kenya Ali Woods" was approved. He and Aaron had long discussions and consulted many books, but Squeak made the final choice of his official name.

Dorinda never contacted Aaron about the treatment plan. One day shortly after the adoption Squeak told Aaron that she had moved out of town. Aaron didn't ask how he had gotten the information, but figured it had come from one of Squeak's old street acquaintances. After that the only sign Aaron had that she was alive was the periodic withdrawals from the bank account that Aaron had set up for her. The fifty dollar draft was automatically made from Aaron's account to hers every week, and he never told anyone about it, especially not Squeak. When he thought of it himself, he felt only shame and quickly busied himself with other matters.

Like playing a good, bruising game of mangle ball with Antelope, who finally showed up at the playground. As Squeak had told him, no one else seemed to want to play with them.

Chapter 7

Big Ed Tower didn't seem very concerned when Perry told him about the nascent campaign at Natural America Club to directly attack the oil, coal and utility corporate clients of APRC.

"They don't have the balls to get into a real battle with us," Ed said while he was clipping the end off of his cigar. He leaned back in the big custom leather chair, looking across the leather top of his massive mahogany desk at Perry, who was seated in one of the upholstered chairs facing the desk. Everything in the office was leather, wood and marble, including gleaming oak paneled walls: massive, rich and meant to impress. There were two walls of windows, one behind the desk and another to Big Ed's right. The office was spacious, which by itself was impressive on K St. where space cost four figures per square foot. Visitors entered through a doorway in the wall opposite the desk after being admitted by the very English Miss Fitchens, Big Ed's personal assistant whose efficiency was exceeded only by her icy beauty. To Perry's right was a six person conference table, mahogany with marble top and leather chairs, of course, and a fully stocked wet bar. Immediately after hiring her Ed had insisted that Miss Fitchens attend bartending school. For what he was paying her she happily attended, adding mixicology to her executive secretary skills.

To Perry's left, in front of the side window wall was a leather sofa flanked by matching club chairs, around a marble topped coffee table with dark mahogany legs. The thick carpet was a deep, rich red and the walls were covered with a green fabric with gold outlined stripes that matched the red in the carpet.

Well under Perry's six feet, Big Ed was broad and squat, weighing at least 260. His jowly red face and generous paunch, which couldn't be hidden by three thousand dollar suits, told one and all that Big Ed had made the most of his 58 years. His head was rimmed by the remnants of still blond hair kept trimmed by a barber whom he had come to the office every Friday more out of habit than need. Anyway, the shave he got with an old fashioned straight razor refreshed him.

"They have a nice little racket going for them now, getting grants and donations to save Bambi and writing three hundred page policies that never get read, much less implemented." Ed continued his thought about the NAC campaign after he got his cigar going. What he called the hypocrisy of environmental organizations was one of his favorite topics. "They don't have a clue of what it takes to do real work out in the real world. Send them out to get a real job and see how far their Masters in Utopian Public Policy or PhD. in Useless Species Ecology will get 'em. Fuckin' eggheads!"

In truth, Big Ed was very comfortable with the role played by the environmental organizations. They created enough of an opposition for him to scare the coal, oil and gas giants into giving him a blank check to fight their battles for them. The "ankle biters," as he sometimes called the enviros in private discussion with Perry, were able to win just enough symbolic victories for things like preventing drilling in the Alaska National Wildlife Refuge to give them credibility as a threat to the industry, but they didn't have the leadership, the real world savvy or the will necessary to get the country to break its addiction to fossil fuels. Ed knew he needed them as much as they needed him, and for the same reasons, to keep the dynamic political balance that drew financial support from their respective backers. Since his backers had the most money to manipulate the media and support the political campaigns and expensive habits of compliant officeholders, he knew he would win most of the battles. He just had to be sure that he kept that balance tilted in the right direction.

Big Ed took a puff on his cigar. "Perry, you be sure you stay on top of that little nature-girl friend of yours and pump her for any information she has on this campaign that might cause us trouble, heh, heh, if you know what I mean," he said with a locker room leer.

"I don't know who's pumping whom. She's a lot to handle, and to tell you the truth," Perry said with a self satisfied grin, "I'm pretty happy to have her stay on top. Don't worry, Ed. She doesn't even think twice about telling me what's going on over there. I just let on I'm getting converted and she gives me the whole pitch. I'm sure this will just be more committees forming and whining about our tax breaks or caribou breeding grounds."

Now Ed got serious. "If you hear them talking boycott or messing with our investors or, you know, anything that'll get on TV or a big splash in the papers, I want to hear about it. Something like that could cost us millions or worse if it gets out of hand. Europe is already goin' to hell for our boys. Global warning shit is all over the papers over there, and in Europe the goddam people read the papers. People all riled up and coal and oil consumption goin' down. India and China are makin' up for it, but right here in the U.S.A., this is the big enchilada. Every American uses four times as much energy as people in those other countries, maybe more, and if Americans start cuttin' back, well our ol' money makin' machine'l stall out big time. Ol' Beat 'um and Cheat 'um will cut us off in a minute if those enviros get something real goin' and we ain't on top of it."

Beat 'um and Cheat 'um was Ed's pet name for the tandem of William Breaker and Rufus Chatham, the respective heads of SPECO and CCCO the leading oil and coal corporations who were APRC's most important backers. Breaker and Chatham had formed a close alliance to sow doubt about the science of climate change in the media and insure the government gave them big funding allowances to cover costs of extracting oil and coal and turn it into energy. They knew that if those government handouts ever dried up and people had to pay what it really cost to use oil and coal their hold on the energy market would disappear, to say nothing of their profits.

"Best investments in history," Ed and Perry had frequently heard "Ball" Breaker tell their cronies about the money spent to curry favor with the politicians and turn out "studies" and "expert testimony" that hid the facts about the coming climate crisis. "Millions out and billions in." The numbers bore him out. SPECO alone had profits of $9 billion in just the last quarter, the fourth record breaking quarter in a row and the rest of the industry wasn't far behind.

"Don't worry, Ed," Perry hastened to mollify his boss, "I'm all over this. That's why I mentioned it to you, even though I don't see any chance of NAC or the rest of the greenies putting together credible boycott or shareholder actions. I mean, they may get a few pickets outside a few gas stations or stand up at a few shareholder meetings, but there just isn't the leadership to pull them all together and focus on us in any really threatening way. Hell, you know how they are, they'll never get that organized, but if it looks like they're headed in that direction we'll know about it and head them off. They'd rather focus on politics, anyway. They're lost when they have to deal with industry or the markets, so I just don't see them going there."

Perry had satisfied Big Ed, at least for that day, but he remained uneasy himself. Over the next three weeks he called Wendy every day, "just to see how you're doing" They had only gone out together twice in that three weeks and the second of those evenings had ended with her leaving early and catching a cab home because she still had to work the phones to the West Coast. Now he had arranged for them to go whitewater rafting on the New River in West Virginia, but Wendy was telling him she couldn't go because her campaign "was really taking off."

"I'm booked to go out of town with Aaron and Tony on the weekend," she told him when he called to tell her about the rafting trip. Her excitement about the progress she was making obviously overrode any disappointment at missing the weekend outing. "We're going to hit three Chapters. We've got meetings set up, to get them committed and to organize them to take action in their state. These folks have always been good at getting their local issues in the local papers and we're going to tap into that for this campaign like we never have before on a national basis. I've made a thousand calls and the staff, well, some of them, anyway, has been on the phone and email constantly, and I'm telling you, Perry, people are ready for this. It's like they've been waiting for something like this to bring them together."

"That's great, honey, although I'm sorry we can't make the rafting trip." Perry's voice always conveyed genuine sincerity because he really believed what he was saying, at least when he was saying it. "I think that it will do a lot of good to get people to begin to understand that at least sometime in the future we'll have to do something about energy issues, and you're the right one to make it happen."

"Perry, you know damn well that we're going to boycott one of your precious clients, and that we want action now, not in the future, so don't bullshit me," Wendy retorted.

"Whoa, I'm not bullshitting you," Perry retreated in an aggrieved voice. He realized he had underestimated her again. He had to keep in mind Wendy wasn't just another pretty face. "I'll never admit I said this, but I know our guys have to change. I don't think your boycott or whatever will kill them and it may help them to realize they have to start moving to renewables, invest more in hydrogen and solar power. And I'm going to be the one to tell them that when they come to ask what to do about your boycott, so I really do want your campaign to take off."

"Well, that sounds good, anyway, although I've told you a hundred times that hydrogen is a non starter." The edge had gone out of Wendy's voice. "I'm sorry I can't go on the rafting trip, too. It would be fun, but I'm going to be really tied up for, well, for now, so we'll just have to do it later. And, Perry, don't think that this is just my campaign. I'm the organizer, sure, but Aaron has been, well, he's been a lot more than we bargained for. He really knows how to connect with people. It seems like he makes them feel like, ah, like they are better than they thought they were before they met him. And a lot of other people are already coming on board. Tomorrow we have an appointment to talk with the Democratic campaign, Aaron, Tony, Phil and I, and that's just a start. We're going to connect with the state and local campaigns, too. Aaron and Tony both say that's more important than trying to get the presidential campaigns interested, and I'm beginning to think they're right. We're going to take this to the people. And Perry, don't kid yourself, we are going to try like hell to bring one of your precious oil giants to their knees. Then the rest will fall in line. Anyway, I got to run. Bye, and thanks for calling."

"Bye," Perry said, slowly putting the phone back on the desk set. He still thought it was no big deal, but he had to think about this the way Big Ed would. Even if it wasn't a big deal, they needed to make it seem like a threat. Then they could shake the money tree and get a few extra million to counter the grassroots attack. They could tap into the Christian Right network across the country, get them to push support for "sound science" and promote fear of the "economic uncertainty" of a "liberal environmental agenda." That kind of effort would need major funding, and whenever the money flowed APRC got wet. Ok, now he had a plan and was ready to go talk to Big Ed.

Perry found out that Big Ed was ahead of him.

"Perry, I've been talking with a few of the boys and they are worried about this talk about NAC putting together a goddam boycott campaign," Big Ed told him when Perry had filled him in on his conversation with Wendy. "We've got to nip this enviro campaign in the bud. They don't want to be seeing their faces on TV as the guys who are fucking up the weather every time there's a bad hurricane or tornado. Next thing, some hot shot will be suing them for the damages of climate change, you know, like the tobacco companies. We've got another 20 years of pumping oil ahead of us. The more scarce it gets the more money we make if we keep demand high and the government in our pocket. When the oil is gone then coal is king again. The oil guys are all buying up coal rights with the big bucks they're making now. They can't be fucking around with carbon limits and law suits and shit like that, they got to protect their shareholders."

"Well, since they already see this as a threat, they ought to be ready to ante up big time for us to push our own grassroots campaign, you know, get our good Christian folks organized to protect their rights to big cars and houses and whatever," Perry answered. He gave Big Ed the outlines of the campaign he had been thinking about..

"Perry, that's a damn good idea for the long term, and we need to keep that in our bag of tricks," Big Ed answered. "It looks like a real money maker for us, and it can be a real image builder. Easy, too. We'll just have to pump some bucks into the conservative network, hand out a few new Cadillacs for the right folks and we'll have our word out all over the country. But the boys want to head this boycott shit off before it gets going. Breaker and Chatham have got some guys they've used when they needed to clean up union organizers and other pests. They swear by these guys. Use them all over the world, in fact. The 'ultimate problem solvers' they call 'em, fast, quiet and clean. They'll be here at 11:30 this morning in fact. I just found out myself, you know how that goddam Breaker likes to pull shit like this, not tell you what's going on until the last minute. I want you here. You're gonna be their primary contact."

Perry could see that Big Ed had already decided what he wanted to do, not that he had much choice if Breaker and the other big time clients had given him his orders. He still didn't think this NAC campaign was ever going to be more than an irritant, something they could use to get some more fees thrown their way. And the way Big Ed described these guys made him a little uncomfortable, but he knew which side his bread was buttered on.

"Yeah, that's a good idea, Ed," he replied with quick enthusiasm. "This hasn't fizzled out yet and there's no reason to let it go any further. So, ah, what do you think these guys are going to do?"

"Hell, I don't know. Maybe leak it to the papers if one of these new hotshot enviros is screwing a live boy or a dead girl. Oh, dammit, that's not gonna scare anyone off any more. That damn NAC guy, what's his name, Albritton, he's already out of the closet. Scandal used to be easier in the old days. Anyway, we'll find out in an hour or so."

That is how Perry found himself back in Big Ed's office at 11:30 when Miss Fitchens opened the door and two of the problem solvers, one white and one black, walked in. Perry thought to himself that they looked like they were casing a bank they were going to rob. The black guy, who led the way, paused and then walked briskly up to Big Ed's desk, stuck his hand out across it, looked him in the eye and barked out, "Fist."

"Ah, hello, Mr. Fist…" Big Ed started in his hearty, men's club manner, but before he got it out Fist pumped his hand once, dropped it, turned and walked over to Perry.

"Fist," he said again, using the name like a weapon. He took Perry's hand in a grip that said he could crush him like an egg if he chose, pumped once and then let go. Fist was wearing black leather gloves with the fingers cut off just short of the first knuckle. He turned and pointed his right hand at his companion, a tall, sallow skinned, whip of a man.

"Grainer," Fist introduced the thin man, who glided more than he walked to a point two steps behind and just off Fist's left side. Grainer nodded his head but made no motion to approach or shake hands with Big Ed or Perry. His eyes moved constantly, looking intently at Big Ed, then Perry, then around the room, then back again. He had a small head, greenish reptilian eyes and thinning non-descript hair combed straight back and plastered to his head before it dropped lankly to his shoulders. His low sharp brow, thin lips, receding jaw and long, corded neck helped give the impression of a snake that could strike out at any instant.

"Mr. Fist, Mr. Grainer, please, let's go over here where we can talk," Big Ed said, motioning the two guests towards the sofa."

Fist looked around the office without moving, then turned to Grainer and nodded. Only then did they go over to the sofa and sit down, Fist very much at ease but Grainer sitting erect, feet flat on the floor, ready to spring.

Fist was fit and powerful. He had a bullet head, thick neck, wide shoulders and deep chest. He moved with economic certainty, about six one and two twenty five, Perry guessed. His muddy skin was pitted and scarred, with patchy stubble. A long sleeved crew neck shirt, leather five button vest, slacks and soft leather shoes with rubber soles were all black and neatly fitted to his well muscled frame. Fist was a cosmic black hole, absorbing all the light and energy from the room and converting it into barely contained rage, hate and contempt. He was a dark contrast to Grainer who wore a sea foam green business suit, white shirt and pale green tie. Perry thought Fist's whole persona was meant to cause fear and it succeeded. Grainer was dressed to blend into the scenery, just another mid level K Street lobbyist or businessman, until you looked into those hooded eyes.

Big Ed moved from behind his desk and sat in a leather armchair with his back to the window, facing Perry who sat in the opposite chair on the side closest to Grainer.

Perry had the impression that the two men seated at his left on the sofa were not impressed with the opulent office and furnishings. In fact, he was sure that they didn't share any of the normal responses to wealth, power, position or human sensitivities and constraints. From the moment they had walked in the door Fist and Grainer had approached him and Big Ed like pit bulls coming into a room and sniffing a couple of poodles. The air around them hummed with a physically threatening force that caused sweat to trickle from Perry's armpits down his sides.

"Ball Breaker and Rufus Chatham speak very highly of you, Mr. Fist," Big Ed started, projecting his friendly but take charge voice from deep in his chest. "We are very pleased to have you work with us on taking care of this little problem. Before we get into the details, can I have someone bring you something? Some coffee or a drink, perhaps?"

Fist leaned forward, his voice harsh and loud, each word a distinct verbal punch.

"Get this straight right now. We don't work with anyone. You have a problem. Certain people see it as a problem for them. We take care of their problems. There will be things we need for you to do, and I 'spect you to do them. The first thing I need is a hundred grand." He reached into a pocket in his vest, took out a slip of paper and extended it to Ed. "Have the money sent to this account today. Any questions so far?"

Big Ed had straightened up in his chair. "Ah, of course. Ah, I mean no."

They were used to dealing with millions and more, but Perry still admired the way Ed had accepted the demand with only slight hesitation. Still, he had seen Ed's face register surprise before it froze into a stiff, blank mask.

Ed took the paper from Fist and held it like it was on fire. He leaned forward and handed it across the coffee table to Perry.

"Perry, ah, here. Ah, make these arrangements for Mr. Fist right away. Ah, I mean as soon as we are done here."

Ed sat back again after Perry took the paper and turned to Fist, recovering a little of his usual assurance.

"Perry will be your contact here. Just let him know anything you need and he will take care of it."

Fist's voice hit him again, this time visibly knocking him back in his seat.

"YOU are my contact here. We'll use your boy for errands, but I want your cell number. Keep it with you and turned on 24/7. That's how I work when I do things for those certain people. Do we understand each other?"

"Yes," Ed rasped out in a whisper, his face now red and clearly agitated. His eyebrow rose up and lowered. Rose up again. He cleared his throat and repeated more firmly, "Yes."

"Good." Fist suddenly smiled broadly, his lips showing a mix of gold and white teeth as hard as tombstones, his eyes still boring into Big Ed's. He as quickly dropped the smile. "When the job is done you will put another hundred fifty thousand into that account."

Fist paused, then went on with the same hard cadence. "Now, you will give me everything you know about Aaron Woods. You will give me your number and junior's number here," indicating Perry with a jerk of his head in his direction but without moving his eyes. "You will give me three credit cards to use to cover our expenses. Then we're out of here."

"Ah, three cards?" Ed managed to choke out.

Fist pounded Ed with a louder voice, still keeping the same steady cadence.

"That's the last time that you question what I say." His tone dropped back to the previous level, steady, hard, full of threat but devoid of emotion.

"Minton is with your secretary watching our coats." He gave another of his smiles that were worse than a snarl, and then it was gone. "He doesn't trust anyone. Now, you," he looked at Perry, "get us the cards, one for each of us. Phone and email contacts for you and the boss man here. Any paper you have on this Woods. Home, work, family, whatever. Get us hotel rooms, someplace central. Not some tourist trap, but someplace we can get in and out without a lot of attention."

He turned back to Ed, who appeared to Perry to have shrunken in his chair. "While we wait you call out for some sandwiches and beer for us. Get double for Minton. He's a big motherfucker and gets mean when he's hungry."

Fist leaned back a little, still expressionless. Grainer remained erect, still and alert.

Perry didn't wait for a reaction from Ed, who seemed incapable of speech or movement. "I'll give the Miss Fitchens the lunch order on the way out and get right on this, Mr. Fist," Perry said as he got up and went quickly to the door, conscious of their eyes on his back. Big Ed had looked at him as though he was being pulled into quicksand and Perry was abandoning him when Perry got out of his chair. He opened the door and stepped into the outer office, pulling the door closed behind him without looking back.

Miss Fitchens sat at her desk nervously pecking at her keyboard, eyes fixed on her flat screen monitor. A mountain of a man stood by the closed outer door to the hallway.

Miss Fitchens had been Big Ed's personal assistant for seven years. Like all the office furnishings, she was intended to impress and intimidate visitors. In Perry's estimation her peaches and cream complexion, high cheek boned beauty, dark chestnut hair severely pulled back into a tight French twist, tailored suits exquisitely fitted to her lushly elegant figure and her well bred British accent made her worth every bit of her six figure salary. A significant percentage of the male visitors to Big Ed's office amused Perry with the contortions they went through to try and interest Ms. Fitchens in an after hours engagement. Perry was among the few who knew that the relatively few female visitors to the office had a much better chance of catching Ms. Fitchens eye than did the men. Perry knew this from having blunted his own lance against the cool, condescending and thoroughly deflating armor of Ms. Fitchens demeanor.

That demeanor appeared to have fallen by the wayside at the moment. She was flushed, furtively darting glances at the man by the door who now commanded Perry's attention as well. He looked to be a head taller than Perry and to outweigh him by 100 lbs. His bald head had the size and shape of a ten pin bowling ball, and looked to be just as hard. Close set eyes in the wide expanse of his medium-brown expressionless face locked onto Perry, with glances back to Ms. Fitchens. His broad nostrils, each of which could accommodate a child's marble, flared wider and then recovered as he audibly inhaled and exhaled. Other than that he was motionless, broad and square with the unnatural weightiness of a stone. His trench coat was still damp from the late April day's rain. Two more coats were draped over his crooked left forearm and a brimmed hat was in that thick fingered hand. His right hand was at his side.

"You must be Mr. Minton," Perry noted, his voice coming out a little high. There was no recognition from Minton that Perry had spoken.

"Ah, Miss. Fitchens," Perry changed gears quickly, "would you please get sandwiches sent up for Mr. Tower and his guests, including for Mr. Minton, here? When they arrive please take them in and provide our guests with drinks or anything else they may require."

"Certainly, Mr. Richardson," Fitchens replied, grateful to have a normal, everyday task to attend to. As Perry gingerly sidled by the silent Minton he heard her relaying the order to the maitre de at Sweet Georgia Browne, the restaurant just around the corner they frequently used for such purposes.

Perry woodenly walked down the hall to his office, trying to get his stunned mind functioning. *What have we gotten ourselves into?* he thought. Now that he was out of the room he couldn't believe that these people, the situation he had left, was real. Lots of their clients, particularly in the oil and coal industries, were pretty rough customers with rumors of dark dealings in their pasts, but Fist and his companions were a different matter altogether. Any of the whispered tales of, well, of people being physically threatened, like union organizers that disappeared and such, those things happened far outside the Beltway, if indeed they really ever happened at all. Certainly those matters had never intruded into APRC affairs. To have such people actually come into these offices and sit where Congressmen and Senators came to visit was just not part of reality.

But these guys are definitely for real, Perry thought, looking down at the account number in the paper on his hand. And they couldn't just send them away. "Oh well, thank you for coming by, but I really don't think we need your kind of help," he imagined himself saying. They would crumple him up like yesterday's newspaper and toss him in the corner. And he couldn't afford to piss of Breaker and Chatham anyway. No, he was best off just playing along and helping them scare off the poor fool who had stirred up this mess so they would go away. That shouldn't take long, he thought, shuddering. This Woods character sounded like just another overeducated liberal with too much time on his hands that had taken up environmental activism as a hobby and was taking himself too seriously. Well, he was soon going to find out that his hobby was very serious indeed when the wrong people decided they were going to take you seriously, too.

"Patricia." He startled his new secretary as he pushed into his outer office. His rooms were smaller and less lavishly furnished than Big Ed's, of course, but they still were sumptuous and comfortable, befitting the high powered politicians and industry leaders he often brought together here. "Forget your fingernails and get busy. Get one two bedroom and one single bedroom suites at the Washington Court Hotel in the names of, oh never mind the names, just have them charged to our account and tell them that Misters Fist, Minton and, ah, oh yes, Grainer will be coming there to stay for, ah, well, at least for a few days and maybe beyond. But before that get me Pincus from accounting on the phone. You got that?"

Patricia, who was blond, attractive and better endowed physically than intellectually, dropped her emery board and scrabbled around on her desk for her pad and pencil, "Yes, sir. Washington Court Hotel." She said that proudly, having already found that Perry favored this luxury address on Capitol Hill for the rooms he reserved for out of town visitors, as well as for assignations he arranged for power brokers in Congress or the Executive Branch.

"Now that was for Mr. Fisk, right? And who was the other one, or no, it was two, wasn't it? And call Mr. Pincus?" She looked up at him with fetchingly wide blue eyes and a tilt headed smile.

Perry slowed and turned as he was about to enter his inner office. Why the hell did he have to keep going through secretaries, one as dumb as the next, he thought for the hundredth time. Of course he knew that his inability to keep his hands off of them inevitably resulted in a short relationship, reduced efficiency at work and inevitable termination, but he felt aggrieved anyway. His preference for selecting his secretaries based on the stirrings in his crotch rather than their resume and skills was something he preferred to not dwell on.

He took a deep breath. He needed to slow down a little and keep his focus on what needed to be done to get this little incident over with. After all he was an expert in guiding some of the most powerful men and women in the world through tough and potentially explosive deals involving billions of dollars, all the while staying in the background as a harmless and pleasant playboy. If he just trusted his skills he could sure as hell get these stupid thugs under control and at the same time brush aside this small time environmental pest.

"I'm sorry, Patricia," he said with a small smile. "I'm just a little rushed right now. The hotel rooms are for a Mr. Fist, with a 't,' a Mr. Grainer, and a Mr. Minton." He spelled the last two names out. "And yes, get me Pincus right away, please."

With that he went into his office and set about taking care of the arrangements that he hoped would bring his comfortable world back into order. That damn Aaron Woods, he thought as he called up his computer file on the man. He had done some preliminary research over the past few weeks since he had first heard about this stupid boycott campaign. Why did these fucking amateurs have to meddle in the affairs of their betters, he thought. They had plenty of trees to hug and meetings to go to without getting involved in things they just didn't understand. He'd do his best to head this off, but if someone got hurt it was their own fault.

Chapter 8

Fist felt good. This looked like it might be a really soft gig. That was all he was interested in, how tough was the job and what could he get out of it. This job didn't look tough, and he knew he could squeeze a good quarter mil over his usual fees out of it, plus some all expense paid time in good old Chocolate City.

The basic facts were simple. Some old fart with too much time on his hands had a bug up his ass about global warming and all that bullshit and was trying to stir up all the other eggheads. For whatever reason, the bosses thought that this asshole might cause them trouble and they wanted to make sure that didn't happen. That's what he did, he made problems disappear, and he was damn good at it. On this one he figured he could squeeze big time bonus money and all the support he needed from the Washington ass kissers with their shiny suits and big deal offices. When Ball Breaker had called him it sounded like he didn't like these hot shit D.C. pricks any more than Fist did, so he didn't expect any blowback from that quarter. This was going to be the easiest job he'd ever done. Shit, compared to other jobs this one was going to be a vacation and he intended to string it out for all it was worth. And take a little skin off the D.C. boys while he was doing it. Make 'em dance to his tune. The thought actually made him smile. Not much of a smile, but a real one, not the one that he used to freak people out.

Fist had been doing strong arm work for the oil industry big shots for ten years now, and for the coal barons the last five. He was one of those rare individuals fortunate enough to find the perfect occupation for their temperament and talents and who has the self awareness to realize it. His earliest memories from his childhood in the back streets of the black section of Tulsa were about pain. First he learned about feeling pain. As soon as he could move, before he could even walk, he started to learn about avoiding pain, learning to slip and evade the kicks and punches of his drunken father, a sometime oil field roughneck. Finally he learned how to give pain. Before he formed his first words he understood that violence and pain were power. Those who gave pain had power and those who absorbed the pain were weak. Using his sharp intelligence and creativity he built his own repertoire of punches, kicks and holds. His mother was a passive target for the old man, but she retaliated to Fist's attempts to practice his punishing skills on her with a whack from a frying pan or other handy home implement. He found plenty of opportunities to test himself among the other children of the neighborhood.

"You a Fist," his father would say, showing him a big, balled up hand. "Here's what a Fist do," and he would knock Fist down, laughing as he bloodied his lip or bruised his ribs. Fist's mother never intervened, hoping that the old man would satiate his need for dealing out punishment before he turned on her. Sometimes he did and sometimes he didn't.

Fist turned his anger and frustrations on the other kids who played in the streets, the alleys behind the stores and the vacant lots. By the time he was twelve he was highly skilled with fists, feet, knees, elbows and any handy objects that could smash or cut. Even the older kids who hung out on the corners or the playgrounds gave him a wide berth. His ferocity and fearlessness became a neighborhood legend, and he had to range farther and farther to find unsuspecting foes who would accept his challenge. Sometimes the older men, hanging on the corner or behind some store, would make Fist fight some kid, usually older and bigger. They'd place bets on the fight and when he won they'd give him a can of beer or a pull on their bottle. He loved the fights, not because of the booze or even the pats on the back and occasional bill tucked into his pocket. He found no pleasure so great as to break the will of another, reducing them to bleeding helplessness: battered, bruised, sometimes marked for life. He took their power and made it his.

That had been childhood, and it came to an early end. He matured early and when he was fifteen his frame had started to thicken. He never had any awkwardness about him and he worked hard to build his muscles. He wanted to give the old man a surprise. For the past three years the father's punches had been getting slower and had less pop when they landed. Still, Fist had absorbed the beatings without attempting retaliation.

That changed on a chilly November evening. The old man came home from a bar, yanked the door open and slammed it back against the outside of the house. He stumbled up to Fist, who was lying on the floor watching TV in the tiny living room of their cramped, run down two bedroom duplex, one of a hundred in the project.

"Get ta' fuck out ta' way, wort'less shit," he slurred. He jabbed at Fist's side with a foot. Fist was ready. He had taken many of these kicks before. He rolled away from the kick, absorbing and lessening the force of the blow as he had learned to do. This time, however, he brought his arm down and trapped the ankle between his arm and his side. He pulled his knees up to his chest and kicked both feet out against the old man's other leg, feeling the knee joint give as the ligaments tore. Pushing off from the floor with his free arm, he sprang to his feet, uncoiling like a steel spring, while still holding on to the ankle trapped between his arm and side.

"Yahhh!" the old man yelled in pain and surprise as he fell heavily on his back. "Yahhh," he continued to yell, interspersing it with grunts as Fist repeatedly stomped him with the heel of his right foot, in the crotch, stomach and ribs. The old man thrashed and flailed, but Fist kept tight hold of his ankle, using the leverage to keep the heavier man on his back and pulling him back when he tried to scrabble away. When the old man's movements got slower and his yells had dropped to wheezes of pain at each drop of Fist's heel, Fist released his ankle, grabbed the front of his shirt and, with a precocious strength that added to his father's shock, pulled him to his feet and propped him up against the wall holding him there with his left hand.

"Motha' fucka'," he said, smashing his right fist into his father's face and body in a steady measured rhythm with each word. "Motha' fucka', motha' fucka'," he went on for a time that he couldn't measure. Each blow forced a pained and unintelligible grunt from his former tormentor.

When he was tired of punching and couldn't hold the limp weight of his father against the wall, Fist let him crumple to the floor. He kicked at him again and again. At first the old man made weak movements to protect himself, but they were futile. "So. You. Show. Me. Wha'. It. Mean. Be. A.

Fist." He punctuated each word with a kick that came from the reservoir of hate formed by the lessons in pain that he had learned from his father for fifteen years.

Eventually, Fist tired of kicking at the bloody form and stepped back; panting, spent, satisfied. As his breathing slowed he became aware again of the room around him, and finally, of his mother, standing in the doorway to the kitchen.

"He dead?" she asked. Fist saw she had a gun in her hand, pointing at either his unconscious father or him, he didn't know which.

"No," Fist said, watching her warily. "Not yet. Whatcha' doin' wit' da gun?"

"Been waitin' for this chance. Gonna blow his fuckin' head off." She gave a malevolent grin, showing the bare patches of gum between her few teeth. "You come an' bus' me up some, make it look like the nigger done beat me again. Den prop'm up an' I shoot him. I call the cops an' it be se'f defense. Ever' body know nigger beat me up all a time. Get ovah heah an' whop me a couple a times. Mark me up. Come on, niggah, dis my chance."

Fist just looked at her for a minute. Slowly he smiled. Old lady wasn't so dumb, after all. He moved over to her.

"Ok, bitch," he said. "This here'll make up for all the shit I took all these years. Jus' you be sure you keep that gun pointed away from me."

As he swung his open hand at her face, aiming to mark her up without knocking her out, he felt something new. He didn't have a name for it, but if he did he would have called it love.

The cops never even brought a charge in the old man's murder, just the way his mom had figured. "Just another nigger shooting" to them, not worth the time and trouble of investigating. Fist replaced the old man's economic contributions to the family support by mugging drunks and the unwary suburbanites who came into the neighborhood looking for drugs. He was a man now.

He sporadically attended school where he was constantly in trouble for fighting, lack of interest, and rejection of authority or rules. He knew that his way to power was through his fists, and he refused to acknowledge that any one had power over him by virtue of their position. This frustrated the few teachers who cared enough to try and engage him, because he was clearly one of the brightest kids in the school. Even when he wasn't suspended he only attended classes for something to do and to meet girls. The notable exception was computer science. To the astonishment of Mr. Evans, Fist was the best student he had in 24 years of teaching. He not only quickly grasped the basics of using the computer: he raced ahead of his classmates. He often spent the whole day exploring both the technology itself and the world of information available on the Web. Because he was feared by administrators and teachers as much as by his classmates, they were happy to allow him to sit in his favorite back corner of the computer lab through the day and into the afternoon after school. Mr. Evans occasionally approached Fist between classes and gave him pointers. He didn't object when Fist brought in a hard drive, opening the case of the computer and installing it himself to increase the storage capacity. Mr. Evans gained a great deal of stature among his colleagues and the students for having the only positive relationship between a teacher and Fist. Years later Fist would occasionally come into Mr. Evans' room without any notice to try and resolve some technological problem. If a student was at his favored station the teacher would immediately move the student and Fist would take his place. Mr. Evans would then help him work out whatever problem he had been having.

Except for those occasional visits with his computer mentor, Fist left school behind at sixteen and roamed the dry, wide lands of the oil patch, ranging from Wyoming down to Texas. He worked the rigs as a roughneck and occasionally rolled a drunk or drug buyer when he went into the bigger towns. He did the muggings as much for the pleasure of feeling the will of his victim give way as for the money. He connected with his victims through his hands; it was how he got close to people. He learned to use a short, spring loaded leather sap, filled with lead buckshot, learning just how much force would break an arm or cause unconsciousness when applied sharply behind the ear. He got canned from numerous oil jobs because of the fights he got into there, and his reputation as a tough spread around the oil fields.

Six years after leaving Tulsa, Fist got into yet another scrape at a SPECO rig near Levelland, Texas. He had been unloading pipe with two other roughnecks. One of them said something, just the usual bullshit banter, but Fist was feeling the need to put the hurt on someone. He worked them both over, breaking one's shoulder and giving the other a concussion. When the two injured workers had been loaded into a van and driven off to the hospital, the site boss came over to Fist, who was leaning on the stack of pipe. Fist figured he was about to be canned again, but it had been worth the fun.

"That's two pretty tough guys you just whipped," the boss said. "Doesn't look like they even touched you."

Fist just shrugged.

"Look, I seen you work on the job here, four months now. So I know you're a smart guy. Now I know you're a tough guy. I'd heard, ya' know, but now I know. I know some guys looking for a smart, tough guy to do some work for them. You interested?"

Fist had expected to get cussed out and shit-canned for putting two workers out of commission. This sounded a lot better than that, damn good, in fact.

"Could be," he said. "I could talk with 'em, anyway."

"Good," the boss said. "I'll get in touch with the big shots and, you know, maybe they'll want to talk to you. In the meantime, think you can finish unloading that pipe?" He gave a little grin. "I'm a little short handed right now, but I figure a tough guy like you can handle it by yourself."

"No problem," Fist answered, and nonchalantly went back to his work.

The next day he got paid off and told to pack up his gear and wait for the company van that ran a route around the SPECO sites in the area. It was another hot, dry day, just like a hundred others that summer. Clear blue sky, wind blowing, dust devils kicking up and well pumps bobbing like chickens pecking at the dirt of the flat prairie. When the van pulled up to where he was sitting outside the shack that served as bunkhouse and office for the surrounding wells, the driver didn't even look at him. Fist waded through the dust kicked up by the van to the passenger side, got in and threw his gear over his shoulder into the back. He was accustomed to people being uncomfortable around him. In fact that was the way he liked it, so he didn't say anything to the driver, a dried up old fart in a cowboy hat whom he could break like a twig if he felt like it. When they pulled out, Fist reached over and turned off the radio that was playing some kind of honky tonk wailing shit. He relaxed and enjoyed the passing fields, broken up by drilling sites and didn't ask any questions. After stopping at two more sites the van headed into Levelland. They hadn't had to think too hard when they picked a name for this town, he thought to himself. The yellow land was as flat as an ironing board for as far as you could see in any direction. The town was a scattering of houses, and trailers with a short main street that had a small grocery, a pharmacy, a couple of offices and not much else. The van driver pulled up at an unpainted cinder block diner that had the usual "Coffee" and "Chicken Fried Steaks" neon lettering in the windows. The diner didn't need any other name; everyone within a hundred miles knew what you were talking about when you said "the diner."

"People you wanta see in there," the driver whined through his nose when Fist made no move to get out.

Fist grabbed his duffel, opened his door and stepped out of the van. He pushed the door closed behind him without looking at the driver, whose head had never turned in his direction, and went inside. There was a blond waitress in a faded red calico blouse and blue jeans behind the counter and two white guys at a table in the back corner with their heads turned to look at him. Fist walked over to the table and dropped his bag on the floor.

"Fist, I'm Breaker." The bigger of the two stood up and reached out a work calloused hand. "They call me Ball Breaker. I'm in charge of security for SPECO."

Fist shook the hand. Breaker was taller than Fist, about 40, same age as his old man had been when he and his old lady killed him. Sun and wind had tanned Breaker's face into rough, seamed leather. None of the lines on the face looked like they came from smiling. He wore jeans and a chambray work shirt that had faded onto his long, lean frame as natural looking as a second skin. He looked like he had spent most of his life humping pipe and fitting bits in the field, but it hadn't broken him down like a lifetime of oiling did to most men, like the old fart in the van. Fist recognized him as one of the men that hard work and rough times made stronger and tougher, just like himself.

"This here is Wayne Twilley," Breaker said, indicating his companion with a nod of his head. "Twilley is from the financial side of the business."

Twilley was short, plump and soft, with the pink skin that comes from a prosperous life of moving numbers around indoors. Fist guessed he was older than Breaker, but out here among hard men away from the city he looked like a baby. He was balding, with gold framed tinted eyeglasses, round cheeks and thin, pink pouting lips. He wore dress slacks, no tie. His once crisp blue dress shirt was wrinkled now and ringed with perspiration under his arms and around the neck, and his face was damp and nervous looking despite the frigid air conditioning that was typical of Texas.

"Pleased to meet you, Mr. Fist," Twilley said as his small pale hand disappeared into the night of Fist's paw. "Please call me Wayne. What do folks call you?"

"Fist," he replied, applying enough pressure on Twilley's wet fish of a hand to make him try to pull it away. He let it go, pulled out a chair and sat down with Breaker on his left and Twilley on his right.

"You want some coffee?" Breaker asked. "We're fixin' to eat."

"I can eat," Fist answered.

Through the ordering, eating and coffee drinking little was said, but Fist was aware that Breaker and Twilley were looking him over as thoroughly as he was checking them out. Fist and Breaker both had chicken fried steak, mashed potatoes and green beans while Twilley had a bowl of soup and a piece of chocolate pie. The soup made him sweat more. Finally, after the table was cleared and the coffee cups refilled, Breaker pushed back his chair, offered Fist a Marlboro, took one himself and lit both with his Zippo. Twilley pushed his chair back and waved his hand in front of his face in annoyance, but didn't say anything.

"Ok, Fist, let's just skip the bullshit and get down to it," Breaker finally said.

To Fist's surprise Twilley broke in, his face flushing as his agitation overcame his nervousness, "First you need to understand that what we are about to talk about goes no farther. In fact, this meeting never happened, you never saw us and we don't know you and we never will know you. If that's going to be a problem then now is the time to walk away."

Fist looked steadily at Twilley, "What if it becomes a problem? What're you gonna to do about it?"

Breaker cut in, "Fist, you're one tough guy. We've checked you out. We know that. But you're not tough enough to fuck with us. No one is. We can get a hundred tough guys if we need to take care of a problem. So we're just telling you, don't be a problem. Now you got that?"

Fist waited a minute, looking Breaker in the eye.

"Yeah, I got it. I ain't no fool," he said calmly, "but long as we're layin' down markers, here's mine. I ain't no one's bitch. Nobody owns me. There's a job to do, I do it how I see it got to be done. You guys ain't buyin' me lunch 'cause you think I'm gonna be you're buddy. You want some heads busted an' you don't want it to get back to you. You need someone off the books who can handle things. That's cool with me, so let's talk business."

He took a drag off his cigarette, flicked the ashes on the floor, poked the cigarette into the corner of his mouth, folded his arms and sat back in his chair.

Breaker and Twilley exchanged a long look. Breaker nodded. Twilley pushed his lower lip up over his upper one, looked away, then turned back and he nodded.

Fist had found a new job.

At first it had just been easy stuff. Independents who needed to be persuaded to be bought out by SPECO. Workers trying to organize in the fields. Politicians and regulators that got out of line. Suppliers who were getting too greedy. SPECO usually could get people back in line with their financial muscle, but a surprising number of people just didn't know when to back down. They were too dumb and full of themselves, thinking they could stand up to the oil giant. A few really were able to keep their independence and frustrated all the approaches, bribes, economic freeze outs, pressure from government stooges and finally threats. That was when Breaker or Twilley would give Fist a call, because, as Twilley told Fist that day in Levelland, "What's going to make us top dog, Fist, is we don't lose. Other people may back down, wait to fight another day or another battle, but for us to get on top and stay there people have to know that SPECO doesn't back down. If we tell someone they need to stop doing something, or they need to do something, those people have to know that if they don't do what we say, bad things will happen to them. And that's what you are going to be. You are the bad thing that will happen."

"If you can cut it," Breaker had added.

"You ain't gonna know that before you see it," Fist had told them flatly. "So I 'spect you have something lined up to try me out. Then you'll see what I already know. I was born to be bad news."

Fist used the first job to show Breaker and Twilley they had the right man. Ray Schweikert was a big, tough field boss who kept sending in reports on some safety shortcuts that SPECO was cutting on their rigs. He was making it uncomfortable for the company and inspectors who had been paid to look the other way. He'd been fired, the mortgage called in on his house (SPECO had a controlling interest in the bank), and blacklisted so that no one would hire him to do anything that had to do with the oil industry, right down to pumping gas, but Ray still was raising hell, writing the newspapers and talking to anyone else who would listen. Eventually he had gotten some young Dallas lawyer to start building a class action case against SPECO for workers who had gotten injured on any of their jobs due to "the purposeful, deliberate and culpable negligence and disregard to basic safety measures," all supported by Ray's eyewitness testimony and documents he had taken from the job site when he was fired. Schweikert had laughed off his former co-workers who had come to him as "friends" to warn him that he needed to back off before "someone really gets pissed off and steps on you like an ant."

"I ain't scared of those goddam SPECO goons," Ray threw back at them, sitting in a Denny's in Dallas. "Get on back to them that sent you and tell them that if they wanta fuck with me, I'm ready. I been the toughest guy on the oil patch for a good long time and they'll find they got their hands full. Shit, they're more scared of me than I am of them, and if they're not, they better be. Now get out of here."

Fist had laid the groundwork for his future when he told Breaker and Twilley what he needed to take care of Schweikert.

"First, I need to go to Dallas and get a place to stay for a month or two," he told them. "I need to have a good desktop PC and access to the personnel records at SPECO. You need to give me everything you have on this guy, and on his lawyer, and everything you can get from the gover'ment or whoever. I need a rental car and some money to live off of and for expenses. I got to study the guy and when I know what I need to know, I take care of him and he won't bother you no more. When I finish the job, we'll talk about what you gonna pay me."

"You're gonna need a month?" Breaker asked with displeasure.

"Don't know. Maybe more, maybe less. You want this done right with no blowback or you want it fast?"

Armed with all the information about Schweikert that the resources of SPECO and their friends, including those in the government, could provide, Fist settled in and watched his prey. Schweikert was staying in a run down independent motel on Westmoreland, in the flight path of Red Bird Airport. His lawyer's office was a ten minute drive away in a small strip mall in Duncanville, a middle class suburb trending in the wrong direction for property values and public services. Trips to see his lawyer were Schweikert's chief occupation, usually with a stop along the way at one of those peculiarly western bars that sat by itself off an exit ramp of Interstate 20; cinder block building with no windows and a broken spring screen door. A handful of pickups could be found in the dusty dirt parking lot from morning until the small hours of the next day.

That was where Schweikert met his lawyer. Carson Carrol had washed out of one of the downtown firms, and was scratching out a living for himself, his wife, two young daughters and a boy on the way, writing wills and acting as attorney of record for mortgages and foreclosures. He was facing foreclosure on his own house, and was four months behind on the office rent. Carson had stopped at the freeway bar on his way back to the office from a house closing, an increasingly frequent occurrence as he slid from depressed to desperate. He knew he wasn't a top legal talent or anything like that, but the thought was growing that he wasn't even an adequate lawyer and he could end up flipping hamburgers or something. Shortly after "How ya' doing," Schweikert had launched into the oft told tale of his battle with SPECO and the attorney had perked up like he had rubbed a lamp and a genie appeared, come to brighten his world and bring him his fortune. Carson realized that up to now he just hadn't had the right opportunity to break into the big time.

The more Schweikert talked the brighter Carson painted their future together. In his office two days after they discovered each other in the freeway bar, the big oil patch boss opened up a shopping bag and pulled out the bundle of safety inspections, injury reports and correspondence that he had taken with him when he was fired. Now Carson knew that their days of glory had arrived. They signed a contract and he started working as he never had before. After three weeks of research he sent his first letter to the SPECO president and CEO. He locked all the paperwork up in his safe and awaited SPECO's reply. On an ordinary Tuesday afternoon almost a month later, Fist delivered it.

Carson was alone, working on his taxes when Fist came in, reached back and turned the deadbolt lock on the door.

"Can I help you?" Carson said, but there was no reply. Fist walked over to the desk, looked at it, and picked up the picture of Carson's wife and daughters, inspecting it.

"What are you doing?" Carson said, rising out of his chair.

Fist held a copy of Carson's letter to SPECO in front of his face, long enough for Carson to recognize it. Then he crumpled the paper, put it into his pocket, raised his hand and casually punched Carson in the face, breaking his nose and knocking him back. The backs of the lawyer's knees hit the chair, the chair hit the wall behind it and he crumpled into the chair, shocked at the pain and the blood that suddenly was everywhere. Fist grabbed the front of his shirt, pulled him up with one hand, the other still holding the picture of his family, and dragged him around the desk and into the bathroom in the back of the office. It took five minutes. Fist had spoken little. Three times he had put the lawyer's head into the toilet and flushed it. Between the near drownings he slowly, methodically beat him with piston-like blows that broke ribs, shut one eye and broke off four upper front teeth. He had the lawyer watch as he tore the picture of his family into pieces and flushed them down the toilet. Then he took the crumpled letter out of his pocket and made the lawyer eat his words, slapping him when he choked, making him swallow every piece of the paper. When they came out of the bathroom Carson limped over to the safe, took out the box of papers that held his dream case against

SPECO and gave it to Fist. Fist grabbed his shirt front again and pulled Carson's broken face to within an inch of his own.

"If I have to come back, it won' be a picture you see go down the toilet, an' that's the last thing you gonna see. You got that?" he said unhurriedly, each word a separate menace.

"Yesh, yesh, pleash," Carson sobbed bloodily.

Fist left him sobbing face down, sprawled on top of his desk

Once the lawyer was out of the picture and all the evidence burned, Fist didn't think that Schweikert would be able to cause any more problems, but he had personal and professional reasons for making sure. He wanted to feel the big oil hand's will to resist run out under his hands, and he wanted to show Breaker and Twilley that any matter they put in his hands would be followed through thoroughly and completely. After leaving the lawyers office Fist went to hunt down Schweikert. Ray's pickup wasn't at the freeway bar or his motel, so he parked in the lot where he could see the room without being noticed. When Schweikert pulled up at 7:00 that evening he showed no signs of agitation, so Fist didn't think he had gotten word that his lawyer had dropped the case yet. An hour later, however, Schweikert burst out of his motel, slammed the door, kicked over a lawn chair that was on the small concrete pad outside the room and banged his way into the truck. He raced the engine, viciously backed out and then threw the truck into gear and out of the parking lot. Fist followed him to the bar, and again, backed into an unobtrusive spot and waited as the sun slid behind the flat horizon and day turned into dusk. When Schweikert lurched unsteadily out of the door three hours later, Fist figured the time was right.

He pulled away from the bar while Schweikert was getting into his truck and went back to the motel. A long minute later Schweikert's truck weaved into the parking lot and pulled crookedly into two spaces, Fist got out of his car and walked over to the truck. Schweikert half fell, half stepped out of his truck.

"Tough day, huh, Ray?" Fist said to him.

The drunken oil man turned his head and tried to focus on him.

"Wha?" he said stupidly.

Fist stepped right next to him and said into his ear, "I said, tough day, i'n it, you dumb fuck."

With a short swing he hit the big man with his cosh just over and behind his left ear. Before he could fall, Fist ducked down and stuck his shoulder into his gut, lifting him up like a sack of grain and shoving him back onto and across the bench seat of the old pickup. He went back to his car and got out the cooler of ice, a jug of water and a gym bag; supplies he had kept on hand for the past two weeks. He took duct tape from the bag, taped Schweikert's ankles and wrists to each other and took a wrap around his head, covering his drooling mouth. The keys were still in the truck. Fist got into the driver's side and drove to an empty patch of prairie that he had scouted out, one of a million empty places under the East Texas sky.

He spent that night with Schweikert, waking him with the ice and water, talking to him and then using his lighter and the pliers, hammer and hacksaw from his bag to punctuate his points until Ray would pass out again. Before dawn, he bandaged up Ray's wounds and took him back to his room, supporting him on the side with crushed toes and a broken heel. Ray was thanking him by then. Fist had become his god, the one who gave pain and stopped it, who controlled life and death itself. Ray would never speak of SPECO or pass a sober day again.

Fist became more sophisticated over the years, but he never lost sight of the fact that his blunt cruelty was what shocked his victims into compliance. He enjoyed introducing people to pain; bringing chaos into what they had thought was an orderly world. He was very good at his job and only once went too far, killing a target unintentionally. He never rushed and was always thorough. Eventually he was sent to Iraq, Egypt and Nigeria to solve problems. He never left a trail that could be traced back to SPECO or been identified by targets who had not been marked for killing.

As Fist eliminated problems, Ball Breaker rose to be Chief Executive Officer and Chairman of the Board for SPECO. Once he used Fist to eliminate a stubborn internal rival who wouldn't step aside. SPECO became the top oil producer in the world, with the highest profits. Their business exceeded the total economies of all but the most prosperous countries. Twilley, now the Chief Financial Officer, set up and controlled the system of accounts that got Fist his money with no connection to SPECO, himself or Breaker.

"Money won't be a problem," he had told Fist in that Levelland diner meeting, and he was as good as his word. SPECO was making record profits, as were all the oil companies, and no accounting audit in the world could keep track of all the money that they had coming in and going out. As fewer oil reserves were discovered around the world the oil companies quit building refineries and new production facilities. What had seemed an endless supply was running out.

"Demand and prices going up, expenses and supply going down, equals big profit," Breaker liked to recite. "You don't need a fucking PhD to figure out how this economy works."

Fifteen or twenty years down the road, when the oil was getting really scarce and the economy tumbled, people would be looking around for scapegoats, wondering why nothing had been done to prepare new energy resources. By then the oil companies would be so rich that they could ride out the transition. Ordinary people would find themselves with SUV's they couldn't drive and big houses they couldn't heat, so spread out that they couldn't walk to the store or work, but the corporations would be stronger than ever.

Fist had figured all that out over the years. It wasn't a secret within the oil industry, and anyone with curiosity could find plenty of evidence on the internet. He had his own top of the line computer and server set up in the house he had bought in a gated suburb of Tulsa. His income as an "independent security contractor" made him acceptable among the elite, not that he had any desire to mingle with them. He kept mostly to himself and followed the energy news like any other player in the business. Everyone in the industry knew that the oil era was ending and that they needed to keep the public pacified to maximize profits while the window of opportunity was still open. So even though this D.C. job was the first time he had been called on to take care of some smartass who was pulling the curtain back and to let people see what the future looked like, he wasn't surprised that it had finally happened. He had expected it.

When he received the e-mail from Twilley he had called Grainer in Vegas and Minton, who lived in a cabin on Brown's Lake about forty miles down the Chattahoochee River from Atlanta. Grainer had been working with him for almost four years now and Minton about three. When he told them to meet him D.C. he knew that they would be there exactly on time and ready to work.

He'd put his team together by using the resources of the internet, where you could get information on anyone but especially on those with a criminal record. Using sophisticated data mining to sort through millions of entries by age, sex, types of skills, (as evidenced by the crimes they had committed) he had spent months tracking down seven that he marked as "possible." Then he checked them out the old fashioned way: talking to people and watching them. He tried one other guy before he picked up Grainer, but he'd proven unreliable; got too heavy into the booze and flapped his mouth. He was fish food now, at the bottom of the Houston Channel. Grainer and Minton, however, had proven to be exactly what he needed. Grainer was unobtrusive and sly. He could mix in with almost any white or mixed groups, do his business, and slip away without anyone noticing he was even there. He liked to use his knife, but he was good with a gun, and could put together some explosives, too.

Minton was just muscle. Everyone noticed him, and that was the idea. His presence alone was enough to scare the shit out of most people. He didn't move very fast and even Fist didn't usually know what was going on behind his silent mask of a face, but if he needed someone immobilized, Minton would grab hold and just crush them.

When Fist left the APRC offices he had everything he had asked for. He took the one bedroom suite next door to the two bedroom unit where Grainer and Minton would stay. He would definitely take his time on this job. Nice comfy digs, blank check on expenses, good restaurants, hot nightclub scene with plenty of women. It all added up to no reason to rush things. His bosses had long ago gotten used to his patient approach to a job, and they wouldn't raise any kind of fuss. He was going to enjoy sticking it to the APRC assholes while he took care of business. They thought they owned the world. He wanted to take a piece of it from them, money, yes, but more importantly, he wanted to make them squirm. First he'd take a month or so to do research on this chump who was causing trouble, this Woods guy. Have Grainer and Minton follow Woods and his kid, make the guy uncomfortable, while he checked out the rest of the family and this Natural America Club bunch of do-gooders. Then they'd find the right opportunity to squeeze this guy. He'd play it cute, be careful to not scare the fool off before he had a chance to enjoy this job. If that didn't work, well then this chump was just too dumb to be walking around. He'd been told to eliminate the problem; no instructions on handling the guy. That left all options open.

Fist opened up his laptop and downloaded the disk he had gotten from Perry Richardson. He didn't know yet exactly how this little problem would get worked out, but he did know three things. It was going to get worked out. He was going to add to his already hefty bank account. And someone was going to get hurt.

Life didn't get any better than this.

Chapter 9

The last questioner of the night had an angry tone to his voice. Typical of the audience he was a white man with grey hair, in his fifties or sixties, casually dressed in the kind of synthetic safari shirt, convertible pants that zip off at the knee and Teva sandals that are accepted summer attire among those who consider themselves environmentalists around the country.

"The government says they aren't sure about how bad this climate change stuff is going to be or even if it is being caused by what people are doing. They don't seem to think there is a big catastrophe happening. Do you really have any evidence? You're not even a scientist, are you?"

Wendy was seated on the right hand side of the well filled meeting room. The NAC members in Charlotte had done a good job of getting turnout for the meeting billed as "A New Climate for NAC and the Environmental Movement." As everywhere she, Tony and Aaron had traveled to over the past month, the hundred and fifty or so assembled NAC members and friends had listened politely as first Tony made the case for needing to take new approaches to revitalize and build a grassroots environmental movement to change the culture of America. Then Aaron engaged them in what he called "a conversation" about what needed to be done. She knew from the dozen and a half or so meetings that they had already held across the country that this question would give Aaron a good chance to end the talk on a strong note. It was amazing just how little even those people who thought of themselves as "green" knew about the biggest damn issue of the century. Not really amazing, she corrected herself, since American media coverage was ten years behind that of Europe, thanks to the skillful disinformation campaign waged by the carbon industry and their political stooges.

"Thank you, sir, for that question," Aaron said easily. "First, I am happy to say that I am indeed not a scientist. I have great respect for scientists. They are the ones who give us the information we need to make decisions. I'm just like you, a citizen concerned about the environment and about our country; concerned enough to be sitting in a meeting on a beautiful May evening. We are the ones who have to look at that information and make the decisions. The scientists won't make the decisions for us about what to do about climate change; how to reduce the economic, social and environmental consequences of it. That's not their job or area of expertise. They will present their best estimates of the outcomes of various choices, but we have to make the choices.

"I am afraid you are wrong about the government not saying this is a big problem. If you go to the EPA web site you'll find state by state information about what the effects of climate change are expected to be, in terms of increased drought, flood, severity of storms, loss of soil moisture, and more. The Pentagon did its own study, and it showed great concern about the geopolitical upheavals that are expected in the next couple of decades due to climate change. It's the politicians that are in the pocket of oil and coal companies that provide big campaign contributions and other favors who either deny these facts or ignore them. They know Americans don't like bad news, and the first target of their wrath is usually the messenger."

When he paused and took a drink from his glass of water one voice called out, "So I guess you aren't going to be running for office."

"No," Aaron said with a laugh, "I don't want any part of that game. Politicians won't make tough decisions unless the corporate donors who support them say they should. The corporations won't make the decisions unless it helps them do what corporations are set up to do, make money and ensure their corporate survival. So if tough decisions are going to be made that will reduce the amount of carbon we are dumping in the atmosphere and reduce global warming pollution, it is up to us, the citizens, to make those decisions.

"You ask about the facts. Here are the most basic facts. For ten thousand years up until World War II, the atmosphere was pretty stable at about 580 billion tons of carbon. Between World War II and the year 2000, the level of carbon in the form of carbon dioxide, increased to 750 billion tons. We know that carbon dioxide is a greenhouse gas that causes climate changes. We are adding about 6 billion tons of carbon to the atmosphere every year.

"We know that before we hit 1000 billion tons of carbon in the atmosphere, those climate changes will be catastrophic, worse than anything I have told you. We don't know where the point of no return is; just that it's somewhere before we hit 1000 billion tons. Unless we stop adding 6 billion tons of carbon to the atmosphere every year, we're going to hit that 1000 billion ton mark by about 2040 or 2050. If we take drastic measures right now, it will take decades to make a difference in the carbon build up, and in the severity of the climate impacts.

"That is what we know. No reputable scientist disputes those facts. Now it is up to us to decide what we are going to do about it. The options are simple. We can take the route that the coal and oil industries and their servants want us to take. Burn as much carbon based energy as possible until catastrophe happens. That makes them a pile of money. For us, it is like closing your eyes while you walk down the train tracks. You can hear the whistle blowing but you don't have to watch what is coming.

"Or we can reduce our carbon footprint. That means burning about 60% less carbon based fuel than we are burning now. The way to do that is to make our buildings more energy efficient, to make our cars get 60 miles a gallon, to build up our light and heavy rail network and focus development around it, and to put all our government subsidies into alternative fuel development and rail instead of into coal, oil and cars.

"So how many of you here want to reduce our carbon footprint, raise your hand," he said, raising his own hand high. First a few hands went up, then more and finally most of the people had their hands in the air.

"Ok, that's great," he said. They all dropped their hands back down as he did. "You are the ones who have to make this happen, and that's why I'm here. To ask you to help."

His voice got stronger as he wound down.

"Tony and Wendy, over there, are putting together a national campaign and we need you to take your part in it. So please be sure your name and contact information is on the sign-in sheets at the back of the room and be ready to help organize your friends and neighbors when we call on you."

Now he visibly relaxed and came back to a conversational tone, "Thank you very much for having me here tonight. Let's break up now and have some of those snacks that have been provided in the back of the room. I'll be happy to chat with you there."

Wendy and several others in the audience started the clapping and were joined by the rest of the audience. As always with the larger gatherings, Aaron had insisted that the podium and microphone be placed on the floor just three feet from the front row of seats, and that there be a center aisle down the rows of seats. He liked to walk back and forth a little while having his "conversations" with the audience, as well as up and down the center aisle, carrying the microphone with him even though his voice easily filled most rooms. He encouraged people to ask questions and both in his talk to the group and afterwards he often responded with a question that let them find their own answers.

"I've been working to save the forests along the Chattooga River for fourteen years," one man had stated during his talk this evening. "Do you expect me to drop that work and start working on just climate change now?"

"How do you think it affects the forests when the insect breeding rate doubles?" Aaron had responded. Several people had contributed with comments about the bark beetles killing off the trees, the gypsy moths eating the vegetation and other local problems that they knew something about.

After listening to the answers from the audience Aaron turned to the man who had posed the question, "You folks know more about your local issues than I ever will. Keep working on those, but just add to what you are doing that we need stop adding to climate change or your good work will be for naught."

The applause was warm, as it had been at all their stops. Aaron just had that knack of building a rapport with people and getting them to embrace new ideas, more so than any of the environmental experts Wendy had worked with before.

Aaron smiled, replace the microphone on its stand and put both hands up. As the applause stopped he started towards the back of the room, but only got a step or two before being surrounded by people who wanted to either ask a question or to demonstrate their own knowledge and experience. If this was like all the other meetings that she had set up over the past month, Wendy knew that he would never get to the back of the room where the food and drinks were set up. She went to the tables in the back of the room, got a cup of the fruit juice and brought it up to him. This had become part of her routine.

Aaron was grateful and she was happy to do it. Then she sought out the local leaders with whom she had worked to put this meeting together. They would be the key to building on the momentum of this meeting and getting The Movement started.

That's how she thought of what they were doing now: The Movement. When she and Tony and Aaron talked about it, they always said "The Movement." One state and one meeting at a time, she thought they were making a good start at recruiting a cadre of beginning organizers. Tony told her that this was step one in taking over the country.

"First we get a dozen people in each state to recognize that climate change is the big one, the issue that trumps all the other issues, and to get passionate about it," Tony had said in telling her how they would implement Aarons boycott idea. "Then we get them to understand that the way to do it is to build up the energy efficiency, solar and wind industries. Third we get them to understand that the energy industries are the ones who have the resources and responsibility to develop those industries, since they got their money by polluting our climate. Fourth we show them that the best way to make that happen is to directly attack those big corporations. The corporations are vulnerable to actions that hurt their relationships with suppliers, customers, financial markets, share holders, insurance companies. We can hurt them lots of ways if we take them on one at a time. Finally, we help our dozen or so key people in each state organize the boycott. After that it is just a matter of building The Movement one house party, one family gathering, one church group, office, hunters and gardeners club, softball team; one anything at a time. Organize and recruit, face to face, building the chain across the country, so that when we say boycott SPECO and picket their gas stations the signs crop up all over the country."

Wendy was responsible for getting that network set up and keeping it connected. Thank God for the internet, she thought, but she knew that wasn't enough. You had to follow up by phone and also give people the chance for face to face contact. That's way she, Tony and Aaron were running themselves ragged going to meeting after meeting across the country.

The three weary leaders stayed until the last local volunteer left at 9:30. It was a Thursday evening and they had rooms in the same hotel where the meeting was held. They had flown down to Charlotte that afternoon and Aaron was going back to D.C. in the morning. She and Ted were going straight to Atlanta and Orlando where they had meetings scheduled on Saturday and Sunday afternoons, but Aaron insisted on going back home to be with Squeak Friday afternoon and evening. He was booked on an early flight to Atlanta Saturday and after the meeting there they would all go to Orlando together. Sunday they would meet with the Florida volunteers in the early afternoon and return to D.C. in the evening. In between the meetings she would get together with the local organizers, building the team.

When Aaron was out of town Squeak stayed with their neighbors, either Antelope, whom Wendy had met, or Baba Ghanouj, of whom she had only heard. Aaron told her that Baba Ghanouj meant "Fat Mama," but she knew that it was some kind of Middle Eastern dish. He had finally confessed that Squeak had started calling his Afghan neighbor that when he first started staying with Aaron, because she brought homemade baba ghanouj, a sort of eggplant casserole, over to their house at least once a month.

"We're having baba ghanouj tonight," Aaron would tell Squeak in the afternoon. When the kindly neighbor from six doors down, a single woman of ample dimensions, would come to the door with dish in hand, Aaron would give a big sniff and grandly announce, "Ahhh, baba ghanouj." The three of them would then share a tasty dinner. When Squeak had started asking, "When's Baba Ghanouj coming over again?" the name had stuck.

Wendy marveled at the relations Aaron had with the people in his neighborhood. He took for granted practices like telling a neighbor that he was going to the grocery store and asking if they needed anything. He had related to Wendy an exchange when Karen, one member of the lesbian couple with two adopted Chinese kids who lived next door, had asked him to pick up toilet paper for her. He had come back with 100% recycled toilet paper, and she reacted with disgust.

"They recycle the toilet paper? Eeyoo, that's dirty! We're not using any recycled toilet paper in this family."

He explained to her that they used other clean kinds of paper, not old toilet paper to make the recycled product but Karen had remained skeptical and didn't ask him to get anything from the grocery for her for the next few months, and even then was very specific about brands, sizes and "fresh, new, not used before."

Wendy contrasted this with her relations, or rather the lack of them, with the neighbors in her big Northwest D.C. high rise. There the norm was to be polite but guarded; say hello but not to build networks of dependencies and shared intimacies. She wondered what it was like to have such comfort with who and what you are that you can be totally open and honest with friends and strangers alike, such a lack of concern about how you are being perceived.

This lack of fear or barriers was part of what made Aaron so effective talking with audiences. It made it easy to accept his ideas, knowing that he would listen to yours in return with the same expectation of honesty and lack of posturing. She had been comfortable spending time with him from the start, and it seemed most other people were, too.

"Whew," Aaron said after the last of the local people had left the meeting room. "I could use a nice anisette. You guys want to go to the bar for a little while?"

"You know none of these places have anisette," Tony said. Aaron always tried to order his favorite cordial made from anise seeds, but nine times out of ten ended up getting a gin and tonic. "But I could use a drink, too. How about you, Wendy?"

"I'll have a beer, but I'm more interested in something to eat. You guys go ahead while I lock up and turn in the key at the desk."

When she got to the bar she found Aaron and Tony sitting at a table not talking and looking pretty glum. Aaron usually was withdrawn after the meetings. He told her that when communicating with people he was trying to give them a charge from his own store of energy and afterwards he needed time to restore himself. A bottle of Sam Adams ale and empty glass was at her place, while Aaron was sipping a gin and tonic and Tony stared at his glass of Chablis.

"I went ahead and ordered for you," Aaron said. "Should be here any minute."

"How'd you know what to order?"

Tony raised his eyebrow and gave a smirk, "He just asked the girl what entre on the menu weighed the most. She had to think but said that she thought probably the bacon cheeseburger with fries. He told her that sounded perfect, to bring that and a salad for you."

"You can be an ass, can't you," she said to Aaron, suppressing a smile as she sat down.

"Hey, I just envy you. You can eat that crap, go to bed, sleep like a baby and wake up slim and beautiful. If I ate it I'd be up all night with heartburn and gain five pounds. It would take me ten weeks of starving myself and working out to it burn off."

"Fact is, that's exactly what I feel like eating," she relented. She poured her ale into the glass and took two deep swallows. "So what's wrong with you guys? I thought tonight went fine. I think I've got three or four people lined up here that will get some house meetings going. We're making some progress."

"Oh, you're right, Wendy," Tony said. "Tonight did go fine and things are going as well as we could hope so far. We're building the network and getting people interested. We are starting to get people to at least understand the problem and the need to do something."

"Yeah, yeah," Aaron said. "As far as it goes we're doing fine."

"So what's the problem?" Wendy challenged them.

"The problem is that I just don't see these nice, white, middle class, well educated people going out and sustaining a high profile campaign," Tony explained. "They understand, but they're too comfortable. We need people that are willing to shout and scream and get angry. Who will sacrifice their precious self image in order to get attention and force action. These people leave the hall understanding what the story is, all right, but I don't see them taking personal responsibility for changing things."

"Right," Aaron said intently. "It isn't so much how many people you have that believe in something that will force change. It is how intense they are. How loud you talk is more important than what you say when it comes grabbing the media and getting the decision makers to come to the table. The intellectual element is there, but we aren't getting the emotional involvement we need; the commitment to go out and talk to strangers."

They all sat back when Wendy's dinner arrived. Aaron and Tony watched her pour mustard on the fries and ketchup on the burger, cover it with the top of the bun and take a big bite. Both of them reached over, Aaron grabbing a fry and Tony a piece of lettuce from the salad.

"That's going to be tough to get," Wendy said, talking around the bite in her mouth. "I mean, you seem to have them more fired up than I have seen our people ever get, but that's a long way from them burning the CEO of some oil company in effigy."

"That is the problem with this kind of issue," Tony said. "This is a disaster, a catastrophe, but it is in slow motion. To get the kind of commitment we need for The Movement we need some precipitating event that people will rally around. The Civil Rights movement had the arrest of Rosa Parks that got the bus boycott going, the Selma beatings at the bridge, the Birmingham bombing where those little girls got killed; that kind of major outrage that gets people to march and sacrifice themselves. The Peace Movement had the Tet offensive and Me Lai massacre. Gandhi had the beatings on the Salt March to the sea. What we have is the biosphere that supports life slowly getting cooked and the sea level slowly rising. It isn't immediate enough to get people out into the streets. Even things like 30,000 people dying in a heat wave in Europe last year didn't bring this issue home to people here in America. Most of them don't even know it happened, and those who do don't understand it can happen here."

"Plus, we haven't clearly identified the bad guys," Aaron added, warming to the topic. "A lot of the rhetoric blames the ordinary people because they make selfish choices, rather than blaming the people who are conditioning them to make those choices; who only give them bad choices to make. Or it is diverted to the politicians who are acting as shills for the corporations that pay for their offices. We haven't defined the enemy, the top bosses of the multinational corporations that extract, sell and promote the use of carbon based fuels. Shit, I'm getting tired of hearing about this stuff, myself. It just isn't personal enough."

They lapsed into silence. Tony ordered another round of drinks and Wendy finished off her late dinner. She had her own ideas about organizing, but wasn't confident she understood how to motivate masses of people.

After the drinks came, Tony summed it up. "So we need to have a big horrible event that is directly traceable to the burning of oil and coal, and we need to tie that event to the bosses of the oil and coal corporations. How do we do that?"

Aaron finished off his drink and pushed back his chair. "I don't know. Maybe it'll happen. We just have to keep pushing ahead with what we are doing. If we can get things going, public demonstrations, media coverage, stuff that will hurt their stock prices or scare off investors, then maybe they will do something stupid; they'll react. That's the way it happens. That's what Gandhi did, what King did, what Cesar Chavez did. You can even say that is what Bobby Kennedy did for the Peace movement. Meantime, I have to do better at getting to our people's emotions. I have to get more heart into it."

He got up from his chair, and unexpectedly went over to Tony and took his hand and gave it a squeeze. "Thank you for taking this on. I am truly grateful to be working with you on this."

Then he took Wendy's hand. "You are a great organizer. These meetings are great. Pretty soon we'll get some demonstrations and such going. I'll find a way to reach them. Please don't lose heart."

Then he bent down and kissed her on the cheek. She felt a rush of warmth from her toes to her head.

"We just have to keep pushing and hope that some day that will be enough," he said.

Wendy was confused as she watched him turn and leave the bar. She couldn't sort out her feelings. She wasn't used to having someone express such naked emotion. It was especially startling coming from a big, powerful, successful, older man. Her father had been a big man and successful at what he did, but he had never seemed to be so vulnerable. Obviously Aaron was urging himself to not "lose heart" as much as her, but he also seemed to be telling her that he needed her to keep his emotional energy high. Thoughts about Aaron, her dad, The Movement, her longing to be a part of making the world a better place, swirled in her head, flashing behind her eyes. She couldn't sort them out.

"Helllloooo," she heard Tony calling, bringing her back to the table. She saw him looking at her with one eyebrow arched high.

"Grow up, Tony," she told him mildly. It didn't really matter how things sorted themselves out. She was committed to The Movement and she needed to keep Aaron energized and involved because without him this whole campaign would fizzle out like a wet firecracker. He was a good man and she was going to support him however she could until The Movement got off the ground and was self sustaining.

Chapter 10

What in hell was I thinking, Aaron asked himself for the hundredth time at 2:00 AM. The image of his bulky old self bending down and kissing Wendy's cheek played over and over in his head. It stayed with him as he lay waiting for the four o'clock wake up call, through his shower, the cab ride to the airport, the 6:15 flight to D.C. National, the Metro ride to Union Station and the short walk home. All day as he caught up on household chores, got some groceries, caught up on email and went to the gym to work out on the heavy bag he alternated from, "I'm an idiot. I've scared her off for sure. She won't want to work with me," to, "What's done is done. That's what I felt like doing and she didn't seem to mind. Maybe..." but he didn't let himself go any further and soon was back to being an idiot.

He didn't really mind being seen as a fool. He had done plenty of foolish things in his life and some of them had actually worked out pretty well. What was different was that now she probably was thinking he was an old fool, a typical dirty old man lusting after young women. And Tony had witnessed it, although Aaron hadn't noticed him at the time. I bet they had fun talking about me after I left, he thought. And why not? He was an old fool lusting after a young woman. Right now, walking back from the gym he could picture her walking up the street towards him. And last night his imagination had been working in overdrive, jerking him awake with vivid close up flashes, the curve of her neck, the thrust of her breasts, the sweep of her hip, whenever he started to drift off to sleep.

Goddammit, that was just normal fantasy shit, he told himself. Any man thought about women like that, at least any healthy heterosexual man. Of course she was in his fantasies, he was spending a lot of time with her and she was a down to earth and sexy woman. He wasn't nuts. He knew she wasn't interested in him, at least not that way, and he hadn't come on to her or anything. That kiss had just been a way of expressing, well, ah, his appreciation for her as a person, an honest, gentle, strong, hard working person.

Yeah, he thought, and a hot babe person, too. He hadn't kissed Tony. He shook his head. Fuck it, he was an old fool.

It was a little before three in the afternoon when the call came that jerked him away from worrying about Wendy and their...what? Relationship?

"Yo, Pops, w'a's goin' on wit'ch ya?" It was his son, Theodore Roosevelt Woods, calling from Zurich. Aaron's own business career had largely been in Europe, with some time in Asia, but he had arranged things so that he and his family would be in the U. S. for Ted's high school years, feeling that his son deserved to have the democratizing experience of American public high school. They had lived in a suburban house in New Brunswick, New Jersey, and Ted excelled athletically and academically. They could have afforded one of the tony private schools, but Aaron wanted his son to be grounded in the values of "real people" not a narrow slice of wealthy elitists. The wider the socio-economic swath of his acquaintances at this stage of his life, the better he would understand how the real world worked and be prepared for his future.

Despite those intentions the de facto segregation practiced in the Northeast U. S. had provided Ted little exposure to African American's during his school days. Blacks and whites lived in separate neighborhoods and school district lines were drawn to limit attendance based on the same ethnic and socio-economic classifications that divided the neighborhoods. In spite of those limitations, Ted's search for expanded boundaries and quality basketball games had drawn him to urban playgrounds where he formed friendships and became familiar with hip hop culture and language. Four years of study at a mostly white, academically rigorous college and three years of graduate study at Oxford had not erased those friendships or pop cultural lessons, and Ted enjoyed shifting into playground argot when he called home or came on a visit. He shifted just as easily into German, French and Italian, all of which were more useful than hip hop in his work with Zurich Finanzampt Internacionale, moving investment money around the world. Aaron could only wonder at Ted's ease with different languages and cultures.

"Ted, it's great to hear you," Aaron said, his voice showing his enormous pride in his son. Ted had managed to remain a warm and loving person despite the shock of his parent's divorce and his own rapid rise in what Aaron perceived to be the cold world of international banking and finance.

Despite the travel and work time demands of his career, Aaron and Ted had been very close when the boy was growing up. He had worked very hard to be there to help coach his son's teams, especially basketball and through sports the many lessons of father to son and son to father had been exchanged. Since the boy had left home and gone to college, however, Aaron had become increasingly unsure of his role with his quickly maturing and increasingly sophisticated son. Ted's career moved to levels of complexity and financial success that outstripped Aaron's own more moderately successful one, but he could not help but still see the young boy who had enjoyed curling up under his arm for a bedtime story. He greatly admired Ted's mastery of virtually any culture or setting, and the glamour and adventure of his expatriate life in Europe. At the same time, however, he fervently wished that his son was living close by so they could share a meal or walk or some other contact on a regular basis. He couldn't stop himself from offering unsolicited advice, and asking about personal details regarding Ted's life and relationships, but then he was washed with guilt that he was invading Ted's privacy and not respecting his independence and judgment by doing so. He suspected that this was the reason why he didn't hear from his son more than once a month. On the whole, being the father of an accomplished, independent adult seemed much more complicated and less rewarding than being the father of a growing child had been. On the other hand, it was far less time consuming.

"Dad, I actually need to talk to you about some strange things that have come up here in the firm that seem to be connected to the latest activist stuff you emailed me about," Ted said after they exchanged health and travel highlights and talked about Squeak's school and social life.

Aaron was surprised. "What's come up? I really didn't think you read most of the activist stuff I send you. Don't tell me you've heard about the organizing work we've started over here? We've hardly even gotten started on it. It isn't even a ripple on the pond yet."

"Well, you know, I don't read all of the stuff you send me, but I went back over the recent emails because, ah, something came up about it at work," Ted replied.

Aaron's surprise turned to concern. Ted's bank handled management of the investments of some of the biggest re-insurance agencies in the world. These agencies insured the insurance companies against the biggest kinds of losses, like hurricanes and tsunamis. Billion dollar stuff. How the hell did his little organizing meetings come up in those circles?

"It isn't in the papers or anything," Ted explained, "but Jurgen called me in to his office this morning to let me know that he had gotten what he called "pointed inquiries" about me from people representing oil industry interests."

Jurgen Anhalt was the Director of the global investment division of Ted's bank and the mentor who had pulled him up the career ladder at great speed. Ted was now an investment manager for several of the largest clients of the bank, a responsibility unheard of for a 30-year-old, to say nothing of a non Swiss national.

"So what did they want?" Aaron asked.

"Basically, they wanted me sacked."

"Sacked? Did they say why?"

"No, that isn't how it works here, Dad," Ted explained. "People don't just say what they want and we don't ask them why they want it. These oil people just talked about increased pressures from outside interests, public exposure that could prove very costly if it got out of hand. They said they needed to be sure that they were not being undermined from within our firm by someone who could be a witting or unwitting conduit to their enemies. Then, they said something like, you know, that they understood we had an American on our staff who was related to, ah, something like reckless and dangerously placed activists who are working to undermine the image of the industry. Jurgen and I had talked about your boycott campaign before, and of course he knew right away who they were talking about. Our clients have a lot of capital invested in those multinationals, so they figured it would be easy to just flick me away like an ant on the picnic blanket."

Aaron's voice rose along with his anger. "Those pricks! Do you know who was behind this? Are you ok? Did they fire you?"

"I'm ok, Pops," Ted soothed. "Dad, people are on your side over here, including Jurgen, the firm and the whole finance and insurance industries.

They take a long range view. They know that the only way to keep from having an economic catastrophe is to move now towards reducing reliance on fossil fuels and figuring out how to cope with the climate change. I mean we see the glaciers melting and the ski season getting shorter right out our windows. So don't worry about me. Jurgen told me to let you know that he admires your work and he looks forward to seeing you over here again next year. He said, 'Tell your Father that when the time is right we will be pleased to support his efforts to bring America into this battle for the future of the world.' Hell, if anything this raises my stature in the firm."

"Well, ok, that's a relief. Still, I wish I knew exactly who was behind this," Aaron said, still angered by this attack on his family.

"Jurgen couldn't tell me who called him. You know how the Swiss are. But I'm pretty sure that it is someone pretty highly placed, because Jurgen doesn't have that kind of talk with just anyone. He did say it didn't come directly from one of the corporations, which makes sense because if it backfired we could cause them a lot of trouble in terms of directing investors away from their securities or insuring their ventures. So it has to be someone who can talk for the corporations but isn't in the corporations, maybe a lawyer or a lobbyist, but my guess is that it was some amateur from the administration. They've filled the embassies with industry guys and they'll do anything the oil guys want. It seems too risky for a big time politician and Jurgen would just laugh at some flunkey, so it has to be an ambassador or top level staff speaking for the ambassador, either here or one of the G8 countries. They spoke our lingo, too, you know, a little too subtle and smart for the politicians or one of their appointees. The most likely scenario is that industry leaned on the administration, they contacted one of their ambassadors over here who then pushed their staff to do the dirty work."

Ted's analysis made sense to Aaron. He worked in a world that was far removed from his father's experience, but he had always found Ted's judgment sound, even when he was a kid.

"Have you heard from your mom?" he asked, thinking he was changing the subject. He missed Elena with the intensity you would miss an arm or a leg. They had been married for over two decades. Elena had been very comfortable with the nomadic international life they led while Aaron's work took them to live in different countries. She spoke more languages than Ted, and could pass for a native in several of them. She had been an equal and invaluable partner in their family and he had relied on her to help him adjust to new cultures. She always made wherever they went to live "home."

When Aaron had suddenly decided that he needed to leave his lucrative business career and devote himself full time to the environmental and social causes close to his heart, Elena's life had lost its purpose and direction. Ted had lived on his own since leaving for college, and now all the expectations for their future were changed as well. There had been a year of deepening depression and diminishing communication, and then the surprise announcement that she had been hired to teach at the International School in Paris. She hadn't taught for twenty years, but she had always kept her teaching certifications current "just in case."

Aaron had been stunned. Within a month she was gone, and soon after came the filing for divorce. He thrashed around for months, dashing across the country to visit scattered friends because he couldn't stand the empty house, throwing himself into one cause after another, trying to make some sense of a world turned inside out.

That had been six years ago. Elena taught in Paris for a year and a half, shedding her depression and building a new French life. She met the divorced father of one of her students and was swept off her feet. Marcel George, Compte de Seuville, was charming, wealthy and extremely well connected. Aaron tried to be happy for her. He even went to their small civil wedding, although he sure as hell didn't give the bride away. He had to face the fact that she was fulfilled in a way that she had never been with him. That not only hurt him, but it made him feel like a selfish prick because he was consumed by hurt rather than happiness for her. He did wish her well and Marcel was a fine man, a good person, but goddammit, he still missed her.

Ted had said something, but Aaron had missed it, brooding about Elena. Even now he would drift off into dark recriminations like that, right in the middle of a conversation. He caught himself.

"Ted, I'm sorry, I didn't catch that. What did you say?"

"Uh oh, first the eyes go bad, then the knees, now it's the hearing. You getting old or something?"

"Hah!" Aaron barked sharply. "You and me, punk, name the game. Hoops, climbing wall, kayaking, weights, whatever, just bring it on." Ted had been blessed with a natural athleticism that Aaron did not share. As early as when he was ten, the youth had been quicker than his father, whose physical gifts were limited to strength, size and fitness. From his early teens the son had dominated their one on one competitions. Aaron never admitted he was hopelessly outclassed, though, and still hoped that he would emerge victorious in their next sports battle. At this stage in life the winning and losing had less importance to Aaron than fighting the good fight, while for Ted a losing result in anything was unacceptable.

"You're on," Ted said. "Next time I come over there or you come here. I think a ski race would be perfect." Ted was an excellent skier while Aaron was merely determined. They both knew who would win that match, and that Aaron would end up in a heap of snow, skis and gloves.

"Anyway, what I was trying to tell you when you were having your senior moment," Ted continued, "was that Mom called me because Marcel told her that some people were snooping around, asking questions. His broker reported to him that there has been an attempt by what he called 'inept and unsavory elements' to get information from his office. He also said that they had detected electronic attempts to break into Marcel's financial accounts. I don't know too much about Marcel's affairs, but I would guess that he is about as secure as…well, as a Swiss bank." Ted chuckled at his own little joke. Aaron just rolled his eyes at what passed for humor in Zurich banking circles.

"So there is nothing to worry about on their account," Ted went on. "I just thought you should know. I think it is more than a coincidence; that these activities against us are all related. You better watch your back, because apparently you have riled up some people with a long reach and a lot of resources."

The line went quiet while Aaron considered what Ted said. Ted let him think for a minute or two. It was a comfortable silence. He knew that Aaron didn't always respond right away when he wanted to give something some thought.

Finally Aaron was ready.

"Ted, thanks for letting me know. Let me tell you what I think and you let me know how you feel about it. I think that there is a chance that I can be a big part of getting a real grassroots effort organized that will make American industry support moving to reduced energy use and a bigger share for clean energy, you know, solar, wind and wave power. I think I have a shot at helping public opinion move towards putting resources into actions that will lessen the impact of climate change and perhaps reduce the intensity and duration of the change that is going to happen.

"Now I tell myself that I'm just some ordinary schmuck and I may be having delusions of grandeur to think I can make a big difference in the world, but you know, that really doesn't matter because if there is a chance that I can be a small part of making a small difference I am going to try to do it. But if I'm delusional, how come some mysterious and connected people are reaching all over the world to try and get a hook into a schmuck like me through my family? This thing must have a chance, otherwise, why are they bothering?

"I think you're right about Elena. She's safe. Marcel has connections that go back for centuries and he's a savvy guy. Besides," here a bitter note came into his voice, "whoever it is will figure out that there's really no connection any more between Elena and me. They'll look for other ways to get at me."

Aaron paused, so Ted would know that what came next was important.

"I really don't care about them coming after me. This battle is more important than me and I will do whatever is necessary to fight it. But I worry about you. If you have any concern about them getting after you over there, I will back off this campaign. I don't want you to hesitate. You just let me know if you would rather I drop this thing. It's not as if I think I'm responsible for the world or anything. I'm just one person, trying to do what I can. If I don't push this campaign, someone else will or things will just happen the way they are meant to happen. So what do you say?"

Ted didn't hesitate, "Good speech, but I'm not buying it. You think you can make a difference and that the work you are doing is important. I think it is, too, and I can tell you that when I talk to people over here about what you are doing they all say that it is very important work and they are glad there are people like you, people willing to stand up and do what they think is right.

"I'll watch my back, but this is Zurich, my town, and I'm really not worried. Anyway, I don't give a damn if they do come after me. You give them hell over there and don't worry about me at all. If there is any real danger, it just means that you are on the right track and this is important enough to go all out. I'm with you all the way, Pops, and if you need anything from me you just let me know. Just watch your back and watch out for Kenya. He's just a kid, but if things get rough you never know what they might do, whoever they are. Do you have any ideas about exactly who could be behind this?"

"Well, it's got to be someone who has to do with the oil and coal industries," Aaron answered. "I'll have to think about it and ask around a little. Tony or Wendy might have some ideas, you know, some people they may have talked to, not that any of this is a secret. Christ, I'd kill for media exposure! Anyway, thanks for your support, son. You know I love you and miss you. We'll have to think about when one of us can get away so we can get together."

"I love you, too, Dad. You take care and stay in touch."

"Ok, bye."

"Bye. Give 'em hell, Dad."

Aaron stayed sitting in his chair. He had about a half hour before Squeak got home from school. It was time for adult stock taking and not just charging forward. There was no question about his willingness to put himself on the line to push this campaign. He wasn't wired to worry about risk, a trait that had come close to costing his life more than once. He kayaked in rapids that were beyond his expertise, climbed rock faces that scared him to death and that stuff was just for fun! In his work over the years there had been death threats a couple of times, once in Turkey when he broke up an illegal strike action and another time in Thailand when he had caused a Thai manager to lose face by chewing him out where, unbeknownst to Aaron, the guy's mistress could overhear. The truth was he relished having some risk in his life. It gave him energy. Besides, the idea that there could be physical danger in this situation really didn't seem plausible. This was the United States of America, even if it had been taken over by corporate interests.

He decided he didn't need to worry about Elena or Ted. Elena was well protected by her powerful husband and Aaron respected Ted enough to take him at his word. That really just left him and Squeak. Squeak was just a kid, and he didn't see how there was any chance of him getting involved. Besides, Squeak had lived with risk, too. Aaron wasn't the kind of parent who thought he could or even should shield his kids from risk in life. They had to learn how to deal with risk if they were going to accomplish anything. And Squeak had been dealing with risk since he could walk. The hell with it, he thought. The best way to deal with something like this that doesn't seem to have a right answer was to just go ahead and do what you think needs to be done. It would all work out or it wouldn't. He got up and went upstairs to sort out some laundry.

As soon as he cleared his worries for his family from his head his thoughts went back to Wendy. All bullshit aside, he liked her. She was fit and athletic, a runner and biker who jumped in to any kind of activity with confidence. She had grown up in Vermont on a small farm, and she had earned the muscle that slid beguilingly under her smooth skin, putting up hay in the summer and mucking out the barn in the winter. She was smart and enthusiastic, and took pride in her competence, not one of those women who felt like they had to feign dependence to maintain their femininity. He liked working with her as a partner, and would have even if she wasn't so damn sexy. He knew she had caught him checking her out when she turned to him, but she didn't make a big deal out of it, one way or the other. She just held his eyes for a minute with a look that he couldn't read and turned back to what she had been doing.

Aaron swore that women had a sense that told them a man was looking at them, or at least it happened to him a lot; probably because he liked looking at women. Still, he never knew exactly how to react when they caught him.

What he had to do now was figure out if he was just going to make a fool of himself by pursuing a smart, attractive woman two decades younger than he. Age had never been a hang up for him, pretty much in any context. Some of the women he'd dated since the divorce had been his age or older and some had been younger, some even younger than Wendy. Truth was that most of them had been a good bit younger than he, but he told himself that was just because those are the kind of people who you meet kayaking the river or pursuing some social justice issue. Most people his age, male or female, were more settled and less interested in taking risks or having new experiences. The important thing wasn't a person's age; it was their maturity as human beings who were trying to grow. Some people were immature brats their whole lives and some young kids already had a strong core of personal pride and principle. Ted had been like that as a kid. "Little man," people called him when he was seven or eight years old.

Still, he had no idea how Wendy would react if he made some kind of overt move on her.

"Might as well be consistent," Aaron concluded. He was risking being a fool by trying to start a new national grassroots movement. Would he be making himself a bigger fool by trying to build a relationship with a young woman? Besides, she wasn't shy about saying what she thought. She'd just tell him to get lost if she found him offensive.

"Yo, Gray," Squeak called as he came in the back door. Aaron was a little surprised, because the boy usually came in the front, but thought nothing of it.

"Hey, I'm upstairs sorting out the laundry," Aaron called back, shaking off his worries. Squeak was his family for right now, and he was determined to enjoy the afternoon and evening ahead of them. Aaron tried to make as many of the trips as possible day trips so that he could be home for the evenings, but he still had been away for one or two nights at a time every week, plus time on the weekends, and that was too damn much. Squeak spent those nights either with Antelope or Baba Ghanouj. Aaron was grateful to have solid, dependable friends, and they both welcomed the chance to have Squeak stay with them, which eased his conscience somewhat, but not completely..

"Sure I like having him over," Antelope had said when Aaron and asked if he was ok with all the babysitting. "You think I like to drink alone every night? Kid can't hold much but at least he hangs in there for an hour or two."

Antelope had been sober for two years and would rather drink gasoline than get back on the bottle to say nothing about exposing kids to booze or dope. Aaron had been there for Antelope when the pull of the bottle got too strong and he needed someone to talk with about it, but this wasn't one of those times.

"Well good, just don't let him get into your stash. I don't like it when the kid gets high without me," he had shot back at Antelope. Aaron had smoked dope every now and then until Squeak had moved in with him, but wouldn't have the stuff around his kid because he didn't think it was good for an immature neurological system or personality. Squeak often expressed his disgust for booze, and drugs, including cigarettes. Aaron felt that the boy blamed drugs and booze for causing his mother and father to abandon him. He and the boy talked often about the kids in middle school who were doing drugs, smoking or drinking. Aaron never passed on the information to anyone else. He wanted to keep the lines of communication open.

Squeak came up the stairs and into the little laundry alcove next to the bathroom where Aaron was loading the washer. He put his arms around Aaron, who reached down and returned the hug, kissing the boy on top of his head. Squeak moved over and sat on the closed toilet seat.

"I beat Antelope in chess," he announced proudly.

"Yeah? That's cool." Aaron and Squeak had been teaching Antelope how to play. "Have you been playing much at school?"

"Oh yeah. Every chance I get. Some of us play at lunch. I'm going to get you next time." Squeak had started a chess club at the middle school. About a dozen kids usually showed up at the weekly meetings. Squeak had never checkmated Aaron, but stalemates were becoming more frequent.

"Well, you get your chance tonight. I picked up some barbecue and salad from Whole Foods. I'll put in some rice and we can eat and then have a game. Wild Friday night at the Woods house."

Squeak turned serious. "Gray, there's someone hanging around here. Could be a perv or something. I've seen him after school for three or four days in a row. I think he's, like, watching me."

Aaron felt the hair rise on his neck.

"What's he look like? What is he doing?" He kept his voice even, not wanting to scare the kid.

"Skinny white guy. Sits in a car, or leans against it. Might be another guy in the car sometimes, I couldn't really see. Across the street from the doors, you know, in front of the school."

112

"So what'd you do? Why do you think he's watching you?"

"I just saw that he was watching me," Squeak said, in the aggrieved tone a teenager adopts when they think they aren't being taken seriously. "Wednesday, when I was coming home I checked back and this geek had walked to the corner and was still watching me. So I cut back into the school yard, hustled over to Fourth St., ducked into the alley and lost him. But I saw that he had come past the school and was looking around the school yard. Now what I do is I check the front of the school before I come out, from the windows upstairs. He's been there yesterday and today, so I snuck out the back of the school and, you know, circled around so I knew he wasn't following me. That's why I came in the back door today. Look, I know if some guy is watching me."

Aaron was quiet while he thought about Squeak's story. Aaron's pauses to think were one of the things that the kid counted on. It meant that his views were important and worth thought. Other people would jump in and say something just to fill the quiet space, usually something stupid or dismissive, but Aaron would wait until he had organized his thoughts. They had talked about people who were afraid of getting new ideas, who tried to control situations by talking non-stop. He and Squeak would exchange glances when it happened, and then silently plot some way to get out of the conversation. Now Squeak waited patiently.

"Squeak, I know you're as alert to what's going on around you as anyone," Aaron finally said. "If you think this guy was watching you, then that's probably what is happening. You did a good job. He could be some kind of a pervert, like you say, but there's other stuff going on, too. I think he could be someone trying to send a message to me. It's starting to look like someone who's pissed off about this campaign I'm trying to get going is looking at my family. Checking you guys out, you know, maybe trying to put pressure on me that way. Ted called and someone tried to get him fired from his job, and he said that someone had been checking out Elena, too. Now you."

"Who's doing this?" Squeak asked, the way some kids might ask about someone not cleaning up after their dog on the sidewalk. His hard early years had given him an awareness of the presence of threats in the world beyond the norm for most people, much less most twelve-year-olds. "What are we going to do about it?"

"I don't know who it is," Aaron answered. "I mean, I know it must be someone connected with the industries that would lose money if they have to take responsibility for the harm they are doing. I'll try to find out some more.

But I'm not sure what we should do. If I drop out of the campaign, then maybe they'll just leave us alone."

Aaron's lips shut into a tight line. The boy just looked at him, not saying anything.

"I think that's what I should do. I mean, we can report these guys to the cops at the school. But then we'll have to keep an eye out for them everywhere else. We'll be looking over our shoulder every where we go. The smart thing for me to do is back off this campaign and let the other people take it from here."

"Are you scared of these guys?" Squeak asked with an edge in his voice.

"No," Aaron answered with his own edge, "not for what they could do to me. I am scared that they could be dangerous for you. I don't want any harm to come to you."

Squeak stood up and looked Aaron in the eyes. His arms were straight down at his sides, fists clenched, chin thrust forward.

"So when I get scared, you tell me about brave men like John Lewis and Geronimo, who get scared but don't back down." Squeak's voice was getting higher as he got angry. "An you, you go walkin' into that gang of drug dealers over by the school and tell them they got to get out, an' I know you were scared 'cause you damn near fainted when we got home. You don't think I was scared then? You don't think I'm scared all the time? You don't think I got scared first time when you had me go up the crazy climbing wall at the gym, or, or you made me take algebra?" His voice broke and his eyes started to water. His voice rose to a shout. "So now what are you sayin'? All that's bullshit? Am I supposed to think we just quit doin' what we think we should be doin' 'cause we're scared?"

"Squeak," Aaron said, pleading for understanding. "Squeak, it's just that I love you. I don't want to be the cause of harm to you."

"When I see you back down from some skinny freak in a suit, that's what'll hurt me," Squeak said, eyes streaming now. "You're takin' away what I count on. That ain't the way we live. It ain't right. You're always sayin' we got to do what's right and take the heat. That's what keeps me goin' on every day when I'm scared."

Aaron raised up his hands out to his sides and let them fall with a big sigh, looking Squeak in the eye. He shook his head and sighed again. A long minute passed. He really wanted to protect the boy, but his words were like ashes in his mouth. That's what people always say when they take away your personal liberty, isn't it? *I'm just doing it for your own good, to protect you.* That's how those who have power keep it from those who don't. It was what the old told the young. Now he was saying that same thing. He just couldn't do it.

"Ok," he finally said. "Ok, you're right. I've got to stay on track. This is an important campaign, but I think maybe we're both over reacting. I'm going to keep on with this fight. But look, that means you're in it too. That's the way it is. What you're in, I'm in and what I'm in, you're in."

Aaron held out his arms. The boy searched his face while slowly realizing that he had won, that he had been right and had said the right things. He quickly moved into Aaron's embrace, clutching his own arms around his Dad's waist.

"This is what we've got. We got to keep it," Squeak said, his voice muffled by Aaron's shirt.

"Yeah, and it's all we need," Aaron said.

Chapter 11

Tony was still feeling pessimistic about their ability to build a national movement when he walked into the Atlanta offices of NAC early Friday afternoon, but at least he was well rested and it was a beautiful summer day. He and Wendy had gotten in from Charlotte at 10:00 that morning, checked into the hotel where the Saturday gathering was going to be held, and had a nice lunch on the patio at Front Page, one of the countless trendy restaurants that catered to Atlanta's large population of young, well paid professionals. Tony thought that Atlanta had one of the best food scenes outside of New York City. The bustling and prosperous commercial center of the Southeast boasted a huge clientele for good restaurants and many renowned chefs had moved there. Combining the southern traditions of good eating with skilled chefs, generous expense accounts and a young clientele generated hundreds of highly competitive and uniquely refreshing dining options. His teriyaki chicken salad and artichoke, leek and fennel soup with beef stock had been tasty and satisfying, and Wendy had devoured her rack of barbecue ribs with sautéed spinach and potato au gratin.

NAC kept a staff of four in the office on Peachtree Street in Midtown, the center of the city's booming economy. With four universities, including giant Georgia Tech, Atlanta was a sociological anomaly in Georgia. Straight and gay bars and entertainment of all stripes abounded. Neighborhoods like Five Corners that were throwbacks to the psychedelic Sixties contributed to a laid back, tolerant and diverse population that was fertile ground for NAC's organizers. Lobbying the Georgia legislature had gained some significant state level victories in the past, particularly on forest and wetland issues, and the young women working there had built up membership through social events that featured free beer, music and soft selling of the issues.

In recent weeks the staff had been instructed to change the focus of their work to organizing small gatherings of members spreading information on expected climate changes in the region and affixing responsibility to corporations like Southern Power and SPECO as the primary sources of the emissions causing those changes. Wendy had sent Ruthann Horowitz and Dante Ferenghi from the head office in Washington to Atlanta for the past week to help convert turnout at those smaller meetings to a big turnout for the campaign meeting on Saturday. This meant that the women that Wendy referred to as "our Atlanta angels" were working more with the middle class suburban population than with the urban students and professionals who had driven much of their past success. He was eager to see if this change of direction was being accepted in this major field office any better than it was among the staff at headquarters. It couldn't be much worse, he thought.

The office was a single large room with moveable partitions, a copier, four work stations, conference and mail sorting tables, a fax machine, some spare chairs, stacks of boxes and two bikes. Despite the largeness of the room compared to D.C. offices, it was always cluttered, and it was especially so now that Ruthann had commandeered one of the work stations for her exclusive use. Dante, a short, slender man with a shock of black hair, was working a phone at a corner of one of the two long folding tables. He looked more like a young intern than a nine-year veteran of the long lobbying effort to increase federal car mileage standards, a campaign that had garnered little public interest or real progress. He gave Tony a wave and a smile, and continued with his conversation, organizing a car pool to get a group of members from Marietta to the meeting.

Two of the Atlanta staff were similarly occupied, and Tony and Wendy quietly greeted each of them, not wanting to interrupt their work. Tony felt his mood lifting as he soaked in the familiar buzz, the smell of left over pizza and the organized chaos of paper and carryout cartons that characterized a real, grassroots organizing boiler room. Everyone had lists of people to call and were checking off the names and making notes as they worked. Wendy had created localized lists for every office where they had an organizer across the country, extracted from membership roles, attendance rosters at actions or meetings and donor lists. Each entry had information about the person being called: family or single, membership status and longevity, type of events attended, donor or not. She had built up this data base over the past several months and could sort the names and numbers based on any one of a dozen variables. A caller would know, for example, if the person had expressed an interest in forests, wetlands, transportation or climate change, what zip code they live in, and if they had family members whom they could be asked to enlist in the campaign. Big donors were sorted into a separate list and were contacted only by the most experienced organizers. The biggest ones were reserved for him and Wendy to call personally; their information downloaded into the hand held organizers they carried wherever they went. Over the past weeks Tony had come to realize what a genius his Campaign Director had for her work, and seeing those tools in action today helped to pick up his spirits.

Bike helmets and clothing that had been carelessly dropped as the wearers got warmer during the day were scattered among the food cartons, flyers, posters and checked off lists on every available surface. This, he thought, is how grassroots organizing is supposed to look.

Ruthann, the longtime policy expert on the Everglades restoration project, was the only one not on the phone. She was reading some recently released article on wetlands restoration on the computer, and she didn't look up from it while Tony walked to her corner of the room, separated from the others by one of the partitions, and greeted her.

"Tony," Ruthann said unceremoniously. Her eyebrows were knotted and her thin face twisted with displeasure. Finally she looked up at him with her head canted to one side. He could feel his irritation rising as her aura of displeasure and unhappiness enveloped him.

"Tony," she repeated, "this doesn't make any sense at all. Why should I call people when most of the time they aren't home? I could just send out emails to them and it wouldn't take any time at all. It is a waste for me to traipse all the way down here, and I don't like staying in someone's house who I don't even know. Why can't I stay in a hotel? And a lot of these people are just stupid and hang up on me when I try to explain energy policy to them."

"Grassroots organizing is tough, Ruthann," Tony said struggling for a sympathetic tone. "I know it gets frustrating."

"It's not just frustrating, it is a waste of time," she retorted sharply in a tone clearly meant to carry over the partition. "None of these people has any power to change the laws or regulate the companies. I need to be working on some real policy, not getting a bunch of ordinary people to come to some meeting. When I do get through to them they get mad at me when I tell them they need to come to get trained. They hang up on me. You're wasting my talents."

Tony had had similar conversations with a dozen of the long time policy experts, including his Chief of Conservation. These people had previously worked in their cubbyholes in Washington, writing up policies, sending them out to congressional staffers, occasionally going to visit with those staffers and talk with them. The closest they had come to doing grassroots work was preparing mailings or email to go out to the NAC members asking them to send letters or emails to Congressmen, Senators, agency heads or the President, and to send financial support to NAC. "Send a letter, have a meeting, write a check," was how one longtime activist member summed up how NAC volunteers had previously participated in national campaigns.

Tony also knew that the staffers on the other side of the partition were listening. Ruthann was talking loudly, playing to her audience and hoping to embarrass him. It was time for him to take off the velvet gloves and show the steel behind the smiles and handshakes.

"Ruthann, you are partly right," he said in clear, even tones that would carry through the office. "You don't seem to have the talents we need for grassroots work. The magic behind grassroots is building positive relationships between ordinary people, getting them to unite and express their passion. It means sharing concerns, triumphs and failures. Staying with members in their houses, eating breakfast with them, talking to them on the phone, finding out about them and how they can fit into the movement. Those are all important skills and you don't seem to be able or willing to master them. That is too bad, because the way you have been working in the past isn't going to build a movement. Since grassroots skills are what we need now in NAC, you will need to make a decision. Next week we will be back in D.C. Contact Arch and tell him I would like to see you early in the week. Now please get your lists together and join the rest of us at the table. I want to go over the arrangements for tomorrows meeting. We'll redistribute your contact lists to the rest of the team and you can work on seating, refreshments, materials, podium, sound system, music and decorations."

What little color there was in Ruthann's thin face had drained out of it. He could see that he had shocked her. Perfect. He needed the word to get around that there was a new, tough regime in place; that they were clearing the decks for battle and only those who could be counted on would be kept on board. He knew that the staff had made an early judgment that he was a mild mannered newcomer and they expected to continue their tight control over the agenda, budget and methods of the Club. After all, they were the experts, the policy professionals, and they had successfully cowed the members, who wanted no part of ugly confrontations, as well as previous directors. He had known when he applied for this job that the day would come when he would have to reform NAC into a true grassroots operation if he wanted to create any kind of historic cultural movement, and that some staff, members and donors would rebel. He had carefully prepared for this task, hiring a few key people like Wendy, learning the ins and outs, building his relationships with the key leaders on the Board and bringing them to see the need for change. Now was the time. He had already forced the resignations of a half dozen obstructive staff members who couldn't or wouldn't change their focus to organizing and away from policy writing and lobbying. Ruthann had provided him just the opportunity he needed to show the staff members in this office that he was driving this train and if they didn't want to go where he was taking it then they could jump off or be thrown off. They would spread the word on the grapevine. Although he kept a stern, even disdainful downturn to his mouth, inwardly he was quite pleased with the way this had gone down.

Tony turned away from Ruthann and walked around the partition to where Dante and the three earnest young local women tried to pretend they hadn't been listening. Wendy made no such pretence and gave him a small approving nod

"Ok, folks, let's have a powwow," he said in a more comfortable voice. "I want to know how many people you have contacted, how many have said yes and confirmed it once, how many have confirmed it twice, what your carpool network looks like, what the local leaders say, what media you have lined up for coverage, the works. This is the part of organizing I love, even better than carrying signs and singing songs."

For the next hour they went over the phone lists, arranged for volunteers to come in and have a last minute phone bank blitz that night, reviewed the plans for the meeting. Ruthann was silent except for when she answered a direct question, but he was gratified to see that Dante and the local women were catching campaign fever. From the jokes, looks and comments that went around it was apparent that a relationship was building between Dante and the local staffer with whom he was staying. Relationships like this frequently sprung up in the intense pressure, long hours and close proximity of organizing work. Before he met Samuel, his partner, he had enjoyed a couple of short term dalliances himself during political grassroots campaigns. This kind of low budget, physically and mentally exhausting, highly personal work attracted passionate and energetic people, many of them young and single. These were people who believed in building a better world, optimists who felt deeply and acted on those feelings. It was only natural that they would hook up. Unlike the more straitlaced atmosphere in think tanks and policy writing offices, casual relationships were an accepted and even welcome part of the grassroots activist environment. Tony was glad to see that loosening up the politically correct, constrained atmosphere that had prevailed in NAC was part of the cultural shift he and Wendy were pushing. The bloom on those young faces took him back to his own organizing days.

"Serena and I will handle the phone banking tonight," Dante volunteered as the powwow was breaking up and they moved to their assigned chores for the rest of the afternoon. "But, ah, we probably won't be in until 10:00 or so tomorrow if that's ok."

"Looks like you guys are a pretty close team." Wendy laughed as he blushed.

"Well, neither of us are morning people, that's for sure," Serena said easily. "Dante has to go back to D.C. on Sunday, so we want to make the most of the next couple of days. Of course, we'll be there to help set up the meeting, run around to pick up stuff and people, and to get out the news release afterwards," she added quickly.

"Ok, that's fine," Tony said. "Wendy, Aaron and I have to fly down to Orlando tomorrow night for Sunday's meeting there, so you folks will have to celebrate without us tomorrow night. It looks like you're going to have the best turnout yet. I'm betting over 200 people. You deserve a celebration."

"Thanks, Tony," Dante said. "We'll help Ruthann take care of getting the seating set up, refreshments ordered and all that stuff today, too."

Tony and Wendy spent the rest of the afternoon calling the local big donors and giving them a personal briefing on the campaign and invitation to the meeting. When that was done they helped recruit people to come in for the evening phone bank and handled their backlog of messages and phone calls from D.C. They stayed until the volunteers came in for the phone banking, making sure there was plenty of pizza, salad, beer and fruit drinks on hand and giving them a personal thanks for volunteering for the tough job of making calls. At seven thirty they got a final report from Ruthann, who was at the hotel getting the conference room ready. It was apparent that Dante and Serena had the phone banking well in hand, so they got a cab to 2 Urban Licks, a trendy restaurant in a converted warehouse that Tony had found out about on digitalcity.com and where he had made reservations. While waiting for their table to be free they savored glasses of wine drawn from the large casks behind the bar and toasted to "The Movement."

"So, Wendy," Tony said, leaning towards her at the bar with an arch look that said he was ready for some juicy gossip. He had planned this dinner with some specific objectives in mind, but he wanted to be able to cover them casually and not put her on guard. "Is anything developing between you and Aaron? What was that kiss on the cheek about last night when he left to go to his room?"

"Huynh," she snorted. "That surprised me. I mean, you know, he gives me looks, like when he doesn't think I can see him, but he hasn't said anything or put a move on me or anything like that."

"Yes and...?" Tony asked. When she didn't say anything he continued. "Are you attracted to him?"

"Oh, Tony, you are such a bitch," she said, the word coming out involuntarily and surprising her. She looked at him to see if he was offended.

"Wendy, I've been called a lot worse than that," he said mildly. "Come on; let's have a little girl talk."

She laughed, took a sip of her wine and leaned back. "Oh, he's an interesting kind of guy, you know, in an older guy kind of way. But a lot of the time we're together we're under pressure and it's all business. We're too focused have time for a lot of, oh, personal bullshit, but he will go off about, ah, the big picture things, you know, social movements, Cesar Chavez, public apathy, and he knows a lot of stuff. He marched for peace and civil rights back in the day. I mean, he thinks about the big philosophical stuff and then he can pull out things he's actually done that show how that stuff applies to the real world. He's mentally running at a hundred miles an hour and once he gets talking it's hard to interrupt him and, you know, make him get back to the schedule or whatever. On the other hand, he is, personally I mean, just as plain folks as any dairy farmer from back home. It's hard to, oh, categorize him."

The waiter came over then and took them to their table. After they settled in and ordered, Wendy came right back to the subject of Aaron without urging.

"I rode my bike over to his house two weeks ago, just to drop in, you know."

"Oh yes! Just to drop in," Tony said drolly, raising his brows.

"Yeah, whatever. Anyway, his kid was there, a skinny, nice looking black kid. He answered the door and I told him I was Wendy and he gives me the once over and tells me Aaron was over at the playground of the school across the street, playing some ball. 'Balling' is actually what he said. So I went over there and he was playing with this other guy, a big guy, not quite as tall as Aaron but more husky. The other courts were real busy, but they had one basket to themselves and I swear that I thought they were really angry with each other. They were banging into each other and pushing and smacking each other with their hands, grunting and calling each other motherfucker and sissy and punk. No one seemed to pay them any attention, though, like it was no big deal. And they were totally engrossed in this, this combat. I watched for a few minutes and finally the other guy notices me, Antelope it turns out his name is. 'Hey, darlin',' he says to me, 'you want to play some ball?' So then Aaron notices me and introduces us. Antelope is apparently his buddy, you know, and here they are, one with a bloody lip, the other with a skinned knee and elbow. I mean, they're like two overgrown boys. Aaron had to introduce me to Antelope's dog. 'What's his name?' I ask. 'Boner,' he says with a straight face. 'He really likes bones.' And they both crack up. When I asked if I could pet Boner they laughed themselves sick, and you can imagine how the conversation went after that. I mean it was funny and wicked and I cracked up, too, but god, how juvenile can you get."

"I see," Tony said with a straight face. "So you haven't thought about him at all."

"Yeah, ok," she said. "I think about him, but I'm not, you know, hot for him. He's as old as my dad would be, for god's sake. And I need to be careful with him, anyway, because we need him now to get this campaign off the ground. I can't play around with this guy, because, you know, he's too intense. Things would get too complicated. Still, I think a little flirting, you know, a little cleavage every now and then can help keep him in line."

"Ha, and you called me a bitch," Tony said. Then he shifted to the other topic he wanted to hear about. "You're still dating that guy from the dark side, that lobbyist, aren't you?"

"Hah!" she barked a sharp laugh. "Talk about opposites. Perry Pierce is all about casual relationships. He's nice though, and charming. He has really been turning on the charm lately, at least when I'm back in town. He's more my age, you know, more in the range that I'm looking for. I think that relationship might be winding down, though. In fact, I told him so last week, but he put on a full court press and really seemed, I guess, stricken and asked me to not push him out the door. Sent me a book of poetry, Shakespeare sonnets, for god's sake, and some flowers. So, yeah, I agreed to go to an Orioles game with him next week when I'm back in town. They have one of those suites, you know, very comfortable and a good view. I think I'd rather be in the bleachers with the crowd and the peanuts and beer, but I love baseball and it should be fun."

Tony just nodded and the conversation moved to other topics as they enjoyed their food and wine, but his interest in Wendy's relationship with her friend from SPECO was much deeper than Wendy supposed. Earlier that day he had retrieved a message off his office phone from Big Ed Tower, that's how he introduced himself, the Executive Director of APRC.

"Mr. Albritton," the message had said, "this is Big Ed Tower from American Power Resource Institute. We've crossed paths a couple of times and it may surprise you to know that I am an admirer of your work, as are some of my clients. I would like to talk with you about how we might work together to advance our common objectives, and at the same time provide you with, ah, personal advantage. Despite common misconceptions, my clients want to find the proper energy model for the future, and they would place great value on your guidance. I'll leave my cell phone number. Please call me at your earliest convenience, regardless of the time of day."

The message had ended with the return number. Through the rest of dinner with Wendy, and in the cab on the way back to the hotel he mused about the coincidence of Perry Pierce Richardson's interest in Wendy and Big Ed Tower's interest in him while they were engaged in a campaign that threatened the cozy status quo for their industry. In fact, he didn't think it was a coincidence at all, and he intended to explore the possibilities. This could work out to benefit him or the campaign, or both.

After arriving back at the hotel, and making himself comfortable, he called the number that Big Ed had left. He used the hotel phone, not wanting to have his cell number appear on Big Ed's records. He glanced at his watch. 10:30 on a Friday night. Let's see how much he really wants to talk with me, he thought.

Big Ed answered his phone on the second ring. "Hey, this is Big Ed," his voice boomed.

"Hello, Mr. Tower," Tony responded. He could hear conversation and cutlery in the background. "This is Tony Albritton, answering your call of earlier today. I hope this is not an inconvenient time."

"Tony, glad you called. Just call me Big Ed, everyone does. 'Cept my boy, he calls me Little Ed. He's a real horse. Let me just move over to a quiet spot and we can talk."

"Gotta take this call," Tony heard him say to whoever he was with. Then the sounds of his deep breathing as he pushed back his chair and walked to an area where the restaurant sounds faded away.

"There, that's better," Big Ed said. "They got this hallway here where it's quiet and we can talk. Where are you calling from?"

"I'm on the road, visiting some of our Chapters," Tony answered, evasively. "Your message said you had some kind of proposal about working together for a clean energy future. I hope you'll pardon my saying that doesn't seem consistent with the past positions and actions taken by your industry clients or by APRC on their behalf. Please let me know what you have in mind."

"Right to the point, that's what I like," Big Ed responded. "Well, Tony, we aren't fools on our side of the fence. We know there are problems with carbon emissions and, hell, we're going to run out of oil sooner or later, although we think it's a lot later than you folks think. Our folks are just like anyone else, they want to see things move in the right direction and they want to be a part of it, too. It's just good business. If we are going to stay on top of this energy business, my clients I mean, then we need to have the best minds available working together to find the solutions. I guess you know we have the resources to back smart ideas and get real programs going. A few of us got together and talked about this, and I'll be damned if every one of us didn't come up with your name as someone who has a real handle on the whole, big picture, I mean the energy industry, the economics, the politics, the environment and all.

"So these boys asked me to reach out to you and see if you want to jump in and have a hand in changing things from right here where the action is, where you can really work on things first hand. You know that's where the money and know-how is to change the energy business, and you could be the key person on putting that all together. So what'cha think of that."

"Well, Mr. Tower," Tony started.

"Come on, now, call me Big Ed."

"Yes. Well, Big Ed, that is one of the most interesting ideas I have heard in a long time. It is quite intriguing. What has caused this change of heart, if I may ask, on the part of your clients who have been fighting tooth and nail for the past two decades to protect their rights to pollute the air, tear up the lands and dump emissions into the atmosphere that will damage the climate for centuries to come? All of a sudden they want to become the agents of change and clean up the harm that they've caused? Is that what you're saying? You understand that I'm a little skeptical, don't you?"

"Tony," Big Ed said in a confiding tone, "I already told you. It's just good business. They want to stay on top. When the time comes that change is gonna happen no matter what you do, then you gotta move to be ahead of the pack. Now I know you're dedicated to doing what is right for the environment and for people. And this is a chance for you to do that. But I'd be remiss if I didn't also tell you that this is a chance for you to do well by yourself, too. You can name your price and they'll be glad to pay it and more to get you on board. That's all I'll say about that, because I know that's not what's important to you, but like I said, I'd be remiss to not tell you. What is important is that they will provide what you need to set up your own think tank here in D.C. and to really become the go to guy for the energy future. Now how does that sound to you?"

Tony waited a moment, wanting to strike the right note. He needed to play this like a big fish, let it run but don't let it get off the hook.

"Ok, Big Ed. This is certainly something I will certainly need to think about. I am sure I will have some additional questions for you, and I will want to meet the people who are involved in this. I assume you understand that this decision will take some time and require some due diligence on my part."

"Why sure, Tony. I mean my folks are ready to go right now and you know they say strike while the iron is hot, heh heh. So don't take too long, because in our business when we hit a dry hole we have to move right on. But you are the guy we all want, so sure, you take some time and ask away. 'Course, I don't have to say that this is a confidential inquiry, right? I mean if this doesn't work out or something it wouldn't be to anyone's benefit if it got out."

"Thank you, Big Ed. Yes, I will keep this to myself and trust you will do the same. Thank you for reaching out to me on this, Big Ed. I am sure we will be in touch with each other."

"Yes, indeed. Ok, then. Let's not let this sit too long. I mean let's get in touch soon," Big Ed answered, pressing hard.

"Very well, good night."

"Right, bye."

Tony put the receiver back on the hook and sat back in the hotel easy chair. I have just been given a great big present, he thought.

Tony had no illusions about the intentions of Big Ed Tower and associates. He knew very well that they were not interested in having a long term relationship with Anthony Albritton, who represented everything that they feared and detested. Queer, geeky, environmental snob city boy that he was, he knew that they were just trying to cut the head off of the campaign against them and once they were done with him they'd just toss him aside like a used Kleenex. Oh, but they didn't use Kleenex, so he would be more like the chewed up butt of a smoked down cigar. But all the same, they had just handed him a key that he was sure would unlock the door to success.

Big Ed's offer meant that this campaign was frightening the oil and coal corporations and their lobbyists. They had exposed to him that they were indeed vulnerable, as Aaron had been so adamantly claiming and as he had long suspected himself. It also gave him an inside channel to use to get information from them and to feed them what he wanted them to know, hiding in some poison pills along with the real meat. And it confirmed his suspicion that the interest in Wendy shown by her APRC boyfriend was not just a coincidence. He would have to be careful about what he told her; try to manage what she passed on to her lobbyist lover.

At some point, Tony thought, he would be able to use this gift as a lever to topple the huge edifice of money, corporations, political cronyism and public misinformation that opposed them. And if he couldn't do that, if it looked like this grassroots campaign wasn't going to work out, he would be able to use the lever to open an escape hatch for himself, setting up a safe position paid for by the very forces he was campaigning against now. It would wound him terribly to have to abandon the dear people who made big sacrifices for their cause, but to survive you always had to make sure you had options from which to choose. And it could very well be true that he might make the biggest difference in moving the culture to a clean power economy by working inside the energy industry itself. He wouldn't be known as a hero of the people, as he had dreamed, but he might have more power to do real good, and be secure for the rest of his life while he was at it.

But he didn't have to make that choice now. For now he could celebrate being in a position of real power, right in the center of the struggle with one foot on both sides of the battle lines. He'd figure out how to use it as the situation developed.

Tony decided to call home and talk with Samuel before getting ready for bed. Someone ought to know how good he felt, even if he couldn't tell his partner of the last seven years why. Tony was very good at secrets, and this was the second biggest one of his life, the first being all the years he had hidden his homosexuality from everyone. Just like that secret, he knew that he would reveal this one at the right time and in the way that would be to his best advantage.

Chapter 12

Wendy, Tony and Aaron got back to Washington National Airport at 6:30 PM on Sunday. Wendy felt that Aaron had been more energetic and compelling than ever in building a connection with the audiences in Atlanta and Orlando. She still felt a ripple of excitement left over from the way he'd closed both meetings.

"When you go out of here and start to talk to people about taking action against corporations that are poisoning the air and the climate, lots of people won't want to listen," he told them. "You won't always be the most popular person in the room. It can be uncomfortable, and some people may act against you and your families. This is serious stuff. But you are not alone in this battle. Look to your left and right. Look up here in the front of the room and look behind you."

He gave them a moment to look in each direction before going on.

"We are in this together and we can count on each other to help out when needed. It only took me two hours to fly down here this morning, so if you need me or Wendy or Tony to come help you, just give us a call. We are committed and we'll get back here if we need to.

"Now everyone join hands with those on either side of you. Join me in a chant I learned walking a picket line in Southwest Baltimore a long time ago. The people, united, can never be defeated!"

He repeated it, and by the third time around the whole room had taken up the chant, over two hundred people holding hands, standing up and shouting.

"The people, united, can never be defeated. The people, united, can never be defeated."

Aaron led them, punching his right fist over his head and walking the aisle. Then he broke into a cheer and started clapping and then reached out to the people around him. The audience clapped and shook hands and hugged, many of them reaching to offer thanks and encouragement to Aaron and receive his gratitude in return.

At the first meeting Wendy and Tony had exchanged looks while they clapped.

"Rock star," Tony said to Wendy. "Just what we needed, a rock star."

"Works for me," she answered. Then they joined in the hand shaking and hugging.

They hadn't been seated together on the flight, and when they got off the plane Aaron was waiting for her. Tony had gone ahead, and they didn't hurry to catch up to him.

"We really haven't had any time to talk to each other the last couple of days," he said as they walked down the concourse towards the Metro station where they would catch the subway to take them back to the District. "Would you like to come back to my place and have dinner with Squeak and me? It won't be anything fancy, but I think I have some ham steaks I can cook up and it'll get us a chance to talk."

"Yes, I would like that very much," she answered right away. Alarm bells were ringing, but this seemed like just a casual, collegial invitation, and it was a chance to build their relationship and keep him engaged. Besides, her refrigerator was empty and a home cooked meal sounded good.

On the Metro and then walking the four blocks from Union Station to Aaron's house they talked about the good crowds and how receptive they had seemed. They both knew it would take a lot of contacts and following up to get those same people to go out and picket their local gas stations or power companies, but at least they were getting a good start.

"You know, I'm satisfied that we're doing the right thing, going about this the way we should," Aaron confided in her, "but I still don't know if it will do any good. People are afraid of big issues, and the people we are trying to mobilize are too goddam comfortable. I'm especially worried because of all the gray heads at our meetings."

"You mean like Sam in Orlando?" Wendy laughed, naming a particularly bald and shiny headed older volunteer leader.

"Yeah," Aaron said, with a smile. "Old Sam isn't very gray haired, is he. It's just that most older people are less willing to take risks, to stand out in a crowd. That's usually what young people do, but the young ones these days seem to be, well, very conformist, not idealistic the way it was in my youth. Plus back then people were protesting because they didn't want to go to war and get their asses shot off, or because they were poor and oppressed by Jim Crow and were getting lynched or the shit beat out of them."

"But look at it this way," she said. "We've got more old people than ever now, and they are the ones that have the time to get involved in things. I think that we'll find that the younger ones will join up. I mean, we have some of them interested now. In the meantime, maybe the older people are the best ones to be working with."

"Yeah, like that old Rolling Stones song, 'If you can't get what you want, you may find sometime that you get what you need.' Not that I don't love the old folks, too." Aaron gave her a serious look. "I really appreciate the work you're doing, organizing things and doing the real work of the campaign. Working with you is great, a real pleasure."

"Well, Aaron, working with you is great, too." Wendy wondered if he was going to go any further. He looked like he wanted to say more, but he didn't so she went on. "I don't think we are ever going to get the kind of passion, the marching in the streets and civil disobedience about climate change that there was about Vietnam or civil rights, but we don't need to. We just need to get a widespread, vocal minority that represents important demographic groups, like churches, parents, grandparents, sportsmen, farmers, young urban students. If we can get a few of them and we can turn the volume up then we can drive the public agenda. That's how it works now."

"Ok, here's Antelope's place," he said as he turned up the short sidewalk to a typical narrow Capitol Hill brick row house. The houses here had mostly been built between 1890 and 1910 and were two or three stories, with postage stamp sized front yards. Many were painted bright colors and most were in good condition, having been renovated as the neighborhood gentrified and became a desirable place for those who worked on the Hill to live. Antelope's house was painted blue with white trim and was clean but hadn't had the full makeover that many of the houses had undergone.

Aaron knocked on the door and Boner started barking inside. He turned the knob and pushed the door open.

"All right, Boner, it's just me," he said, reaching down to give the excited dog a quick scratch behind his ears. "Anyone home?"

"No, go away," Antelope answered from the dining room. "I don't want you to see me beat the shit out of your kid when he checkmates me."

Aaron and Wendy walked through the small living room and into the dining area. Antelope and Squeak were seated at the table with a chess board between them. Like most old houses, the rooms were small and the floor creaky. Antelope kept his house clean and had a minimum of furniture. The few decorations were an Indian blanket hung on one wall, a hand made spear with flecked flint point over the fireplace and a drum in the corner. The shelves of the single cabinet held some Hummel figurines and a German wooden nutcracker in the form of an eighteenth century soldier. In the dining room one wall was dominated by a picture of the Alps with a small village in the foreground.

Aaron had told Wendy that Antelope's wife, Grendle, was from that village in the foothills of the Bavarian Alps. They had met and married when he was a soldier, stationed in Munich. She spent several months a year with Antelope, but spent the rest of the year with her aging parents in the farm house where she grew up. Antelope went there for a visit every two or three years, but her parents and the people in the village had never accepted the fact that Grendle had married an auslander, and a Schwartze to boot, so he didn't stay long. They didn't have any children, Aaron didn't know why, and their arrangement seemed to suit both of them very well. Grendle was a sweet, loving girl with country manners and no pretensions. Aaron thought she and Wendy would enjoy each other's company and she looked forward to meeting her. Unfortunately, Grendle was "back in the village" now, so that would have to wait.

Squeak came over and gave Aaron a hug.

"Kenya, this is Wendy," Aaron said a little formally. "Wendy, this is Kenya, or as we call him, Squeak."

"We met the day I rode my bike over here," Wendy reminded them as she shook his proffered hand. "So do I call you Kenya or Squeak?"

"Squeak if you're calling me to dinner," he said, smugly. "Kenya if you're my teacher."

"Is this some kind of championship match or do you want to come home and eat," Aaron said to the boy.

"Ain't no championship match, get him the hell out of here," Antelope huffed. "I'm tired of getting whipped. It's a stupid game, anyway. Boy should be learning how to play football."

"Yeah, let's go eat," Squeak said. "Baba Ghanouj said she was going to bring over the casserole you asked her for, and some of her flat breads." He turned to Wendy. "He's planning on impressing you with a fancy dinner. Got the table all set and the house all cleaned up before he left yesterday. He even got candles out."

Wendy laughed while Aaron swatted at the boy, "Ham steaks, huh. Looks more like a plot to me. What if I hadn't agreed to come?"

"Then I'd have lots of leftovers for tomorrow and this miserable snitch wouldn't get any," he said. "Antelope, are you coming? I'm sure there's plenty of food."

"No thanks," Antelope said. "Having the kid there will be bad enough when you're trying to put your moves on this poor girl."

"You guys are so funny," Aaron said sarcastically. "Wendy and I work together and are friends, so try to get past your bourgeois junior high imaginations." Then to Wendy and Squeak, "Come on, let's go while I have a shred of dignity left."

She chuckled when Antelope gave her a broad wink as they were leaving.

Aaron's house it was indeed neat and clean, with the table set as advertised. A casserole of mixed lamb and beef with eggplant, figs, pine nuts, mint, garlic and other assorted spices was warming in the oven and filling the house with its rich scent. Assorted warm flat breads were in a basket on the table, covered with a quilted cloth, and Aaron pulled a bowl of tabouleh, the mid-eastern salad of parsley, lemon, pine nuts and, of course, garlic, out of the refrigerator. Within minutes Aaron had lit the candles, punched on some low jazz on the digital music channel, opened and poured wine for himself and Wendy and milk for Squeak, and filled plates with casserole and tabouleh.

"If this is what you call your moves, I've got to tell you, it works for me," Wendy said as she sat at the table and they passed around the bread basket.

Dinner was a leisurely feast. Wendy enjoyed the easy exchanges between Aaron and Squeak. It was homey, reminding her of similar relaxed exchanges at family dinners when she was growing up in Vermont. They moved seamlessly across topics large and small, from light banter to events of their respective days to discussion of the Presidential elections. Squeak's opinions were accorded full respect, and he had no hesitation in questioning or challenging statements from her or Aaron, or defending his own positions when they challenged him.

At one point Aaron had returned to their discussion earlier in the day about whether the American public was too selfish and insular to support any kind of grassroots campaign.

"How many people have you heard say that they want to work for change, but they won't stand on the corner and hand out leaflets or take part in picketing or any kind of public demonstration. Their so comfortable in their own little cocoons that they won't shed them and come out as grown up butterflies," he complained. "And the young people are no better than their parents. They only want to participate in a campaign if it will help their career, for Christ's sake."

Squeak jumped in. "So now you're putting all the young people and all their parents in one basket. How about me? I'll help you hand out flyers and hold demonstrations or whatever, but what do you have me do? Stay home with Baba Ghanouj or Antelope. So who is building a cocoon here?"

"He's right," Wendy put in. "You have to give people a chance to do the right thing; to stand up for principles and work for the future. I think that we are doing that with our campaign. I keep telling you, we don't have to get a hundred thousand people to march on Washington. We just have to get a vocal, widespread minority that represents important interest groups, voter blocks. If we get a well placed, vocal 5% to take part in events, question candidates, demonstrate and write letters, then we can dominate the media and the rest of the country will follow. That's what the Christian conservatives have done."

"I'm not sure if I hope you're right or if I'm appalled that you are," Aaron answered. He started to go on but stopped himself in mid sentence and held up his hand in a "stop" sign. He and Squeak started listening intently to a guitar putting down an insistent, rolling beat to introduce a song on the music system. Squeak got up and turned up the volume as another guitar and then some drums picked up the beat, riffing against each other in turn before strong, low-key vocals were added on top of the instrumentals.

"Sweet Emotion," Aaron said to her along with the first two spoken words of the song. Both man and boy tapped fingers and nodded, letting the music flow through them. She sat back and felt herself letting go, enjoying the play of instruments and voices weaving in and out of each other while pressing forward along the beat of the drums. When the song was over, Squeak returned the volume to background level and sat back down.

"That's Leo Kottke and Mike Gordon," Aaron told her. "That song reminds me of a mountain stream. The percussion is the force of the current, steadily and insistently moving from source to the end. The guitars come in like two joining streams, mixing their essences together, building the current. The voices are like a fall, mixing it all together and adding the power of human emotion."

"I can play the vocals on my sax," Squeak added. "It's called 'Sweet Emotion.' I'm working on the guitar riffs, you know, translating them into sax."

"That's very cool. You guys are into music, aren't you." It was a statement, not a question.

"Oh yeah," Squeak said. "Of course, Gray isn't really up to date on the new stuff, but, you know, some of the old stuff is good. Like classics, you know. I mean, you're a lot younger than he is. Are you into the new stuff? Snoop and Li'l Bow Wow and stuff?"

"No, I'm a country girl at heart. You guys are way too hip for me," she answered. "Anyway, why do you call Aaron 'Gray'?"

"That's just, you know, what I call him. People on the street, ones that I know from way back, they call him 'the gray dude.' Everyone knows him, so it's like, just like when black guys call each other 'nigger.' I don't do that much anymore 'cause Gray just can't deal with it, but for black guys it's just an inside kind of thing. Anyway, 'gray dude' is just old school for what you call a white guy and, I don't know, you got to admit he's an old school white guy. Way too old for, you know, whatever." Squeak said this last with a mischievous smirk.

"Enough," Aaron said. There was some irritation in his voice. Wendy reminded herself to be careful around the age issue. Anyway, it really didn't seem like as much an issue as just a, well, a social convention around Aaron. He expressed such disregard for conventions in general that it made him look foolish to be even concerned about it. But still, he seemed to be a little sensitive at all the kidding.

"Why don't you go hit the books and get ready for school tomorrow," Aaron told the boy. "Make sure you have clothes for the week. By the way, did you see that guy hanging around this weekend?"

"No, but I did see another guy that looked like he was in the same car. He was parked down on the corner of F. He stayed in the car, but he looked, like, huge. A big black guy wearing some kind of doofy hat. You know, like that one you have with the brim all the way around."

"That happens to be a Stetson fedora and it's cool, not doofy." Aaron objected mildly, but then turned serious again. "When did you see him?"

"Saturday, it was in the afternoon. I was out, you know, just scoping things out to see if that other guy was around."

"What are you guys talking about?" Wendy asked. "You have someone stalking you or something?" This kind of thing hadn't been part of her pastoral upbringing nor did she have any experience with them in her current social or professional world. Of course, like any young woman she was aware of the existence of sexual predators and stalkers, but she never thought about them on a personal level. It was too chilling.

Aaron had Squeak tell her about the guy he had spotted watching him after school during the past week and then he related to her the information that he had gotten from Ted about the attempt to get him fired and his report on Elena. This was the first that Wendy had heard more than the barest mention about his son and ex-wife, and she really didn't track much of what he was saying about the mysterious inquiries. There was too much to absorb all at once. Elena had married a rich French Count, or whatever it was Aaron had called him. It was hard for her to relate the very urbane sounding Ted and sophisticated Elena to the Aaron she knew, the hard headed activist of modest means with a black twelve-year-old son. She knew that he had been "in business" and had lived "in Europe and Asia," but hadn't really thought about the huge difference in the scope of their experiences. Their interaction had been focused on organizing and the issue. Of course he was always coming up with unusual stories and examples to illustrate different points that made you think "where did he come up with that," but now she felt unsure of herself and she didn't like it. She was used to feeling that her brains, energy and looks gave her the balance of control in dealings with men, and she felt that balance going the other way. She felt like she needed to break away and sort things out. When they had finished relating the situation the room went quiet and she realized they were waiting for her reaction.

"Are you sure that you aren't being a little paranoid?" she asked, knowing right away that it was a little lame, but it was the best she could do. "Why do you think someone would be, what, spying on your family? It seems to me that you're reading a lot into these things. Maybe they aren't related to each other or to you at all."

"I suppose you could be right," Aaron said, doubtfully. "On the other hand, it doesn't seem likely that it is a coincidence that Ted, Elena and Squeak are all reporting these things at the same time that we are pushing a campaign that would upset the bosses of very powerful and ruthless corporations and cost them a lot of money."

"Yeah," Squeak was obviously offended, "I didn't just imagine these guys I seen."

"Guys I saw, not I seen," Aaron said automatically.

"Ahhngh," Squeak said in disgust, waving his hand as he got up from his chair. "Guys I saw, alright? I gotta go do some homework." He went upstairs to his room, giving the door a slam for emphasis.

"Aaron, I'm sorry. I didn't mean to make him angry," Wendy said, getting up with him to help clear the dishes from the table.

"Wendy, that's not angry. That's just being twelve years old. You'll know it when you see angry." He gave a little chuckle and asked, "So you think that I may be putting two and two together and getting ten, huh?"

"I just don't think that is the way things work," she explained. "I mean, I know people who work for the oil and coal corporations, high level executives and lobbyists. I think what they do is wrong, of course, but they are, I mean they just don't go around spying on people like us or threatening them or anything sinister like that. They don't need to. They have other ways of getting what they want."

They took their wine into the living room after the dishes were stacked in the sink and the leftovers covered and put in the refrigerator. She sat on the sofa and he sat back in his easy chair with a thoughtful look on his face. The music system was obviously high end, what you would expect of a music lover. A mellow alto saxophone was playing in front of a piano, bass and drums now. She took a sip of her wine and looked around the room. It was a man's room, scuffed leather furniture, walls painted a deep mustard with brown wood trim, thick green curtains drawn back from the windows and shelves filled with books, magazines, files and assorted artifacts: shells and polished stones, a long, carved meerschaum pipe, odds and ends from around the world. But no pictures, she noticed.

"Well, you may be right," Aaron finally said. She could tell that he really didn't think that she was right.

"This is a nice room, Aaron," she said, changing the subject. It pissed her off to be patronized and she wanted to say so, but she thought it best to suppress her feelings and ignore it. "I notice you don't have any pictures out, of Ted, or you or Squeak. Of anyone."

She didn't know what kind of reaction she expected, but the force of his response surprised her. He sat up straight, piercing her with a hard look. Then he got up and moved across the room. When he turned around she could see pain in his compressed lips and lowered brows. Finally, he took a deep breath and said in a low, clipped voice that he was obviously working to control, "I keep the pictures put away in albums. I don't like to see them every day. They remind me that people I love are far away."

Wendy was at a loss for words. She was swimming in unaccustomed depth. She didn't know how to find the words that could match his openness, or even if she wanted to go deeply enough into her core to respond.

She got up and went over to him and put her hand on his arm.

"Aaron, that is very sweet," she said, and stretched up and kissed him on the lips. He responded more hungrily than she expected, putting his hands on both her arms and pulling her to him.

They held the kiss for a brief moment, and she leaned back and turned her head to the side. "It's been a long week for me and I guess I should get home. I really enjoyed seeing you and Squeak. Thanks for having me." She regretted her words as soon as she rushed them out. She wanted to say more, but wasn't sure what or how to say it. She knew that she had to be sure of her words with him, so she didn't dare say anything.

Aaron smiled ruefully and released her arms. "Thank you for coming," he said. He went over to the door and picked up her carryon. "I'll walk you over to the Metro."

They walked the four blocks to the Metro at Union Station in silence, both afraid of saying too much or too little. At the escalator she gave him a kiss on the cheek and said, "Hey, nobody really thinks you're too old for anything, you know. They just aren't used to anyone with your kind of energy."

"Well, I have to admit that I had been thinking about the same thing, you know, age getting in the way of, well, approaching you," he answered thoughtfully.

Now she was uncomfortable again, not knowing how to answer him without either leading him on or offending him.

"Well, let's not worry about that now," she said carefully. "I'm sure we won't let your age get in the way of doing what we need to do."

"That's not what I meant. I was thinking you may be too old to keep up with me. I usually hang out with younger women." He smiled, chuckling.

She stepped back and hit him hard on the shoulder with her fist.

"We'll see who can't keep up," she replied with mock anger. She took her bag from his hand and moved to the escalator. She waved as she went down, but he just smiled and rubbed his shoulder where she had hit him.

On the subway ride home she tried to sort out exactly where she was with this guy, but couldn't put it into any category. She wanted him to be the figurehead for her campaign, the biggest campaign she had ever worked, but he kept moving into a more personal space. He continually surprised her with the breadth of his experience, the depth of his thought and the intensity with which he lived every moment without doubt or regret. She enjoyed being with him, but at the same time he was very demanding and made her unsure of herself, of her ability to maintain her personal sovereignty.

She tried to push all her personal feelings aside and to sort out her schedule for the coming week. This campaign was bigger than any of their personal concerns and she needed to stay focused. She took out her cell phone and scrolled through the calls that had come while it was turned off at Aaron's, sorting out which to answer now, which could wait and which to delete. She started her calls. This campaign was the work she had prepared for all her life. Any thoughts about Aaron's warnings of danger from unknown sinister forces were forgotten, buried under layers of larger and more realistic concerns.

Chapter 13

"They're still behind us," Squeak reported to Aaron, checking out the big Lincoln Town Car that had been following them all the way from D.C. This Tuesday afternoon was one of the hottest days of the early summer. The night before as he was going to bed, Aaron had told Squeak that they were going to go for a hike in the mountains and see if the "spies," as they called them now, would follow them. Finally he was being taken seriously and given a role to play. He was supposed to make sure and walk by the spies if they were at their usual place in front of the school and come straight home.

When Squeak got up that morning Aaron had already left, leaving a note propped up on the cereal box on the table to remind him of their afternoon plans. Like he was about to forget! It was an early dismissal day, so at 11:45 Squeak had waltzed right out the front door of the school, and turned to the corner to head straight for home, not taking the evasive action that had become part of his routine. The car was parked in its usual spot and this time both the white guy and the big black one were there. The white guy was leaning against the car and the other one was in the driver's seat. Both of them were giving him the fish eye. Probably they were tired of him giving them the slip every day and had decided to team up to try and keep up with him, Squeak thought to himself. He put a little swagger in his step, but kept watch on the guys out of the corner of his eye as he turned the corner, crossed the street and walked down the half block to his house.

Gray was sitting on the steps that led up to their front door.

"Let's go," he said. The Beemer was parked in front of the house and Squeak saw that his hiking boots and their day packs were in the back seat. Gray already had his boots on, which was unusual. He usually drove in sandals and changed into hiking boots when they got to the trailhead. They got in and waited for a minute until, sure enough, the Town Car slowly nosed around the corner. They took off slowly, turned left on F St., left again on 3rd and right on D. That took them straight to the tunnel and onto I395 out of town with the Lincoln a block behind.

"Keep checking your side mirror," Aaron said. "Make sure we don't lose them." He noticed that Gray wasn't driving as fast as usual and made sure that he didn't rush through any lights about to turn red or make sudden lane changes.

The Town Car stayed behind them on the freeway, not too close, but he still was able to keep them in sight when he turned around and looked out the back window. When they got onto I66 heading west towards the mountains he reached into the back seat and brought out the bag with sandwiches from Baguette and Bagel and apples Aaron had put there. Hot turkey pastrami for Gray and steak and cheese for him on fresh baguettes. They munched quietly as they rolled out past the Beltway, through the ugly sprawl of the suburbs. The 'burbs always amazed Squeak. Having to drive to get anywhere, the library, market for a quart of milk, school…whatever. What a waste of time! Friends of Aaron that they visited in the 'burbs were almost totally disconnected from their neighbors. They frequently complained about the so called "loss of community." Why didn't they recognize that they had built their own isolation with their decisions to live in castles with moats of grass that sucked up time and energy that could otherwise be spent doing fun things with their neighbors? He and Gray laughed especially at the gated communities. They called them "prison farms for middle class minds."

"Ok, now we know they're following us and they aren't perverts," Aaron said an hour and a half later as they made the last turn onto the country road that led to the trailhead for Old Rag mountain. "Let's see if they want to go for a walk or if they just hang around in the parking area. I'm betting they'll follow us; try to corner us when no one else is around. When I park, grab your pack and let's haul ass up the Weakly Hollow fire road." He sped up now to get as much room as possible between them and their followers when they stopped. This dead end road was familiar to them, because it provided access to several of their favorite hikes and streams, but Squeak had never seen Gray take the corners and gun the straights like he did today, putting the Beemer through its paces. He quickly lost sight of the big car behind them.

There were only four other cars in the small, gravel parking area, probably because of the heat. Most people started summer hikes early in the morning so they could be finished before the heat of the afternoon. He had put on his boots while they were driving, so Squeak was ready to roll when they skidded to a stop. Ten seconds later, as the Town Car came into sight around the last bend, they were briskly walking down the fire road to where it crossed the Hughes River. It had been a wet early summer, so the river was running high, tumbling through the rocks and splashing overhanging brush and fallen logs.

They moved fast enough to put some distance between them and the two followers, but not so fast that they disappeared from sight before the spies knew which trail they were taking. The foliage was in heavy layers: ferns, blackberries and golden ragwort on the ground, a thick under story of holly, red mulberry and black gum and up to the high tops of the white oak, black oak, beech and hickory that shaded the trail. It was hot with little breeze and Squeak could see spreading sweat circles under Old Gray's arms and in the middle of his back. The heat never bothered him and he hardly ever sweat himself.

"Don't look back unless you're screened by the leaves. We have to pretend we don't know they are there."

Squeak was excited. "What're we gonna do, Gray? We gonna ambush them?"

"No, I just want to fuck with them a little. Give them something to think about. Let them know we know they are there, but under our terms, on our turf." Aaron snuck a peek back as the trail turned and he was screened by the bushes. "Good. They're coming. Look like they aren't happy about having to jump rocks to cross the river. Their feet are going to hurt in those shoes."

They stayed ahead of their pursuers, teasingly in and out of sight for about ten minutes. The fire road was a steady upward incline, but it wasn't hard walking in good hiking boots; fairly well maintained dirt and stone. Shortly after they crossed Broken Back Run, which fed out of Corbin's Hollow into the Hughes, Aaron stopped at the head of a side trail that went up Robertson Mountain, looming steeply on the right.

"Ok now, we have to be sure they see us make this turn. Let's grab a drink of water while they catch up."

"We went up here last winter," Squeak said. "I remember this gets steep and rough pretty fast and it's a good seven mile circuit up it and then down the other side and back out along that creek, isn't it?"

"Exactly," Aaron said. Squeak could see Gray was pleased that he recalled their winter hike and knew where he was in the woods, but he wasn't loose and relaxed the way he usually was when they went hiking. This was serious business, Squeak knew, but he felt protected.

"We're only going up to the second switchback," Aaron went on. "I came down here and scoped it out this morning. There's a kind of chute there that we're going to take down to Corbin's Hollow. If we do it right they'll think we kept on going up while we double back through the hollow to the fire road. Ok, there they are, and they see us, let's go." He slung his pack on as he started up the trail. Squeak had to rush to keep up now.

After some steep uphill hiking and a little rock scrambling, they came to the second switchback with some distance between themselves and their followers. The trail cut sharply back to the left and went up under a rock overhang, not technical climbing but still a somewhat steep scramble that required complete attention. On the right at the point of the switchback was a big granite boulder with a narrow, rough shelf running around the bottom of it and overlooking a sheer drop of a hundred feet before it went out of sight in the tops of the trees below.

"Ok, quick and careful now," Aaron said. He put his toes on the narrow shelf, hugged the rock and started to slide his way around it. Squeak took a look down. Big mistake. He felt his stomach churn.

"Don't look down. Just stay next to me," Aaron commanded.

Squeak jerked his head up and looked into Aaron's eyes.

"Piece of cake," Aaron said. "You can do it easy."

Squeak took a big breath and stuck first his right foot then his left foot onto the shelf. His smaller feet fit more easily than Aaron's and he quickly shuffled after him until they were around the rock and completely out of sight of the trail. There was another big rock beneath the one they had circled around with just enough room for them to stand on top of it. On this side of the mountain shoulder Squeak could see that there had been a rock slide down the steep drop and these two rocks were part of a group that had gotten hung up. The slide and the place where they stood were hidden from the trail by the big boulder. He didn't see why these rocks hadn't just slid down the drop along with all the others he saw littering the base of the trees below and he sure hoped they didn't go crashing down now. The face of the slide was loose dirt, exposed and stripped of vegetation by the rocks that had gashed it out of the mountain side on their way to the bottom.

Aaron put his finger to his lips. They both were still, barely breathing. Soon they heard the two guys coming up to the switchback. They were talking in low voices and breathing hard.

"Shit! I keep slipping. These fucking shoes." *That's the white guy*, Squeak thought. "Come on, Minton. Let's catch up to 'em, kick their asses so they get the message and get the fuck out of here."

"So (gasp) git (gasp) th' fuck (gasp) goin'." That was the big guy. His voice was high pitched, almost girlish, Squeak noted with surprise. They had stopped right at the switchback, just the other side of the boulder.

"Ok, ok, I'm goin'," the white guy said. "Just be sure you keep up." They heard shoes scraping as the two hoods started up again. The black guy only answered with an angry grunt that he repeated with each exhale. "Ungh (wheeze), ungh (wheeze), ungh (wheeze)…"

Aaron waited for a minute after they could no longer hear their pursuers. Then he whispered, "Ok, now we go straight down. Face the hill and dig your hands and toes in to slow your slide and walk your way down, like rappelling but without a rope. Just don't get over balanced backwards, lean your chest into the slope. Your chin should get dirty." For the first time this afternoon he smiled.

Squeak looked at him. "You're crazy."

"Yeah, but like a fox. This way they won't catch up to us even if they figure out that we doubled back on them and turn around. I'll go first. Wait until I get to the bottom, then you come down." With that Aaron stepped off the rock onto the slope and began climbing down, hands and feet digging at the dirt on the face of the slope, barely controlling his slide with his feet still slipping three, five, six feet in the steep, loose dirt with every step. In seconds he was at the bottom, dust flying, loosened rocks and dirt rushing down and pelting his legs and feet. He waved his hand for Squeak to follow as he stepped out of the way.

"Oh shit," Squeak muttered. He stepped over and it was like trying to climb down the side of a pile of greased sand. He moved his feet but mostly he just slid down, trying to slow himself with his feet, hands, chest, anything. Dirt got up his nose, in his mouth, shirt, everywhere. His hands and cheek got scraped and when he got to the bottom the back of his legs thudded into a rock, making him lose his balance and fly over backwards. Aaron was right there though, and half caught him and half collapsed under him so he didn't break any bones or anything. He opened his mouth to shout at the crazy old bastard, but at the last second stopped, remembering the mean looking pair that were now chasing them up the wrong trail.

After that it was a rough but quick bushwhack through the brush the rest of the way down the rocky slope. In the hollow they crossed Broken Back Run and picked up the trail back to the fire road. The Run was a favorite fishing stream for Aaron, and he and Squeak had camped there once for a couple of nights. Ordinarily when they hiked along mountain streams they would stop and inspect pools, looking for wild, native Brook Trout that Aaron would catch and then return to the water. Squeak understood the need to put back the wild fish so that they didn't clean out the stream, but he still preferred to camp on the stocked streams like the Robinson River so that they could clean and cook up a couple of trout for dinner. Often they wouldn't fish at all, just enjoy the music and the ever changing, cool light and boil and bubble of the running water. This time they just marched through, moving with a purpose and carrying concerns that had never been part of their time in the woods.

When they got to the fire road Aaron turned to Squeak. "Ok, I think those bastards are a ways back now. If they keep on going it'll take them hours to get back here. You did great back there, partner. Didn't make a sound when you came down that slide and hit the rocks."

"I was too scared to make a sound but I'm makin' a sound now and I'm telling you, you are crazy," Squeak complained. But he couldn't hold his pique for long. "Those are a couple of real badasses, aren't they?"

"Oh yeah, they're badasses, all right. And it'll be serious business if they get a hold of us. We'll have to stay on guard, but at least now we aren't just toys for them to play with. I've got a few more surprises in mind." Squeak heard a new hard edge in old Gray's voice. They didn't talk any more as they hustled down the fire road back to where they had left the car. Squeak liked it when Gray talked to him seriously, as an equal, not treating him like he was "just a kid" the way most adults did.

"Now they'll know that we're badasses, too," he said proudly, breaking the silence.

"If they don't know it now, they soon will," Aaron answered. "We're not going to just let them fuck with us."

When they got back to the cars, Squeak found out what other surprises were planned for the spies. As soon as they got there Gray opened the back of the Beemer wagon and got out a small sledge hammer and some big railroad spikes. Squeak could see that the point on the spikes had been filed and sharpened and had some kind of lubricating jelly smeared on it. Quickly looking around to be sure they were alone, Aaron walked over to where the Town Car had been carelessly parked, taking up space for two cars. He gave Squeak three spikes to hold, leaned down, put the point of the remaining spike against the right front tire and with three quick, hard swings of the sledge drove it right into the sidewall of the tire. He yanked out the spike and the air came out with a whoosh. He walked to the back and punctured that tire, too, then went to the passenger side and punctured the back and then the front.

"Didn't need the extra spikes. Bring me the crowbar," he ordered Squeak, as he straightened up from the last tire. Squeak ran to the back of their car, tossed in the spare spikes and grabbed the crowbar he found there. He looked up when he heard a big thud. When he rushed back he saw that Aaron had driven the sledge hammer through the passenger side window.

Squeak handed Aaron the crowbar and Aaron gave him the hammer and spike. He stepped back while Gray used the crowbar to knock away the shattered but still intact safety glass that surrounded the hole he had made with the hammer, then reached the crowbar inside and pried open the glove compartment door. It popped with a ping as the lock gave way. He reached in and grabbed the papers he found there.

"The rental agreement on the car," he told Squeak. "Let's get out of here."

They ran back to their car, dumping the tools in the back. Aaron closed the rear of the wagon and they both got in. "Hold on to these," he told Squeak, handing him the papers from the Town Car.

Within seconds they were down the road and on their way back to D.C. They hooted and war whooped and gave each other high fives and bumped fists as the tension drained out of them. Squeak was awestruck at old Gray's total disregard for rules and caution, the planning and daring behind this strike against their enemies. So that is what you do when you get angry, he thought. You plan it out and then fuckin' go to war!

After they had settled down on the road home, Aaron said, "Ok, look, this is just the beginning, buddy. Take a look at those papers. See who that car is rented to."

Squeak unfolded the pink sheets of paper and took a minute to find the right line. "Ok, let's see. Is that the lessee? Ok it's leased to something called American Power Resources Council. Um, lemme see, got a name here. Its

Perry Pierce Richardson, then it has the initials A. P. R. C., whatever that means."

"Ah ha," Aaron said thoughtfully. "What that means, my son, is we know who is behind those thugs, and probably who is behind the people bothering Ted and Elena, too. Now we know who we are dealing with and we can start to figure out how to take the fight to them. We can go on the offense."

"Hey, Gray, I got to tell you, I think we went on the offense already," Squeak told him.

"Yeah, we got a start on it," Aaron admitted. He was quiet for a while and Squeak waited while he finished his thought.

"Listen, Squeak. We can't tell anyone about what we did today. This has to be our secret, for a lot of reasons. Some of what we did is against the law, of course, but what is really the problem is that people won't understand that we had to take the initiative, to jack things up and hit these guys before they decided to hit us. And they won't understand me including you, because you're a kid, you know. So not a word to anyone, except Antelope. You got it?"

"Yeah, Gray, I got it," Squeak said and gave him a short punch on the shoulder to cement the pact.

Aaron grunted, nodded and fished his favorite Dave Mathews Band concert CD out of the holder on the back of his visor and put it into the player.

"We've got a long way to go, but this has been a very good day," he said before he cranked up the volume on "One Sweet World," making speech impossible. Squeak settled back and they rocked their way back to D.C.

Chapter 14

Fist got the call on his cell phone just before eight in the evening. He saw it was Grainer when the number flashed on his phone's screen. "Where the fuck are you?" he growled, biting his anger back behind clenched teeth.

Over the past weeks it had proven difficult to follow the kid or get the old man isolated on the busy streets in town. This morning he had told Grainer to press for an opportunity to corner them and bust them up enough to make the bastard back off his stupid do good campaign. Grainer and Minton were supposed to call in every three hours. Their last report had been shortly after noon when they said they were following Woods and the kid out of town. Fist told Grainer then that when he and Minton found their chance they should jump Woods and the kid, break a few bones, and tell the old fart that if he kept stirring up trouble neither one of them would get a chance to see what global warming would look like.

Fist's frustration had been mounting and he had decided that it was time to go back to old fashioned head knocking. The bosses had talked him into letting them use the political and business power of the oil companies, their network they called it, to put pressure on this bastard. Some fucking network.

It was worse than useless. The bankers in Zurich hadn't even blinked when the consulate there pressured them to trash the old guy's grown kid. And the guys they hired in France were total jerk offs. They were trying to get information on the ex wife and her new husband, some kind of goddam Count of some damn thing, when someone pulled some strings and got the French feds on their ass. Their French guys had to hightail it out of the country and now were down in Martinique laying low in some fishing village on the back side of the island. The fucking big shots had been so proud of their connections "from the top of the U. S. government to the bottom of the European underworld" when they talked to him about how they wanted this handled and it had turned out to be pure bullshit. He'd had enough of their way.

On top of that, Grainer and Minton had only gotten glimpses of the goddam kid as he went into school in the mornings. He never seemed to come out of the school and then when they did catch him slipping out a back door a couple of times they lost him in two minutes. The whole point had been for the kid to see them and get scared and tell the old man, and Grainer wasn't even sure if the kid had noticed them. He was some kind of ghost kid who appeared and disappeared with no reason.

He hadn't had any luck trying to access Wood's bank and investment accounts either. The money was locked up in annuities, trusts, bonds, cd's and treasury bills. He could look at it but there was no way to get at it. He hadn't pushed on this job very hard at first, just enjoying the ride, but in the last couple of weeks he'd gotten tired of D.C. The place was changing fast. It used to be Chocolate City, with the best concentration of black culture, both legal and illegal, anywhere south of New York and north of New Orleans. Now the whites were taking over, moving into the old neighborhoods, converting apartments to condominiums or tearing things down and replacing them with offices and upscale residences. There was still plenty of night life, at least as far as clubs and music were concerned, but it was different. It wasn't pure black anymore. And the illegal trades, the whores and dog fights, games and drugs, they were nothing like they used to be; no class, no real players and a lot of the action moved out to the black suburbs in Prince Georges County. Not that he had ever been much of a user, but the drug money was behind most of the good action, and that money was drying up from the streets. It was sticking to the hands of the big time distributors who looked and acted more like stock brokers than players. They didn't even live in the city, for Christ's sake. They had big houses in Potomac or McLean and spent as much time watching their kids play soccer as they did watching their action on the streets.

Fist had decided to stop playing around and put the pressure on the old bastard, but so far the damn guy just didn't seem to have any handles he could grab hold of to shake him up. Finally he had gotten fed up with it and told Grainer and Minton to double up and get hold of the kid; rough him up and leave a message for Woods that if he didn't wise up next time it would be fatal. When Grainer called this morning and told him that they finally had the two of them together driving somewhere out of town he figured it was the perfect chance to get back to the tactics that had always made his targets cave in before. Nothing like a good beating to jerk someone out of their normal, soft, comfortable life and make them realize that they had stepped into hell, and if they wanted to get back to the world as they knew it they had to dance when the devil told them to dance and stop when he said stop.

So now, after eight fucking hours of waiting for a call to tell him that this job was just about done and he could collect another big paycheck and move on, his anger and frustration had gotten as high as it could get. When he heard Grainer asking someone for the name of the town they were going to, he was ready to explode.

"Sperryville," Grainer said. "We're in a tow truck on our way to a town called Sperryville to get four new tires."

"Grainer," he said in the slow, hard grinding voice that meant he was ready to rip someone's head off. "What the fuck is going on?"

"Ah, I can't talk much now. Someone, ah, you know, someone, got us lost in the woods. Ah, up a mountain. And, ah, it looks like someone, you know, ah, punched holes in the tires. An', you know, the cell phones don't work in the mountains. So, we had to walk to get to a phone and, ah, now is the first that the cell would work. So I'm calling in and, ah, it'll probably be about 11:00 or so before we get back."

"Is Minton there with you?"

"Ah, yeah, Minton and the tow truck guy. The Town Car is on the back of the truck."

It took all of Fist's control to keep him from raging at Grainer on the phone. It had been hard to find Grainer and Minton, and up to now they had been the perfect tools. He didn't want to lose them. They did what he told them to do, they were ruthless and efficient. Grainer was excellent with a gun, knife and small plastique bombs. Minton was as strong as an ox and could break a man's bones with little effort and no remorse. They cost him a bundle but both were reliable and didn't talk to anyone. So Fist, grimacing with the effort, kept his voice on an even pitch. "Get the fucking car fixed and get back here. We'll talk when you get here. Got it?"

"Yeah, I got it."

Fist broke the connection. He didn't know what had happened out there, but now this was personal, not just a job.

Chapter 15

Perry Pierce Richardson was reviewing the new energy policy statement that the President was going to deliver to Congress. This baby was loaded with money for the oil and coal industries, as well as a big boost of money for alternative energy research that was structured so most of that would go to their clients, too. He was very pleased with himself. He had been the chief architect of the strategy behind issuing this statement. He knew that it wouldn't get put into an energy bill by Congress. He knew that the President knew that it wouldn't be enacted by Congress, and so did the Congressional leaders. And they all would be very happy about it, because industry friendly Congressmen were pushing a bill that gave even more billions of dollars in subsidies and other favors to his clients. In fact, Perry had helped write much of that bill himself. He didn't do the actual writing, but he put together the policy writing experts from his clients with the staff people of his friendly Congressmen and they came up with the magic wording that would send tax dollars their way. The President's statement was just political cover.

Perry's strategy was for the President to present his relatively "clean" and responsible energy proposals, and make some noise about not needing to give all that money to the already healthy oil and coal industries. That would take the wind out of the sails (or wind turbines, Perry mused) of the President's critics who delighted in tagging him as a lackey of big industry. He wouldn't make too much noise or push Congress too hard, and they would pass the big give-away bill that the Congressional leadership had put together, making small concessions towards the position the President laid out in his statement. The President would sign the "compromise" bill, loudly touting the little bit left for solar, wind and energy efficiency initiatives, and not mentioning the big giveaways to his oil and coal industry patrons. He would laud the bill as an energy plan that would give "certainty," a favorite word, to the energy industries and "move the country forward while protecting the economy" and call it a "victory for the people."

And why not? Perry Pierce thought. *We're people, too. And this is certainly a victory for us, guaranteeing the flood tide of money to the oil and coal industries would continue.* As oil became increasingly scarce the prices and profits would go up, especially if demand remained undiluted by major efforts to reduce consumption and develop alternative energy sources. That was the way the market worked when you had control over the government and the public stayed dumb and happy.

Perry's happy contemplation of the wealth he was creating for himself and for the clients of APRC was abruptly ended when the outer door from the hallway was thrown open, banging against the wall behind it. Fist strode through the outer office, paying no attention to Patricia's startled shriek of, "Oh...what...who?"

Fist walked through the open connecting door and up to Perry's desk. Perry pushed himself to his feet and took a step back, as Fist leaned over, put his hands flat on the desktop and snarled, "Where's all this inside information you're supposed to be getting me? You ain't done shit; none of you bitches in your shiny suits."

"Ah, Mr. Fist! What's the matter? What are you talking about? I got you everything you asked for." Perry's voice was high and unsteady. The blood drained from his face, his body tensed, his shoulders came forward and his legs came together. He had to fight the urge to curl himself into a protective ball. This was the way he always felt when threatened with physical harm. He felt like a child now, and he had no doubt that Fist was a physical threat.

"What I want is to know when Woods will be coming and going, asshole," Fist said. "You're keeping tabs on your girlfriend over there at the NAC, aren't you? The one he travels with, right?"

"More or less, yes." Perry tried to straighten his spine and control his voice. "She doesn't always tell me when and where she is going, and they don't always travel together."

"Fuck that. It looks to me like that old man is dippin' in your honey pot. Can't you hold on to your woman?"

"That's not the way it is with us, I mean with Wendy and me," Perry said. He didn't want Fist to think that he meant anything racial by "us" and the more that he could get Fist to talk with him the more he felt he could gain some control of the situation. "She and I have a relationship, but it isn't exclusive."

"So you're pussy whipped, is what you're sayin'." Fist straightened up, taking his hands from the desk. "Anyway, I wanna know when he is goin' out of town and I wanna know it before he goes. I've had enough of you bitches and of this town. I'm gonna take him out a the game."

Perry felt a chill. "What do you mean?"

"I told you don't ask questions, pissant. You don't get me what I need and you'll know what I mean."

Perry recoiled involuntarily, as spit sprayed from Fist's mouth with his words, feeling moisture hit his lower lip. He hastily wiped it away with the back of his hand, then dropped his hand as though he were guilty of some offense.

"Sure, ok. So what you want is to know when he's going out of town," Perry said. He didn't want to think about what Fist meant, or let the conversation go further in that direction. How the hell did he get into this mess? He just had to find a way to get all this over with as soon as possible and get Fist out of his life.

"You get your girl to tell you where he's goin' and when," Fist commanded. "And as soon as you know, you tell me. When you see her next?"

"Thursday," Perry retorted automatically. "Tomorrow night. We're going to a dinner."

"Well, you get her talking and find out what I need to know. I gotta set things up and I don't want to wait around. You call me Friday, got it?" Fist glared at him.

"Yes. I understand." Then when Fist's glare didn't waver Perry added in complete capitulation, "I've got it."

"Bitch, you better get it," Fist spit out. He straightened up, turned and took one step to the door but then he stopped and turned back to Perry, fixing him with a glare. He pointed his finger at Perry's face.

"Don't fuck with me, bitch. I could split you open for no fucking reason at all, so just don't fuck with me."

He turned and strode back out of the office, past the terror stricken Patricia and disappeared into the hall. Patricia was frozen in her seat with her mouth open, eyebrows high, stunned.

"Shut the fucking door!" Perry yelled at her after Fist was well gone and safely out of hearing. He had never yelled at anyone in the office before.

Patricia jumped up and moved on wooden legs to the middle of the floor before stopping and looking from one door to the other fearfully. "Wh, wh, wh, which door?" she finally managed to squeeze out.

"Both fucking doors, goddammit," Perry exploded. He rushed around his desk and over to his office door and slammed it shut. He walked back to his desk and sat down, unable to think or do anything. He could still see the contempt on Fist's face. "Bitch," he'd called him. His hands were trembling on the desk in front of him. He slowly dropped his head into them, trying to stop the sights and sounds reverberating inside his head.

It may have been five minutes or fifteen before he was able to get control of his thoughts, he didn't know. When he finally did raise his head back up, he had one clear thought. He had to get this monster out of his life. Goddam Ed for bringing these, he searched for the right word, these hoodlums, this scum, these terrorists, into their lives at this critical time. He looked down at the printouts that he had been reviewing earlier with such satisfaction. Damp prints showed where he had rested his face on them. Here they were well on their way to securing at least another five years of unprecedented riches for themselves and their clients and instead of focusing on greasing the skids to get their carefully crafted tax credits and subsidies through the Senate he was having to deal with a...a...a...thug. Perry almost let himself think of more accurate and much worse words to describe Fist, but he couldn't do it. If he didn't let those words come into his head then he didn't know what Fist was going to do.

He got up to go talk to Ed about Fist's visit, but stopped on his way to the door. Yesterday Ed had told him about the offer he'd made to Tony Albritton. "He's sniffing at the bait," Ed said. "He's interested. I mean, this guy may be queer, but he's no virgin in D.C. politics. He knows this 'save the world' campaign isn't going to be a winner. No matter what facts and figures they trot out, people don't want to hear it. They don't understand it and if they do understand it they say it's just too big for them to deal with. They'll tune it out. He knows his best chance of influencing the way all this climate change shit is going to work out, and for sure of making big money, is to work from our side of the fence. He'll play around with it for a while but sooner or later he'll take the bait. Then we sink the hook and pull him in."

"If you're so sure that this grassroots stuff won't amount to anything and you can cut the head off NAC with a simple buy out, how come you called in Fist and his goons?" Perry had asked him.

"Perry, I told you I don't want to hear about those guys," Ed had said, his face turning red and switching from smiling to angry in an instant. "It wasn't me. Ball Breaker and Chatham want to cover all the bases and they're the ones that pay our bills. Those guys got where they are by snuffing out little problems before they become big ones. You just give Fist what he wants and make sure he stays away from me. That's the last I want to hear about him. Period."

So Perry turned back to his desk. Big Ed would cut him off in a minute if he thought it would help him keep his distance from any dirty business. No, it wouldn't do any good to go talk with Ed. He knew what he had to do. He had to get Wendy to give him Woods' travel schedule. He'd been getting the feeling lately that she was losing interest in him. Maybe she was falling for Woods; what did he know? Ordinarily Perry would have just dropped her. She was good looking and well built, but she wasn't like his usual women; too serious, a little older, smarter and more sure of herself than his usual. The women he preferred were just fun girls, out for a good time and not encumbered with concerns about long term commitments or the problems of the world. Not bimbos, as he protested on occasion when confronted by friends, or more often by the wives of friends. Just girls who made him feel young and who wanted a good time. Wendy was good looking enough and certainly sexy and a good lay. But even in the looks department, she wasn't his usual blond bombshell, and she did have a pretty big nose, not Barbra Streisand, but kind of Roman. And the sex was maybe too intense, and there were things he liked that she wouldn't do.

He hadn't broken things off with her earlier because he found her attractive and challenging in a way that was different from his other women. And also, he had to admit to himself, because he had bragged to Ed that he was getting inside information from her. Pillow talk, he called it, and that had added a little extra spice to his status as a ladies man. And when Fist had found out about his "inside pussy" as he called it, he was under pressure to keep the relationship going. Now the pressure had been turned up. He was on the spot and he had to deliver. He'd give her a call; see if she wanted to meet him for a nice dinner tonight, just the two of them. Cancel whatever he had scheduled. He'd tell her he wanted to see more of her, let on like he was getting serious and wanted to go exclusive with her. Then they could both pull out their planners and compare schedules for the next few weeks to see what days they could get together. He could ask, just because he was interested in her and her work, what was happening on each of her trips and then he'd know if Woods was going or not. Maybe even let on that he would like to go to one of their meetings, like he was getting turned around on the climate change stuff and wanted to find out more. That should give him what he needed to get Fist off his back.

Perry paused as he reached for the phone. It's not like he wasn't really interested in her, he told himself. Right. She's a great girl, different from other girls. She's a woman, a real woman, and I just want to spend more time with her.

Perry pulled his arm back from the phone, opened the left top drawer of his desk and pulled out his hand mirror. He looked himself in the eye and said, "Wendy, my feelings for you have just gotten, well, they're just different from anything I have known. You're different from other women. I just want to spend more time with you." Then he repeated it, searching his face for sincerity, trying for the right look and tone. Serious, but still a little abashed, like he was grappling with the issues and was realizing he may have had some wrong ideas in the past but wasn't sure how to move forward. He repeated it two more times, getting it just right. Yes, he thought, I really mean this.

His conscience clear, he put his mirror away, picked up the phone and punched in her speed dial button.

Chapter 16

Squeak woke up Saturday morning with an uneasy feeling. On most weekend mornings, if he didn't have to wake up to an alarm or Aaron calling him to breakfast, he enjoyed drifting in and out of sleep for hours until he couldn't hold onto the last snatches of dream. Then he would half open his eyes and take inventory of all the familiar things in his room that were the same every day: the Alan Iverson poster over his bed, the crack in the ceiling where a nail head showed through the plaster and paint, his precious saxophone on its stand, waiting for him to put in the reed and blow some tunes, his small music system, the clothes he had taken off the previous night placed always exactly the same way on the back of his desk chair, his desk with the Hulk cup filled with pens and pencils, the pencil sharpener, the rest of his glass of water from the night before, the desk lamp, his favorite bookmark peeking out of a book placed squarely in the middle of the desk top, the alarm clock right where it should be, in easy reach. He would look at each wall, the small rug on the wood floor, the door to the hall, the window, the blinds and the curtain. He would look at the dresser, knowing his clothes were folded inside exactly in order and in the same place they had been yesterday and the day before. He would look at the closed closet door, knowing everything was hung in the exact order he had determined, unchanged. It took him several minutes each morning to be sure that nothing had changed, that this was his place in the world for another whole day and for the day after that and after that. Only then was he ready to get up and take his place, his known place, in the world.

But today his eyes jerked open and he didn't see his poster or all his familiar things. He looked around frantically, pushed back the covers, swung his feet around and sat up. *Ok*, he thought, *it's ok. I'm just stayin' over at Antelope's 'cause Gray's out of town saving the world.* He had stayed here before, lots of times, but whenever he was away from his little piece of heaven, a room of his own, a home, a family, he woke up like this: uneasy, jumpy, afraid it all had been taken away and he was back to the old days of not having a place, any place, that was his, where he belonged. The only times he could wake up away from his home without this fear was when he went out to visit the streets overnight, seeking some of the old timers and the places he had known before old Gray gave him a home. Those times he would be alert but confident when he woke up in some cubbyhole under an underpass, in an empty building or in the dark, back corner of a recessed office doorway. He knew that he was just visiting, touching base, validating that he had come from those streets and that his place, his room and desk and lamp and horn, and Gray, the strange, complicated, contradictory but solid man who had given him a real family were all waiting for him to come home. Those mornings waking out on the street, he didn't know why but he didn't feel the fear.

Gradually his nerves settled down as he came fully awake. He padded barefoot out of the spare bedroom and into the narrow hallway, down to the next door and into the bathroom. He peed, showered, brushed his teeth, ran his comb and wide bristle brush through his short hair, thinking about letting it grow out and getting corn rows like A. I. or some other kind of do. He knew he wouldn't do it because he liked the clean feel of short hair he could wash every day, and no way he could sit for hours while someone fussed over him, but he liked the feeling that he could do it if he wanted to. Gray wouldn't object. He let Squeak pick his own clothes and hair styles, sometimes even urging him to "get some kind of wild do," but Squeak liked a more understated look and wouldn't cave in to pressure from Aaron or the kids that sometimes teased him about it. He didn't tell anyone, but he wanted to be as much like Ted, Aaron's grown first son, as he possibly could. When he and Gray had visited Ted in Zurich, Squeak had begged the young executive to take him shopping and he'd come home with a whole suitcase full of European style clothing that made him look like a small, darker, more casual version of his step brother. They had gotten close over the years and talked frequently on the internet phone hookup that Ted had got them to set up when Gray complained about the bills.

Carrying his under shorts, he went back into the spare bedroom and got dressed; clean drawers and socks, same shirt and pants, and went down to the kitchen to see if Antelope was up yet.

In the empty kitchen he got down a bowl, some cereal and a spoon. He got out the milk and some dried blueberries to put on the cereal. Neither Antelope nor Aaron would let him buy any of the marshmallow, chocolate, or fruit flavored cereals he had craved when he was running the streets. Back then when he had cadged or begged some money he would buy a box of those sugary sweet cereals from the store and eat them straight from the box, like candy. Sometimes now he still found himself wishing he could get some of those sweets, but Gray had gotten down books from his shelves, and more books from the library and gone over with him how the sugar was just like a drug and how if you wanted to be strong you had to eat the stuff your body could use to build muscle, nerves and bones and store up energy. Back when he first came to stay at Antelope's for an overnight he had thought he could get his friend to buy some of the sweet stuff, but damn if he didn't say the same thing, sneer at him for wanting a "sugar fix." He had come to see how the kids at school who ate all the sweet and fried stuff, a bag of chips and soda for lunch and stuff like that, how they would get hyper for a while and then sleepy; how they didn't have the energy to keep up with him. That was just exactly how Gray and Antelope said the food would affect him and had showed him in the nutrition books, from the very beginning before he could even read. He felt stronger every time he ate good food now, like he had a secret power that other kids didn't have.

At least Antelope had real whole milk instead of the soy or 1% that Gray kept in their refrigerator.

As Squeak poured and drank his juice and ate his cereal, crunchy granola that came in big bags instead of boxes, Antelope came into the kitchen in his baggy white boxer shorts and a tee shirt with holes of all sizes in it.

"How come you didn't make any coffee?" Antelope growled as he got out the old fashioned percolator and filled it with water.

"I don't drink coffee. How come you ask me that same thing every time I stay here?" Squeak answered.

"How come you never know the right answer?" Antelope retorted. Satisfied with their morning ritual, Squeak continued to eat his cereal while Antelope fixed his own bowl, coffee and juice and sat down across from him.

"You think old Gray is gettin' it on with Wendy?" Squeak asked, breaking the silence. He tried to make it sound casual, but they both knew it was a serious question.

"Is she stayin' over at your place nights?" Antelope queried.

"Nah, and he isn't spending nights there, you know, at her place, but still, they could be, you know, in hotels…"

"Well," Antelope considered, "I don't think they're shackin' up. Not because I don't think Aaron doesn't want to." As always he dragged out the "Aa" when he said Aaron. "I think he's serious about this woman, so he's like taking his time and trying to build something bigger than the old slam, bam, thank you, ma'am."

Squeak thought about this as he scooped, chewed and swallowed two bites of cereal and followed them with a drink of juice. "Yeah, I think he's serious, too. You think she might move in with us?"

"Ha, if old Aaron is really lucky and she's half blind and can't see what an odd ball old fart he is, then she might move in with you. I mean, maybe you're too much of a punk to notice it, but that woman is hot. She could have her pick of a lot of men with more sex appeal than Aaron. Me, for example." Squeak rolled his eyes while Antelope paused. "So, you think it's a problem if she moves in with you?" Antelope asked.

Squeak finished his cereal, put the bowl and spoon in the sink and sat back down to finish the rest of his juice.

"Goddammit," Antelope said in exasperation, "you're getting just like your old man. How long you got to think about this before you answer me?"

"We're gettin' along real good, me and old Gray," Squeak answered. "If she moved in, it'd be a big change." This was what had been on his mind all along.

"Yeah, that's true," his old friend told him. Now it was just man to man, no jiving each other. "Do you get along with her ok?"

"Yeah, she's ok. I mean, you know, she hasn't been around black people too much so she has that, you know, guilt thing like she's afraid of saying something wrong, but she's cool."

"I know what you mean. She's probably more like that with you than me because you're like Aaron's boy and she's got to get along with you. I mean, even if she isn't digging him, they got this campaign and I think she needs him for that. You know how it is with Aaron, if he's in something he's in it all the way and he kind of takes over. She's less like that with me."

160

"So you think she's serious about him?" Squeak asked.

"Well, duh! She's come clear across town at least twice just to stop by. What do you think?" Antelope said, riding the kid a little. Then, "I got no way of knowing if even she knows, you know? I mean, she may be getting interested in him without knowing it. Listen, you trust Aaron, don't you? I mean, he isn't gonna kick you out or anything. He adopted you for Christ sake."

"Yeah, I trust him," Squeak said. "But like you said, she is hot."

"Yeah, there's always that." There was a long moment while they thought about the power of a woman to wreak havoc in the affairs of men.

"Still, I don't think ol' Aaron is one to drop his friends because of some hot babe," Antelope finally reassured him. In the first three years he had known Aaron, before he had gone into recovery, Aaron had bailed Antelope out of jail twice and finally had stayed with him for two weeks while he dried out. He had gone with him to his first five AA meetings. Squeak had been around then, so he knew that Aaron stood up for his friends.

"Yeah, I guess it'll be ok. Anyway, what's the chance of old Gray hooking up with a fox like Wendy," Squeak concluded with a satisfied chuckle. "Even if they did shack up, she'd wear him out pretty quick." He felt relieved, like a cloud that had been hiding the sun had blown away. He pushed away from the table.

"I'm gonna go out, go see if Tayshawn is doing anything," he told Antelope.

"You keep an eye out for those hoods," Antelope said. "If you spot 'em come back here. You got your cell phone?" When they had gotten back from their scam in the mountains with the two hoods, Aaron had gone straight to the wireless phone store and gotten three new phones with walky talky connection between them so he, Antelope and Squeak could be in touch with the push of a button.

"I'll watch out," Squeak said with the typical teenager's aggrieved boredom at any instruction. "And I got the phone and it is charged up and it's turned on and I'm gonna wear my rain jacket, and anything else, Big Momma?"

"I'll Big Momma you, punk," Antelope said, taking a half hearted swing at the kid as he skipped past him and upstairs to get his rain jacket. He watched fondly as Squeak went out the door. "Just don't go by your house unless you come get me," he called, but the door closed before half the sentence got out.

Squeak pulled up the hood on his rain jacket as he started up the street toward Tayshawn's house where he figured his friend's mom would press him to eat some eggs and bacon, and maybe some of her homemade biscuits. It was raining harder than he had thought, and just as he was thinking about spreading strawberry jam on a fluffy biscuit he remembered: Shit, I left the window open in my bedroom yesterday. The wind was blowing towards the front of their house and his bedroom and window were on the back, but with this much rain some could still get in and get his desk wet. And you never knew if the wind was going to change directions and then it would really be a mess.

He went down the hill to the corner at F St., but instead of continuing north on Fourth he turned right and cut past the school playground. Antelope lived across the street from the west side of the playground, a block away and almost directly opposite his and Aaron's house across the street on the east side. He checked around to see if the hoods were watching in their car, but he hadn't seen them or their car since their "ambush" of the hoods, and he figured they wouldn't be hanging around on the weekend anyway, since no one was staying at the house. He crossed to the north side of F St. and as he crossed Fifth he looked up and down the block. His house, 537, was just the second one up from the corner of Fifth and F, and he couldn't see anything suspicious there or see the hood's Town Car, so he figured he was clear. Just to be sure he circled around to the alley in back of his house. Sure enough, he could see his bedroom window open, but he didn't see anyone lurking in the alley and the garage was closed up tight.

He went back down the alley and around the corner to go in the front, checking again and not seeing anything wrong. Gray had told him to stay away from the house until he got back from his trip, but Squeak thought he'd be pissed if the house got flooded from rain coming in the window. He'd just run in, close the window and get out, maybe take his horn with him so he and Tayshawn could jam a little. Tayshawn played keyboards and they liked to fool around with the music, talk about starting a jazz band. Gray had taken them to a couple of jazz clubs and playing in a club seemed pretty cool to the boys. Gray invited some of the musicians to come to their table for a drink between sets. The players were real friendly and talked to the boys about the music and some of the big names they had played with. Squeak thought they were even cooler than The Answer or Kobe.

Squeak unlocked and opened the metal security grate and then the deadbolt on the front door, pushed it open and stepped inside, rushing to get upstairs. By the time he took his first step, he knew something was wrong and he started to step back and pull the door closed. Too late. The door was pulled the rest of the way open and a hand grabbed his arm that was extended on the doorknob, yanking him into the room. A big black guy, but not the huge guy that they had tricked in the woods, lifted him right up into the air by his arm like a bug and pushed the door closed with his other hand. All that Squeak saw was the big toothed mean smile on the guy's face, his angry eyes, yellow around the black iris and pupils, the dull, dark pitted skin and black clothes.

"Grainer, come look at what we got here," Fist said in a rough voice that scratched in Squeak's ears like sandpaper. "Little tadpole, looks like." He shook Squeak and it felt like his shoulder was being yanked loose from the socket. Cries of pain ripped out of him as he dangled in the air. Flames of pain shot from his shoulder down to his fingers.

"Shut your fuckin' mouth," Fist ordered and threw Squeak into the lamp table at the end of the sofa. Squeak hit the table with his chest and arms, knocking it into the wall and then crumpling onto the floor. The lamp crashed on top of him. His brain slowed down, dazed, but he fought to stay alert. He grit his teeth together, stifling his cries down to whimpers.

Squeak saw the skinny white guy, one of the watchers that he and Gray had tricked in the woods, come in from the dining room. That must be Grainer, he thought.

"You little fuck," Grainer snarled and took two quick steps to where he was huddled in a ball and kicked at him, catching his thigh with the point of his shoe. The pain exploded in Squeak's leg, forcing out another cry before he could bite it back. Now he was sobbing. Fluid streamed from his eyes and nose, but he still stayed alert. He'd heard old Gray and Antelope talk for hours one day about controlling pain, telling stories and comparing scars and techniques. He focused on building a box around the pain, then closing the box, shrinking it and setting it off to one side. He had practiced what he had heard the men saying before, burning himself with a candle to try it out, so now he could deal with it and not let it take over his whole mind. It was hard, though, especially since he had pain from his shoulder and from his leg, plus from his arms and chest from crashing into the table, but he focused on putting the two worst pains, one at a time, into the box, while at the same time watching Grainer and the other hood through his tears.

"What're we gonna do with 'im, Fist," Grainer said. "How 'bout I cut him up and leave 'im all over the house. I'm still sore from chasin' these fucks around the woods."

"You're a dumb shit, Grainer," Fist said. "We kill the kid now and leave 'im here and the cops'll be all over us so hard we'll never get to his old man. I want that prick. I'll think about what ta do with 'im. You find a computer or anything in there?"

Grainer snarled his answer. "I didn't have any time before the kid got in the way. I'll check up stairs."

As Grainer turned towards the stairs they heard a horn blow outside. No one moved while the horn blew once, twice, three times.

"Shit," Fist said. "Someone's here to pick up the kid. What a cluster fuck." He looked around, and then he came over to Squeak, grabbed the front of his jacket and picked him up in the air again and pulled him up so their faces were just inches apart. Squeak hung limply, too scared to move. He didn't make a sound except for his sobbing breath pressing in and out through his closed teeth. Nostrils so wide he could fall into them and teeth like tombstones filled his squinted eyes.

"You tell the old man this is just a taste." Fist's hot breath scorched the boy's skin. "I'm gonna come back here and cut your nuts off, both of you. Then I'm gonna break every bone in your body, both of you, and watch you bleed to death. You tell 'im Fist'll be back. I'm fuckin' tired of you shits."

They heard a car door close out front. Fist dropped Squeak back into a heap on the floor. He strode through the dining room, heading for the back door. Grainer followed, but stopped long enough to aim another kick at Squeak, this one grazing his already throbbing shoulder. Just as Grainer disappeared through the dining room Squeak saw the knob turn on the front door and Antelope push it open.

"Squeak," he started to call out, but then he saw the boy on the floor, the overturned table and lamp. "What the...where are they?" he said. Then the back door slammed. He pounded out to the kitchen and pulled open the door. "Shit," Squeak heard him say.

Antelope rushed back into the room and knelt down by Squeak. "Come on, kid. What'd they do? Where'd they hurt you?"

Antelope picked him up in his arms, resting on one knee and cradling him against his chest.

"Are they gone?" the boy asked.

"Yeah," Antelope said. "I just got a look at one of them, skinny white guy going over the neighbors back fence. That must be how they got in. They musta jumped into the neighbors yard, then into yours 'cause they couldn't open the garage. Then they pried open the security grate and busted the window on the back door and reached in and opened it. Ok, now, buddy, what'd they do to you?"

Squeak slowly unfolded himself from Antelope's arms and stood up, wincing as he put weight on the right leg, the one Grainer had kicked. He slowly raised his right arm, groaning as the strained muscles and tendons in his shoulder shot pain from his fingers right up into his brain.

"Nothin' much," he said, trying to choke back a sob. "I...I think I'm ok. I got their names."

"You don't look ok," Antelope answered. "You got their names?"

"Yeah, I beat it out of 'em." Squeak forced a smile through his snuffling.

Antelope just looked at him, for a minute before letting his face relax. "Well, I'm glad you're such a tough guy. Sorry to have busted in on you when you were working those bastards over. Now you have to keep ol' Aaron from whipping on me for letting you get messed up."

"How'd you know I was here?" Squeak asked.

"I didn't, 'cause when I called your cell phone to see if it was on it wasn't on, you dumb shit. I just figured I'd check because it's just like you to ignore what I told you and come straight over here for something."

"Oh, yeah, the cell phone. I forgot," Squeak said.

"Well, now let's turn the damn thing on, call Aaron, call the cops, and get hold of someone to get the door fixed here. Then let's go back to my place and you don't get out of my sight until your old man gets back."

Squeak thought that sounded just fine.

Chapter 17

Aaron got the phone call from Antelope at the desk of the Nashville Ramada Convention Center. He had just finished talking with 150 Tennesseans who charged him up with their readiness to strike back at the corporations that were ripping the tops off their mountains to get coal, fouling and heating up their rivers with waste and power plant effluent and poisoning their air and climate with unfiltered emissions. Wendy pushed her way through an excited group who were reaching out to shake his hand, and said, "Aaron, there's a call for you at the desk. They said it was urgent."

Instantly he no longer heard or saw the people surrounding him. He had no recollection of getting from the meeting room to the phone. Dread, like an icy hand, grabbed and squeezed his heart. One word, Squeak, was repeating in his head. Nothing more, he didn't dare think further, just the name, Squeak.

"Squeak's ok," Antelope said when he got the phone to his ear. He said more, but Aaron didn't hear it. His knees felt weak and he put both forearms on the counter and laid his head down on his arms. The phone clattered to the top of the desk and then to the floor behind it. After a minute the desk clerk's voice pushed its way through the fog in his head, repeating, "Sir, are you ok? Sir, would you like a chair? Are you ok, Sir?"

He raised his head and saw the young man's face stretched with alarm. The clerk was holding the phone he had dropped. "I'm ok. Thank you." He reached out and the clerk handed him the phone again.

"Antelope? Ok, I'm back. All I heard was that Squeak's ok. Thank God. What happened?"

Antelope told him about Squeak going to close his window and getting jumped by Fist and Grainer, how he had gotten a hunch and, on his way to the grocery had stopped by the house, seen the front security gate open and come in and found Squeak. He recounted chasing but just getting a glimpse of one of the two hoods as they went over the back fence of the neighbor, calling it in to the cops and then calling someone to come fix the jimmied back security door. Aaron listened without interrupting until he was finished.

"So they roughed Squeak up?" he asked. Angry red flooded his face, replacing the white of shock

"Yeah, got some bruises and a sore shoulder, but he's bragging about how he was about to whup their butts when I scared 'em off, so he's ok."

Aaron thought of the cell phones he had just bought. "Why didn't you call me on the cell phone?"

"Check your phone. You're just as dumb as your kid," Antelope answered.

Aaron pulled the phone out of his pocket. "Oh yeah, I guess I turned the ringer off. I thought it would vibrate."

"Yeah, right. You are just not ready for this century, Aaron. Anyway, when I couldn't get through to your cell I just waited until the cops left. They damn near took me in, you know, cause of my record, but the gay guys next door came over along with some of the other people on the block and gave them hell. I'm probably still their top suspect, maybe me and Squeak both, but they backed off for now. They couldn't get hold of you, but there should be a message on your cell to call them. I mostly just told them that you were having trouble with some guys and you could fill them in. I got a guy to come fix the back grate next week and I'm going to nail a board on the window they busted to get in the back door."

"Antelope, thanks. Thank God you're there. I'll get on the next plane out and get back there. I'll come by your place as soon as I get there."

"Ok, man. I think the kid's cool and all, but I understand you wanting to get back. Call me on the cell when you land in case we're out having dinner at Charley Palmer's on your credit card." Aaron had long ago given Antelope a card on his account to use when he was taking care of Squeak. Charles Palmer is a very up scale and expensive steak house just blocks away from their neighborhood on the Hill, frequented primarily by high rolling lobbyists on expense accounts.

"Have at it, man. Get the best dinner in the house," Aaron said. "See you later."

He hung up the phone and became vaguely aware of Wendy at his elbow. He had no idea how long she had been there. "I've got to go," he told her flatly. "Where's my bag?"

"It's in the meeting room. I'll get it. You have the desk call you a cab." She was cool and efficient, leaving him at the desk and wasting no time on questions. Aaron gratefully turned to the desk to get his cab called.

While he was waiting for the cab Wendy took his ticket and called the airline on her cell, changing his flight and getting him on standby for the next flight, leaving in an hour. He gathered his wits and started to tell her what had happened, but she interrupted and asked if Squeak and Antelope were ok and told him to fill her in later, when he had things settled down. He weakly thanked her and stumbled into his cab, still only vaguely aware of what he was doing. His mind and emotions were on a roller coaster ride from the morning's events, moving from blank numbness to blazing anger. His focus shifted from Squeak getting mugged to their ambush of the hoods in the mountains to the great crowd at the morning meeting. He was filled with guilt for exposing the boy to danger, for abandoning him to go on the trip, for abandoning the campaign events planned for Memphis that evening and Kentucky the next afternoon, for leaving Wendy in the lurch.

It was nearly six o'clock when he found himself in front of Antelope's house. He tried to open the door, but it was locked. That usually meant no one was at home, but he knocked anyway and heard Antelope come to the other side of the door and look through the peephole.

"It's your old man," he heard him call as he flipped the dead bolt and opened the door. When Aaron stepped inside Squeak limped in from the dining room. He dropped his bag and the boy came into his arms.

"Ow, careful of my shoulder," the boy's muffled voice came up from Aaron's chest.

"I'll try to be careful," Aaron said, loosening his hold. Hah, he thought, like I even know how to be careful.

The rest of the weekend went quietly. Aaron quickly agreed to Antelope's suggestion that he and Squeak stay at his house in case the intruders came back. He could see that his friend was surprised that he was so cooperative. On Sunday they all went for a walk past the Capitol, to the national Mall and over to the National Gallery of Art. They spent a half hour looking at the Gauguin's and Van Gough's but Squeak was still feeling some pain in his shoulder and thigh, so they cut up to Chinatown and got some carry out, then caught the Metro to take them back to Union Station. They ate their Chinese food in the D St. park, just north of the Senate office building. For the most part Aaron was sunk in deep thought through the weekend despite the other's cheerful bravado talking about the encounter with Fist and Grainer. They all were on high alert throughout the day, especially as they made their way by a circuitous route back to Antelope's house.

Aaron left Squeak and Antelope there and, again taking a round about route and keeping watch for observers, went to his house to clean up the mess there and get the things he and Squeak would need for an extended stay at Antelope's. Along with the mess in the living room, the contents of drawers and shelves in the dining room and kitchen had been dumped onto the floor. Aaron had no idea what they had been looking for, but the violation of his privacy felt like they had put their dirty hands all over him. He spent an hour on the phone talking with the detective who caught the case, but came away with no sense that there would be any kind of active investigation or that the cops believed his claim that the oil industry was behind the attacks. His guilt over exposing his child to harm vied with anger at the scum who had dared to attack the boy and threaten them in their home. Squeak had told him about Fist's threat to "cut our nuts off and break our bones while we bleed to death." The boy had bounced back quickly and seemed ok both physically and mentally but he was not so resilient himself. He just couldn't sort out all the emotions that he was feeling so he retreated into his shell until he could figure out what he should do.

Aaron knew that leading a campaign that challenged the most powerful interests in the country placed those around him in danger. His modern day heroes had all faced the need to put others in harm's way in order to achieve their goals. He knew he wasn't any Chavez, King or Gandhi, but that didn't mean that he didn't aspire to have their courage, their willingness to sacrifice all for their cause. He felt his cause was worth the sacrifice; that if the people didn't demand action now millions would suffer from the coming droughts, floods, disease and more. Having that courage for himself was one thing, but his commitment was melting away in the face of real danger to the boy who had become a big part of his family, who had rescued him from his loneliness and depression after Elena had left him. Squeak trusted him completely, the way only a father can be trusted, and he knew he couldn't guarantee that the boy wouldn't be hurt more, or even worse.

Monday morning he walked Squeak the block to school. Antelope had left early for his job as site manager on a construction job in Annacostia. The District was booming with construction of new offices, apartments, stores and condominiums and Antelope was a highly sought after site manager who knew the building trade from the bottom up. He had worked his way up from laborer despite not having a college degree, and could discuss blueprints and stress tolerances with the engineers as well as sink hot rivets with the iron workers. After spending the morning desultorily doing laundry, Aaron finally got disgusted with himself. I'm acting like a goddam wimp, he thought. It is time to make a decision.

Wendy was at her desk, talking into the phone cradled between her shoulder and ear while reading her computer monitor when Aaron came to her office door that afternoon. He paused before going in, feeling awkward and embarrassed at the decision he was bringing. She was wearing an old tee shirt and jeans that molded themselves to her strong, graceful body. Her shoulders were high and square and the smooth muscles in her arms played under the silk of her skin. Her dark cloud of hair was more disordered than usual, tied loosely back with a bandanna at the base of her neck, but with tendrils of soft curls escaping randomly. Her back was sinuous but erect, neck canted left to hold the phone against that shoulder while her fingers flew over the keyboard. Standing out of her view on her left, he admired the elegant, somewhat aquiline profile that announced intelligence, beauty and character in equal measure, from high forehead to firm chin. How will she react to what I'm about to tell her, he thought, but dismissed that immediately. Sure, he wanted to have a relationship with her, but doing what he had to do was more important. Besides, any possibility of a relationship had to be based on each respecting what they felt they needed to do.

"Ok, Jerry, I'll let you know when we firm up the plans for next weekend. Bye," she said, deftly letting the phone drop into her left hand and placing it on its cradle. She caught sight of him out of the corner of her eye and he came through the door.

"Aaron, how is everything. I'm glad you came by. Sit down and talk to me." She pushed her chair back but didn't get up, trying intently to read his expression.

"Squeak's ok. I'm sorry, I should have called you. He's bruised up some, but he seems to be taking it in stride."

"Thank God," she said.

Her relief was obviously deep and genuine and he was moved by it. "I need to talk with you and Tony. Can you get us in to see him?"

"Of course. Let's just go. I know he wants to see you, he, we both were very concerned." She got up and started to the door. As she passed him she gave his arm a small squeeze. Her touch was electric, briefly short circuiting the carefully constructed reasoning he had prepared for this visit. She led him the short distance down the hall and into Tony's outer office. "Hi, Arch," she called to the administrative assistant as he looked up at them. The door was closed to the inner office. "Who's in there?" she asked breezily.

"Hey, Wendy," Arch answered comfortably. He had been working for NAC for twenty years and had been one of the few immediate allies Wendy had found among the old guard. "He has Jeremiah, Ruthann and, oh another guy, I can't remember his name. They're going over new responsibilities, new priorities, new this, new that…" Arch gave Aaron a wry look. "This place has sure livened up since you started coming around here."

Aaron gave him an automatic smile, not sure if Arch was being ironic or appreciative; not really caring at the moment. Wendy went straight to the door and opened it. She motioned to Aaron to follow her and marched right in.

"I'm sorry to break in on you like this, guys, but we really need to see Tony right now. Can you possibly give us a few minutes?" She gave them her brightest smile but spoke in a tone that made it clear that they were leaving. They looked at Tony, who had been surprised when the door opened, but he left them with no doubt.

"Aaron, thank goodness you came in. I have been very anxious since you left on Saturday. Quinton, Ruthann, Jeremiah, please do excuse us. This is an emergency. We'll get back together later. I am very enthused about what you are doing with the Southwest." With that he went over to Quinton, the older of the men, clasped his hand and practically pulled him out of his seat while shaking it.

Soon they were alone, Aaron seated on the sofa, Wendy beside him and Tony in a side facing chair. Aaron gave them a full account of the events of Saturday both the actual events and the frightening imaginings of possible harm to Squeak that had been crowding his head. He tried to express his own mixture of guilt and anger. He had never opened himself up so much to anyone outside of his family, perhaps not even to them. Having such a sympathetic audience was unusual and liberating despite the depressing

171

nature of what he had to say. He felt as though they were taking on some of the weight that had been pressing down on him, not for just the past couple of days, but since the start of the campaign. As he was talking, Wendy took his arm again, this time sliding her hand through and resting it on his forearm. Tony grimaced at the descriptions of the attack on Squeak and Fist's chilling threat. Both of them nodded and murmured in understanding as Aaron poured out his guilt at putting his son in such danger.

He didn't tell them about the trip to the mountains and disabling the hoods' car, or the information he had gained from the car rental papers. That was a secret between him and Squeak and, besides, even though he was about to drop out of the campaign, he still didn't want to lose their respect, especially Wendy's. They just wouldn't understand the need to take action instead of waiting to be a victim.

Aaron finally finished, feeling as though he had stripped his soul bare despite some guilt at holding back his secret. He was relieved but still didn't know how they would react when he gave them his decision.

After a pause, he looked them both in the eye, first Tony and then Wendy. "So I've decided I need to back off of this campaign," he said firmly. "I just can't put Squeak at risk any more. I…" he paused as he searched for words that felt foreign as he said them, "I need to play it safe, to consider his safety and future." He sat back and waited for their reaction.

Wendy just nodded her head and tightened her grip on his arm. Was she looking at him differently, he asked himself. Is that pity? Has she lost some respect for me? He couldn't tell.

"Aaron, of course we understand," Tony said after a long moment. "Everyone has their limits and you have done more than anyone can ask to move this campaign forward. If you walk away from it to protect your family, no one will blame you. But I have to tell you that we can't build this movement without you. You saw in Nashville on Saturday how you were able to get the people fired up and ready to take action, get out and do public advocacy. It's been like that everywhere, and you get better at it each time you give a talk. Or have a public conversation, as you put it. Well, yesterday in Memphis Wendy and I had to do it without you and that excitement, that personal connection, just didn't happen. You have a gift of creating community and inspiring a vision that we don't and we aren't likely to find anyone who can take your place."

Aaron felt pressure in his temples and his face flushing as Tony spoke. He stood up, took a pace towards the desk, turned away, and then turned back, his arms extended down to his sides with his fists clenched. "So I'm supposed to let them cut my kid's nuts off and break his bones because you can't find a new speaker," he flung in Tony's face.

"You have to protect your son, of course." Tony remained precise, unflustered. His voice was sympathetic, but his words bored in without mercy. "I'm not sitting in judgment over you, only you can do that. As I said, you have done more than anyone can ask. Yes, we can find another speaker, but it is doubtful if we can find someone with your combination of experience and effectiveness. You started this movement. It is built on your ideas and initiative. I wish I could take your place, but I can't."

"Look, we're talking life and death here. These guys are not fooling around."

"I have known that from the start and I thought you did, too. We are fighting ruthless people who are willing to sacrifice thousands, even millions of lives, including that of your boy, in order to protect their private and corporate interests. At the same time, I have to say that I am not convinced there is a connection between the campaign and the break in at your house or the nebulous reports of inquiries about your family in Europe. The reasoning is plausible, but thin and there is no hard evidence. This goes against my entire experience with the tactics of industry. They have too many other ways of opposing us to resort to base thuggery and I am sure they will use them as needed. I never thought they were fooling around and I didn't think you were fooling around, either. If I had I wouldn't have staked my own reputation and that of this organization on this campaign."

Wendy stood up. "Aaron, you have done more than enough. Sure you have been the key to this campaign, but we will keep on fighting without you. You are not expected to sacrifice the safety of your family." She directed the last at Tony, whose lips were set in a grim line.

Aaron looked at her and then at Tony, who returned his glare with a level look. "Well, I guess I don't have any more to say." He dropped his eyes, then raised them and looked first at Tony and then at Wendy. "I...I'll be in touch," he said, and turned and walked to the door.

"Aaron," Wendy called as he opened the door. He stopped. "Yes, stay in touch," she said, shrugging, seeming to not know what else to say.

He walked out the door, closing it behind him.

Chapter 18

Although he could see Aaron was waiting for him on the steps outside the entrance when school let out that afternoon the way they had agreed, Squeak still gave the street a good scan and made sure that no danger was lurking before he went out the door. Old Gray could see things that Squeak would never pick up when they were out in the woods, and he was pretty good at picking up what was happening on the street, but he would never match the savvy ingrained in Squeak by his first seven years. Squeak was more embarrassed that he had walked right into Fist and Grainer in the house on Saturday than he was about going there alone after telling Aaron he wouldn't. How could he have missed the broken window on the back door? What a sap he was! The easy living of the past five years must have made him soft despite his occasional overnight forays back to his old street haunts. He would sharpen up from now on. You can't take things for granted, he reminded himself. You just never know when some shit is going to go down and you'll be scrambling to stay alive. He wouldn't be such a chump the next time. He had to look out for himself and for Gray, 'cause that Fist guy and Grainer would eat them alive if they slipped up.

He didn't see anything that set off any alarm bells, so he went on through the door and gave old Gray a hug. Some of the kids hassled him because he would hug and kiss his dad in public, but he didn't really care about that any more than he did when they chided him for working hard on his school work or carrying books around and reading them just to find out things. The other kids didn't know what it was like when you didn't have anyone to take care of you, or any chance that you could have a future beyond surviving the next day. Lots of the kids had messed up families. Most of them were being brought up by their mothers or grandmothers or maybe an auntie, but still they at least had someone and someplace to call family and home. He tried to explain it to them and had written about it in class assignments, but most kids couldn't see how easy it is to slip across the line from a normal life to being homeless and hopeless and how hard it is to cross that line in the other direction; what a big deal it was to actually do it. He knew he was lucky and he was going to do whatever it took to stay on the right side of that line, including taking care of old Gray and being the best student he could.

A couple of times some punk ass kids who thought they were bad had gone too far and tried to push him around. He exploded. His thrashing, kicking and shouting hadn't done much harm to anyone because he was so out of control, but it got him suspended from school and none of the punks bothered him any more. They just called him "crazy ass nigger" and "the perfessor." Squeak kind of liked both of those labels, often using them to describe himself. He found his own friends and a place of respect in the school. He didn't worry about the opinion of losers who tried to pull down anyone who was trying to earn their place in the world.

He felt good that Gray was there to get him. He figured that between them they could handle those hoods or anyone else that wanted to cause them problems. He could see that Aaron was still in a funk, though, and they were quiet as they walked away from the school. They were staying at Antelope's house for now, but they didn't walk directly there. They took a route that would be hard to follow, staying on busy streets where they had the cover of crowds to protect them but where they would also be able to tell if anyone was on their tail. That way they could be sure that no one followed them and found out where they were holed up. So they headed down the tree shaded streets of old, restored town houses, past the Folgers Shakespeare library and the Library of Congress, down 4th St. to Pennsylvania Ave. on the Southeast side, cutting around whole extra blocks and backtracking through alleys. When they knew they were clear they ducked in to the Starbucks on the corner of 3rd, so the old man could get his afternoon latte. Squeak got a mint mocha frappachino and a cookie, a rare sweet treat, and they went upstairs to get a table and enjoy their snacks. Usually they sat at an outside table on the shady side of the building, but they both knew that wasn't possible now.

"Hey Gray," Squeak said between a sip and a bite of his cookie, savoring it. "What's up with you, man? You been down in the dumps since you got back Saturday. Did your girlfriend dump you or what?"

"No, it's not that. Anyway, she isn't my girlfriend. Probably won't ever be," Aaron answered gloomily. "No, I've been thinking about our situation. Those guys jumping you, the threats, this has all gotten out of hand."

"Yeah, it's some heavy shit," Squeak said. "But, you know, it's kind of, like, exciting! It's like a TV show or a comic book or something. Pow! Bam!"

Aaron just looked at him for a minute. "This isn't any TV show or comic book, Squeak. I'm in way over my head with this stuff, and I've dragged you in over your head, too. I'm supposed to be the adult, here, and I'm acting like it's some kind of TV show or comic book, too. Let's face facts, I'm no Batman and you're not Robin. This is real life."

Batman and Robin were Squeak's favorite comic book and movie characters. The relationship between the two heroes, guardian and ward, was a lot like the relationship between Gray and Squeak. Except, as he would remind himself whenever he engaged in Robin fantasies, he had it better because Aaron had gone ahead and adopted him and Robin was just Bruce Wayne's ward, whatever that was. Now he quickly reminded Gray, "No, we're tighter than Batman and Robin. We're family and no one can mess with family, right?" Squeak's voice had gone from certainty to questioning, asking for Aaron to affirm their bond.

Now they were both sitting up straight and looking directly at each other. They both sensed that this discussion would have deep ramifications on their relationship, was maybe the most important discussion they had ever had. Their drinks were forgotten.

"Squeak, no one can mess with us and break up what we have together. We are a family and we are going to stay a family. But there are some powerful people in the world and I am messing with them. Those people can crush us, like ants under a steamroller. I can't let that happen. I'm the dad and I have to make sure that you don't get crushed because I'm acting like some big, I don't know, hero who can change the world. I'm not a hero; I'm just me, even if some people are trying to make me more than I am. So I told Tony and Wendy today that I was backing out of the campaign."

It was Squeak who took a long moment to examine Aaron now. He wanted to shout, he could feel his arms and legs twitching and tears starting to come to his eyes but he knew he couldn't succumb to tears this time. Losing control would only cause Gray to think he wasn't able to deal with this rationally. That he was just a kid who didn't have to be taken seriously. So he didn't say anything until he could speak past the scream that was like a rock in his throat. He reached both hands up and brushed away the moisture that was starting to roll down his cheeks, but didn't look away from Aaron's eyes. That was another thing that Gray had taught him, you have to look someone right in the eyes if you want to be taken seriously. He was damn well going to be taken seriously this time.

When he finally had enough control, he said in a small voice that had to squeeze out past all his emotions, "Gray, I thought we agreed on this already. You said you weren't going to quit on this. We are in it together."

"Squeak, I know that's what I said," Aaron answered, his face as scrunched up as Squeak had ever seen him. "But I think I was wrong. I got caught up in the emotions of the moment. You getting beat up, well, it just opened my eyes."

"I don't know what you mean by opening your eyes. That doesn't mean anything."

Aaron's eyebrows knit tighter in frustration. "I mean that I saw I was being selfish and not looking out for my responsibilities."

"What responsibilities are you talking about?" Squeak persisted.

"Responsibilities to take care of my family; to take care of you." Now there was a note of testiness in Aaron's voice. Squeak had never questioned him like this before, and maybe no one else had either. Gray was usually the one doing the asking, leading the way with questions that made you answer in ways that you didn't necessarily like but that you knew were the truth. Squeak had been on the other end of those questions more times than he could count. Plus he and Ted were in regular contact by email and text messaging. Aaron's ways and how to deal with them were frequent topics, so now Squeak had more than his own experience on which to rely.

"But I have to take responsibility for me, that's what you always have said. And you have to be responsible for what you believe in, right? And you believe in this campaign and that the guys who are trying to fuck us up are bad guys and we have to stand up for what is right against them, right? If we don't do that now then you're gonna be teaching me that if it gets tough we shouldn't stand up for what is right. So how is that taking care of me, of your responsibility, to teach me to cut and run?" Squeak sat up straighter, leaning forward. *I got him now*, he thought.

Aaron pursed his lips and shook his head, losing eye contact. "You may not understand this now, but as you get older and have a family of your own you'll see it differently."

"That's not fair," Squeak shot back. "That's odd hominy."

"What? That's what?" Aaron asked with asperity.

"Odd hominy, you told me about that. Attacking the man and not the message, I remember that. You can't say what I said is wrong so you say I'm just a kid so what I said doesn't count because I'm just a kid." Squeak rapped the table with his knuckles to punctuate his words.

"Ad hominem," Aaron said. "Christ, why do I teach you this stuff. Ok, that was an ad hominem argument, you're right."

"Right." Now Squeak thought he might win! He had to win, because if Gray quit doing this big campaign because of worrying about him then it would change everything between them. He didn't know how it would change, but he knew it wouldn't be good. "Right, and when you use...ad hominem..." he said the words carefully, "you're disrespecting me. It's avoiding dealing with my point. And here's my point. You don't quit doing what's right because of me, because I think what you're doing is right and this climate stuff is about my future and we don't quit just because we're getting the shit kicked out of us. You don't quit because of me. You gotta respect me."

"What if you get hurt some more? What if they kill you or kill me or both of us?" Aaron said. "What am I supposed to do then?"

"Hey, whatever! We do what we gotta do. If one of us goes down the other one keeps fighting." Squeak saw that other people were looking at them and lowered his voice. "What is right is what is right, and you can't quit because of me." He could see Gray was coming around. It was just going to take him some time to think about it. "Anyway, if you do get killed, you won't be doing nothin' so why worry about that?" he added triumphantly.

Aaron picked up his latte and slowly drank the rest of it without answering. Squeak did the same with his frappachino. After they finished, Aaron said, "Let's go," and they got up and headed home. They crossed Pennsylvania Ave. and walked up 4th to East Capitol St. in silence, both of them keeping an eye out for any sign of trouble, zigzagging around the streets that they knew so well. They had to stop at a crosswalk at East Capitol, and as they stood there, Aaron put his arm around Squeak's shoulders and hugged him tight to his side.

"Ok, punk," he said with rough affection. "All right. I'm back in this thing; I mean we're in it. We'll see it through. No more backing off. But it's going to mean that you have to come with me on the road and we've got to watch our backs all the time."

Squeak put his arm around Aaron's waist and they crossed the street when the traffic cleared. As they headed up the next block he said, "So you better tell your girlfriend that you're still in the game. Maybe that'll help you out there."

"Yeah," Aaron said. "I'll tell her and I'm gonna let the creeps know that sent those hoods around, too. I'm in this all the way and I want them to see me coming."

"All right, Batman," Squeak said comfortably. Aaron looked at him, shook his head and let out an exasperated sigh. Squeak's world was back in order.

Chapter 19

"Hi, Mom, I'm sorry it's been so long since I called you, but I really have never been so busy in my life. Anyway, how are you doing? Tell me about the farm and cousin Winny and everything." Wendy hated to start out her calls by apologizing, but she knew that her mother would really like her to call every day and it had been over two weeks, maybe three since she had called. Actually, her mom would be happiest if she would move back to the farm outside Middlebury and marry a nice Vermont boy, settle into the old farmhouse and have six grandchildren for her. Since that wasn't going to happen, she always felt like she had somehow disappointed her mom, and until he died two years ago of a heart attack, her dad, too. She wasn't alone in feeling that way, of course. It seemed like all her friends had the same kind of unease with their parents, the sense that they couldn't fulfill their expectations no matter what they did, even the ones that had stayed back in home and had kids. Somehow, that didn't make any difference. She always apologized and dreaded the "well, when am I going to see you" question that found its way into every call.

"Well, darling, it is so good to hear from you," Mom started, as usual twisting the blade of guilt, although Wendy knew, or was pretty sure, that it was unintentional. Her mother had stayed on the farm after Dad's death because, "I just don't know where else I would go." Wendy's beloved cousin Winny, short for Winston, was two years younger than she was, twice divorced and possessed of a high school diploma, iron constitution, three sets of coveralls and no ambition other than to keep alive the tradition of old fashioned New England small dairy farming. His second divorce, due no doubt in part to his frequent unhappy periods of unemployment and low wages when he did get farm work, had coincided with Dad's death and it had been natural for him to move in with Mom and work the farm for her in return for room, board and an equal share of whatever little profits they made. As the older female cousin, Wendy had been the object of Winnie's true affections from childhood and she had fond memories of torturing him with peeks of her growing womanhood through supposedly careless but really carefully staged clothes changing behind half opened curtains and skinny dipping in the Otter River while pretending not to know he was peering through the bushes. She loved Winny like a favored Labrador that you had to kick off your leg when he got amorous, and there was that cousin thing anyway. It was soothing to hear Mom talk about him, though, and the spring crop of calves, the start of haying season, putting in the kitchen garden and how he had gotten the old 1926 Farmall tractor running and was going to use it to pull a float in the Middlebury Summer Festival.

"Well, enough about us, tell me what has been keeping you so busy down there in Washington?" Mom finally said.

You mean so busy that I don't even call my poor mother, Wendy thought before she answered. "Well, I'm still working on the big campaign to stop climate change, running all over the country, reorganizing the way the staff work here and building the base of activists we need across the country," Wendy started. She had found that since her dad died, Mom had become increasingly interested in the big national and international issues on which Wendy worked. She had started reading the New York Times. Dad had always gotten it and read it to Wendy sitting on his lap when she was just a baby, but Mom had never had time or interest in affairs of the wider world, immersing herself in family, Wendy's schools, the church and rural, small town social life. Wendy was pleased to find that Mom reacted to the loss of her spouse of over thirty years by trying to expand her horizons. It seemed that she was trying to fill the hole left by Dad's death by focusing her warm and loving attentions on the rest of the world, or at least as much of it as she could reach out to. Now Wendy enjoyed sharing her environmental activism with Mom and getting her view of how "things could be if people would love one another and try to get along."

Wendy had a lot to tell her mom today. Aaron's departure from the campaign in the face of the threats to his family had thrown her life into turmoil. When he left the office she and Tony had a horrible argument. Tony thought she was weak and disloyal for not helping him persuade Aaron to stay with the campaign, and she had been equally distressed with Tony's lack of compassion and concern for Aaron's situation. After a long, loud exchange of accusations she had stormed out of his office, faced with the bleak prospect of trying to restructure the whole campaign. She had greatly underestimated just how much their work depended on having a credible, capable figurehead who was willing to spend the time and energy necessary to build their activist network. She had spent the rest of the day calling her key contacts around the country, feeling them out and concluding that none of them would be close to adequate as a replacement, even if they had been willing to try. By 5 o'clock she was ready to just go out to some bar and get shit faced to try and forget her troubles, something she hadn't done since she got over the break up of her marriage. Then, just as she was getting up from her desk, Aaron had called to tell her that he and Squeak had "thrashed this thing out," and asked if she and Tony would take him back, and if Squeak could travel with him when he had to be out of town. He wanted to "get back on board."

"There won't be any more indecision or quitting," he said with steel in his voice. "We are in this one way or another, come hell or high water, until we win, if you'll have us back."

Of course, she had welcomed him back into the fold and agreed to his conditions, thinking what an asset Squeak would be in front of their audiences. After their short but happy conversation, she had rushed down the hall and into Tony's office, interrupting a phone call and wrapping him in a big hug before telling him the good news. They had gone out together and washed away their earlier angry words in enough celebratory beverages to leave them both silly and unsteady as they caught cabs home late that night. She had vowed to Tony that she would do "whatever it took" to keep Aaron in the campaign until they got it built up to a national level and it could move forward under its own power. Tony promised to do everything he could to hasten that date and to protect Aaron and his boy, which she appreciated even though when she thought about it on the way home she didn't see any way her elegantly mannered and slightly framed boss could provide protection against the brutal elements that they seemed to be facing.

Mom was very upset about the threats and harm to the child. This sort of thing was alien to life in Middlebury, and reawakened her long held fears for her daughter living in the big city. Wendy spent a long time reassuring her mother, but the subject was exhausted without either of them feeling it was settled and both of them knowing it would come up again.

"All right, now tell me about that rich Perry Pierce fellow. Are you still seeing him?" Mom said after Wendy had brought her up to date on the campaign. "It seems you are talking a lot about this older man, Aaron. Are you sleeping with him, too?"

"Mom, I wouldn't call Aaron an older man," she replied with a little exasperation. "No, I'm not sleeping with him, and yes, I'm still seeing Perry," Wendy said. "He has gotten a lot more, umm, intense over the past couple of weeks. Calls me every day and we go out a couple of times a week. He gave me the most beautiful sapphire earrings and necklace, it's scandalous. I feel like a whore taking his gifts. He is very nice and handsome and rich. And amusing, I guess, and I think eventually I'll get him to see things the right way, but, you know, I just don't think the spark is going to ever light up there."

"Yesss. And how about this Aaron? How old is he?"

"Mom, I'm not really sure. I guess he's maybe 50." Wendy knew exactly how much he was over 50 but didn't want to say so. Her mom was 56. "No, I'm not sleeping with him. Not yet. I thought about seducing him to get him back into the campaign when he quit, but didn't have to when he changed his mind."

"Wendy, that's shameful," Mom said, but Wendy could tell she was as entertained as she was scandalized.

"Yeah, well, now you know why I've been so busy," she said mildly. It always felt good to talk to her mom, despite the guilt trip. Mom's love was so unconditional that she didn't have to worry about keeping any secrets or hiding how she really felt about things. "I've got to go now, Mom. Monday was my first day back from the Tennessee trip and Tony and I went out drinking, last night I went out with Perry, and tomorrow I'm going on a trip with Aaron to Delaware, New Jersey and Pennsylvania. We won't get back until Sunday. His son is out of school and he's going on the trip with us, so I don't think you have to worry about me seducing him, at least this week anyway. I need to get my laundry done, pay some bills and just get myself together tonight."

They said their goodbyes and Wendy put down the phone. Talking with Mom helped her sort things out. Passing the complex issues of her work and urban social life through the prism of the simpler world in which she had grown up seemed to make choices simpler. She felt like she had summed up the past, tidied up loose ends and now she was ready to move on to whatever happened next. She whistled while she got her laundry together to put in the wash.

She still felt refreshed from her talk with her mother when Aaron and Squeak picked her up at the office on Thursday, just before noon. Tony wasn't coming along this time and right from the start the day had a family outing feeling to it. Aaron insisted on taking his car, saying he didn't want to risk riding in her old Wrangler, calling it a "death wish on wheels." She preferred the comfort of his Beemer for an extended trip, so she only put up a pro forma defense of her beloved rag top. She had bought it very cheaply and liked the worn feel of it, despite the occasional breakdown. She had driven it home to Vermont once in the winter and wouldn't ever do that again. The heater was a joke, the canvas and plastic top did little to block out the cold and wind and the suspension was strictly "back country," but tooling around town in a rough, old open jeep with her hair flying loose was fun and suited her self image. It drove the guys crazy, too, and added some spice to short trips around D.C. or hiking, fishing and camping excursions into the surrounding countryside.

Squeak asked her to sit in the back seat with him to keep him company. Indicating Aaron he told her, "He mostly just listens to music while he's driving and sings, which is no treat and he doesn't talk much anyway so there's no point sitting in front with him." She wanted to get to know the boy, so she agreed despite Aaron's mild objections. It didn't take long before she wondered if she had made a mistake. Squeak handed out the sandwiches from Baguette and Bagel they had picked up on the way over to the office so they could eat while they drove, but before she got the first bite of her chicken salad on sun dried tomato bagel the boy started plying her with questions. "Do you have a boyfriend? Have you had any kids? Why not? Do you like kids? Where are you from? Do they have any black people there? How old are you? What do you weigh? Do you have PlayStation? Are you ever going to get married...?" She felt like she was being interviewed for a very important and highly classified job, a feeling that was magnified by her determination to build her relationship with Aaron as a way to keep him from quitting the campaign before the time was right. She knew that the kid was going to be important factor. It was unsettling to have Squeak taking the initiative in this whole process, although he really was cute and smart.

"Hey, are you just going to let me get the third degree back here?" she finally pleaded with Aaron. "I can hardly get a bite out of my sandwich."

"You could have sat up here with me. I don't say much, remember," he answered with a laugh.

After wrestling to answer a dozen awkward questions she decide to just relax and treat Squeak like any other person and assert herself without gauging her effect on him.

"Ok, enough already, Mr. Inquisitor. I'm not saying any more about me. It's my turn to find out about you. Do you have a girlfriend? Why not? How tall are you? What do you weigh? What do you think about women? What are your grades…?" By the time they had finished their sandwiches and apples and were crossing the state line into Delaware they both felt like they knew the basics and the usual social barriers to communication had been battered to the ground. Wendy reflected that people would all be a lot better off if they just asked people what they wanted to know the way Squeak had done, but knew that it could only work for kids because adults forgot how to be so honest.

She found out that Squeak's school year actually wouldn't end until the next Tuesday, but Aaron had taken him out early since he had already done all the work and grades were already in. Squeak told her that he and Aaron had to stick together in case the hoods came back to kill them. "We got to watch each other's back," he said with such aplomb that she didn't know how to react. As they rode down the highway he and Aaron both constantly checked out the cars on the road behind, in front and next to them and compared their observations to be sure that they didn't see anyone following them. At one point Aaron pulled into the parking lot at Chesapeake House, a rest stop on I95 in Maryland to see if anyone pulled off behind them and then pulled right back onto the highway after they both agreed the coast was clear. Despite having heard about what had happened in the house, this kind of intrigue and suspicion seemed unreal and theatrical to her and she asked if they weren't being a little paranoid. Squeak pulled up the leg of his shorts and showed her the yellow and purple bruise on his thigh. She started to check out the cars around them and compare notes, too, but still felt like she was playing a part in some fantasy game.

After they checked in to the Holiday Inn and Conference Center in Wilmington she got to work, checking out the meeting room and contacting the local Chapter leader. This was the real world for her and she gratefully forgot about plots and gangsters. She spent the rest of the afternoon on her cell phone and computer, confirming the turnout for tonight's meeting, checking on the arrangements for the next meetings in New Jersey and Pennsylvania and catching up on her calls and correspondence. Aaron and Squeak headed for the swimming pool.

She didn't see them again until just before the meeting started at 6:30 and didn't talk with them until it ended after 8:00. Only half of the 48 people who showed up were NAC members, but they all ended up giving an enthusiastic reception to Aaron's call for action. The projected rise in sea level was their main concern. Even a small rise would be devastating to their beloved shores and wetlands, to say nothing of all the development near sea level, and to hear that a rise of between one foot and three feet could happen in the coming decades was enough to make them ready to take action.

She was mildly surprised when Aaron introduced Squeak, using Kenya, his real name, and made him part of the "conversation" with the audience. She counted only three African American's in the gathering, but as she would have expected everyone was captivated by the "cute young man" and, of course, intrigued by the "odd couple" father/son relationship. Squeak's initial discomfort, resulting in a high pitched and stumbling delivery of his obviously rehearsed little speech, only made them more receptive to him, Aaron and their message. I have to figure out how to capitalize on having Squeak part of the show, Wendy thought to herself. We've got to get pictures out of him and Aaron together, push their back story. Maybe that'll help us get more black and brown faces in the audiences.

"This is for everyone's future," Squeak interjected near the end of the talk, having gained ease as he got used to being the focus of so much attention. "Black, white, yellow or brown. If you care about us kids you've got to join the fight to protect our future." That sparked a standing ovation, which Aaron channeled into group chanting before breaking off to exchange handshakes, hugs and promises to "be there for each other and spread the word" while the local leaders handed out brochures on energy efficiency and alternative fuels.

When the crowd thinned out, she gave both Aaron and Squeak big hugs and praised them for their great pitch. "Oh, man you guys are dynamite. They loved you. Now we're really getting the ball rolling," she said, flushed with excitement. "We've got to keep the momentum up. That's my job. I'll get

186

these people out on a picket line or pack some public meeting or demonstrating in a protest this week, I promise you. The Movement is happening!"

After the meeting room had cleared and she had made arrangements with the local leaders to set up some kind of action for the next weekend, she met the guys in the hotel snack bar. Wendy got fried chicken, vegetables and a milkshake. Aaron and Squeak had eaten before the rally, but Wendy had not and Squeak was always ready to eat. He got a shake and a chicken salad sandwich. Aaron just sipped water while they talked about the crowd and how to keep people involved after they went home. It was after nine when they said their goodnights and went back to their rooms.

Wendy pulled off her slacks and blouse and flopped down on the bed, futilely trying to relax. She was just too excited about the way the meeting had gone, about being involved in building something big and good and real to help people and the country. She stared at printouts of demographics in Philadelphia, their next stop, but couldn't focus and tossed the papers aside. Giving up, she pulled out her "travel stash," took a couple of hits off a joint and thought about how the day had gone before the meeting, how comfortable she was with Aaron and Squeak and what a good team they made. Aaron was a good man, she thought, honest and loving in his tough kind of way. She thought about her talk with her mother, how she had said that Mom wouldn't have to worry about her seducing Aaron on this trip. *Oh well, sorry, Mom*, she thought with a giggle. She reached for the phone and dialed Aaron and Squeak's room.

"Hi, Aaron. Look, I'm wired right now, I can't settle down. Can we talk for a while? Can you meet me in the bar? How about fifteen minutes? Thanks." She jumped off the bed, shed her bra and panties and got into the shower. Ten minutes later she was pulling the "special little dress" she had brought along out of her travel bag. She slipped on white bikini panties and then pulled the dress over her head, reached in back, zipped it up and took a look in the mirror. The dress was simple, gauzy cotton with spreading slashes of white, red, green and black going from top left to bottom right. It had spaghetti straps and a tight bodice that ended just below her breasts. From there it fell loosely to a couple of inches above her knees. The white panties showed clearly through the gauzy material, and the light behind her outlined her figure. It was obvious that she wasn't wearing a bra, and it became more obvious as she thought about the impact she would make on Aaron. She added a little lipstick and eyebrow pencil, admired her skin, rosy from the shower and from the tarty boldness she was feeling. She put some mousse on her hands and worked it into her hair to give it some sheen and body, but left it loose and wild, because that was how she felt. When she tossed her head her hair bounced and shone. Very nice. She checked the time. Humph, have to wait a few minutes so he gets there first and will see me come in, she thought. She re-lit her joint and took another hit and then sat on the end of the bed to file her nails. Before leaving the room she sprayed around some of the air freshener that was part of her travel kit to clear the pot smell from the room.

She entered the lobby of the hotel on the side opposite from the bar, which was open to the rest of the lobby but distinguished by a lower ceiling and a waist high barrier of planters with assorted greenery. The bar itself ran along the wall opposite the plants. The near end was open, flanked by the end of the planter barrier and the end of the bar. Aaron had taken a table at the far wall, in the corner formed with the planter barrier, and was seated with the wall at his back so he could see all through the lobby and the bar. Like a bear in his den, she thought, waiting for him to look her way before starting to walk across the lobby, past the hotel desk and to the entrance of the bar. She walked slowly; smooth but with a practiced, loose hipped stride. She had a good walk and she wanted to be sure he saw it. From the corner of her eye she could see that she had his complete attention. When she walked into the bar where the lighting was softer she exchanged "good evenings" with the bartender and passed by two men seated at the bar and the three occupied tables among the dozen that filled the bar area. She heard the break in the buzz of conversation. Hah! She thought, that's in sandals, too. If I had brought heels they'd fall off their stools.

Aaron stood with his mouth in a kind of half open dopey smile as she came to the table, but didn't come around to pull out a chair for her. She pulled it out herself, choosing one at right angles to him and facing the lobby, leaned over the corner of the table and gave him a kiss on the cheek before she sat down. *That's to pay you back for the kiss in Charlotte,* she thought.

"Good lord," he said as he sat down, "you, ah," he hesitated then shook his head with a smile and spread his hands helplessly, "well, you are beautiful."

She smiled, leaned back in her chair and crossed her legs. "Thank you." The waitress came and she ordered a rum Collins. Aaron took a sip of the gin and tonic in front of him, trying to keep his gaze on her face but unable to resist his eyes slipping to her bare shoulders and lightly concealed breasts.

"What is Squeak doing? Is he ok?" she asked.

"Ah," he said dismissively, "who cares?"

She laughed, reached over, picked up his glass and took a drink from it. "Well, I'm glad you're able to get your mind off the threats and, you know, all that. I've got to tell you that I still have trouble processing that, ah, that violence, you know, and connecting it with our campaign. Squeak seems pretty resilient."

"Yeah, he's just happy that I got him out of the last few days of school. For him that was worth getting a beating, having his life threatened and running around looking over our shoulders for however long this lasts. For now it's still some kind of adventure for him, and I guess I have to admit that I'm not, well, you know this sure beats some dull nine to five job. They don't do anything productive in school the last few days of the year, anyway, and he pretty much gets all A's. He went through some tough times as a kid. I mean, really tough. Mom was a drunk and an addict. Never knew his dad. Far as I could find out he was a con man and hood and blew town for who knows where years ago. His mom left town, too, at least that's what Squeak told me he had found out from old acquaintances. I never knew her before I met Squeak and arranged the adoption with her. She seemed, well, she was a troubled woman, but you'd think she would have shown more interest in the kid over the years."

Wendy could see the disgust on his face. The waitress came back with her drink and another gin and tonic for Aaron. After she had gone Wendy said, "Well, you're giving him a good home and a shot at a good life."

"I'm not giving him anything," Aaron replied with a force that surprised her. "He is giving me a shot at a good life. My first son is a wonderful guy, bright, kind, hard working. He doesn't need me, though, and he's off living his own life, and I can't be making demands on him. When Squeak came along I was going down hill fast. I really didn't feel like I had any role to play in this world. I wasn't important to anyone. He changed that. He fills that need for me."

Wendy matched his serious tone. "Aaron, I, uh, I can tell you this. The work you are doing is important to many people. When you left Tony and me in Nashville and we had to go to Memphis and do the Sunday meeting without you, we both knew that there wouldn't be any movement without you. We knew you were important before then, but that showed us just how different it is when you are there to connect with people in a way that neither of us or really anyone else we know can do. You have the vision, you have the ability to get other people to share that vision and you're able to open your heart to them to make it ok for them to care. So you are important to the movement and all the people who are involved and who will be touched by the movement. Not in the same way as you are important to Squeak, but very important."

Her voice softened and she reached over and put her hand on his arm, "And you are becoming especially important to me."

Aaron looked into her eyes, losing the frown that had come to his face and easing back into a smile. They took each other's hands, leaned towards each other until their lips met. It was a chaste kiss at first, but their lips lingered together and explored. She put her hand on the back of his neck and it turned into an eager, open kiss; tongues touching and playing..

She broke away, eyes wide, just inches away. "Let's go some place where we can get laid," she said.

"You mean by each other or do you have some third and fourth parties in mind?" he answered, keeping a straight face until she hit him with the side of her fist on his forehead. They quickly paid the bill and left the bar, oblivious to the envious looks that they left behind.

They went straight to her room, embracing for deep kisses in the elevator and in the hallway before she fumbled the key card into the slot, and pushed open the door so they could stumble inside. He clasped her to him with one arm as he kicked the door closed with his heel, reached behind her with the other arm to find the zipper on her dress and pull it down. He reached down with both hands, one on either side, and ran his hands slowly up her legs, from above her knees to her hips, lingering there to slide them around to the round cheeks of her ass, and then sliding them up her sides, pulling the light cloud of her dress up and over her head. They embraced again, mouths together, tongues meeting first in her mouth and then in his. He bent his head down to her breasts and ran lips and tongue over them, sucking loudly on first one hard nipple and then the other. They both gave soft grunts of building excitement. His hand reached down to caress her belly, thighs and rub the mound of her pubis. She felt like she was on fire, and pulled at his shirt, then his belt, pulling him toward the bed. They broke apart and each finished undressing, she first, discarding her panties and then lying back and rubbing her hand on her mound and down between her legs. She watched him take a condom from its pack, she didn't know where it had come from, and put it on, watching her all the time. She spread her legs and welcomed him, lunging at first, wanting to be fulfilled now, right away. He was patient, though, starting slowly and calming her with hands and lips, building to the point where they were bucking wildly, her arms and hands clutching him tightly while her heels beat against the back of his knees faster and faster. He brought her to first one orgasm, then slowed again before finally releasing himself with hard thrusts and a loud, "Aaaaahhh," bringing her to climax again, with him this time.

Some time later Wendy propped herself up on her elbow and looked with satisfaction down their naked bodies. They were on their sides, facing each other, legs entwined. Aaron had taken off the condom, reaching behind himself to drop it on the floor beside the bed, and now was resting his head on the pillow, looking at her face while she enjoyed her own lazy inspection.

She was frank in her interest in his body, touching him here and there, squeezing and occasionally tasting with her tongue. He was fit, strong but not sculpted like body builders who devoted themselves to some strange idea of manhood. He had the muscles that come from a lifetime of testing oneself in different ways just for the pleasure of the action and the testing. He was hard but thicker in the middle than any programmed Adonis, or than the more slender Perry Pierce Richardson and those like him for whom a slim appearance was the goal of exercise and diet. His skin was older, not so elastic, but not unpleasing. He had no more pretense physically than in his person. She thought he appeared as he was, a man who spent his years grasping for the fullness of life, now as before and more than any other man she had known.

"So, did I pass the test?" she asked.

"What test?" He was running his hand over the contours of her back; from below the shoulders in to the small of her back and then across the high flare of her buttock.

"Am I young enough to keep up with you? Remember you said I might be too old for you."

"Oh, yeah. You're probably good for at least a few more years."

"Well, ditto for you," she answered, bending her face down and kissing him, letting him feel the smoldering embers of her passion.

"Were you an ice skater?" he asked as he continued mapping the curve of her ass with his hand. "You know, figure skating."

"Ha! I played ice hockey. With the boys, mostly. In fact, I played on the boy's freshman team in high school. I had to quit when I was a sophomore. My mother got upset when I got this."

She pointed out a small scar on her chin.

"Besides, the boys kept trying to feel me up when we went into the corners after the puck. Then the coach would get mad when I hooked them in the crotch with my stick. It was time to move on to other things, anyway."

After a while he got up and went into the bathroom where she heard him urinating. She was amused that he closed the door. He came back, collected his clothes and sat on the chair by the desk.

"I have to go back and stay with Squeak," he said. "He isn't comfortable when he wakes up in a strange room. Plus I just feel better if I stick close to him now. I don't think we were followed, or that those hoods or anyone from APRC would know where to find us, but I still feel better staying close."

Wendy sat up quickly, knees up and back against the head of the bed, pulling the sheets up over her breasts.

"Why are you concerned about APRC?" she asked. "What makes you think that they're involved with the guys who hurt Squeak?"

His face went through a series of expressions, like he was weighing what to tell her and he didn't answer her right away. Finally he said, "I can't tell you how I know, now. Sometime, but not now. But I know that there is a connection, a direct connection."

She considered that, obviously not satisfied but then was overcome by the realization that she had a big problem.

"Oh my god!" she said.

"What?" he asked. "What's the matter?"

She dreaded what she had to say. "Aaron, I think I may have been a sucker. I've been seeing a man. We have been dating for months now; from before I met you and we started the campaign."

"Are you still seeing him?"

"Yes, I have been. We went out just this past Tuesday."

She saw he was processing that, trying to sort out what it meant to him, what to say. He started to get dressed. After he put on his under shorts and pants and sat back down on the chair, he stopped.

"Look, I know that everyone has different views on, uh, relationships and I respect that. I know that people have relationships with more than one person at a time, and I wouldn't tell you anything about what to do with your life. But I can't deal with having a relationship with you if you are sleeping with another guy. I'm not judging you or saying it is wrong for you, it's just wrong for me. I can't do that."

"Aaron, it isn't that. He works at APRC. Perry's their chief lobbyist. And lately, the last couple of weeks, he's been really insistent about finding out when I was going to be in town and this week he wanted to know where I was going. I thought it was just, you know, that he was serious about me and .... God damn him. I think he was using me to get information. I'm so sorry. Shit!" Her eyes started to well up and she put her head down on her drawn up knees so he wouldn't see her tears. She never let anyone see her cry and it made her furious at herself and him that her weakness was being exposed.

Aaron came over to her and gripped both her arms just below the shoulder. "Wendy," he said roughly. "Look at me. We don't have time for that now. Just tell me, did you tell him where we were going this week? Think! Think!"

"I'm trying to think!" Her voice was scratchy and her breath started to catch in her throat. "Let me go."

He sprang over to the phone and called his room. She could hear it ring twice, then, "Squeak, are you ok? Yeah, I know it's late. I'll be right there. You're ok? Good, I'll be there in a minute. Never mind about that." He hung up, went back to the chair and started to put on his shoes and socks.

Wendy had gotten control of herself. The tears wouldn't stop, but she could talk, although her voice sounded weak and childish in her own ears. "No, I didn't tell him where I was going to be this week. Where we were going. I remember. I'm sure."

"Ok," Aaron said as he pulled on his shirt and buttoned it. Two buttons were missing, popped off in her hurry to undress him or in his own hurry to get undressed earlier. "Look, I gotta go. We...we'll talk tomorrow."

"Go," she said. "Just go."

He went out the door.

Chapter 20

Aaron had a good view of the house on Mason Place from the back window of the recreation center that was beside the elementary school. The house was on the middle of the block of row houses, across from the baseball field that filled the block behind the center and school. Officially it was a vacant property, but it looked just like the other house fronts on the block, just a little shabbier. At 4:30 AM there was no traffic going in or out of the house and street was quiet as dawn crept across the sky from the east. Aaron figured that the occupants were all sleeping, since their business hours usually ended around 2:00 or 2:30 AM.

Miss Dixon had been more than happy to let Aaron, Squeak and Antelope come and use the center, where she had been the director for as long as anyone could remember. Two years ago Aaron had organized the neighbors, parents, students and school administrators to demand that the police take action and clear out the drug dealers who'd hung around in front of the school and center for two decades. Miss Dixon was grateful for the removal of the bad influence on "her children" who attended the school and spent their free time in the center. Aaron stopped by the center to chat every now and then, sometimes with Squeak and sometimes alone and they helped each other on various local projects. She was a short, round woman of indeterminate age with smooth chocolate skin. Thick black and gray hair pulled back into a round bun topped a large round head that sat directly on her soft, round shoulders. Viewed from behind, her round buttocks rode high over thick round legs. Her large bosom, which had smothered the cries of two generations, almost smothering the children, rested over her round waist, hiding from her view round feet firmly planted on the floor of the center over which she had reigned for her entire adult life. Her desire to help her friend only grew when she found out that they were going to do something to disturb the new crop of dealers who had established themselves in the vacant house visible from her back store room window over the past couple of months. "Just like cockroaches, you got to keep cleanin' them out," she had agreed when Aaron told him his plan.

It was early Tuesday, two days after Aaron and Squeak had returned from the road trip with Wendy. They had been waiting at the window since eight the previous evening, watching for a sign that Aaron's latest scheme would work. It was a hot, sticky night, not as bad as it would get in July, but still not comfortable in the stuffy storeroom. The window wouldn't open and there was no air conditioning in the center. Little air made its way from the open windows in the main room to where he sat waiting. The long hours had given Aaron plenty of time to tell himself that this was a foolish waste of time, an opinion strongly voiced by both Squeak and Antelope, but that he would not admit out loud. Instead he did the bulk of the watching while the other two played cards and then slept on the recreation mats that Miss Dixon had pulled off of their shelf and stacked in the main hall next to the storeroom door for them. She had long ago gone to her office and fallen asleep on the sprung seated sofa that she kept there for the slow periods of her endless work days.

As the evening turned to night and the night slowly moved towards morning Aaron had more time than he wanted to go over in his mind how he had handled Wendy's revelation of her relationship with Perry Pierce Richardson of APRC, and the swift cooling of their short affair. After returning to his room and getting Squeak to quit playing video games on the hotel TV and go to sleep he had brooded in the dark. Sleeping with the enemy, the stupid phrase kept repeating in his mind while he sat propped up by pillows waiting vainly for his racing thoughts to slow and allow him to rest. He pictured them in the throes of passion, then in the warm afterglow of satisfaction, and then he would see her with another man, experiencing that same passion and then whispering secrets about him and Squeak into an evil ear. Sleeping with the enemy, and maybe it was as applicable to him as it was to her since she apparently didn't find their opposition as completely distasteful as he did. He knew that in D.C. people routinely put aside their professional differences when they left their offices, and that was probably necessary to keep the government running with even the current low level of civility. James Carville and Mary Matalin, respectively the arch liberal and arch conservative political operatives who shared an apparently happy marriage were only the most prominent example of the "strange bedfellows" that populated the Capitol City. Still, in this case, he could not understand how she could share secrets and her bed with someone allied with those who were ruthlessly exploiting the planet for profit, and who would send gangsters after him and his family.

The remainder of their trip bore no resemblance to the easy pleasures of a growing relationship that had led up to their night of passion and betrayal. When he looked at her the next morning he still saw the beauty, the warmth, the honest spirit of adventure that so attracted him, and he reacted by closing down his feelings so that he wouldn't be drawn back in to her trap. She hadn't apologized, in fact, she displayed a growing hurt at his polite but distant words and manner, and finally that hurt had turned into anger. By noon she had pulled him to one side of the next meeting room, outside Philadelphia, and told him that she didn't think she had anything for which she needed to apologize and that he was acting like a self-righteous ass…and then she turned and stalked away on legs stiffened by anger, unable to continue. Squeak was a puzzled victim of their frosty battle, at first trying to engage them in the joy of days on the road with no responsibility except to meet and talk with people at their rallies. Finally he had confronted Aaron, asking, "What's with you and Wendy? What'd you do the other night?" When he couldn't get an answer he had given up on them and turned to his own books, Game Boy and mp3 player between enjoying the attentions of the audiences.

And the audiences did love the boy, which helped to make up for what Aaron considered his own less than stellar performances over the rest of the weekend. Squeak quickly became comfortable in front of the crowds, and on Friday and Saturday nights he had stayed in the homes of volunteers from Pennsylvania and then in New Jersey, making friends and being spoiled. Meantime, Aaron and Wendy spent miserable nights in their solitary rooms in the hotels.

By the time they finished the last meeting Sunday afternoon and were headed home, Aaron had concluded that he was, as usual, an idiot when dealing with a woman. Why should she apologize to him for having a sex life, he asked himself? How was she supposed to know that those APRC bastards were behind the attack on Squeak when he had hidden his evidence from her? Who was he to judge her, with his own secret about luring the hoods into the woods and disabling their car? Goddammit, she had been betrayed by those same bastards who had chased him out of his house. It was them he should be getting even with, not her! In fact, he should get back at them for her sake now, as much as for him and Squeak. Oh yeah, and don't forget that this is really just one more example of those bastards fucking up the world for everyone else, too, just so they can make more money ripping up the wild places and pumping poisons and carbon into the air and water. Perry Pierce Richardson, he turned the name over in his mind. You're going to some special ring of hell and I'm going to do all I can to help you get there as soon as possible.

But when he had turned to her while driving from one meeting venue to the next, now seated in front with him at Squeak's suggestion "since you are just as uptight as he is these days," he saw the firm set of her jaw and her ostentatious avoidance of his eye. She rebuffed any attempt at conversation that did not directly pertain to the rallies, the campaign or the movement. He couldn't find the words to get them back to where they had been just two nights ago, especially since he wasn't sure where it was that they had been. Could he say it was love? Was it love for her? Was it just a good lay? Had it even been as good for her as it had for him? How do you get all that across to someone who is so pissed off at you, and rightly so, that they wouldn't throw you a line if you were drowning?

And that further stoked his determination to strike back at the bastards that had put them into this situation, starting with Perry Pierce Richardson.

It was after he dropped her off and he and Squeak had parked the car three blocks away and gone through the alleys to Antelope's place that he had figured out how to take a swing at his enemies, and maybe break through the ice with Wendy. It was risky, but, hell, he was lost if he didn't try something. So he had called her and given her the plan. She was guarded at first, he thought she might even hang up on him, but he had pleaded with her to hear him out and hurried through it and she had listened, and finally, after he got it all out, she had thought about it, not speaking, but at least staying on the line.

"Ok, let me get this straight," she had said, finally. "You want me to call up Perry, just to talk with him, and get him to ask me out for tomorrow night, but to say that I have already committed to help you move into a neighbor's house who is away on a trip, what is that address? 275 Mason Place, N. E. Ok, I got that. And let slip out accidentally that you will be staying there hiding out for a night or two. Is that right?"

"Yes."

"Ok, and you are going to set up some kind of trap for whoever comes, if they come to harm you. Is that right?"

"Yes, Wendy. I…I am going to…look, those guys have been fucking with us and I'm not going to sit back and just let them mess us up," he answered.

"Aaron, are you going to do anything illegal."

"No, Wendy. This is all legal. I am just going to set them up to get caught doing something illegal. If they fall for it and if it works. It's not a sure thing, but at least it gives us a chance to, ah, take the initiative. Wendy, can you do this? I'll understand if you don't think you can."

There was a long pause. He felt the sweat build up under his arms and between his shoulder blades.

"Yeah, I think I can do it," she finally said, her voice still frosty. "So now you think you can trust me to do this and not tell Perry your secret plan?"

"Wendy, yes. Yes, I trust you and I was stupid and foolish for the way I treated you." He was elated that he had a chance to apologize. If she went along with this then at least they were moving back to being on the same side, fighting the enemy and not each other.

"Ok. Look, this plan is crazy," she said. He crossed his fingers while she thought about it, sure that anything he said had as good a chance of pushing her the wrong way as not.

Finally she sighed and continued. "Ok, I'll give him a call right now and I'll call you back and let you know if he sounds like he took the bait."

"Great, Wendy, thank you, that's great." He thought he had a chance of getting back to whatever their relationship had been before he pushed her away, but he wasn't going to press his luck, so he just said, "Take your time, however long you need. I'll be waiting right here by the phone." Which was stupid, since he was calling on his cell phone, so where else would he be except by the phone and she presumably knew that, but she said again that she would call him back and they had hung up.

He was startled out of his thoughts as the door to #275 was quickly pulled open. A head in a red, black and green knit cap poked out and jerked first right then left and then was pulled back inside. "Showtime," Aaron called over his shoulder. Squeak and Antelope both lifted their heads and then scrambled to get over to the window next to him. Meantime he punched the last digit of the 1st District police substation number on the new cell phone he had been holding for the past four hours. While he waited through six rings for the desk sergeant to get on the line the morning quiet was punctured by the muffled sound of gunfire, "Pop," then "Pop, Pop, Pop."

"Officer, shots fired at number 275 Mason Pl. NE, that's 275 Mason Pl. NE, First Precinct. Get all units here now. It's a war. Repeat the address back to me." He was unnerved by the gunfire, he hadn't expected it, but his voice was steady. When the sergeant started to say, "State your…" he cut him off. "Shut up," he yelled. He heard more shots. "Continuing gunfire, 275 Mason Pl. NE, repeat that address or I hang up." The officer repeated the address and he disconnected. He put the cell phone in his pocket. It was a disposable one that he had bought at a Radio Shack in Virginia on Monday and he would throw it away later in a trash can at Union Station.

As he hung up Miss Dixon bustled into the store room and stood behind Squeak with her hands on his shoulders, looking out at the row of house fronts. They saw the door of 275 pulled all the way open by the same man that had looked out earlier, still wearing his cap, plus an oversized tee shirt, dark green baggy pants held up at the waist with one hand and no shoes or socks. He scurried out to the porch, but turned back and lifted the gun they now saw in the hand that had been holding his pants and fired rapidly back into the house. He clumsily spun around, losing his balance, took a step, fell down the stairs, pushed himself back up onto his feet and started running east on the street, towards them. His face was strained, eyes wide and his mouth open, tongue out. His pants had sagged down and were impeding his progress, and he pulled at them with his free hand.

"Fist," Squeak said, and Aaron thought he was referring to the running man. Just then there were rapid shots and the man fell, legs collapsing and arms loosely flailing like a wooden puppet. His momentum and the force of the bullets skidded and rolled him forward down the sidewalk. Aaron looked from the now motionless figure on the sidewalk back to the door just in time to see the back of a dark figure going back in. Where's the goddam cops, he thought.

"Fist shot him," Squeak said excitedly.

"Ohhh Lord! Oh, sweet Jesus! Ohhh," Miss Dixon moaned, first trying to cover Squeak's eyes, and then covering her mouth when he pushed her hand away, her moans continuing.

They heard the sirens then on 7th St., coming from H where Aaron knew there was almost always a cruising patrol. They saw the lights of the patrol car as it raced up 7th, past G, on the other side of the ball field. It turned left onto Mason and then it screeched to a stop in the middle of the street in front of 275. The single patrol man jumped out, staying behind his half open door with his gun in his right hand resting on the roof and pointing at 275, the handset of his car radio in his left. Sporadic gun shot reports continued to come out of the house, then several in quick succession and finally, quiet.

"I saw him. That was Fist shot that guy," Squeak said, his eyes big, pulling on Aaron's arm.

"Ok, let's clear out of here before the place is crawling with cops and we're boxed in," Aaron said. They all turned from the window. Miss Dixon had taken her hands away from her face and was looking at Aaron. Her eyes were bulging, her mouth open and her head shaking left and right in short jerks.

"Come on, you too, Miss Dixon," he said. "We were never here this morning. Let's all get home."

"No, Mr. Aaron. I'll be staying here," Miss Dixon told him. Fright and anger competed in her voice. "Don't you worry; I won't tell anyone you were here or that I saw anythin' or heard anythin'. I'll just go back to my office an' be stayin' there like folks know I do lots a nights. You take that child and go now, Mr. Aaron."

She hadn't called him "Mr." in the past two years. Aaron knew that he had lost his friendship with her.

"Don't you be coming back here, Mr. Aaron," she continued, anger overriding her fear. "You've gone too far. You shouldn' be showin' that child what he just seen. That's a bad thing you've done. You go now."

Aaron looked at her for a moment, not knowing what to say. He was in shock himself at the firestorm he had set up. He heard an echo of Wendy's voice at the motel after he had found out about her affair with Richardson. "Just go," she had said.

"Come on," Antelope said roughly, pulling him by his arm. "We gotta get out the front and across the street into the ally and still three blocks to get to the car. Let's go."

He turned and ran.

By noon Aaron had heard enough from the news reports so that he was pretty sure that Fist, Grainer or the big guy who had followed them into the woods hadn't been killed or caught. The story was a sensation on TV, leading every report and even breaking into some local shows as they identified one dead man and two wounded, a man and a woman, in the "wild dawn shootout, apparently between rival drug gangs on a quiet street on Capitol Hill." He hoped that the bastards had at least gotten wounded, but most likely they had gotten away through the back of the house and into the alley, the way they must have sneaked in, expecting to surprise and execute him.

He was pacing in Antelope's living room, fighting to control his building rage. Antelope and Squeak were in the dining room eating sandwiches.

"Hey, man, maybe you better slow down," Antelope said to him. "You may want to think about what Miss Dixon was telling you."

"Right, I slow down and what happens. They come after me and blow me away. No, I've got to fight this through to the end."

"So when is enough, enough?" Antelope said. "And how about your kid?"

"It's ok, Dad," Squeak said, quickly. "I'm with you, don't worry."

"Shit, we're all with you. I mean, what choice do we have?" Antelope said dismissively. "But where are we goin'?"

"I don't know," Aaron said angrily, frustrated that he didn't have the answers that they depended on him to provide. "I don't know when it's enough. When I don't have any more to give, I guess that's when it's enough. Right now I'm just going as far as I can, to where ever it takes me."

He broke away from their eyes and strode over to the door and out of the house, escaping from questions that didn't have any answers. He stalked up the street to D and turned right, walking to the parks north of the Capitol and Senate office buildings. Summer flowers bloomed, trees were in full leaf and the grass was green and fresh, but the usual solace he took from these public gardens eluded him.

One man had died in front of his eyes, and others were wounded and might die. He was responsible, but he couldn't fool himself into thinking that responsibility was what troubled him. He had no remorse for his actions. When he looked deep into his soul, he only found anger that Fist and the other thugs he had set up got away. Was he some kind of monster? Where were the normal feelings of a civilized person, of compassion for the people whom he had caused to die or be hurt? That was why Ms. Dixon had turned away from him. When she saw that man gunned down in the street, falling like so much trash without the least dignity that a human being should have in death, she saw him as the boy he once had been, who had spent summer days and after school afternoons in her recreation center. She saw a child she had given love and discipline and laughter. And she knew that Aaron only saw that dying man as a tool to use in fighting his battle against his enemies, enemies of whom she had no knowledge. When that man had served his purpose, she thought that Aaron just discarded that dead body with no more remorse than a broken shovel. And Aaron had to admit that she was right. He was as much a thug as Grainer or Fist or the other guy, or the drug dealers that he had tried to push out of his neighborhood for years.

He had set this whole thing up with the idea of killing two birds with one stone: getting Fist and his thugs into a dustup with the drug dealers and having the cops pull in all of them at once. Well, it hadn't worked the way he planned. The cops had only picked up the dealers, and Fist's crew had gotten away. He knew that he would never be lucky enough to lure Fist into another trap, and that next time they had a chance they would kill him. They might lay low for a while, but he knew that they would be back and with a vengeance. Metropolitan Police didn't have Fist and Grainer high on their priorities because of the break in at his house. That had been a minor incident with little damage and no significant injuries and they didn't give much credence to the report that he and Squeak had given them. That one was buried in the "don't care" files. He didn't have any evidence to tie Fist, Grainer and the big guy to the Mason Place shootout or the break in. Just the rental car contract and the story about how he had set them up, and he couldn't use any of that because then they would hold him responsible. It would look like he had instigated this whole war, instead of just taking action to keep the bastards from harming his family.

Perry Pierce Richardson, that name kept intruding on any attempt at thought in his head, throbbing like a festering cyst that shot pain through your system whenever you touched it. All right, he thought, I've got what I've got and I can't depend on anyone else to do anything with it. I can either just sit back and wait to get myself and probably Squeak, Antelope, and who knows, Wendy and anyone else that gets close to me picked off by hired thugs or I can take what I have and go with it.

I'm not going to wallow in any more indecision, he thought. Action is the answer. No one is going to tell me I can't work on the things that I know are right. I'm going to pay a call on APRC and Perry Pierce Richardson, take the ball right at them. See how they like dealing with me face to face. I can't be worrying about who I am or what I feel or don't feel. I am what I do, and this is what I do. I act. Let them do the worrying.

Aaron stopped pacing the gardens and turned towards the Union Station

Metro stop. His steps were spurred by his anger and buoyed by the feeling that he had found the right target for both his personal emotions and his determination to stop the continued destruction of the natural world by selfish interests. Those bastards at APRC and the bastard corporations they fronted for were responsible for both his personal problems and harming the earth. The man and the mission were now one, perfectly matched.

He called APRC before he got on the Metro and was told that "Mr. Richardson is in but in conference, would you like to leave a message on his voicemail." He had declined but verified the office address and what floors the offices were on from the obliging secretary. Aaron found the APRC building easily and gained entrance by showing the guard at the reception desk the expired D.C. Government identification card he had been given by his City Councilwoman two years ago. She had found it easier to just give him a staff badge instead of someone having to vouch for him every time he came to her offices when he was organizing people to get rid of the drug dealers.

When he burst into Richardson's office he was met by the same voice that had answered the phone, issuing from an attractive but nervous blond woman. Her head jerked up, blue eyes and crimson lipped mouth wide.

"Oh! Sir! You startled me. What can I do for you?" she said breathlessly.

"Is Richardson in his office?" Aaron barked, peremptorily. Not waiting for a reply he went directly to the inner door and opened it. "Where is he?" he demanded when he confirmed that the office was empty.

Patricia was having trouble getting her words out. She had been on edge since that first week when Mr. Richardson had changed from the very smooth, sophisticated and sexy playboy who had hired her to a snappy grouch who cursed at her and made her feel stupid. She had gotten a pimple on her chin, a huge ugly thing that wouldn't go away. She wasn't sleeping, she couldn't keep food down and her hair had lost its luster. This job, which had seemed to be a dream with the high pay, great benefits, hunky bachelor boss and swanky surroundings had become a nightmare This was the last straw. She started to stand up, but then sat back down as Aaron reached the front of her desk, leaning his angry face close to hers.

"You heard me. Don't waste my time. Where is he?" he demanded, his voice cold and hard as winter ice.

"Oh, I'm...he...he's in Mr. Tower's office." She sobbed twice, then regained enough composure to speak. "Left and two doors down on the right. I quit."

Her sobbing receded behind him as he marched down the hall and through the door to Ed Tower's office. He paid no attention to the meticulous Miss Fitchens, who was saying, "Sir. Sir. Sir! You can't go in there!" as he pulled open the inner office door and walked in, pulling it closed behind him. A heavy, florid faced man whom he presumed to be Ed Tower was seated behind the desk and a sleek, younger man that must be Perry Pierce Richardson was in an armchair in front of the desk. Both turned to him in surprise.

"Who the fuck are you?" Tower said angrily, his face going from florid to crimson.

"I'm Aaron Woods," Aaron said as a challenge and walked up until he stood two steps from the desk. "You ought to know that, since you sent your goons to kill me. You're Ed Tower, right? And this must be Pee Pee Richardson."

"Get out of here. I'll have you thrown out." Tower reached for the phone.

Aaron took another step, grabbed the big communications console off the desk, stepped back and threw it into a corner. "I'm gonna talk to you and I'll leave when I'm done," he said.

Tower yanked open his desk drawer, clumsily grabbed a gun and stood up, thrusting the gun at Aaron. Richardson was standing now, too, his face white, looking back and forth between Tower and Aaron.

"I'll blow your fucking head off," Tower spit out, froth flying from his mouth.

"Perfect," Aaron said, not backing down an inch. "Put that together with the proof I already have and you'll go straight from here to jail. You think I'd be stupid enough to come here without someone watching my back?" That he was exactly that stupid entered his mind, but he didn't flinch.

"You can't have any proof of anything," Richardson whined. "We have no connection to you."

"You are a dumb prick," Aaron told him. A savage smile bared his teeth. "Pee Pee from APRC, you are connected to Fist and Fist is connected to me." He turned to Tower, whose now purple face was contorting as he tried to unravel how he had lost control over his office with a gun in his hand. "Put that gun down or use it before I shove it up your ass, Tower."

Tower looked at Aaron's eyes, then at the gun. He lowered it. "We got nothin' to say to you, Woods."

"I'm not here to listen anyway, asshole. I've got something to say to you," Aaron said. "I'm going to bring you down. You and your goons made a big mistake coming after my family. You've been fucking with people too long, you and your fat oil and coal companies, but you're day is over now. I may die doing it, but I'm bringing you down."

Aaron took a last look at Richardson and deliberately spat on the floor. He turned around, opened the door and walked out past Miss Fitchens, standing to one side and two men who stepped back from his path to the hall.

Chapter 21

Tony reclined on a chaise lounge in the tiny but tidy back yard of his row house on Q St., N.E., a block off DuPont Circle. It was hot and sunny, Monday, July 5th, and he was luxuriating in the first two consecutive days off he had taken in months. He wanted to do nothing but rest and enjoy the comforts of home and Samuel, his partner for the past seven years, had made it his mission over the Fourth of July weekend to spoil Tony. The compelling complexities of a Thelonious Monk CD were floating out of the outdoor speakers to the sound system, a Mockingbird was jamming with Monk from the neighbor's dogwood tree, and the afternoon sun baked his bare oil lathered torso. A glass of cool Sangria rested on the flagstone terrace within easy reach.

Tony turned his head and appreciatively appraised Samuel, sitting at the round patio table that held the Sangria pitcher, working the Sunday Times crossword puzzle. He never took for granted his good fortune in having such a solid relationship with a wonderful human being. They had been introduced at a gallery on Connecticut Ave. during one of the free Thursday evening showings, when all the small, private art galleries on Connecticut are open to the public with wine and cheese and a little music. They had exchanged remarks about a particularly brutish and primitive work in oil and acrylic that reeked of sexual anger; he still shuddered when he pictured it in his mind's eye. That led to talk about other comparable works they had seen, and other galleries and other nights. They moved from gallery to gallery together and ended the evening at Teaism with lotus tea and biscuits. Talk ranged from art to more personal matters, as they discovered a rare ease of communication. Schmuel was Samuel's real name, he disclosed, a legacy of his Orthodox Jewish upbringing. Samuel revealed the fresh pain of recently coming out to his dear mother and clueless father in their very kosher Brooklyn home. Samuel was the most beautiful man Tony had ever seen. He could have modeled for classic Greek depictions of Adonis and sometimes did work as a life model. He was remarkably sensitive, composed and intelligent, without a trace of the bitterness or cynicism that infected so many in the extensive D.C. gay community. Samuel had taken his hand that evening in Teaism and suggested that they go to Tony's house. He knew right then and there that this beautiful man was going to be his lover and they would be partners forever, and here they were, their bond growing ever stronger and still exciting each other in bed.

"Samuel, I've been boring you all weekend talking about my dreary meetings, dour employees and the dramatic Mr. Woods. Now I'm refreshed and able to focus on something other than my own worn psyche, so please tell me of your adventures at Ellington." Samuel taught art for D.C. Public Schools at the selective Duke Ellington High School that specialized in the performing and graphic arts.

"Ah, dear, it's always a challenge, if not with the children then with the adults. I had one student do some beautiful work with marking pens. Unfortunately the dear girl rendered her grand visions, in three colors, of a penis and vagina on the doors to the boys and girls rest rooms, respectively. "Much more expressive than those 'Boys' and 'Girls' signs, don't you think, Mr. Liebowitz?" she said to me. I had assigned them the task of showing how art could be incorporated into everyday objects to enrich our lives. Of course I had to give her an A plus, it was marvelously done, but the administration was unmoved and suspended her for two weeks."

Tony smiled, truly relaxed for the first time since Aaron burst into his office almost two weeks ago to tell him that he had just confronted Big Ed Tower at APRC. When he had pressed Aaron for his evidence that APRC was behind the attacks on his family, he had produced a copy of a rental agreement that he said he had gotten from a car that the threatening thugs were driving. He wouldn't explain how he had obtained the original of the agreement. He had to agree with Aaron; it looked like his life could very well be in danger, but Aaron gave no sign of wanting to back off and he didn't him to do so either. He had been surprised that Aaron didn't want to have Wendy come in to the office to talk about his confrontation of Tower and Richardson, but that too he had decided to leave without further examination.

Aaron's visit had been followed shortly by a call from a very angry Big Ed, demanding that he "keep that fucking wild man away from here or I won't be responsible for what happens." Tony had, indeed, kept Aaron on the run ever since, and had even gotten a friend to let Aaron use his beach condo in Ocean City for the Fourth and today. Aaron took his boy and some hulking friend, keeping them all safely out of the way so that Tony could enjoy this respite and have a chance to evaluate the campaign. Aaron's direct confrontation with APRC turned up the pressure for him to make his own decisions. Should he stay with the NAC, dealing with the angst and complications of turning it into a vital national grassroots activist force while pressing a difficult but critically important campaign? Or should he step aside and take the plum offered by Big Ed and the energy multinationals: his very own think tank, advocating cooperative solutions to the energy and climate crisis?

He knew that the oil industries' intent was that his departure would leave the Energy and Climate Protection campaign floundering and that his new think tank would divert the public into thinking that there were going to be easy technological solutions that wouldn't require any change to the current wasteful use of energy and dumping of poisons into the atmosphere and waters of the world. Tony knew better. Changing to a less wasteful, secure, clean energy economy was not only necessary, but clearly possible with currently available technology. A combination of conservation, energy efficiency measures and building a modern rail network would reduce greenhouse gas emissions by 60% in 30 years. It would mean, however, convincing Americans that bigger was not always better, that sustainability rather than growth was the foundation for a sound economy, that rail transit should be the basis for the transportation system and economic development. The switch from concentrated sources of energy that required massive investment which only huge multinational corporations could provide to dispersed sources of energy, like solar and wind power that could be harvested and marketed on a small scale by individual investors challenged those multinational corporations in a fundamental way. All the politicians, economists and financial networks that equated economic well being with the growth of the large corporations were equally challenged and were fighting the very idea that an economy could be based instead on the well being of the eighty percent of the population who were going to bear the brunt of expensive fuel, lack of alternatives, higher food prices, increased disease, insect infestation, and severe weather events. Tony believed with all his heart that the Energy and Climate Protection campaign was a key component in getting the public to recognize the harm that was coming their way and to demand that changes be made now that would prepare the social, economic, agricultural and health infrastructure for the future.

Still, he also knew the obstacles the campaign faced. Not only the ruthless opposition of the most powerful interests in the world, but also the unwillingness of the public to consider taking action now to prevent long term harm. Any actions to reduce carbon emissions today, he knew, would only have impact on the climate thirty, fifty or a hundred years from now. History was littered with the remains of societies that failed because they were not prepared to sacrifice today to secure a future for the next generation and the ones that followed. Chances are that only the onset of more hurricanes, tornadoes, floods, droughts, epidemics, geopolitical upheaval...the list was as long as it was dreary...only then would people be ready to take decisive action. At that point they would recognize that the oil and coal corporations, and all their political servants, had been selfishly duplicitous in obscuring the true cost of inaction from the 1990's to the present. That realization would likely happen sometime in the next 20 years, Tony thought. If I can build this campaign into a real movement, that is when I will be recognized as a prophet, one of the great men of history.

"Tony," he finally heard Samuel say, obviously not for the first time. "There, I finally got your attention. You need to pull your chair back into the shade. You're turning pinkish."

"Oh, yes. I'm sorry. I just have to make some decisions about this campaign and, oh, you know how focused I get," Tony answered. He got up and moved his chaise back towards the house so that it would be in the growing shade. He propped the back up a bit more and sat back down, taking a drink from his Sangria.

Samuel stood up, folding his paper. "I certainly do know how you get, a million miles away, just the way I do when I'm working out an art problem. Take your time and work out whatever decision you need to make. I'm going in to prepare a special dinner for us tonight; a recipe from Provence that I want to try. Nothing heavy, but it should put a tingle on your tongue."

"That sounds wonderful," Tony answered, leaning back into his chaise. Samuel was a good cook and his plates showed his talent as an artist. "I'll be in and choose a wine as soon as I get this thing worked out."

Samuel patted him on the cheek as he passed him on the way inside. The kitchen was at the back of the house, just inside the door, so he could hear Samuel getting out his utensils and ingredients.

Ok, he thought, should I stick with the campaign or should I bail out? Well, if the campaign has a realistic chance of growing into a major movement, I really want to stick with it.

He enumerated the things that the campaign had going for it. First, it was a good cause and would be recognized as such eventually. Second, they were starting with a good organizational base and making it better, more motivated and action oriented. Third, Wendy was proving to be a great organizer, a demon for details who still saw the big picture, soft and sweet when it was called for and tough when that was needed. Very smart and very energetic. If he did leave NAC, he was going to have to take her with him. Fourth, Aaron Woods had a rough genius for building the bonds that led to group consensus and at motivating people to stretch themselves. He exuded an animal energy, intelligent but still primal, that drew people to him. He was someone you trusted, without question.

Ok, now for the negatives. All the organization and bonding and motivating had laid the base, but the movement would eventually fizzle without some dramatic turn of events. It was like the Civil Rights movement, whenever it would get bogged down, something would happen, like the marchers getting beaten at Edmund Pettus Bridge in Selma, or the church getting blown up in Birmingham, killing those four little girls. Unless something dramatic happens, this campaign will never get kicked up into a movement.

And then, he thought, there is Aaron Woods again. He could be as much a negative as he is a plus. He is so emotional and unpredictable; you never know what he will do next. Not only that, he really may be in danger. Without the drive, the bonding, the (he hated to say it but it was true) leadership that he provided they would have difficulty maintaining the gains they had made, to say nothing of moving forward. The NAC staff was still shaky. The transition from being policy experts and lobbyists to being organizers was going predictably. Some were doing well, some were being left behind and some had already departed. But they weren't ready to hold the volunteer organization together if Aaron were to be taken off the board.

So they needed a dramatic event and they needed Aaron Woods to keep going. Unless, he thought....no, he didn't want to think like that. But he couldn't help it, it was there and it had to be thought through. Unless, Aaron were to be...martyred! It could happen. Woods himself seemed to be trying to provoke such a reaction. Not that he would wish for such a thing, he just had to be ready in case it did happen. If it did happen and he were ready and handled it properly, then it could be just the thing to kick the campaign up to national prominence and make it a movement.

Well, Tony thought, that really makes a difference. If Aaron keeps pressing ahead and he and Wendy keep building the funding and structure of the campaign, and if something dramatic happens, like an Exxon Valdiz, then they may get the movement to the next level as a national phenomenon. Or if Aaron gets martyred, then that could be the dramatic event to galvanize a movement, if it is handled properly. So for now, he needed to keep stringing things along on their current path, put off Big Ed and his offer but don't reject them and in the meantime continue to build the NAC campaign and see if anything dramatic will happen. And, of course, make sure he was ready if something big does happen. If nothing big happens, then he will know the time when he should make the deciding call to Big Ed. He had to stay alert to any possibility to push things along and create opportunities to go in either direction. He could play the waiting game just so long.

"Tony," Samuel had opened the window and called him. "Come on in now. Give the wine time to breathe and get ready for dinner."

"Ok," he said. "I'm ready now."

Yes, he thought, *I'm ready for whatever happens.*

Chapter 22

Every day that passed since the shootout at the house on Mason Place Fist felt his rage ratchet up another notch, pushed by frustration and embarrassment. They'd been holed up for over two weeks in their safe house in Southwest Baltimore. This was the kind of neighborhood where people didn't notice you if you were standing right in front of them and even if they did notice you they would certainly have forgotten about it if anyone asked. One house in three was boarded up and only used by addicts and other squatters. Nobody talks to anybody in Southwest Baltimore. They're only there because there isn't any place else for them to go. If there was, they would be gone.

Townhouses lined all the streets, some still showing the last rags of proud dressing from the days when this was a middle class neighborhood noted for freshly scrubbed marble doorsteps and working class camaraderie. No trees graced the trash strewn streets, all victims of urban blight and municipal neglect. Rats roamed gutters and vacant lots in broad daylight. At night the rats were joined by dealers on every corner and one in the middle of each block, each jealously guarding their territory. Cars from across the city and suburbs cruised slowly, stopping at each dealer station until they found their drug of choice at a reasonable price. On the main drag, Wilkins Avenue, whores shared posts with the dealers. This drive-in one-stop vice market was the main economic engine of the neighborhood, and young people got introduced to it early, recruited as runners and holding the drugs since they would only get a juvvie conviction if they got caught. Not that there was much chance of running into a cop; they left the neighborhood when it got dark because it was too dangerous on the streets. Trouble for the vice trade came from turf disputes, or hard cases and suburban crazies who would try to rip off a dealer's stash. The six block area surrounding Wilkins west of Route 1 boasted at least one murder a month and three or four was unremarkable.

As he gained professional experience over the years, setting up a safe house had become part of Fist's preparation for a job. He always picked one in a different jurisdiction from his operating area, just in case things went wrong and he needed to disappear. This house was on a side street, a block off of Wilkins, and Fist had picked it largely because it had air conditioners in both the upstairs and downstairs windows. The owner, a small time dealer and addict temporarily in recovery, had been more than happy to take a pocketful of cash and an extended all expense paid trip out of town, turning over his keys and not asking any questions.

Fist didn't think that they'd left any evidence behind at the shootout except for bullet casings and slugs. None of their guns were traceable, and he had ditched them all at the bottom of a reservoir on the way up Rt. 29 from D.C. He had called Richardson at APRC and told him to settle up the hotel and other loose ends in D.C. He figured they'd gotten away clean except for Minton getting grazed on the side of the head and a flesh wound in the shoulder. That was the big dummy's job, to go through the doors first, and absorb any shit thrown their way. He healed up fast, and would be ready to go when he was needed.

But for two weeks they hadn't gone anywhere except to the store for papers, smokes, groceries and booze. They fixed cereal, eggs, bacon, beans and franks, or at least Minton fixed them since he was the only one who could cook anything, and got a lot of Chinese take-out and pizza. They watched the news and he did searches on his laptop every few hours, looking for any sign the heat was after them, but the story had faded after the second day even in D.C. He did his workouts and spent time on his computer in his room, Grainer cleaned his knife and his new gun endlessly at the dining table and Minton watched TV.

They were safe for now, and it wasn't like doing time, but Fist felt that Grainer and Minton were looking at him differently. And why the fuck not? He'd been suckered in by a gray haired do gooder and some ditzy broad. They had walked right in to a house full of hop-head dealers who must have figured that some other crew had come to off them and swipe their stash. They probably still thought that, and according to the papers and TV reports, that's what the cops thought, too. He knew he had hit one of the bastards, Grainer said he got two and Minton claimed one, although the news only reported one dead and two wounded. What a fucked up mess. They had barely gotten to their car at the end of the alley behind the house and out of the neighborhood before the cops closed up the streets. Must have had four cruisers roar by them with lights and sirens going when they turned onto Maryland Ave. and headed out of town.

It was six in the morning and he had been awake for at least two hours. Enough was enough. He was going to move before they all went crazy. The heat had probably forgotten about them now. They didn't really care about drug gang banging as long as bystanders didn't get killed. He called Tower, woke him up and told him to be in his office at noon and wait for them there. Fat shit tried to tell him to stay away and meet him somewhere else, but Fist hung up on him. One fuck up and now no one was giving him respect. He was going to mess up that Woods real good, had to or he was dead meat himself. The bastards that had paid him to do their dirty work for the past ten years would turn on him in a minute if they thought he was getting weak or could turn into a liability. They might even give Grainer or Minton a call; give them the word to put a slug in the back of his head when he was asleep or even if he just turned his back. Hell, they may have gotten the word already, or have some kind of arrangement set up long ago. Breaker and his pals wouldn't have any second thoughts about getting rid of him. In fact now that he thought about it, he was sure they had a plan in place to do just that. The question was not if, but when they would do it and now might just be the time.

The boys had plenty of guns. He'd stocked up the safe house before they started the operation, just in case. Now he was sorry that he'd given them to the boys already. Should have held on to them until it was time to go into action. Once he got this mess cleaned up and wiped out the asshole that had started all this trouble and made him look bad, he'd have to deal Grainer and Minton out, too. Get a new crew.

214

That thought raised his anger another notch. What a waste! These were the best guys he had ever put together, his team, the only team he had ever been a part of. Now, because of that lying Woods and that dumb prick Richardson, who had passed the word on from his bitch, setting up the ambush, he was going to have to wipe this team out and start all over. And in the meantime he had to watch his back every second to be sure they didn't off him first. He was going to smash that fucking Woods up good, piece by piece, until he begged for a bullet. He may just take out the bitch and that prick, Richardson, too, just to feel their bones and flesh break and tear under his hands.

Fist knew his anger was getting in the way of thinking straight, but he didn't give a damn. Rage was the engine that drove him to where he was today. He channeled it, but he didn't try to control it or tamp it down. The combination of the power of his rage, the sharpness of his brain and the hardness of his fists had overcome every obstacle that he'd faced since his old man started beating him up as a scrawny kid. Now it would blow away this new old man, this bastard that had been setting traps for him and making him look like a stupid kid again. And it would blow away anything and anyone who got in his way.

When he pushed open the door to Tower's office just after noon Fist was glad to see that Richardson was there along with the fat bastard sitting behind his desk. How he hated these white bitches with their fancy clothes and big offices, thinking they were the kings of the world. They weren't shit. They ripped off more people than any mugger ever dreamed of and their poison spread all over the world, killing off people every minute. They thought he was stupid, but they were the dumb bastards, never suspecting that he could do the research and see what pollution and global warming was all about. They took him for just a dumb nigger, but now they were his niggers. He liked the way they popped out of their chairs when they saw him come in the room, the way they didn't say anything until he did.

Fist walked over to Richardson and jabbed him in the chest with his finger, knocking him back a step with each jab. "You set me up." Jab. "You stupid bitch." Jab.

"No!" Richardson whined. When the back of his knees hit the coffee table he scurried around it out of reach. "I just told you what she told me. I had no way of knowing."

Fist took another step towards him and Richardson flinched back against the sofa. "That's what I said. You set me up by being stupid." He turned to Tower. "I had enough of this shit. I been goin' slow because some people didn't want to ruffle any feathers in this town. Fuck that. I'm gonna end this game, now. What do you know about Woods? Is he in town?"

"Fist, we've done everything we could to help you," Tower said, trying for a reasonable tone. "Everything you asked. That's what I told your, uh, the people who sent you here to do this job. They were surprised when I told them that I'd paid you a hundred grand and put another one fifty on account for you. 'We pay him plenty. We don't know anything about you paying him,' they told me."

Fist took that in, cocking his head to one side. "So, you want to know why you gotta pay me extra," he said in a flat tone. He stepped over to the desk. "Well, here's why." He leaned forward, left hand on the desk and the other in front of him in a fist. "You pay extra, you cocksucker, because I can barely stand to see you without putting my fist right through your head. 'Cause you make me sick with all your pretty clothes and big offices and fancy cunt secretaries. 'Cause you're pussies who wouldn't last a minute in a fight, but play tough guy, all show and no go. So just to keep me from cutting you from your ass up to your eyes, you pay me whatever I say. Now, and for the last time, what do you know about where Woods is."

"I know right where he is and where he's going to be," Big Ed said.

Curiously he was calmer now. Fist could see that he had lost a lot of his menace with Tower. That damn Woods, he thought. He has them all disrespecting at me.

Tower continued. "I got my information from my own source at Natural America. Right from the top. Tomorrow night Woods is speaking at the Charles Sumner School, downtown. The meeting's scheduled to end at 9:00, but he figured that they would stay until after 10:00, so Woods won't be getting home until 10:30 or so. He's staying right back in his house, but there's a private guard there now, front and back. I'm not sure who is paying for that, but the house is sewed up tight. My guy at NAC told me that, but he didn't say anything about any bodyguards on Woods when he's running around town, going to meetings and going home."

"This better be the straight scoop," Fist snarled. "Because if it isn't, I'm coming back for both of you. You got that?" He looked first at Tower, who nodded back, not saying anything. Then he turned to Richardson, who looked down at his hand, rubbing his chest where Fist's finger had poked him.

"We got it," Perry said quickly when he felt Fist's eyes on him.

Fist walked out the door. Oh yeah, he thought as he went through Miss Fitchens' office, where Grainer and Minton had been waiting. After I take care of Woods, those two are going down.

Chapter 23

Aaron didn't even notice the drizzle as he wearily walked home from the Metro stop at Union Station. After months of talking he was sick of hearing his own voice enlisting people in activism for a better future, tired of hearing the same stale objections and excuses from people about why they couldn't keep a picket line going or get their church or school involved. Tonight's meeting at the Charles Sumner School had brought together the directors of twenty six environmental groups that had their headquarters in D.C. Astonishingly, this was the first time that an attempt had been made to gather the directors in one place to collaborate on climate change, the most important issue of the century! They all saw the issue the same way he did, they all acknowledged that their work would be devastated by the effects of climate change over the coming decades, but they still came up with multiple reasons why they couldn't work in concert on this campaign and no ideas on how they could. It had taken all his skills to bring about agreement to form a coalition that would look for ways they could pool resources, but there was no real sense of urgency or bond of trust among these intelligent and well meaning people. The professionals were harder to get motivated and organized than the ordinary everyday folks whose first priorities were their kids and mortgages. Aaron concluded that it all came down to them having to compete for funding from the same sources. If they joined together it could affect their ability to survive independently. Careers would change, maybe even be lost and that was very threatening. Besides that, they were all preoccupied with the election that was going on and they were afraid that if they put their energies into climate change it wouldn't "resonate with the electorate."

They weren't wrong, of course. It was going to be a long, slow process to get good people across the country to elevate the slow motion disaster of climate change to an issue of immediate importance, especially with the oil war in Iraq turning sour. He thought of the election as an opportunity to tie the increasingly problematic war with the need to reduce oil use, while these careerists felt it was better to focus on the short term objective of electing the more environmentally enlightened challenger. The debate over matters that had a lot more to do with organizational survival than building a viable movement for cultural change had dragged on until almost 11:00, when the janitor had finally thrown them out.

Aaron was more convinced than ever that the best way to get The Movement going was to go straight to the people, bypassing the mass of environmental interest groups. When the oil got scarcer and the industry jacked up their prices for it then people would start to get concerned about conservation and having alternatives to oil and coal. When people were stuck out in suburbia and had to choose between gas for their SUV's or beer they'd be wondering why their government hadn't been preparing for this. That wasn't likely to happen before the election, however, and unless something else came along that would capture the attention of the public, he figured they should write the election off and focus on long term cultural change. Still, Tony and Wendy both wanted to at least keep the doors open to engaging additional resources for the cultural campaign, and they knew more about these political dealings than he did, so he had done his best tonight to build the needed collegiality.

A wild storm had raged outside while they had been in the meeting, and the streets were wet and filled with trash and debris from the trees. The rain had stopped except for occasional drops and gusty winds of heavy air howled and swirled through the expanse of Columbia Circle in front of Union Station. Thunder rumbled in the distance, and lightening flashes lit up the western sky on the Virginia side of the Potomac, portending more heavy storms. Aaron barely noticed, but did momentarily become aware of the unlit heavy metal three-cell flashlight in his hand. Wendy had given it to him after the meeting.

"Here, I wanted you to have this," she had told him as they were leaving to catch their separate Metro trains. "I worry about you walking around at night."

He'd been surprised but truly grateful despite knowing he'd just take it home and leave it there. He was just happy that she was thinking about him. They were gradually getting past their awkwardness, he thought, one ray of light in the evening. Maybe I'll get another chance. Then his thoughts returned to gloomy review of the unproductive discussions at the meeting. His feet automatically followed the route home, past the Thurgood Marshall Building, left down 2nd St. and crossing over at E.

He was too preoccupied to enjoy the varied colors of the old row houses as he passed them on the next two blocks, or the swaying of the trees against the thick clouds in the dark sky. He barely noticed a figure coming from the right down 4th St. to intersect with him at E, automatically registering that it was a big man, huffing and puffing, dark clothes, some kind of hat. You automatically saw those things when walking in the city at night, but he wasn't really paying attention.

Just as he came to the corner he felt a crawling of the skin on his neck, his ear twitching. He jerked his head up and really looked at the guy who was now just five feet away and closing.

"This guy is locked in on me," flashed through his head, but the guy quickly grabbed his right arm just above the wrist, pushing and twisting it at the same time to get it up behind his back..

Aaron automatically stepped back with his right foot and then forward with his left, keeping himself face to face with the attacker. He knew who it was now, and that this was about survival, not a mugging. He pivoted, pushing off his left toes, turning his hips and whipping his left hand, wrist cocked, up into the right side of the big guy's head right in front of the ear.

Over the years since his days of club fighting in college, hitting the heavy bag had been one of his favorite workouts. "Expressing his aggression" he called it. Never in his life had he thrown a better punch than the left hook he unleashed at that moment.

"Unnh" he grunted, the sound coming from an animal place deep in the back of his brain controlled by instinct, not thought. His fist connected like a hammer hitting a steer on the head at the slaughter house, every muscle and ounce of weight in the left side of his body behind it. Only then did he realize that the flashlight was in that hand. The force of the blow jerked the massive head left as his hand continued through its arc.

"Sshhuhh!" the mugger said, his hold on Aaron's right arm loosening and his body going slack as the air seemed to leak out of him.

Aaron continued his turn and pulled his right arm free, feeling the rush of joy that combat brings to some men, but at the same instant he saw more figures rushing up from behind him on E. St. What looked like a black leather sock, but stiff, come whistling down as they got to him. But the blackjack missed him as he continued his turn and it hit the shoulder of the first guy, who was now falling between him and the others. He desperately pushed the bulk of the first attacker away and regained his balance.

"You," he thought or yelled, he didn't know which. He saw it was Fist and Grainer that had rushed up and he knew this was his time to die. It was happening fast but the seconds seemed to stretch endlessly

The big guy fell like a pole axed ox into Fist and Grainer as Aaron yanked himself away, stumbled once and started to run. He headed up 4th towards Massachusetts Ave. where people would be, sprinting for the first time in a decade, pumping arms and legs as hard and fast as he could. He heard them scrambling, cursing behind him.

He got maybe eight steps.

"Pop!" A gun went off. Fire ripped through his right leg and he found himself thrown to his left onto the front fender of a Ford Explorer.

"Pop, pop!" The right side front window on the Ford exploded right behind him. Glass fragments stung his left hand and the back of his neck.

"Whoo, woo, whoo, woo," the car alarm went off and he turned back as Fist and Grainer closed on him. The huge guy was still back on the corner, slower to get up from where they had been tangled but coming to his hands and knees.

Aaron threw himself at them. Fist was in front and Aaron bulled right into him, getting into his chest with his head and pumping his fists into his belly and groin. The blackjack thudded his back, shoulders, neck and head like a hammer, but he kept his face buried in Fist's chest so that Fist couldn't get a full blow. Grainer was trying to get around behind Aaron to get in a final shot with his gun, but he was blocked first by Fist between them and then by the Explorer as Fist gradually pushed Aaron back up against it. They were locked together, grunting and hammering. When Fist tried to step back so he could get a full swing with his blackjack, Aaron pressed forward, keeping his face pressed to Fist's chest. His nose was filled with the heavy smell of testosterone laced sweat coming off both of them like two stags he had once seen fighting for dominance over female elk.

Finally the blackjack hit a nerve, taking away control of his legs and Aaron went to his knees on the sidewalk, clutching at Fist's legs. Fist swung the blackjack more freely, driving Aaron flat but still impeding Grainer from getting a shot. Grainer tried to push past Fist but only succeeded in hindering some of the force of his blows with the blackjack as Fist pushed him back.

"Motherfucker! You gonna hurt. Fuck wi' me. Die." Fist's words burst out with each explosive breath as he changed from the blackjack to kicking at Aaron who was curled into a tight ball now.

"Get back! Get back, Fist! Gimme a shot! We gotta get outta here!" Grainer's voice was a small sound behind Fist's chant, somewhere behind the pain, behind the foot pounding into him, behind the sound of the car alarm.

Then he didn't hear Grainer any more.

"What the fuck," he heard Fist say from way above him, as the foot stopped breaking his ribs.

He couldn't see. Pain was everywhere. Aaron uncoiled his balled up body, felt the broken ends of ribs grating and pushing into him, inside. He didn't care. He had one thought. One more shot at the bastard before I die. He reached up and grabbed at Fist's crotch. Fist had twisted to see something. Something else was going on, but Aaron's being was focused on pulling himself up, feet scrabbling to get under him.

The Explorer horn was going now. "Honk, honk, honk," pause, "honk, honk, honk."

Fist twisted back to him, but Aaron had gotten his legs under himself and now he grabbed both of Fist's legs with his arms and drove forward with his legs, using all the pain and force of life that was left in him. He didn't even feel Fist pounding with the blackjack in one hand while he tried to grab hold on Aaron's shoulders, head or back with the other.

Fist went over onto his back, tripping over Grainer who was flat on his stomach right behind Fist. Aaron was dimly aware of Grainer as a lump on the ground. His humanity was gone. He was an animal now, exalting in rage and death. He clawed up with hands and teeth, going for Fist's throat. Every cell was focused on ripping that throat out, every fiber of his being hungry for the blood of his enemy.

It wasn't enough. Fist was stronger and younger. He turned them over so Aaron was under him. The blackjack came down and Aaron's last thought was, "Not enough." Then his head exploded and the world went from red to white and he was gone.

Chapter 24

When Squeak alerted Antelope that Aaron would be coming home late that evening they agreed they should wait for him at Union Station; follow and keep watch over him until he got home. They didn't want to make it obvious, grabbing him as he got out of the Metro and escorting him the rest of the way, because that would just piss him off and who knows what reckless stuff he might do then. Gray wasn't so sharp and watchful these days, since the shootout on Mason. They all agreed that Fist, or someone just like him, would be back sooner or later, but there hadn't been any sign of the hoods and it seemed to Squeak like Gray was deliberately being reckless, like he was daring those hoods to come back and kick his ass. He was running all over to meetings and rallies at all hours of day and night doing his save the world stuff. Ok, that's just what he did and it was understandable, but he refused to have anyone go around with him and offer protection, despite the NAC offer to provide security. He had only agreed to have security on the house, where he tried to keep Squeak penned up as much as possible. Squeak didn't doubt that Gray would find a way to get his movement going, but he would have to stay alive to do it. Those crazy bastards were going to try to get at Gray and this time it would be for keeps because of the way he and Gray had fucked them up in the mountains and tricked them into the shootout with the Mason Place crew.

Gray didn't have any sense of fear like normal people with good sense anyway. That was one reason he had cred on the street, part of why people looked up to him, including Squeak. He was a big, tough guy, and he never quit until he won, so people just felt that they would be safe following his lead. But Squeak knew that on the street it didn't matter how tough or strong you were. Anyone could get killed if they weren't careful and Gray was never careful. Ordinarily that was cool, but not now.

He and Antelope had agreed to do what they could to keep an eye out on Gray as much as possible. If they were careful maybe they would catch sight of anyone who looked like they might be going to jump him. Tonight wasn't the first time they had waited for him to come up from the Metro, and they had worked out a routine. From where they watched at the bus stand on Columbia Circle they blended in with people waiting for busses, even at that late hour. They had a clear view of both the front entrance of Union Station and the side where the Metro let out directly to the sidewalk.

When Aaron came up from the Metro and headed across the front of Union Station towards home they started to follow but then Fist and Grainer came out onto the sidewalk from the Metro escalator and they held back. The big dude, wearing that dorky brim hat, came out of the little alcove at the front corner of Union Station and met up with Fist and Grainer. The three of them talked for a minute then the hat dude took off fast, crossing over to Columbia Circle and up Massachusetts Avenue, parallel to the route Gray was taking home. He was hustling; huffing and puffing, arms pumping and shoulders rolling with every step. That big guy wasn't meant for moving fast, Squeak thought.

"He's trying to circle ahead of Aaron," Antelope said.

Squeak had already figured that out, but he didn't say anything. They moved in behind Fist and Grainer, who took off slower, following directly after Aaron but staying a good ways back. Squeak spread out to the left and Antelope to the right, as they left the cover of Union Station and crossed 2nd St. to the Thurgood Marshall Justice Center. The area in front of the Center was wide open and he could see Aaron just turning left at the end of the building to go east on E St. The big guy in the hat had stayed up on Mass. and was working hard, heading toward D.

Probably going down D St. to get ahead of Gray, Squeak thought. *Got to think this out. What's going to be their move?*

224

Then it came to him. Just like Gray had done to him the last time they played chess. The hat dude was a Knight and would go up a couple of blocks east on D and then cut back north to E St. Grainer and Fist were the Queen and Rook. They'd go up E behind Gray and trap him on the corner of 4th or 5th. Check and fucking mate.

He started running to the left, cutting behind Thurgood Marshall and, leaving Antelope to keep tailing them all. This was familiar territory. He got to 2nd just in time to see Gray cross and head east on E. He stayed hidden until Fist and Grainer crossed, following Aaron up the right side of E and then ducked across 2nd himself and raced east on the alley between E and F. He moved silently through the deep darkness of the alley screened from the view of Gray, Fist and Grainer by the solid wall of row houses on the north side of E. As he crossed 3rd he saw Antelope cross on the right side of E, laying behind Fist and using the trees and cars to hide his bulky frame. Antelope was solid. He'd be there when the shit hit the fan. Squeak started racing now. He had to get to 4th and E in time. He was betting that was where they were going to checkmate Gray.

As he cut around the corner of the alley onto 4th Squeak picked up a brick from the house where they were putting in a new brick sidewalk. He already had his blade out in his left hand, open and ready. It was a short folding survival knife Gray had given him to use in the woods. He was scared, and could feel his heart pounding to get out of his chest. He cursed himself under his breath.

"You little punk, you're nothin' but tough talk. You tell Gray you know the streets and can handle yourself. Now he's gonna need you and you're scared shitless. You gonna just be a worthless little shit and watch him die? You gonna be a man when it counts?"

He got to the corner of 4th and E at the same time as Gray did on the opposite side. Suddenly it started. Squeak was right across the street, but he froze. He started to cry. The hat dude appeared, running down 4th just the way he had predicted. He grabbed Gray and the other two came rushing up behind. Somehow, though, Gray whipped around and blasted the big dude with his left hand. They all fell in a heap but Gray got his feet under him first and started to pull away up 4th. It was happening too fast, faster than he could think and his feet were stuck to the sidewalk.

Then he heard the shots, "Pop, pop, pop," and saw Gray fall against the Explorer. The car alarm started blasting out and he found his feet moving. He was running across the street, still crying but not thinking about that, not thinking at all.

Antelope got to the corner just before him and clubbed the hat dude who was trying to get up on the arm with the pipe he carried around. Squeak saw a gun clatter to the sidewalk as he flew past them like a shadow to where Gray, Fist and Grainer were in a grunting, heaving knot: Gray was backed against the car with Fist pounding him and Grainer trying to get a shot past Fist. One, two, three steps and he came up behind Grainer and whipped the brick up and out with every bit of his strength and the momentum of his speed. He caught Grainer right in the temple with the end of the brick, right where dudes said you needed to get someone if you were in a fight to the death. Grainer dropped to one knee and Squeak set his feet and swung again. Thud. A solid hit on the back of the head.

Grainer dropped, but not straight down. Fist and Aaron's struggling pushed him into Squeak as he fell and Squeak went down with him. He dropped the brick. Fist fell backwards over them, and Aaron came right after him, both of them snarling and growling worse than two pit bulls in a dog fight. Gray was on top for a minute and Squeak struggled to pull out from under Grainer, stabbing at him with the knife and pushing with his other hand.

He pulled his legs loose and stood up, tears still streaming and gasping for air. Fist and Gray were locked together right next to him. Fist was on top now and he raised his arm up high and took a big swing with a blackjack. Squeak went right in over Fist's shoulder with the knife as the blackjack came down and crunched into Gray's head with a sound like a watermelon breaking open. At the same time his razor sharp four inch blade sunk into Fist's neck, right up to the hilt. Blood spurted into Squeak's eyes, blurring his vision. Fist turned towards him with his eyes and mouth wide in surprise.

Fist swept him away with an arm, knocking Squeak over Grainer's still form and into the Explorer. Squeak bounced off the car and onto the ground while Fist got to one knee and pulled out a gun. Then "Whop," Antelope came out of nowhere and clubbed him down with the pipe, the elbow joint of the turnbuckle crushing Fist's cheek and dropping him to the ground. Antelope swung again, smashing the pipe into Fist's head. Fist stopped moving.

Nobody moved, for five, ten seconds. The Explorer alarm stopped honking and whooing, and Squeak could hear sirens in the distance. He pulled himself up to his knees. Antelope rolled Fist off of Aaron, where he had fallen. Both lifeless bodies were covered in blood, limbs awkward and limp, no sign of breathing.

"He's dead." Squeak's voice was broken, high and ragged. "I couldn't do it. I tried. I wasn't big enough or fast enough. They killed him."

Tears running, nose running, Squeak crawled over to Aaron, reached his arms around him and put his head on down on his chest.

"No, no, no. Now what? I'm back on the shit heap where I belong." He groaned.

"Whoa, Squeak! You did good, man." Antelope's voice rasped, his chest heaving. He wiped the length of pipe with his shirt and threw it into a front yard three doors up the street. Then he reached down and pulled the knife out of Fist's neck. He wiped that off, too, and threw it into another yard.

Squeak felt Antelope's big hand on his shoulder.

Then, "Wait a minute, Squeak. Aaron ain't dead. Look at his lips."

Squeak picked up his head and looked, "What? What?"

Gray's lips moved, just a little. Squeak got up and tore at his pockets. "Shit, shit, shit," he spit out as he yanked out his cell phone, flipped it open and dialed 911.

"Send an ambulance to Fourth and E Street, North East, right now," he screamed into the phone when he heard an answer. "Shut up! Aaron Woods been shot and smashed up and he's dying. Don't you let my dad die. Fourth and E Street right now. Don't ask questions. You got that ambulance coming? Just tell me you got the ambulance coming, goddammit. Ok. Fourth and E Street North East right now."

He shut the phone and dropped down and grabbed Aaron's shoulders.

"They're coming. They're coming. Don't you die on me, Gray. You stay with me. You're my dad. You gotta stay with me." Squeak wasn't crying now. He had to tell Aaron the way it was going to be. He focused on willing his own life and energy and strength into his battered protector, barely registering the rising scream of the fast approaching cop cars.

With sirens blowing, lights flashing, one MPD car came up E St. then another came down 4th. The cops started yelling at Antelope, who was the only one standing.

"Put your hands up and step away." They had their guns pointed at him and Squeak heard a shrill edge in their voices. Fucking cops! They were all yelling and edging around Antelope, him and the three still bodies next to the Explorer. One cop stayed at the corner of 4th and E, watching over the big guy whose brim hat was lying in the gutter. He was coming around and the cops didn't know who was a good guy and who was a bad guy. Two white guys down, two black guys down. A kid on one of the white guys on the ground. One black guy standing over them, with his hands up now.

"Call an ambulance right now," Antelope said clearly as he kept his hands

227

high and backed away from his buddies on the ground. "Don't hurt the kid. These three jumped the kid and his dad. His dad's hurt bad. Get an ambulance."

"Shut up," one cop screamed three, four times. Round, smooth face. Young guy, scared and new on the beat.

His partner, a Sergeant, gray whiskers showing against his brown chin, stepped closer and said more calmly, "Ok, let's take it easy now. There's a kid here. You," he indicated Antelope, "lie face down, hands behind your head and spread your legs."

Antelope knelt and then lay on his face on the ground, moving carefully and slowly.

"Get my dad to the hospital," Squeak said to the sergeant, speaking clearly, firmly, man to man.

"That one's your dad?" Sergeant Pendleton was skeptical. "Are you ok, kid? You need to step away from him."

Squeak didn't move. He just turned back to Aaron, talking to him, telling him to hold on.

"Get on the radio," Pendleton told his young partner. "We need three ambulances. We need more backup and we need a detective here, Code 10. Go do it. We got this covered."

Squeak watched as the young patrolman moved to the car, moving quicker but keeping an eye on the scene. He was just starting to take it in himself. Blood everywhere, all over him. Big pool of blood under Fist. Big guy groggy and sitting up on the corner. He was huge! Antelope lying face down, hands behind his neck, not moving. The young cop, face pale and steps disjointed as he took the scene in; but he got to the car and started calling.

"We got 'em coming, kid," Pendleton told Squeak. He started to sort things out. "Frisk your guy over there and keep an eye on him," he told the patrolman from the other car who was watching the guy on the corner. "Sixteen years on patrol and I never saw nothin' like this."

Squeak only knew he wasn't going to be separated from his father. He had another chance and he wasn't going to let Gray down.

Chapter 25

Wendy had just pulled off her wet clothes and plopped face down on the bed when the shrill ring of the phone cut through the thunder crashing outside. She'd had another long day of calling NAC leaders and visiting with staff: pushing, pulling, prodding, pleading and pandering to get more action going on the boycott campaign. Then the meeting tonight with the assembled directors of the other major, and some minor, non profit environmental groups had gone on forever. That goddam Aaron, she thought admiringly, he could herd chickens through a dog pound. He looked tired as hell, and every now and then she detected a look of angry impatience cross his face as the assembled environmental leaders strayed "from how to win to why it will be hard," as he put it, but he had managed to keep them moving in the right direction without ruffling too many feathers. Tony was a big help and she felt she had done her part, but Aaron just had that knack. When she gave him the flashlight after the meeting she considered asking him to have a drink, maybe get their thing going again, but she decided they were both just too tired and it could wait for another day.

"What?" she groaned out, after fumbling the phone off its cradle.

"This is Kenya. I'm at the hospital. Gray's busted up. There's cops here and Doctors. Look, I need you to come here. Now. I think he's dying." Squeak's words tumbled out fast, and urgently, his voice barely controlled.

Wendy sat up and swung her feet around to the floor. She got up and started to pick up the clothes that she had just taken off, but dropped them when she felt how wet they were. She stopped and put her free hand to her head for a moment, forcing herself back from the threshold of sleep.

"What? Squeak, that's you? My God, what happened?" She stepped to the dresser, pulled open the drawer to get clean jeans and a tee shirt, but there weren't any there.

Squeak started to tell her about the attack but she cut him off. "Never mind, I'm coming. What hospital are you at?"

"Washington Hospital Center. Wait a minute." She heard him asking someone a question. "Neurosurgery, the waiting room. They're going to operate. I need help."

"Ok, Squeak. I'm on my way. I'll be there in ten or fifteen minutes." She pulled some dirty jeans out of her hamper and struggled to get into them with one hand.

"Good. Hurry," he said and closed the connection.

She ran every light, blew past every stop sign and broke every speed limit on the way to the hospital, pushing the jeep through its paces. One storm ended but then another rushed in with a crash of thunder. Lightening bolts seemed to be trying to spear her from above and cold water streamed through the tattered canvas top and plastic windows. Adrenalin and anxiety had erased her tiredness. When she pulled into the hospital parking garage, out of the wind and rain, she felt like a primitive cave dweller escaping the wrath of angry gods.

She raced down the hospital corridors, stopping only to check the directional signs to neurosurgery. Her wet, uncombed hair, tightly drawn brows, clenched teeth, shallow, explosive breaths and haphazardly buttoned shirt all bespoke the kind of crisis all too familiar in the hospital but with which even the most experienced night shift staff avoided contact. Finally, cursing after two wrong turns, Wendy charged around the corner and burst into the neurosurgery waiting room.

"Squeak," she cried out as she saw him sitting in a chair next to a heavy, dark man in a rumpled brown suit. Squeak jumped out of the chair as she ran to him and they hugged, neither of them able to speak but both gaining composure and comfort. For a moment, just a second or two, she felt Squeak shudder as a sob was wrenched from deep in his chest. But then he firmly pushed back from her and brusquely wiped his hands across his eyes, pushing away his tears.

"Squeak, my God, you've got blood all over you. Tell me what happened." Wendy reached out and touched the side of his face.

"Look, I'll tell you it all. But now I need you to help me here." Squeak took hold of her hand resting on his face, lowered it and held it in his. He turned to the suited man still sitting in the waiting room chair. "This is Detective Sowonga. You got to tell him who I am and talk to the nurses and doctors. Tell them Aaron is my dad and who we are. And don't call me Squeak no more."

Wendy looked at the detective. He had a wide face, dark, almost purple black folds of skin, receding hair in a brushy, natural cut, a broad nose with wide nostrils, thick purplish lips. He observed her calmly through large eyes under drooping lids, thick, permanently etched circles underneath speaking of permanent weariness from seeing too much of life's underside. He afforded her a small smile as he unhurriedly stood and took his badge holder out of the left outside pocket of his brown suit coat and flipped it open to briefly show her his badge.

"Good evening. I'm Detective Sowonga of the Metropolitan Police Department. Could you give me your name and show me some identification, please?" His voice was deep, weary, commanding but not unpleasant, a slight African accent adding melodious cadence. She felt an instinctive trust for him, but remained cautious, wary about talking to the police.

"Um, yes. I'm Wendy Sparks." She fumbled open the flap of the handbag that was hanging from her shoulder, pulled out her wallet, opened it to the plastic window that showed her driver's license and handed it to him. As he took it, she added, "I'm a friend and colleague of Aaron Woods. And this is his son. Anyway this is Squea…uh, I mean Kenya. Woods. Uh, Aaron's other son, his real son, I mean his natural son, his other son is grown and lives in Zurich. Uh, Switzerland."

"Ahh, that Zurich," Sowonga said, keeping his slight smile and handing back her wallet. "Please, Miss Sparks is it? Please sit down." He indicated a chair in the row across from and facing the one in which he had been sitting. She sat and Kenya sat next to her, holding her hand again. Sowonga eased his considerable bulk back into his chair and took out a notebook and pen. He opened the notebook and wrote what Wendy presumed was her name and other identification particulars. He was unhurried, not speaking until he was finished.

"Now, Miss Sparks, I understand you are under considerable stress. The doctor told me and young Kenya here that he would be back as soon as possible. He asked Kenya to call an adult member of the family or friend, and he did so, calling you. The doctor will fill you in on Aaron Woods' condition when he returns. He had already been in surgery for an hour or so before I got here. Now in the meantime, Miss Sparks, I would like to ask you some questions. I am the responding detective. The crime scene was very confusing. One dead man, three badly injured. And young Mr. Kenya Woods was there along with a Mr...." he paused and flipped back a page in his notebook, "Mr. Carleton Antelope."

"Antelope!" Wendy blurted out. "Is he ok? He's Aaron's best friend. He's a neighbor."

"Mr. Antelope seemed to be unharmed when I last saw him," Sowonga said after making another note. "He also says he is a neighbor who was just on his way to the corner grocery to get a lottery ticket when he chanced on the scene and came to the aid of Mr. Woods and his son. He was curiously unaware that the grocery closed at 10:00 and he was over an hour late."

"Where is Antelope? He should be here, too," Wendy interrupted.

"They took him in. The cops took him to jail," Kenya blurted. "I tole you he was our friend," he directed at the detective.

"He's just being questioned," Sowonga said mildly, directing his comment to Kenya and then turning his eyes back to Wendy. "We're just trying to get this sorted out. Now what can you tell me about the other three men?"

"It was Fist and Grainer," Kenya interjected. He was working hard to keep himself under control. "Same ones that been after us since summer. I don't know the other guy, the big guy in the hat, but he was with them. They jumped us and tried to kill us. Me and Gray, Aaron, my dad."

Sowonga gave Wendy a questioning look, but didn't say anything. He was the best detective in the District because he knew how to listen. People wanted to tell him things.

"Them," Wendy said, shaking her head. "This is...it's preposterous. They tried to kill him to stop the campaign? Aaron said that they would stop at nothing to keep people from seeing what they were doing. Oh, God. I've never been involved in anything like this." She reached into her handbag again, replacing her wallet and taking out some tissues to wipe the tears that started to run down her cheeks. She felt Kenya give her hand a reassuring squeeze.

"Ok, Miss Sparks. Now I need you to tell me why these people would want to kill Mr. Woods. Who are they and what have they been doing that they want to keep a secret."

Wendy nodded, sat straighter and took a deep breath. "Ok, these guys, Fist and Grainer and I guess the other guy, are hoods. They've been hired by the big oil and coal companies to stop our campaign against them. They, the oil and coal companies, are responsible for dumping poison gasses in the air that are killing people and causing climate change. Aaron was working with us; I'm the campaign director for the Natural America Club. We're trying to get a national grassroots campaign started to make people aware of the harm they were doing, the oil and coal companies, and to hold them responsible. He was having some success, not a lot, but he told us that they have been threatening him and trying to stop him. I... I didn't believe him at first. I thought he was just being paranoid. He was really just getting things going, but I guess they didn't want to take the chance. He reported them to the police, you know, when they broke into his house and hurt, ah, Kenya."

Sowonga leaned back and just looked at her for a minute. "Well, now," he finally said. "This sounds very interesting. You are going to have to go back to the start and fill me in. Climate change. You're talking about global warming, aren't you? Well, you're going to have to help me understand all this."

The doors to the operating rooms burst open just then and a thin man in surgical scrubs came out, pulling his mask down under his chin. He had a narrow face with sallow skin, a great sword of a nose, dark bushy eyebrows and mustache.

"I'm Dr. Paravizian, the neurosurgeon. Are you a relative of Aaron Woods?" he asked Wendy.

"No, I'm his friend," Wendy said. "His son is in Europe, his grown son. Kenya is his only family that is here in D.C. How is he?"

"Is he going to live?" Kenya said. He was standing as though expecting a punch that he couldn't avoid.

"He's alive," Paravizian said. "He's lucky to be alive and it is going to be touch and go. Come, let's sit and I'll give you what I can."

They all sat down, Paravizian next to Detective Sowonga with an empty seat between them, and facing Wendy and Kenya. Kenya had taken Wendy's hand again.

"Here's what we've got," the doctor told them. His voice was serious but calm. "Blood loss and shock trauma had dropped his blood pressure drastically. When we brought the blood pressure back up we got swelling in his brain and spinal cord. We put a shunt in his skull to drain fluids off his brain and repaired the fracture in his skull. One lung has been punctured by the broken ends of two ribs, and Dr. Cooper, our thoracic surgeon is operating now to stop the internal bleeding. There are contusions to his spleen, kidneys and liver, I don't know what else. The bullet that went through his right leg miraculously didn't hit an artery, but it left a big hole at the front of his thigh when it exited. His left clavicle and wrist are broken, and so is one cheekbone, his jaw and nose. Half his left ear was torn off."

He paused, "We've done what we can for now. He has a fighting chance. He must be pretty tough to even be alive now. We won't know about permanent damage until the swelling goes down in his brain, but you should prepare yourself that if he lives he could have brain damage and maybe some paralysis. He was unconscious when he came in, and we will keep him in a coma until the brain swelling goes down. We're good at what we do and we're doing all we can, but you need to prepare yourselves for the worst. His injuries are grievous."

"What can we do?" Wendy asked for herself and Kenya.

"Just be there for him. Pray if you pray," the doctor said, rising. They all rose with him.

"I won't leave here until he does," Kenya said. "I'll be here for him. He's been there for me, the only one who ever was."

Wendy felt a powerful urge to protect and support the boy and put her arm around him.

When he was moved out of the operating room and onto the intensive care ward Aaron was hardly recognizable. Machines kept his breathing steady and monitored all his bodily function. Tubes snaked in and out of him, including the shunt into his brain. He had seams of stitches on his scalp, where much of his hair had been shaved away, and his skin was pale and gray where it wasn't bruised purple and yellow or covered by bandages. In three days he had two operations to deal with internal bleeding in his chest and abdomen, remove bone splinters and set his ribs. They found another one fractured, making three broken ribs. The lack of improvement increasingly concerned Doctor Paravizian, who was the primary physician, and his daily warnings to keep expectations down depressed all of them except Kenya, who steadfastly refused to acknowledge that Aaron might not recover. He not only insisted that he no longer be called Squeak, but he no longer called Aaron "Gray." Ted had flown in on the second day, taking charge of all the official duties. He spent most of each day at the hospital, giving Kenya some relief, and allowing Wendy to get back to work.

Kenya refused to leave the bed side except when Aaron went into surgery and he had to go to the waiting area, watching the doors. His devotion, his determination, his eagerness to learn every detail about Aaron's condition and his willingness to do any task suggested caused him to be adopted as part of the hospital family. Even in the Intensive Care unit he became an unofficial junior member of the staff, complete with slightly oversized hospital scrubs. Wendy watched in amazement as the boy metamorphosed into a totally focused and very serious young man with a mission. His bearing became more straight and certain and he visibly gained physical stature. Everyone agreed that his steady, calm voice and positive presence would play a big part in keeping Aaron focused on living, and he made it easy for them to bend the rules so that he could be there and play that part.

"We frankly don't know a lot about what people in his condition can hear and sense," Paravizian admitted to Wendy and Kenya in his second briefing. "But there is evidence that the voice of a loved one can promote healing and help bring them back from where ever they are in this state." So rules were ignored and Kenya kept his vigil.

Wendy brought food and changes of underwear and socks every day. She relieved Kenya some nights so he could get a few hours of sleep in the hidden corner where the nurses would wheel a cot for him. Antelope came in on the second day, after the cops had figured out that he was not one of the bad guys and released him. He also took turns relieving Kenya and swearing at Aaron in his normal way. Along with Ted, who was splitting his time at the hospital and at the house, the four of them kept a steady vigil, but hope wore thinner as Aaron seemed to shrink and fade in front of their eyes.

"Ted's the best, you know, like a real brother," Kenya told Wendy on one occasion when she arrived and Ted wasn't at the hospital. Kenya had taken on responsibility for keeping spirits up and building solidarity on what he called "the team."

"He's on his cell phone and laptop and that little computer that looks like a Gameboy, his PDA, all the time, but he's taken care of the paperwork and insurance and all that stuff and he sits and talks with Aaron about, you know, stuff from when he was growing up. He speaks French and German and some other languages, on the phone I mean, not to Aaron. Aaron's no good with languages. He's really smart, Ted I mean, and he's teaching me stuff on the computer and how to say some things in French. He's going to buy me a laptop so I can get on the net here in the hospital. That'll help when I need to look up stuff when the doctors tell me things. He said he wants us to be closer, like I said, we're real brothers now."

When she was sitting with Aaron Wendy followed Kenya's very precise instructions; encouraged him to keep fighting and come back to them. She found herself talking things out that she would have had trouble saying to him when he was conscious. It was like those therapists that you talk to and they don't say anything, they just listen. She felt that Aaron was listening, and there weren't any of the usual bullshit barriers to speaking from the heart, none of the thoughts about how your words were going to be received or how you were going to be perceived.

"Come back to me," she said in a low voice, surprised at how strong the feelings were that washed over her when she said it. "We had something, I mean we have something. We connected like…like I haven't connected with anyone else. The damn movement got in the way, it distracted us, along with your sensitivity about being older, but now I can sort out what I feel about you in the campaign and what I feel about, about just you. I…I guess I love you. I mean, I don't know, but I want to have another chance to work out things, to try to build a relationship with you." How stupid she had been to wait until now to tell him how she felt.

Detective Sowonga frequently came in to check on Aaron and whenever Wendy was there they discussed the developing case. Her trust in him grew each time they met. He was surprisingly open and provided her details about what had happened the night of the attack. He even had called her on two occasions to see when she would be at the hospital so that they could meet. Fist had been dead when the ambulance arrived, he informed her. Grainer and the big guy in the brim hat, whose name was Harlan Minton, a.k.a. Harold Morgan, a.k.a. The Mint, had been taken to the hospital in ambulances and were being held on a prison ward as material witnesses. Both had long arrest records for assault, attempted murder, suspicion of murder, assault with a deadly weapon and other charges in six or eight states. They had convictions on reduced charges and both had served jail time, six years for Grainer and two years for Minton. Both had concussions, but were able to exercise their right to a phone call by the morning after the attack. Whoever they called had hung up on them. They immediately clammed up and demanded to talk to lawyers.

Sowonga encouraged Wendy to tell him what had been going on in Aaron's life up until the attack. He listened intently and she told him all about the campaign and trying to build a movement. Sowonga was skeptical at first.

"So this guy has been building up a public campaign that will make people think that big multinational oil and coal companies are responsible for messing up the climate and the air, is that what you're telling me? And that's why they tried to kill him on the street?"

"Yes," Wendy answered. "They, the oil companies, are afraid he could be a big problem for them. You have to realize that they have been pulling the wool over people's eyes for years, pretending that there is no global warming, or that it isn't harmful, or that it isn't because of burning coal and oil. Aaron has been the first one to really have a good handle on how to build a grassroots movement so that people will realize they've been duped and need to make changes fast. The oil and coal companies make millions of dollars every day that they keep people from realizing that we have to stop burning their products. Every day! That's why they needed to shut him up."

Sowonga considered what she said. He had seen some things in the papers, he told her, but nothing that had seemed to relate to him. Like everyone else, he had a life to live and didn't really have time to read about this global warming stuff. It was too distant, too far from his world. By the second day they got together and talked he seemed to have put aside some of his doubts.

"Miss Sparks," he said, as they sat in the waiting area outside Intensive Care. Ted was in with Aaron and Kenya had gone down to the cafeteria. "I have done some research. Isn't it true that some scientists don't believe that global warming is a big problem or that people are causing it?"

Wendy sighed. "Detective, that is what the coal and oil companies have been pumping out for years. There are about four scientists who question global warming. They are all on the payrolls of the oil and coal companies. None of them have done any respected scientific work in years, but when the papers report on this they use the old 'he said-she said' format, balancing those four paid jerks against the collected wisdom of thousands of respected scientists. They spend millions on their disinformation campaign. Don't get fooled. Global warming is real, we are causing it by burning coal and oil and the companies are trying to keep us doing it so they can keep making money."

On the fifth day after the attack, Paravizian didn't make his rounds to see Aaron until 9:00 in the evening. Ted had just left and Wendy and Kenya were talking in the waiting room. Only one person was allowed to visit in Intensive Care at a time, and they always had to leave when the doctor was doing his examination. When he finished he came and sat across from them, letting out a long weary sigh before he spoke. They waited while he gathered himself, fearful of what he would say.

"This has been a long day," he finally said. "And not a particularly good one for me. I lost a patient that I had hoped to save."

Wendy felt like the bottom had dropped out of her stomach. Her face blanched.

Then he sat straighter and gave them a smile. "Sorry, another patient, not Aaron. Aaron seems to be doing better. The swelling has gone down significantly. That isn't unusual, when it goes down it can happen fast. His heart has remained strong, remarkably so, and that is an excellent sign. If the swelling continues its present recession, we will start to reduce the coma inducing drugs in the morning. Then we have to wait and hope he comes around. I would say his chances of surviving are much better now, although you can't get your hopes up too high. He could go the other way just as fast, I've seen it happen too often in these trauma cases, and we have no idea yet of how much permanent damage there will be."

Despite the caution, Wendy felt her spirits lift for the first time since she got Squeak's call in the night.

"Oh, that's great, Doctor, thank you. Isn't that good news, Squeak, sorry, Kenya?" she said.

His face started to relax into a smile but it was only fleeting.

"I told you, Aaron was going to make it. We need to just keep up what we're doing. I'll call Ted and Antelope and let them know." He stood up and shook the doctor's hand.

Three days later Sowonga, Wendy, Ted and Kenya were in Aaron's room, a gathering the detective had arranged. Aaron still couldn't talk and they didn't know if he understood what they were saying, but he was breathing on his own and had been moved out of intensive care to the neurology ward. He drifted in and out of sleep and sometimes moved his eyes towards them when he was awake.

The day before at a similar gathering, Sowonga had made it clear that he didn't have enough to tie Fist and his gang to APRC, all the time looking at Kenya as though he knew that the boy was keeping a secret. Reluctantly, Kenya, with Wendy and Ted urging him on, told them about the ambush in the mountains and produced the rental agreement from his backpack.

"It was our secret," Kenya explained. "But I think my dad would agree to give it to you." The detective had taken the paper, looked at it, and quickly left the hospital.

Now Sowonga was excited.

"Several days ago I traced numbers on Edgar Fist's cell phone to the private lines of Perry Pierce Richardson and Edward Tower at APRC as well as top officials at several major oil and coal corporations. We retrieved the messages that Fist had saved on his phone, including references to planning the attack on Aaron, but I needed more. Thanks to you, Kenya, thanks to you trusting me with your secret, now I think I have what I need, or I will have it pretty soon. I got the rental company to pull the records on the car. It turns out, the car where you, ah, found the papers had been returned because of a broken window, but another had been rented and delivered to the hotel where Mr. Fist was registered. He had departed the hotel more than two weeks prior to his death, but the rental car records, plus the hotel records, gives us a tie between Mr. Fist and APRC. And best of all, we were able to find the replacement rental car. It was parked in the Union Station lot. Damn if there wasn't a laptop in the car. We've only just started, but this laptop is linked to what appears to be another computer, I imagine at his home. Once we get through all the firewalls and encryption he has set up, I'm sure we will find a treasure trove of connections. Mr. Fist appears to have had excellent technical skills and kept very good records. The prosecutor is already very interested, so we are keeping this to ourselves for now. She doesn't want the Fed's to step in before she gets a crack at this one, because it looks like it has big time possibilities. She's pulling together a case to put in front of the Grand Jury. I'm confident Grainer and Minton will become eager to talk when she tells them she can give them a good deal if they point their fingers at the big guys in the suits who they did jobs for. Quite frankly, this could go anywhere. I'm hoping to bag some very big shots in industry, and who knows where it can lead from there, perhaps into the administration. Of course, this could all fall through, but if it works out," he paused for a moment, "well, I should make Lieutenant, at last!"

Wendy felt the airs on her arm and the back of her neck rising. She looked over at Aaron.

"You hear, Aaron?" she said to him. "You stubborn, bull headed fool. We just might get those guys. You just might have pushed them over the edge."

"Look," Kenya said excitedly. "Look at his right hand. He's moving it."

First it was just his index finger. Slowly, almost imperceptibly, it moved up and down. Then his hand rose at the wrist. Finally his arm bent at the elbow and his whole forearm and hand went up one, two, three inches!

Wendy looked in his eyes. She could see that now he wasn't just looking at her, he was seeing her.

"Aaron," she cried. "Oh my God, Aaron! You're coming back."

"Yes!" Kenya yelled. "Yes, yes, yes." He high fived with Ted and then with the beaming detective. "I told you he wouldn't leave me."

Wendy and Kenya reached across the bed to each other in a hug that included Aaron, half laying on him and each slipping an arm under his neck, while Ted and Sowonga shook hands. Wendy felt joy, pure joy, for the first time since, yes, since that night they made love in the Delaware hotel room before APRC intruded between them.

Chapter 26

On the night of Aaron's mugging Wendy had called Tony while on her way to the hospital. He later admitted to her that he had immediately called the NAC media chief, got her out of bed and had her call and email all her media contacts. She provided the papers with a picture the campaign had been using of Aaron and Kenya posing with an award the boy won at the regional scholastic science fair. When Wendy dragged herself directly from the hospital to the office on the morning after the attack, she immediately went in to see him.

"Deadly Attack On Local Activist," he read from the headline of the story below the picture on the lower left side of the front page of the Washington Post he held front of him. "The picture is on all the local news shows this morning. We got mention of the campaign but we've got to find a way to get the media to tie this to APRC and the oil and coal bastards. That'll take it out of local and put it into national news. They just eat up the black and white, single father family angle. Just showing the picture and not having to mention race or single parent they get huge demographic and human interest points. They love it."

Wendy shuddered.

"You creep," she said, weary contempt in her voice. "Aaron could be dying this minute and you gloat about media coverage."

Tony slowly put the paper down and gave Wendy a long, cold look. She was a mess. Wrinkled blouse with buttons in the wrong button holes, dirty jeans and flip flops, her hair dull, uncombed and frizzing around her head, dark circles under eyes shot with red. The corners of her mouth were pulled down in distaste as she balefully regarded him across the desk.

Tony knew that this could be the big event they had been hoping for. If the scandal spread deeper into industry or even the administration and was handled correctly it would make Enron look like a scalping scheme at the county fair. It would push the campaign from just another stagnant and fizzling conversation piece in the hard core environmental community into a major movement that played out on network news and front pages across the country. This was his chance to lead that movement. He also knew that he needed lots of luck and he needed Wendy's help if he was going to move into the rarified ranks of people who are remembered in history as making a difference in the world. He drew in a big breath and let it out.

"Wendy," he said, his eyes and voice softening. "I am concerned about Aaron, too. He is a great man. We need him and love him. If there is anything I can do to help him recover I will do it gladly. Please sit. You look dead on your feet."

She took a seat on the sofa, but her look didn't change. Tony stayed behind his desk.

"We need to think about this from Aaron's viewpoint," Tony went on. "He has devoted himself to this cause. He has seen the future and he wants more than anything for everyone else to see that future and prepare for it. I don't have any doubt that he would lay down his life if he thought that it would be the boost that this campaign needs to succeed. In fact, that is exactly what he has done."

Tony stood up, stepped away from the desk, and then turned to her, his left hand palm up, open and his right fist closed on top of it. He raised that right fist up, pointed his index finger and brought it down onto his open left palm as he made each point.

"He has done his part and now it is up to us to do our part. We have to honor his sacrifice by taking this horrible tragedy and making sure we pin it on those responsible. We have to control our passion and use it to drive us as professionals. We must manage the news about this attack; build the story day by day and week by week. We have to devote every ounce of energy we have and every bit of professional knowledge to link the responsibility for this event and the responsibility for global warming to the coal and oil bosses. If we are very good, if we are very lucky, if things break our way, we just may make this the event that turns the tide in this battle."

Tony came to the front of the desk and leaned back against it, one hand on each edge beside his hips. Wendy wasn't looking at him now, her head down looking at her arms folded across her chest. Her lips were closed and chin trembling as tears leaked from her eyes.

"Wendy, this is what Aaron would tell you he wanted you to do, isn't it? He needs you to do this. I need you to do this." He sat down next to her and took her right hand into both of his hands.

"We need you, Wendy."

She took a long minute. Finally she pulled her hand away and used both hands to wipe the tears from her face.

"Oh, fuck you, Tony," she said in a tired voice. "Ok, you bastard, ok."

"Ok," Tony said, firm and louder now, showing his own anger. "Let's get those bastards now. That crazy Aaron is still showing the way. This is our chance and we have to take it. We just cannot let this be wasted."

She reached over and lightly punched his upper arm and then moved away, putting some distance between them.

"He's in a coma, you know. They say he's stabilized, that's why I came here, but he's in critical condition and could turn for the worse at any time. If they call me I have to go and stay with Kenya."

"Kenya?" Tony asked, puzzled.

"Oh! That's Squeak's real name, and he is, ah, he wants to be called Kenya now."

Tony nodded. "Ok, Wendy. Please do all you can to support, ah, Kenya and Aaron right now, and try to keep me informed as much as possible. Here's what we can do to use this horrible event to press the campaign the way Aaron would want. I am going to be talking with the donors and build up our funding. An event like this is, forgive me, a way to encourage them to increase their giving. It makes them angry and that translates into dollars. They will also see this is a media opportunity and some of them will want to take advantage of that. You need to do the same thing marshalling the troops to take grassroots action. Keep them informed of the attack on Aaron and his fight for his life. Make them angry at the people we know are behind the attack. Tie it to the campaign and get them to do picketing at SPECO stations, vigils and other media events. Can you do that? I'll get the funding if you can get the events happening."

Wendy stood up. She was weary and had aged five years, but her voice was determined.

"Alright, Tony, don't worry about me. I know what to do and I'll do my part. You're right, we have to use Aaron's…his…his fight for his life to advance the cause he…he might die for."

Tony stood up, and they looked at each other. He held out his hand.

"Oh, hell, Tony," Wendy said. She stepped to him and they embraced. She sobbed just once, then broke away and left the office, her chin up and step firm.

Tony pursed his lips and let out a long breath. "Whew."

Thank you, Aaron, he thought. I'm not going to let this chance go by. You hang in there and give us time to work this thing and I will make it the real deal.

It might not be what most people would call sympathy, but it was definitely sincere.

Three weeks later Tony could see that Wendy was on the ragged edge of exhaustion. Still he pressed her mercilessly to move forward with the now surging campaign: boycotts of SPECO stations across the country; vigils at statehouses and corporate offices; flyers distributed at public meetings or just on busy streets; news releases and letters to the editor flooding papers, radio and TV stations. Climate change and the rapacious practices of SPECO and other energy multinational corporations became a prime topic as the calendar moved towards the November elections with NAC members speaking up in churches, schools, hunting and fishing clubs, neighborhood associations and around the water cooler at work. The opportunities were endless and as the number of actions grew across the country Aaron achieved something approaching cult status.

"Aaron Woods put his life on the line for a better future, and the dirty corporations beat him down. He's lying in the hospital fighting for his life right now. If he can do that, then we can give up one hour a day to man a picket line." This was the pitch that the three dozen staff people Wendy had commandeered were giving over the phones, all day, every day and into the night, reaching out to any activist who had ever done anything in the past, imploring them to organize or participate in some kind of action. Press releases to local papers in the vicinity of each action tied the local action to the national campaign. Whoever wasn't on the phones in the head office was out in the field helping to organize and get turnout for the events, building networks with local organizations to which members belonged and bringing them into the effort.

Tony was bone tired himself from his constant fundraising efforts and media events, but Wendy was far worse off than he. She was not only being drained by the constant work; her worry about Aaron's struggle to overcome his injuries etched deep lines in her face and reduced her nails to ragged stubs. For the first week she had despaired that Aaron would ever come out of the coma and she was still haunted by the fear that he would be hopelessly damaged.

She spent any free hours at the hospital. It was common for her to come to work in the same clothes for two and three days in a row now, showering in the room provided for bike commuters. Occasionally he saw her napping for 20 minutes at her desk or on a sofa wherever she could find a vacant office. Her power naps, she called them. When they took a few minutes to talk, she agonized over the pace and uncertainty of Aaron's recovery. The bond between Wendy and Aaron seemed to have grown enormously since he became incapacitated, a development that Tony felt was not healthy for her but which he did nothing to dissuade.

Tony couldn't cut Wendy any slack. Her melding of the latest information technology with the oldest grassroots actions was brilliant and essential. He also pressed her to provide him with the latest information on Aaron. He needed to build his own secret plans. He was delighted by her friendship with Detective B'Akili Sowonga, and had gotten her to invite the detective to come visit the NAC offices. When the detective arrived Tony asked Wendy to leave them alone and he personally had provided a tour through the campaign operation before they closeted themselves in his office for over an hour of very fruitful discussion. They parted with a friendly handshake and exchanged regular phone calls as the days passed. He was ending one of those calls as Wendy came into his office:

"That is excellent, Detective Sowonga. If we can make it happen in a week it will work out perfectly. Can you arrange it on your end? Ok, let me know how it goes. Thank you."

Tony hung up the phone and turned to Wendy, who slumped on the sofa, propping up her head with one hand, her elbow on the arm rest.

"That is one fine detective," he told her. "Things are moving along very well. What do you hear from the doctors?"

"They had to operate on his leg again today, but they say that his recovery is a miracle. He has control of all his body functions and is eating and drinking normal food. Use of his arms and legs is coming back, although his muscles are atrophied. They took the shunt out of his head, because the swelling is completely down in his brain and spine. He's so weak, though…"

Her voice trailed off and her eyes looked away.

"Wendy, of course he's weak. He almost died. He will get stronger now."

"Yes, I know." She turned back to him and straightened herself up. "I know. It is just so hard to see him like that. It isn't…he just is such a …you just have to think hard to remember how forceful he was, and you wonder if he will get that energy back."

She paused a minute.

"And he still can't talk. He understands what you say and he tries to talk, but he can't form the words. He can't write, either. He just can't make words."

"Do the doctors think he will get it back?" he asked gently.

"They don't know. Paravizian says it is early. They do tests but he says that they just don't know exactly what was damaged and if other parts of the brain will take over those functions or even if the original cells were destroyed or not, and if not, if they can recover. His skull was broken, and…" She stopped, waving her hand dispiritedly. "They say we just have to wait and see."

"Wendy," Tony said, in a crisper tone now, "I want you to take a message to Aaron. You've been keeping him up to date on the campaign, haven't you? How we have been able, with the help of the good detective, or, I mean, the un-named source, to build this story every day and point it closer and closer to the oil and coal giants. You have kept him up on it, haven't you?"

"God, yes. He's worse than you. He makes Kenya read him the papers every day and he waits for me to bring him up to the minute. Sowonga stops by there every day to see if he can talk, too. Right from, what was it, a week ago? When Sowonga had him pick out the pictures of his attackers and you two got the picture of Fist and that story in the paper he wants to know everything. "Victim awakens from coma. Fingers attackers. You wrote that press release up yourself, didn't you?"

"I helped," Tony said with a small smile. "What's more important is that across the country this story is growing. Still, if we are going to make this more than just a short term thing we need one more big event to tip it over the edge and start the landslide."

"Tony, you have something in mind." She was suspicious. He could see that she was much less naive than just a few weeks ago.

He could hear out of both ears, now. His thoughts were getting better organized, less confused. He could keep a train of thought going longer. If he focused he didn't lose track of an article in the middle of the kid reading it the way he had a week ago. His vision was ok in both eyes now, but he still couldn't read, write or talk. Tried it again this morning and the words just didn't make sense in his head when he looked at them. He could think the sounds of words, but he couldn't say them even though he could move his jaw with only minor pain; it just came out in grunts and moans. This was his biggest fear now. What if he lost the world of words? But he pushed those thoughts back. It would come or it wouldn't. He'd just keep pushing and adjust to whatever happened. Thank God he had the kid.

"Hey, you ain't listening." Kenya broke off his reading. "I guess you don't want to hear about this press conference tomorrow."

Aaron waved his right hand in a "bring it on" motion.

"Ok. It's only on page 6 of the A section, so we've dropped off the front page for a whole week now. Still, that's not bad for just talking about something that's going to happen tomorrow. It's in the national news section, in a little box. See?"

He showed Aaron the page.

"'Energy Initiative To Be Announced'," Kenya read. "'The Natural America Club and oil and coal giants SPECO and CCCO have called a press conference for 11:00 AM on Wednesday, August 18, at the National Press Club to announce progress in moving towards a clean energy economy. In a startling departure from the deep differences that have characterized relations between environmental groups and the energy industry, Mr. Tony Albritton, Executive Director of NAC announced that 'NAC will recognize the efforts of energy companies such as SPECO, CCCO and others, as well as initiatives from their Washington industry representative, APRC, to transition to new energy sources that will reduce poisonous and climate changing emissions.' Relations between NAC and the named energy organizations have been especially contentious since the July 13 Capitol Hill attack on Aaron Woods, a prominent NAC activist who has targeted the energy industry as the cause of ongoing climate change in a growing national campaign. Mr. Woods is recovering in hospital. NAC has repeatedly drawn a connection between the attack on Mr. Woods and his activities to reform the practices of the energy industry, a charge that Edward Tower, Executive Director of APRC, has called 'fantasy.'

"'Mr. Albritton announced that 'NAC will present rewards to recognize

249

the roles that industry has played in the past and will play in our new campaign to unite industry and the American people in building for a better energy future.'

"'I am glad to see that we are putting behind us the divisive rhetoric of the past and will be happy to join NAC in saluting efforts to secure America's energy future,' noted Mr. Tower.

"'Mr. Albritton declined to reveal the details of the awards to be given or the upcoming campaign, saying only, "I am sure it will surprise many and mark a major change in the relationships and practices of the past."'

Kenya closed the paper and turned to Aaron.

"What are they doing, man?" He was clearly agitated. "It looks like they're ready to sell you out. That's bullshit."

Aaron smiled, and shook his head. He pointed to the paper and motioned to Kenya to give it to him. When it was on his lap, he opened it to the page with the announcement. Then he pointed at Kenya.

"Mmmoomf," he got out, concentrating hard. Not right. He shook his head.

"Mmvveee," he said, pointing to himself.

"Mmnnuh," he said, pointing at the box with the article in the paper. He repeated it, pointing at Kenya, himself and the box while making his mooing, grunting noises again. Then again.

"What?" Kenya asked, his brow furrowed. "What are you saying? You want us to go to this press conference? Is this what you and Wendy have been whispering about?"

Aaron nodded, emphatically. Then he repeated it, again pointing.

"Mmmooo, Mmnnee, Mmngo," then he raised his hand from the paper and pointed out with his whole hand.

"Mmooom," he looked fiercely at Kenya.

"You want to go to this press conference, right?" Kenya asked.

Aaron nodded. "Mmmnnn, Mmoom." He swept his had down his body and then flung it out towards the door."

"And then you want to go home?"

Aaron nodded and smiled. Fear be damned. He was going to beat this. He sat back and motioned Kenya to come to him. They hugged each other for a minute.

Kenya got up.

"Ok, old man. All right, Dad. We're gonna go raise hell at the press conference and then we're going home. I don't know how we're going to do it, but I'll call Ted and have him come over. He's probably on the way, anyhow. We'll let the doctors know and he'll get the papers done and tomorrow we're going home. Ted'll make it happen."

Aaron just kept nodding and smiling. He had more work to do to get ready for tomorrow. Tony better have his shit together, he thought, because I'm damn well doing my part. Wendy had warned him that she wasn't sure about this press event when she had relayed Tony's message, demanding that Aaron get there. She couldn't give him any details and was suspicious of Tony. But sometimes you just have to trust, and with him as laid up as he was now, he figured this was that time.

Paravizian was a real pain in the ass about it.

"I need you here for another week," he said, storming into the room after Ted told him that Aaron was insisting on checking out in the morning. "You have had major head trauma and you are just getting back your normal function. Any shock or minor trauma or infection and you could do yourself irreparable harm. Now just be sensible. I've done some of my best work on you and if you go running around you could put it at risk."

Aaron just shook his head. Life was all about taking risks, and he wasn't going to back away from this one. Ted prepared a letter relieving the hospital of liability due to the early release and the doctor reluctantly signed the discharge. Throughout the day and into the night the very prospect of getting back into some kind of action seemed to make Aaron stronger. He barely slept through the night, tensing and relaxing his muscles and making sounds, trying to form words that wouldn't come.

"We got to wait on the detective," Kenya said for the third time as Aaron motioned for him to push his wheelchair out of the room. It was 10:30 Wednesday morning, the time scheduled for their departure. "He said he'd be here and drive us to the press conference. That's one cop I trust, so just hold on."

Five minutes more crawled by, seeming like an hour, before Detective Sowonga came into the room. He had a crisp, new blue suit on, a white shirt and red tie. He was standing straight and moving briskly, unlike his usual slow shuffle.

"Ah, very good. We are ready to go?" he said brightly.

Aaron waved his hand impatiently for them to get going.

"Here, let me push the chair," the detective said.

"No, I got that," Kenya told him, firmly holding on to the handles.

Sowonga exchanged a glance and a shrug with Ted, who had a small bag with the books, radio, Ipod and odds and ends that Aaron had accumulated during the last couple of weeks of his hospital stay. Kenya had his own gear in his backpack.

"I think we just better get going, Detective," Ted said, "or these guys will try to wheel their way on over to the Press Club on their own."

"After seeing what they did to the three guys that jumped them I certainly don't want to get in their way," the detective replied, reminding them that he knew there was more to the story of the mugging than they had told him. He had let Antelope's role stay hidden, and he didn't want Kenya and Aaron to forget it had been his decision to do so. He led them out of the room, through the halls and out to the police cruiser in the no parking zone at the entrance to the hospital.

"I thought the marked car would make our trip a little easier," Sowonga said as he opened the back door. He held the door while Kenya helped Aaron out of the wheel chair and into the back seat of the car. The detective put the wheelchair and their bags into the trunk. Kenya got in the other side of the back seat and Ted sat up front.

"Everyone else is already at the Press Club," Sowonga told his passengers as he started down the drive. "Everything is ready."

Aaron saw a satisfied smile crease the detective's fleshy face. He certainly looks pleased with himself, Aaron thought. I can't wait to see what kind of mousetrap he and Tony have rigged up.

He turned to look out the window as they came to the stop sign at the exit from the hospital. His eyes widened and he sat up straight as he looked at the sign intently.

Stop, he thought. The letters on the sign clearly said *Stop* to him. He could read them.

As they pulled away he mouthed the word to himself. He felt his lips part, teeth together, tongue tip against the bottom of his mouth, then moving to the top as his teeth opened. Then the mouth opened wider and finally he brought his lips together and expelled a small explosion of air pushing them apart.

"Sssst...o...phh." He said it quietly. Then a little faster. "Sstop." He put it together, still very quietly, "Stop."

He turned his head to find Kenya to looking at him intently.

"Stop," he said, still very quietly. Kenya's eyes widened and mouth dropped open. He grinned and nodded his head.

"Ok, let's go rock and roll," the boy said and reached over to clasp Aaron's left hand.

Yes, Aaron thought. *Let's go rock and roll.*

They pulled up to the entrance of the Press Club, ignoring the no parking zone signs. Sowonga turned back the doorman who approached with a wave and a brusque, "Police business."

They got out of the car, leaving the flashers on, and went through the lobby, taking an elevator to the fourth floor auditorium where the press conference was being held. Aaron had been there before, but despite that familiarity everything was going very fast for him now. He felt overwhelmed and confused, but tried to not show it He held onto his focus tightly, lips compressed and brow furrowed as Kenya pushed him from the elevator across a smaller lobby area and into the back of the auditorium where they stopped. There were ten rows of chairs, more than half filled with about 60 people. A table with cold cuts, bread and chips was along the right side of the room. Basic rules of media handling: always have food for the reporters, Aaron thought, getting his bearings.

Three TV cameras pointed at the raised stage in front where Tony Albritton stood at a podium. He was on the right side of the stage, to Aaron's left, beside and slightly in front of a row of six chairs facing the audience, the closest of which was empty. Ed Tower was in the first filled chair. The heavy executive looked comfortable and pleased with himself. Next to him were Perry Pierce Richardson, and then two other executives, all with the smug, satisfied look of very successful men about to enjoy a public moment of triumph. Wendy was in the last chair in the row.

The audience seemed to be mostly bored looking reporters, some looking at handouts and some with notebooks at the ready. There were about a dozen people from NAC. Near the front were a half dozen men in cheap suits that looked out of place among the casually dressed reporters.

Antelope, who had been sitting in a back row aisle seat, came over to Aaron's side. Aaron gave him a nod and turned his attention back to the stage.

"You will all find the background information about the impacts of climate change in the materials we have provided to you." Tony continued with what was apparently the opening part of his briefing. Aaron saw that he had noticed his arrival, but Tony made no acknowledgment. This was exactly according to the script that Wendy had gone over with him at least half a dozen times this past week.

"The consequences of climate change are indeed dire. Sea level rise, increased breeding and biting of insects, increased infestations of disease causing parasites, species loss, reduced soil moisture, increased frequency and intensity of heat waves and hurricanes, more flooding and drought; these will have harmful and even fatal impact on many millions of people over the course of this century."

Aaron watched as Ed Tower and the two industry executives exchanged speculative looks. Perry Pierce Richardson maintained his cool exterior.

"But that is not why we are here today," Tony continued. Ed and the executives relaxed again. "Today we are going to recognize the role that the oil, coal, gas and utility industries are playing in preparing America to deal with the transition to a new energy future."

Tony turned and swept his left hand toward his guests on the stage, while Wendy rose to stand behind them and nodded to Aaron. This was the moment. Aaron raised his right arm and pointed forward, and Kenya started to slowly wheel him towards the stage.

"I am very pleased that Mr. Ed Tower and Mr. Perry Pierce Richardson from American Power Resource Council, the voice and truly the leadership body for the giants of the energy and utility industry have joined us today as we look to the future," Tony said with a flourish in his voice.

Ed and Perry both stood as their name was called. Aaron, pushed by Kenya, was about halfway down the aisle, followed closely by Detective Sowonga, but no one gave them any particular notice.

"And we also have with us the Chief Executive Officer of SPECO, Mr. William Breaker, and Mr. Rufus Chatham from Consolidated Coal Corporation. These are truly the giants of the industry and we are very happy to have you here today, gentlemen."

Tony then turned back to the audience and moved his hand to indicate Aaron, who had arrived at the front of the room with his entourage following.

"And we are very fortunate that we also can have with us today, released just this morning from the hospital where he has been recovering from the attack that nearly took his life a month ago, Mr. Aaron Woods. Mr. Woods, as you all know, has been the driving force behind the campaign to get the energy industry to accept responsibility for the climate change crisis and to use the vast profits they have gained from poisoning the atmosphere to lead the transition to a low emission economy."

Ed Tower now was frowning and turned to Perry Richardson. Breaker and Chatham looked at Tower.

"What the fuck is going on?" Tower growled at Perry, his face turning red.

Tony went on without taking notice of the four squirming executives. The TV cameras were zooming in, swinging from Aaron, who now was in front of his prey, to the four angry, suited men.

"I understand that Mr. Woods will now make a statement regarding his attack," Tony said smoothly.

The room fell silent as Aaron slowly rose from his wheel chair, pushing himself up with his good arm. Ted handed him the crutch that he had been carrying and Aaron put it under his right arm. He stood as straight as he could, knowing that the picture he presented was of an old, beaten and broken man. He didn't care. His face was still discolored from the operations that had reset his left cheekbone, eye orbit and nose. His head was patched with bandages and hair growing back from having been shaved for his operations. He had a light cast on his left arm, hanging in a sling. His right leg had another light cast from the top of his thigh to below the knee, over top of his pants leg. He held his head high, though and his eyes fixed each of the four executives in turn, then returning to the first.

The room was silent. He took one small, halting step forward, obviously weak and still in some pain, breath coming hard but head steady, eyes unwavering. Left foot forward, then the crutch and drag the right up to it. Then another. A third step brought him to the foot of the stage, just four feet away from his quarry and two feet below. The cameras rolled as Tower and the others looked left and right, but always had to come back, transfixed by the glare of Aaron's eyes, shot with blood and filled with rage.

Slowly, Aaron raised his left arm, lifted it out of the sling, and straightened it, pointing at Ed Tower. Pinning his prey.

A rattle came from his throat. Then something more like a growl.

A deep breath and then, with a voice that could have come from the grave, low, wheezing but steady and clear, "Yooouuu!"

He turned to Perry Pierce Richardson, with that finger extended from the cast, and said again, "Yooouuu!"

And again, in turn, to William "Ball" Breaker and to Rufus Chatham, that condemning finger and chilling voice, "Yooouuu! Yooouuu!"

"Goddammit, this is bullshit, I'm getting out of here," Tower roared. He slammed his arm into Richardson, knocking him back into his chair and to the ground.

"You stupid shit. You let them set us up!" Tower shouted. He started toward the stairs at the end of the stage, pushing a frozen Breaker and pale Chatham ahead of him.

"Stop," came a loud, deep and commanding voice, as Detective Sowonga came up the stage on the very steps towards which Tower was pushing his two stumbling clients. Sowonga held his badge out in front of him in his left hand and had folded papers in his right. He was followed by two of the suited police men who had been seated in the front row of the audience. There were flashes of light as some of the audience pulled up their cameras. Even the most jaded of them had been caught totally by surprise at the unfolding spectacle, but their instincts took over.

Tower shot a look to the right side of the stage, but two more police were approaching from that direction.

"Mr. Edward Tower, I have a warrant for your arrest for conspiracy to commit murder of Mr. Aaron Woods, for withholding evidence from the Metropolitan Police Department and for other charges related to the attempted murder of Mr. Aaron Woods," Sowonga toned deeply, flashing one of the folded papers for the TV cameras to see.

"I also have warrants for the arrest of Perry Pierce Richardson, William Breaker, also known as Ball Breaker, and Rufus Chatham, issued by the grand jury sitting in Washington D.C. for charges of racketeering, conspiracy to commit murder and other charges related to the attempted murder of Mr. Woods."

Sowonga showed the folded papers in his hand to the audience and TV cameras, spread out like a hand of cards. The other four plainclothes police then moved in and grabbed the four energy executives, cuffing one hand then pulling it behind the prisoner's back and cuffing it to the other. Tony had made a point of telling Sowonga to use metal cuffs, not the less impressive plastic ones, and to maximize the visibility. Cameras flashed. Tower started to struggle against the officer who was cuffing him, but was quickly subdued. Richardson, Breaker and Cheatham were in shock as they were led away, but their eyes all turned to that avenging figure that stood in front of them and the world and declared their guilt. Only as they left the stage did Aaron lower his pointing arm, and his gaze never wavered. He held their eyes until they were off the stage and out the door, followed by the smiling B'Akili Sowonga, soon to be the most famous Detective in the Washington Metropolitan Police Department, if not in the entire country. Sowonga and Tony exchanged a satisfied nod as the detective left the room.

The audience was a wild stampede of shouting reporters waving notebooks, calling questions at the arrested executives and Sowonga until they went out the doors at the back of the hall. Then they streamed back in, rushing the stage where Tony Albritton was still at the podium, ready to give them the story of the most dramatic arrest of the year.

Unnoticed in the pandemonium, Kenya pushed Aaron's wheelchair up behind him. Aaron lowered himself to the chair, dropping the last foot with a thump as his trembling left leg wouldn't hold him any longer. Ted took the crutch. Wendy had come off the stage, and she leaned to Aaron's ear.

"Let's go home," she said. "We're done here."

With Ted leading, Kenya pushing, Wendy by his side holding his right hand and Antelope bringing up the rear, they left the hall. Aaron took a last glance back at Tony, coolly fielding questions from the shouting reporters and referring to the charts that his media relations director had now set up in front of the now disarrayed chairs. He looks perfect, Aaron thought. He is the perfect leader for this day, this Movement.

They left the tumult behind and crossed the lobby to wait for the elevator car to come up. Sowonga and his prisoners had been whisked down in elevators held for that purpose and the lobby was quiet. Kenya came up to Aaron's left, Ted and Wendy were on his right.

"You ok, Dad?" Kenya asked.

He nodded and smiled, looking around at his family and feeling a deep peace, such as he could never remember feeling before. Finally he had reached that point where the outcome may be in doubt, but you know that you will never have to say you could have done more.

"Enough," he said aloud. "Enough."

Owl came without sound or warning. Sharp talons thrust down through Aaron's shoulders, grasping deep inside. Pain seared through him but quickly passed as the great wings silently beat and he was pulled up above the broken vessel of his body. He took a last look at his two sons, so different but sharing the essentials of courage, compassion and commitment that defined them as men. They would be well. Wendy was looking back at the stage. That was where she needed to be.

He passed through the roof, up into the sky and quickly out of the city, past the sprawling suburbs toward the green canopy of the forest, borne easily by the great Owl. He was going to the nest, the wild home he had sought since those sunlit days and moon shadowed nights as a boy in the woods.

Printed in the United States
73944LV00006B/34-51